Praise

‘This brilliant and witty b ... ed!’
Star

‘Thoroughly enjoyable . . . Had me smiling from start to finish’
Erica James

‘A wickedly comical read’ *Heat*

‘A fabulous novel which addresses real-life issues with wit and humour’
Closer

‘From the author of the superb *Ex-Wife’s Survival Guide* comes another wicked treat’
Daily Mirror

‘This fast-paced romantic comedy is perfect bad-weather escapism’
She

‘Clever and surprising’ *Daily Mail*

‘A deliciously funny, gently ironic novel, Jane Austen-like in its elegance and playfulness’
Woman’s Weekly

‘I absolutely love this book. It is as funny as it is wise and I couldn’t put it down’
Katie Fforde

‘One to curl up with on a winter’s evening’ *Oxford Times*

‘Laced with wise and witty humour, this is great fun’ *Woman*

ALSO BY DEBBY HOLT

The Ex-Wife's Survival Guide
Annie May's Black Book
The Trouble with Marriage
Love Affairs for Grown-Ups
Recipe for Scandal

ABOUT THE AUTHOR

Debby Holt was a shambolic supply teacher until she (and her pupils) were saved by her writing. She lives in Bath with her nice husband and her horrid mortgage.

Visit www.debbyholt.co.uk

Friends, Lies and Alibis

Debby Holt

London · New York · Sydney · Toronto

A CBS COMPANY

First published in Great Britain by Simon & Schuster, 2011
An imprint of Simon & Schuster UK Ltd
A CBS COMPANY

1 3 5 7 9 10 8 6 4 2

Simon & Schuster UK Ltd
1st Floor
222 Gray's Inn Road
London WC1X 8HB

www.simonandschuster.co.uk

Simon & Schuster Australia
Sydney

A CIP catalogue record for this book is available from the British Library

ISBN 978-1-84739-655-6

Typeset by Hewer Text UK Ltd, Edinburgh

Printed and bound in Great Britain by Cox & Wyman Ltd, Reading, Berkshire

For James and Sophia

ACKNOWLEDGEMENTS

Thanks to –

Chris and Saija Leaning who gave me the idea for this novel.

Dr Nick Whitehead who answered all my medical enquiries with his customary patience and wisdom.

Jenny Bower of Reside, Bath Ltd for sharing her professional life with me.

Ned Sawdy for putting me right on the likes and dislikes of seven and nine year olds.

Teresa Chris, my agent, whose contribution has been massive.

Suzanne Baboneau and all the team at Simon & Schuster, especially Libby Yevtushenko for her wise, generous and essential editorial notes.

David as always.

'So we agree that Merrily needs our help,' Alison said. 'The question is: what can we do?'

Leah stared thoughtfully into her wine. 'We could break up her marriage.'

Alison frowned and then slowly nodded her head. 'Of course! That's it! That's what we have to do.'

'Alison,' Leah said. 'I was joking.'

'I'm not,' Alison said.

CHAPTER ONE

Alison Has a Surprise

It was ridiculous to be thrown by such a trivial accident. She had broken a cheap picture frame. It might be annoying but it was hardly earth-shattering, although, come to think of it, it *had* been glass-shattering: the floor looked like it had been invaded by frost.

And now she would be late for Sally, but only by a few minutes, and that wasn't the end of the world either. On balance, Sally had kept her waiting more times than she'd kept Sally waiting.

Alison's cloakroom-cum-utility-room housed two coat stands, a washing machine, a dryer and an ironing board. Felix had long ago christened it the History Room. This was because Alison had mounted on its walls sundry old photos belonging to Alison and Felix, many of them taken prior to their marriage and their children. It was one of these that Alison had inadvertently knocked down onto the unforgiving stone floor, after reaching for her anorak.

She knelt down and gingerly extracted the photo from its now jagged casing. It had been taken fifteen years ago, in her parents' garden, on her twenty-third birthday. There she stood, flanked by her two best friends, grinning broadly because she was pregnant for the fourth time and she loved being pregnant. On her left was Merrily, in jeans and a T-shirt, her head slightly lowered so that her pale brown hair obscured half her face, with a shy smile that betrayed her discomfiture at being photographed. And there, on her right, was Leah, with dyed red hair piled up on top of her head and enough eye make-up to stop a bee in its tracks.

Alison stood up and put the photo on the washing machine. She knew why she was upset. Most of the time, she hardly noticed the photos in here. This was, after all, a room for action rather than reflection. Liberated from its frame, this photo, more than any other, had the power to blow her off course and distract her with old, unresolved questions. She and Leah and Merrily had all lived next door to each other. They had spent most of their childhoods in and out of each other's houses. There was a difference in ages – Alison was a year older than Merrily and three years older than Leah – but somehow that hadn't mattered. They were the best of best friends. Fifteen years ago, Merrily had chosen to disappear from their lives and Alison and Leah still had no idea why.

She glanced at her watch. She must go. She collected her anorak, unhooked the dog's lead from its place on the second coat stand and shut the door firmly behind her. She would clear up the mess later. She went through to the kitchen and waved the lead at Magnus, who was lounging in his basket and looking as if he wanted to stay there. It was absurd that she should be made to feel guilty for taking him out for a walk, particularly since she was only going for a walk in order to give *him* some exercise.

As she walked out of the drive and into Parsley Lane, Alison's customary good humour reasserted itself. It was a beautiful September morning. The birds were twittering in the trees, the sky was a seamless blue and there was a tangy scent of cow parsley in the air. Any dog would be happy to go for a walk on such a day. Any dog except Magnus, who had to be the laziest giant-sized retriever in the world.

She was, she felt today, an exceptionally lucky woman. She lived in one of the prettiest villages in Somerset. She had, in Felix, a husband who was commonly regarded as an exceptionally popular GP, one of the few doctors around who preferred to look at his patients rather than his computer screen. She had four gorgeous teenage children, the eldest of whom was already living an independent existence in London. Best of all – and this was probably the reason for her cheerful state of mind prior to the picture-crashing accident – her two youngest children had this morning returned to school after the long summer break. She had absolutely no reason to feel so discombobulated. Discombobulated was one of Alison's favourite words. She had gone through a period of trying to learn ten new words every day and discombobulated was one of the few lasting legacies.

She pulled at Magnus's lead and told him to come *on*. She was anxious to see Sally and tell her about the holiday she had organized for the autumn half-term. Sally, she thought, would be impressed by her energy.

Last week, she and Felix had gone with Sally and Michael Bracewell to the Rushtons for supper. Jenny and Jonathon Rushton lived on the other side of the village, by the church. It had been a very jolly evening and at some point they got talking about a programme they had all watched about Hadrian's Wall. Alison had suggested the six of them go for a short break there at half-term and everyone agreed that that was a brilliant idea. Alison couldn't wait to tell Sally she had already planned the expedition.

The Bracewells lived near the bottom of Parsley Lane and Sally was waiting at the end of her drive along with Billy, her cocker spaniel. As always, the sight of Sally had the effect of making Alison dissatisfied with her own appearance. Alison knew she possessed enviable features: she had good skin and her shoulder-length blonde hair retained its sheen without any artificial aids. It was only that, unlike Sally – and Leah, for that matter – Alison never felt she was able to nail the cool and contemporary look. It was her contention that women with big breasts never *could* look cool and contemporary, whereas both Sally and Leah had lean, boyish figures.

Today, Sally wore black trousers tucked into shiny crimson wellington boots and a red shirt that matched to perfection her short auburn hair. In her twenties, Sally had been an artist. These days, she promoted and set up art events and exhibitions. Alison had been to see quite a few of them. She had been particularly struck by one installation, a ten-minute black-and-white film of a small child thrusting her hand into a chocolate cake and then throwing bits of it at the wall. Alison had thought it was a horrid film and a terrible waste of what looked like a delicious cake. Sally's husband, Michael, was an independent TV producer and Alison was rather proud of the fact that she and Felix had such stylish friends. Tucking Friary might be a small village but no one could say it didn't have interesting residents.

Sally's cocker spaniel showed great excitement at the approach of Alison and Magnus, an excitement not shared by Magnus, who stood staring into the distance while Billy sniffed his backside. Alison apologized for being late and then, as Sally fell into line beside her, said in a voice that was pregnant with anticipation, 'I have a present for you in my pocket. Don't go home without it. It's a guide book about Hadrian's Wall!'

'Oh,' Sally said, 'thank you.' She sounded baffled rather than excited, which was disappointing, but then she often said she wasn't really a morning person so perhaps she hadn't really woken up yet.

'I've dropped a copy through Jenny's door,' Alison said. 'And I've organized everything! We *shall* go away at half-term! I spent hours on the Internet and eventually I booked two pubs for us to stay in, one on the Thursday night and one for the Friday and Saturday. I've even worked out the route we'll take *and* you wouldn't believe all the research I've done. If you want to know anything about Hadrian's Wall, you can just ask me. And if you can't get your parents down to look after your two, I can always lend you my Harry.'

'Right,' Sally said. 'I hadn't realized . . . I didn't think you'd organize things so quickly. You are frighteningly efficient.'

'I find,' Alison said, 'that it's best to do things as soon as one thinks about them.'

'You're probably right,' Sally said. 'Of course, if you do

things as soon as you think about them, it doesn't leave you much time *to* think about them.'

'I'm of the opinion,' said Alison, 'that too much thinking is counterproductive.'

They crossed the lane and walked over the small narrow bridge that spanned the river. A heron stretched its long neck, unfurled its wings and glided effortlessly and elegantly away from them. The two women let their dogs off their leads and Billy bounded off with a joyous bark.

'Go on, Magnus,' Alison said. 'Go and play with Billy!'

Magnus gave Alison a pained stare and then cheered up at the sight of a dog turd amongst a clump of straggling soapwort. Magnus loved sniffing dog turds.

'Do you remember my friend Grace?' Sally asked. 'She came to stay a few months ago. She teaches at Newcastle University. You said she reminded you of your friend, the one who vanished.'

There it was again: a twist of apprehension or anxiety, like a stone being thrown into a still pond. Alison looked sharply at her companion. 'That is so odd, you mentioning Merrily. Do you know why I was late for our walk? I broke one of the framed photos in the cloakroom. And do you know who was in the photo?'

'I presume it was Merrily.'

'It was the last picture I have of Merrily and Leah and me. After that, we never saw her again. I mean, I haven't thought of her for ages. And now I break a photo of her and a few minutes later, quite randomly, you bring her up. That is quite spooky.' Alison frowned. 'And now I've forgotten why you *did* mention her.'

'You said Grace's voice reminded you of Merrily. Grace rang me last night. She's going to have a baby.'

'Is she?' Alison said wistfully. 'She's a lucky woman.'

'That's not the word I'd use. She's throwing up all the time at the moment.'

'I've been reading a book,' Alison said, 'by a woman who used to be a midwife in the East End in the nineteen fifties. She had to deliver this baby and it turned out to be the woman's twenty-fourth child.'

'That's appalling.' Sally glanced at Alison with eyes that were only half joking. 'Tell me you agree that's appalling.'

'Apparently, she was blissfully happy and so were the children and so was the husband. I'm not saying I'd like to have twenty-four children but . . .'

'Right,' Sally nodded. 'You'd probably be content with twenty-three.'

'I always loved having babies. You always know where you are with them.'

'You certainly do,' Sally said. 'You know they're going to wake you up night after night, they're going to leave trails of sick over all of your clothes, they're going to make your house smell like one big soiled nappy and they'll ruin your sex life. Of course I haven't said any of this to Grace.'

'I should think not,' said Alison.

'I had my first child at thirty and I remember thinking I was too old. Poor Grace is thirty-nine. You did it the right way. You had your first baby at nineteen and your last at twenty-three. And soon you'll be free of all of them. Very clever.'

The path along the river melted into a huge clearing that led on the right to a small copse, a favourite hunting ground for Billy. Since there was no sign of him, Sally went on ahead to check he was still in the vicinity while Alison waited for Magnus to catch up. She was glad the conversation had been interrupted. There was no point in telling Sally that she hated the fact that her eldest child now lived in London, and that she was dreading the imminent departure of her second to Manchester. Sally would only laugh and tell her to get a life. Alison had no need of such advice. She knew very well she had a perfectly good life. It didn't stop her from missing her children, that was all.

She picked up a stick, and pushing back invasive stinging nettles she walked on towards Sally, who had retrieved Billy and was extracting burrs from his fur. 'There was something else I had to tell you,' Sally said. 'Grace had another reason for ringing me. She has a friend who's come to live in Bath and she wants me to look after him. He's a historian. He's written two books and has another one out in a few weeks. He's been on television and he's done lots of radio documentaries. Grace says he's gorgeous and clever and single.'

'It doesn't sound like he needs you to look after him.'

'Grace says he does. Apparently, he's nursing a broken heart. He'd been going out with some woman who was newly divorced and she told him they had to break up because her children weren't ready to watch their mother going out with new men. So David – that's his name, he's called David Morrison – David was very sad and he was even sadder when he found out that she'd told him a load of old bull. She'd already started seeing a millionaire property developer. Grace says he'll tell us he's moved down to Bath because he's taken a teaching post at Bristol

University. But Grace says the truth is he left Newcastle because his heart was broken. Grace says he needs the love of a good woman. Perhaps we should introduce him to Leah.'

'I'm not sure I'd describe Leah as a good woman,' Alison said. 'And I've given up finding men for her. I've introduced her to three eligible males since she moved to Bath and each time it's ended in disaster.'

'Will you and Felix come if I invite him to supper? I'll try to fix a date this evening.'

'I'd love to meet him,' Alison said. 'We can chat about Hadrian's Wall.'

'Right,' Sally said, in a voice that Alison couldn't help feeling was unnecessarily sarcastic. 'That will really cheer him up.'

Once back home, Alison cleared up the mess in the cloakroom and went upstairs to change into her work clothes: discreet heels and short-sleeved grey dress, which she would team with her navy-blue jacket. She gave her hair a quick brush, applied a smattering of make-up and put on her pearl earrings.

Alison liked to describe herself as the Rumpelstiltskin of the property world. She might not be able to spin straw into gold but she could make the dullest apartment sound like a highly desirable residence. There were three property magazines for which she supplied glowing articles on flats and houses. In her own, possibly partial, opinion, no one could winkle out positive qualities like she could. Last week, for instance, she'd transformed a muddy frog-infested piece of land into a 'magical, fairy-tale garden with its own little army of frogs ready to eat any greenfly daring to intrude'. She'd been proud of that.

Alison went downstairs, gathered up her bag and was about to leave the house when the telephone rang.

As always, her eldest child was in a hurry. 'Hi, Mum! I can't speak for long, I'm at work, but are you and Dad free on Saturday? Lennie and I are having lunch with his sister in Reading and we thought we could drive on and spend the night with you.'

'How lovely,' Alison said. 'I have to dash – I've got a train to catch – but I'll look forward to seeing you both.'

Which was partly true, she thought defensively. She did look forward to seeing Phoebe. It was just a pity that Lennie had to come too.

Twenty-five minutes later, she stood on the platform at Bath Station, wondering, as she always did when she travelled to Bristol, whether it wouldn't have been easier to drive. She gazed at the platform opposite, her eyes drifting past the elderly couple perusing a map, the group of Chinese women taking photos of each other, and the elderly man with the stylish fedora. Her attention was drawn to a tall, thin woman who was chatting to a teenage boy in baggy jeans and a white T-shirt. The woman wore a terrible raincoat; Alison suspected its last owner had been a Gestapo officer. Her hair was held back from her face by a blue Alice band that was pushed behind two prominent and oddly familiar ears. She had sensible, if unattractive, brown walking shoes but what interested Alison was not the shoes but the fact that one foot was tucked round the other like a corkscrew. Alison had only ever known one person who stood like that.

As she stared with increasingly painful concentration, the woman sensed her scrutiny and looked across.

Another morning, Alison might not have turned on her heel and thundered down the stairs. Another morning, Alison would have assumed her mind was playing tricks. But now, as she raced through the station and up towards the other platform, it struck her that the broken picture and her conversation with Sally added up to more than a casual coincidence. As she reached the woman at last, she put a hand to her stomach and managed to gasp out just one word: 'Merrily?'

CHAPTER TWO

Leah Makes a Big Mistake

It was Friday evening and Leah's ex-husband was twenty-seven minutes late. The children had had their tea, they'd changed out of their school uniform and their rucksacks were packed and waiting. Fred sat at the kitchen table reading his latest book, *One Hundred Top Facts*, brushing his fringe away from his eyes. She must cut his hair again soon. He was, she thought, without a hint of partiality, a remarkably attractive little boy. Like most boys of seven and three-quarters, his mouth looked like it had been spray-gunned with teeth that were far too big for his small round face, but it didn't detract from his beautiful brown eyes.

The difference between the two children was particularly marked this evening. Although Molly was the elder by twenty months, she idolized her brother and generally fizzed around him like a sparkler, constantly vying for his attention in the hope of provoking one of his rare slow smiles. Tonight, while Fred displayed his usual calm tolerance of adult ineptitude, Molly was awash with anxiety, her eyes constantly drawn to the big kitchen clock above the notice-board. Molly had darting blue eyes, flyaway hair the colour of mink and a face which flagged up every thought in her head as she thought it. She loved going to stay with her grandparents and had been to the front door at least three times to see if her father was coming. Leah was currently plaiting her hair in a half-successful attempt to calm her down.

Molly swivelled her eyes upwards. 'You won't forget to feed Stephen, will you?' she asked.

'I won't,' Leah said. She wouldn't dare, even though she secretly wished Stephen would quietly expire. Molly had won him in a fun fair a few months ago and he lived in a bowl on top of the fridge, along with the fruit dish and her three cookery books. Leah felt guilty every time she watched the poor creature swim round and round his small home. She had read that every time a fish swam round his bowl he immediately forgot he'd already done it, but Stephen looked quite intelligent for a goldfish and she did worry that his eyes seemed to betray an awareness that his life might be a shade repetitive.

'When you see your friend tomorrow evening,' Molly said, 'will you ask her why she disappeared?'

'I'll play it by ear. I haven't seen her for fifteen years. She might not want to talk about it.'

Fred raised his head from his book. 'But if you don't ask her,' he said gravely, 'she'll know you *want* to ask her and she'll probably be waiting for you to ask her, so you might as well do it straight away.'

'I suppose you're right,' Leah said. Not for the first time, it occurred to her that adults would get on a lot better if they conducted their relationships with the same simplicity that governed her son's actions.

'Perhaps she lost her memory,' Molly suggested.

'No,' Leah said. 'I remember Alison's mother telling us that Merrily sent a letter to her parents saying she was all right but didn't want to stay in touch.'

'Perhaps someone hypnotized her,' Molly said.

'Well, I'll try to find out,' Leah promised. She tied the second plait with ribbon and said, 'Your hair's done. Do you want—'

But Molly had heard the doorbell ring and she flew off the chair and ran through to the small hall. Leah could hear her open the door and tell her father off for being late. A couple of moments later, Jamie was in the kitchen doorway, showing a distinct lack of contrition for keeping them all waiting and smiling appreciatively at her. 'You look nice.'

There was no point in returning the compliment since Jamie knew he looked nice. He was tall and narrow-hipped, with cornflower-blue eyes, short dark hair and a sensual mouth. It was a constant irritation to Leah that she continued to find him attractive. 'And you're very late,' she retorted. 'I bust a gut to get them ready by half past five and it's now,' she paused to look at her watch, 'twenty past six.'

'I know, I know, what can I say? I've been in London most of the day. All right, kids, into the car.'

Leah bent down to kiss first Fred and then Molly before following them out into the hall and handing them their rucksacks. Jamie opened the front door and hustled them out towards the pavement. Glancing over at Jamie's gleaming black BMW X1, Leah noticed that the front passenger seat was occupied and that the occupant had long, blonde hair.

Jamie, following Leah's gaze, said quickly, 'Charlotte's coming with us. She said she'd like to meet Mum and Dad.'

Charlotte was Jamie's latest girlfriend. 'That's nice,' Leah said. She forced a brisk smile onto her face and clapped her hands together. 'Well, have a good weekend. Send my love to your parents.'

'Will do. We'll see you on Sunday.'

Leah waved goodbye until the car turned the corner and disappeared from view. She went back into the house, shut the door behind her and went through to the kitchen.

'Have a good weekend, Jamie,' she said. 'Have a really wonderful weekend.' She took out a half-empty bottle of Sauvignon from the fridge and poured herself a glass.

What was it Jamie had said? *You look nice.* She wondered if he suspected that she always made an effort with her appearance when she knew she was going to see him. Today, for example, she had put on her pencil-slim black leather skirt and close-fitting jersey shirt. It was a pathetic way to carry on; in fact it was deeply sad and ultimately rather humiliating.

She took a sip of her drink and caught Stephen's eye. 'What?' she demanded. 'There's nothing wrong with having a drink on a Friday evening.' She stared irritably at him. 'There *is* something wrong about trying to talk to a goldfish.'

She and Jamie had split up three years ago. They were divorced. He was never coming back, which was fine because why would she want a man who was programmed to have sex with any pretty woman who wanted him? Especially since, as Leah had found to her cost, there were queues of them waiting to take their turn.

She'd known from her children that he'd been seeing Charlotte for at least a couple of months. What hurt, what really, really hurt was that this was the first time Jamie was taking a girlfriend along with his children to see his parents.

The first time Jamie had taken *her* to see his parents, she had adored them almost immediately. Mary Payne was elegantly dressed, with immaculate silver hair and perfect skin. Unlike her husband, a big man with a ruddy complexion and a white moustache, who had instant opinions on everything, she chose her words with care and was far more interested in hearing Leah's views than in voicing her own.

Leah's mother, Sylvia, had always been a lukewarm presence in her life. Her father had died when she was eighteen months old and her mother had married again soon afterwards; she never stopped being slavishly grateful to her second husband for rescuing her from poverty and she never tired of telling Leah that his wishes must always be paramount. Unfortunately, it was quite obvious that while he loved Sylvia, he did not love Leah and didn't actually like her much either. Leah learnt from an early age that her mother would always put her husband before her daughter and that Leah's best chance of pleasing them both was to keep out of their way as much as she could.

Six years ago, her mother and stepfather retired to Corfu where they lived in a bright yellow villa with views overlooking the sparkling bay of Kouloura. For the last three summers, Leah and her children had gone out to visit them and she wasn't sure whether she or her stepfather dreaded the annual fortnight more.

It was impossible not to compare the chilly bleakness

of her own upbringing with that of Jamie. Mary and John adored their son and they extended their warmth and interest to Leah, blithely accepting her as part of the family. When she and Jamie split up, Mary rang to assure Leah that, as far as she and John were concerned, she would always be important to them. Inevitably, as time passed, Leah had seen less and less of them. It was ridiculous to be jealous over one's ex-parents-in-law but there it was.

Leah caught Stephen's eye again. She was just as bad as he was. In fact, she was worse. Stephen might keep swimming pointlessly round and round his bowl but she – even more pointlessly – kept letting herself be hurt by Jamie and she didn't even have the excuse of amnesia. She gulped down the rest of her wine and made a sudden decision. She was aware that she had a tendency to respond to emotional turmoil in a way that was often reckless and irresponsible. Tonight, she had no intention of changing the habits of a lifetime. She could stay at home and fester in a cesspool of self-pity or she could go out and drink too much and behave badly. She had no need of babysitters, she was looking good and she wanted company. More specifically, she wanted male company. 'No offence, Stephen,' she said, 'but you're not quite enough.'

Leah lived in a small terraced cottage in Widcombe, a part of Bath that had its own distinct and uniquely laid-back atmosphere. Its short high street possessed three excellent restaurants, a couple of wine bars and two coffee shops. One of the many plusses of living where she did was that she could walk from her home to Widcombe High Street in a matter of minutes. Another plus was that Terry's Wine Bar was in the middle of the high street and Terry's

Wine Bar was a great place to go to when she had no children at home and nothing in the diary. The eponymous Terry was a short, middle-aged man whose life seemed to proceed precariously on a permanent tightrope below which professional and personal disasters were constantly lying in wait. He and Leah were fond of each other and he often said they were kindred spirits. Leah had never liked to ask *why* he thought that.

Tonight, the place was pretty empty. There was a bulky, middle-aged man reading the paper at one table, a trio of young men talking business at another and two girls speaking earnestly to a third at the table by the door. 'The trouble with you, Rachel,' one of the girls was saying, 'is you never say no. If you act like a doormat he'll treat you like a doormat. Next time he tells you he's coming round because he's horny, just tell him what he can do with his pathetic little penis . . .'

Too right, Leah thought. She would have liked to join in the conversation. She walked up to the bar and greeted Terry with an affectionate kiss on his cheek.

'Ah, Leah,' Terry said, 'my evening has suddenly got better. A glass of your usual?'

'You bet,' Leah said, watching him pull a bottle from the ice bucket. 'I'm in need of cheering up.'

'Tell Uncle Terry. I presume it concerns your charming ex-husband?'

Leah nodded. 'He's taken the children to Winchester for the weekend. He's also taken his latest girlfriend. I know it shouldn't matter but,' she paused to take a seat, 'it does.'

Terry scratched the stubble on his chin. 'Leah,' he said, 'how old are you?'

'I'm thirty-five.'

'You're thirty-five, you're great-looking and you have a good job. I'm forty-three, I'm losing my hair and, as you can see tonight, I need more customers. I also have a wife who I'm pretty sure is doing her best to make me lose my sanity. Do you know what she did to my favourite shirt the other evening?'

Terry always did this, he always had to prove that his problems were worse than her problems. He was a competitive man. It was quite comforting to know someone who was better at screwing up relationships than she was and normally she would be all ears as Terry related the latest episode to hit his troubled marriage. Tonight, however, she became increasingly aware that the middle-aged man with the newspaper was watching her. She was unfazed by his attention, in fact she welcomed it. She wanted to forget the sight of the blonde in the front seat of Jamie's car and a bit of ego massage was just what she needed. At one point, she flicked her long, dark hair back from her face and let her eyes meet his. He was quite old but rather impressive-looking with his mane of charcoal-coloured hair.

She was not surprised when, a few minutes later, he came up to the bar. In a pleasingly deep voice, he asked Terry for another drink and then looked down at Leah. 'Your glass is empty. May I buy you a drink?'

He was tall – always a plus for Leah who was five foot eight in her stocking feet – and looked reassuringly solid in his black corduroy jacket and pink linen shirt. His voice had a slight hint of a Scottish accent. Leah was reminded of Sean Connery. She smiled and told him she'd love a margarita.

By the time she accepted a second margarita, she knew she would take him home. He had unnervingly mesmerizing black eyes and it was undeniably exciting to be the focus of such undiluted concentration.

She invited him back for coffee and knew that he knew that coffee was not on the menu. Once in the house, he took her in his arms and told her that he'd wanted her the first moment he'd seen her. This seemed to Leah to be incredibly romantic. She was aware that after two glasses of wine and two margaritas she would probably think that Attila the Hun was romantic, but she decided that if Jamie could have fun, so very definitely could she. The man not only had the voice of Sean Connery but he looked rather like an older Heathcliff in *Wuthering Heights*. She had always believed that Heathcliff must have been tremendous in bed.

As it turned out, this particular Heathcliff was a considerable disappointment. His foreplay was abysmal. He squeezed her breasts like a child grappling with playdough, rummaged briefly between her legs and then went straight for the kill, which, quite literally, took an age to come. She was reminded of a faulty bicycle pump trying to inflate a punctured tyre. At last, after what seemed forever, he rolled off her, said in his deep gravelly voice, 'That was good,' and went to sleep almost immediately. And he snored.

She awoke at seven with a thunderous headache and slipped out to the bathroom in search of paracetamol. He was still asleep when she came back and he continued to sleep through the sound of her hairdryer and a long, ill-tempered discussion about the economy on the radio. She switched off the radio, sat down on the bed and shook the man's arm.

One eye opened. 'You're dressed,' he said. 'That's a pity.'

Leah scratched her head and forced a smile to her face. 'I'm sorry to wake you,' she said, 'but my ex-husband is bringing back the children this morning.' Leah had just spoken two falsehoods in one sentence and she didn't feel even slightly guilty. 'I don't want to hurry you but he's coming over in an hour and I'd rather they didn't see you, so if you wouldn't mind . . .'

He opened the other eye. 'I can't get up without a cup of coffee,' he said. 'I like it black with just half a teaspoon of sugar.'

'Right,' Leah said, 'I'll go and get it for you.'

'Thank you. And if you could manage a piece of toast and a soft-boiled egg, I'd be very grateful.'

In the kitchen, Leah put on the kettle, slipped a slice of bread into the toaster and threw a saucepan on the stove. What had she *done*? Of all the stupid things she had done in her life, this had to be one of the stupidest. What other woman would bring home an overweight, middle-aged stranger, *have sex* with him, let him stay the night and end up making breakfast for him? She couldn't believe she was making him breakfast. He had so blithely assumed she *would* make him breakfast that she had found herself unable to contradict him. The man had a sort of spooky authority about him. She couldn't wait for him to go. His presence in the house made the self-disgust rise in her throat like bile. She wished her head didn't ache so much. She should never have drunk those margaritas.

When she went back upstairs with coffee, egg and toast,

he was still lying in bed. He sat up when he saw her, taking her pillows and placing them behind his back. 'Thank you,' he said, 'how very kind.' He studied the contents of the tray with care. 'Do you have any salt?'

'No,' Leah said firmly, 'I don't.'

'Never mind.' He took a sip of his coffee. 'Very nice.' He patted the duvet. 'Won't you join me?'

His hair fanned out around him as if he had been electrocuted and while he might sound a little like Sean Connery, he certainly didn't look like Heathcliff, because there was no way that Heathcliff had man boobs. 'Actually,' Leah said. 'I have quite a lot to do downstairs and the children will be here *very soon* . . .'

'And you'd like me to go.' He completed her sentence with a smile that implied his insight into her feelings was both admirable and unusually prescient. 'Don't worry. I won't be long.'

'Thank you. You'll find a towel in the airing cupboard to the left of the bathroom.' She gave him a cheery wave and went downstairs, muttering, 'Stupid, stupid woman! What were you thinking of?'

She felt slightly less angry with herself when he finally came downstairs. He looked better with his clothes on and his hair was now smoothed back from his face. He handed her the tray and said, 'Shall I see you again?'

'I don't think so,' Leah said. 'The children are here most of the time and at the moment they don't leave me much time for a social life.'

'I quite understand,' he said, a bit too quickly for her liking. It was all very well for her to find *him* a disappointment in bed but it was a blow to her pride that he obviously hadn't found *her* overwhelming either. 'Well,' he paused and she realized he couldn't remember her name, any more than she could remember his. 'Thank you for a very happy evening.'

When he'd gone, she murmured, 'At last!' and went through to the kitchen to make some fresh coffee. She wished she could bottle the way she felt at the moment so that the next time she was tempted to get drunk and behave badly, she could open the lid and smell the repugnance she was feeling now. It was stupid and immature and downright dangerous to pick up strange men when she was drunk. It wasn't as if she was particularly perceptive about men when she was sober.

She could still remember, as if it were yesterday, the first time she had seen Jamie. It was at a party. She had entered the room and had immediately caught his eye. He smiled at her and she felt as stunned as if he had called out her name. He had looked at her as if he *knew* her, as if he really knew her; he had looked at her as if he *understood* her, as if he felt they had a connection. It was fanciful, it was ridiculous, it was exhilarating.

There would be occasions in the future when she would see him giving that look to other women and would recognize in their faces the same effect it had had on her. He'd probably spent years perfecting it in front of the mirror.

She sat down at the table with her mug of black coffee and stared gloomily into the dark liquid. At her age it was pretty appalling to go to bed with a man whose name she couldn't remember. And as for his mesmerizing black eyes, he'd probably stared at her in that flattering way because he was too vain to wear his glasses. At least her headache was receding, which was more, she thought penitently, than she deserved.

Later that morning, she flung open her bedroom window and changed her sheets and duvet cover. A subsequent visit to the densely populated supermarket seemed punishment enough for her reckless behaviour and in the afternoon she settled down to the much more pleasant business of creating a Welcome to Bath card for Merrily.

By the time she left the house at half past six, Leah was, physically at least, completely recovered from the excesses of the night before. She was wearing one of her more successful finds from the Oxfam shop, a genuine 1940s dress with a ruched waist. She had been drawn by the ultra-feminine print of light yellow flowers on a sky-blue background and when she wore it she felt very much the demure young lady. Leah had a theory that what one wore affected how one behaved. It was a pity, she thought, that she hadn't worn this outfit last night.

She walked down the hill and felt her heart beat a little faster as she approached her destination. On the phone, Merrily's voice had sounded just as it used to: breathy, uncertain, slightly husky. When Alison told Leah that Merrily was moving to Bath and passed on her number, Leah discovered that Merrily was moving just half a mile away up the hill. In her excitement, Leah suggested a drink out to celebrate her first proper evening in Bath. Now it dawned on her that after moving down from London today, the last thing Merrily would want to do was to go out and be sociable. Well, she thought, going through the door of the Ring O' Bells, it was too late to worry about that now. She bought two large glasses of Sauvignon Blanc and found a table near the window. Alison had told her she'd easily recognize Merrily, but Alison had also told her she'd not been sure Merrily was Merrily until she had spoken.

In fact, when a thin woman with anxious, searching eyes came in, Leah knew at once who she was. She called out her name and stood up. She could see that her old friend was as nervous as she was. For a moment neither knew what to do and then Leah kissed Merrily's cheek and said, 'I bought you a white wine. I hope that's all right.'

Merrily sat down. 'That's lovely.' She stared at Leah for a moment and shook her head. 'You look so different!'

Leah laughed. 'I got rid of the red hair some time ago.'

'Your hair looks great. I like it longer like that. You look lovely.'

Leah would have liked to respond in kind but the fact was that Merrily did not look lovely. Her hair was scraped back from her forehead with a metallic blue band, she had dark shadows under her eyes and her large mustard-coloured cardigan did her no favours. Leah said, 'You must be exhausted after moving down. It was thoughtless of me to ask you out tonight. We'll make it short.'

'I wanted to see you. My husband's not around at the moment and I was only too happy to leave all the cases and come here. It was so nice of you to ring. I can't believe our new house is so near to your place.'

'I can't believe I'm talking to you. I never thought I'd see you again.' Leah watched Merrily's complexion darken and decided now was definitely not the time for an in-depth interrogation. She took the card out of her bag and presented it to her friend. 'That's for you.'

'Oh Leah!' Merrily blinked very hard and her mouth

wobbled dangerously. 'That's so kind. You and Alison have both been so kind. She's invited me and Christopher to supper next week.'

'I'm coming too. I've got it in my diary. It will be a grand reunion! She's quite jealous that I'm seeing you now. She'd have been here as well but she's got her eldest daughter staying the night.'

'I couldn't believe it when she came up to me at the station. And then my train arrived and we only had time to exchange phone numbers. I gather she lives out in the country.'

'She lives four miles away in a village called Tucking Friary, and when you see her house you will be green with envy. It's very old and it has an enormous garden and views to die for.'

'It's funny that you and Alison should end up living so near to each other.'

'That's all down to Alison. I used to live in London. I worked in a big letting agency. When my marriage broke down, Alison came up to see me. She suggested I make a new start down here. She's a property journalist, so she could help me with contacts. I got a job here in Widcombe with a woman who lets out flats and small houses, mainly to students and retired couples. It couldn't have worked out better really. Eighteen months ago, she and her husband decided to go travelling round Europe in their camper van for three months. They're still there now and we're talking about me buying her out. So I owe Alison a lot.'

'She was always great at organizing people. I presume she and Felix are still together? I liked him so much. Is he still a hospital doctor?'

'He's been a GP for years. He's the same old Felix. I

think you were still around when they had Phoebe and Eva and Harry?'

'I remember them. Phoebe was a plump little thing and she was always smiling . . .'

'She still smiles a lot but she's not plump. She's tiny. I always feel like a giraffe beside her. She works for an animal charity in London.'

'And what about Eva? The last time I saw her, she seemed to spend the whole time on her potty.'

'Eva has long dark hair and is just like a Hollywood film star except she's far more intelligent and will probably end up being prime minister. Then there's Harry, who looks very tough but is actually lovely. You wouldn't believe how many games of Connect 4 he's played with my two, and then there's Nathan, who's—'

'You have two children? Tell me about them.'

'Molly is nine and Fred is seven. I hope you'll meet them very soon.' Leah had a sip of her wine. 'Now I want to hear a bit about *you*. I know you have a son and that's about it. What made you decide to move to Bath?'

'Well,' Merrily hesitated, as if she was trying to remember the answer. 'My husband's aunt died in February and left Christopher her house down here. Christopher decided he'd love to live here and so,' she paused and blinked a few times, 'here we are.'

'Am I right in thinking,' Leah asked tentatively, 'that you aren't as enthusiastic as he is?'

'I'm sure I will be eventually,' Merrily said. 'It's just that I had a job I liked and I'll miss my friends and . . .' She paused and took a sudden gulp of her drink. 'Our son, Tom, is thirteen. It's difficult leaving Tom.'

'You've left him in London?'

Merrily managed a faint smile. 'We haven't left him on his own. I'm not quite that bad.'

Leah said quickly, 'No, of course not. Is he at boarding school?'

'No. He . . . he's moved in with Isobel.'

'*Isobel?*' Leah tried belatedly to contain her astonishment. 'So you're back in touch with your sister?'

'Yes. Do you remember she had a daughter? She went on to have a son. He's the same age as Tom. I like him very much. They get on really well and Tom didn't want to leave his school so . . . so Isobel offered to have him live with them during term-time.'

'Right.' It dawned on Leah that fifteen years was a very long time. The Merrily of fifteen years ago would never have asked her elder sister for a favour for the very good reason that Isobel had never shown the slightest desire to help Merrily in any way at all.

'I have a photo of Tom,' Merrily said. She delved into her bag and took out of her wallet a passport-sized picture of a young teenager with a broad grin and curly hair.

'He looks nice,' Leah said.

But Merrily's attention had been diverted. She smiled as a new arrival came through the door, and said, 'Christopher, you've joined us after all!'

Leah dragged her eyes away from the photo, and as she raised her head she felt her mouth turn to sandpaper. Merrily's husband smiled at her and said in a voice that would henceforth make the very name of Sean Connery repellent to her: 'You must be Leah. I've heard so much about you.'

CHAPTER THREE

Alison Receives Another Surprise

Alison's daughters had once been close companions. Breasts were responsible for the initial cooling of relations. At the age of eleven, Eva, like her mother before her, developed a pair of generous-sized breasts while Phoebe, nearly two years her senior, remained stubbornly flat-chested. Other differences soon emerged. Eva was loathed by her teachers because she was stroppy and mouthy and eager to seek out injustice wherever she found it, which usually seemed to be in the exasperated figures who tried to teach her. Phoebe was quiet and well behaved and constantly embarrassed by her sister's behaviour. Eva gathered round her a group of like-minded friends who loved politics and strange music. Phoebe divided her time between the Claverton Dogs' Home and a series of good-looking boys in near-identical leather jackets. She showed a far greater constancy towards the former than she did towards the latter.

Appearances, as Alison often observed, could be deceptive. Eva's flamboyant exterior concealed a deep shyness and lack of confidence. As far as Alison knew she had yet to form any romantic relationships and had dithered about university courses until the very last moment. Phoebe's gentle, gamine appearance concealed a core of steel that revealed itself in the sixth form when she steadily resisted all attempts to persuade her to apply to university. Instead she started work with an animal charity in London and found herself a grubby flat in Streatham.

And now here she was, looking ridiculously young with her short blonde hair and her oversized army jacket, climbing out of the car of a man who resembled a throwback to the 1950s with his slicked back hair, his quite extraordinary yellow winkle-pickers and his three-quarter-length coat with shiny lapels. Alison had been telling herself all day that just because she had disliked Lennie on his first visit, there was no reason for not making an effort to like him on his second. So now she smiled brightly and moved forward to greet him.

She was rewarded with a kiss on both cheeks. 'All right, Mrs C?' he said, patting her shoulder. 'May I say that you look extremely shapely? And as for your cardigan, it shouts out: look at me, here I am. Great stuff.'

It was possible that he *did* like her cardigan but it seemed to her that he gave the compliment an ironic flourish. Alison, who already possessed doubts about the aesthetic value of the pink and green stripes on her sleeves, decided she would take it off at the first opportunity. She wasn't at all sure she liked being called shapely, either. It was the sort of word one would use to flatter someone who was overweight. Which she wasn't, although it was true she hadn't weighed herself lately.

'It's so good to be home,' Phoebe said, giving her mother

a hug. 'I'm sorry we're so late. Lennie's mother made a cake for tea, so we felt we had to stay . . . Hello, Dad!'

Alison knew only too well that Felix disliked Lennie as much as she did and was relieved to see that after kissing his daughter, he greeted her boyfriend with at least a semblance of civility. Nathan, who had followed his father out, nearly spoilt the happy scene by admiring Lennie's shoes, but Alison, immediately sensing that Felix was about to say something he should later regret, hastily ushered everyone into the kitchen whereupon Phoebe spotted Magnus and cried, 'Oh, I've *missed* you!'

Magnus, thrilled to have his biggest fan back, promptly rolled over onto his back in the happy knowledge that Phoebe would scratch his tummy.

'Harry sends his love,' Alison said. 'He's had to go out tonight but he says he'll be back in time for Sunday lunch.' What Harry had actually said was that there was no way he was going to spend a Saturday night with Lennie telling him what music he should be listening to. It had taken some hefty negotiation to extract a promise that he'd be back in the morning.

'What about Eva?' Phoebe had dropped down onto her knees in order to attend to Magnus. 'Is she around tonight?'

'She's been getting ready for at least an hour,' Alison said. 'She'll be down soon. She's going out for a Thai meal. I think it's somebody's birthday. You'll see her properly tomorrow.'

'*I'm* here,' Nathan said. 'I refused to go out once I knew you were coming.'

'Oh Nathan,' Phoebe sighed. 'That's so sweet.'

'Also,' Nathan said, 'Mum promised to make chocolate bread and butter pudding if I stayed in.'

'Great,' Phoebe said. 'Eva and Harry are out on the town and Nathan has to be bribed to stay with us.'

'Nathan is teasing you,' Alison said quickly, 'and Harry and Eva had made their plans and couldn't—'

'Mum, I don't mind! I don't mind anything!' Standing up, Phoebe smiled and took Lennie's hand. 'I can't wait for Eva,' she said, 'I'm far too excited. We've brought some champagne with us! Lennie even bought a cool bag to keep it cold. You'll never guess! Lennie and I are engaged!'

For a second, Alison was aware that her face had become set in concrete, imprisoned behind a sickly smile. Felix looked like he'd just seen a vampire.

'Well?' Phoebe beamed at her parents. 'Isn't it amazing?'

Alison, with a huge effort, set her facial muscles to work. 'Yes,' she said, 'it's very, very amazing.'

Phoebe radiated happiness as she looked at her mother. 'Do you remember telling me that the first moment you met Dad you knew he was the one you would marry? That's how I felt about Lennie. It was love at first sight.'

Alison looked at Lennie. He had a smug smirk on his face and she couldn't for the life of her see what Phoebe saw in him.

'I didn't stand a chance,' he said. 'When your daughter makes up her mind, she's a terrifying woman.' He reached for his bag. 'Let's break open the bubbly. It's time to celebrate!'

Alison sincerely hoped she'd never go through another celebration like this one. Felix lapsed into a shocked silence, which was fortunately obscured by the fact that

Magnus started barking when Lennie opened the champagne. Then Eva came down and when given the news, asked simply, 'Why?'

'Why not?' Phoebe's voice held a hint of irritation. 'We're in love.'

Eva accepted a glass of champagne from Lennie and said, 'Cheers! I think you're crazy, but cheers anyway!'

'Why am I crazy?' Phoebe demanded.

Eva shrugged. 'For the first eighteen years of your life you had to do what Mum and Dad said. In another ten years you'll be stuck with children. This is the only time you're free to do what you want and go where you want to go. Why get married when you're only nineteen?'

'That's an interesting point,' Felix said hopefully.

'Well, you can't talk, Dad,' Phoebe said sharply. 'You married Mum when she was only eighteen!'

The sound of a car horn punctured the darkening atmosphere and Eva, sensing she might have been more tactful, said quickly, 'That'll be my lift. I'd better go. I'm sure you'll be very happy and it is very . . . very romantic. I'm just saying it's not something I'd want to do until I'm at least thirty. I'll see you later.'

There was a short silence after she'd gone and then Phoebe said in an uncharacteristically petulant tone, 'Lennie's family were really pleased when we told *them*.'

'Of course we're pleased,' Alison said quickly. 'It's a bit of a shock, that's all.' She added almost absently, 'It's my second shock of the week.'

'Why?' asked Phoebe. 'What was the first?'

'On Monday,' Alison said, 'I was at the station and I looked across the platform and saw Merrily.'

'Merrily? Oh my God!' Phoebe turned immediately to Lennie. 'Eva and I used to act out stories about her. When Mum was a child, she had two best friends. They all lived next door to each other. One of them, Merrily, went to university in Exeter. She stayed on to do a teacher training course and then she vanished.'

'Perhaps she was murdered,' said Lennie, who had obviously been too busy picking up Eva's discarded glass to follow the conversation.

'Of course she wasn't, you idiot.' Phoebe gave his arm an affectionate push. 'Mum's just told us she's seen her and besides, she vanished deliberately. She sent a letter to her family saying she wouldn't be seeing them again.'

Alison, pleased that Phoebe's good humour had been fully restored, continued the story. 'To tell the truth,' she said, 'Leah and I were rather pleased she'd cut herself off from them. Her parents were always putting her down and they made it crystal clear that they preferred Isobel, Merrily's elder sister. But we never thought she wouldn't contact *us* again. We'd always looked out for her. And then, on Monday, after fifteen years, there she was. She and her husband are moving down to Bath. In fact, I'm pretty sure they moved down today. I've invited them and Leah to supper next Saturday and hopefully we'll find out what she's been doing.'

'Well,' Lennie said, 'that's great news.' He beamed at his future mother-in-law. 'I think it calls for another glass of champagne, don't you?'

Felix had a face that was naturally mournful in repose. Possibly that was due to his dark hooded eyes and his high Slavic cheekbones. His antecedents actually hailed from

Hertfordshire but Alison was sure that some Slav had got mixed up with them at some point. He also possessed a pair of dimples that frequently belied the apparent gravity of his demeanour and Alison did sometimes find it difficult to know if he was being serious or not.

He certainly looked pretty grave tonight. When she climbed into bed beside him, he was staring at the Winifred Nicholson print on the wall opposite. It was a charming depiction of two flower arrangements but Alison was pretty sure that Felix was currently oblivious to its charms.

'Do you remember that dinner party we went to several years ago?' he asked. 'One of the guests turned out to be a patient who was convinced I'd misdiagnosed her and then the hostess's son got ill and she asked me to have a look at him and he threw up all over me.'

'I do remember that,' Alison said. 'And we ate braised veal tongue and it was disgusting and someone else spilt red wine all over your trousers. It was a terrible evening.'

Felix turned to look at his wife. 'Tonight was worse.'

'That's a bit excessive.'

'I would rather watch a hundred Hugh Grant films,' Felix said, warming to his theme. 'I would rather listen to the Archbishop of Canterbury talk about God for twenty-four hours. I would rather have my teeth extracted.'

'Well, *that's* not true,' Alison said. 'It wasn't that bad.'

'It was. For me, it was. Eva was right and I should have said something. I kept wanting to say something but Phoebe looked so happy . . .'

'You heard what Phoebe said to Eva. I was eighteen when I married you. How could we possibly say she's too young to make up her mind?'

'She *is* too young.'

'I don't know that she is,' Alison said. 'Phoebe's had loads of boyfriends but this is the first time she's met anyone she loves as much as Magnus.'

'You're comparing Lennie to *Magnus*?'

'You know what I mean. She's never been like this before. She loves Lennie.' She sat up and repositioned her pillows before settling back against them. 'I think we're looking at this the wrong way round. I think this is our problem, not Phoebe's. She has no doubts at all. I think we need to work out why we don't like Lennie. Let's try to make a list of our objections. You start. What's your first objection?'

Felix stared thoughtfully at the duvet. 'Well,' he said, 'I just don't.'

'You just don't what?'

'I just don't like him.'

'Felix, that's a pathetic objection. You can't say you don't like him without explaining why.'

'Yes, I can,' Felix said. 'I just don't like him.'

'Oh for goodness sake . . . What's your second objection?'

'He's older than Phoebe.'

'You're older than me.'

'I'm six years older than you. He's eleven years older than Phoebe. He's only eight years younger than you.'

'My father's twelve years older than my mother and they're still happy.'

'Of course they are. Your parents were made for each other. They also happen to be two of the nicest people I know. Lennie, on the other hand, is one of the most irritating people I know. In fact, he *is* the most irritating man I know. He talks about his job as if it's the most important job in the world. He designs the sort of brochures that people throw straight into the wastepaper bin. And he makes jokes that aren't funny.'

Alison sighed. 'It's possible we bring out the worst in him. When people are nervous, they're never at their best.'

'That man doesn't have a nervous bone in his body.' Felix switched off his light. 'I tell you something,' he said. 'I wouldn't marry him if you paid me a million pounds.'

'Well, that's all right,' Alison said, reaching out to switch off her own light, 'because I don't think Lennie would have you.'

In the darkness, Felix sighed. 'I'm too depressed to go to sleep,' he said.

'Think of something cheerful,' Alison told him. 'Merrily's coming here next Saturday. You always liked Merrily.'

There was a long silence. 'Sorry,' Felix said, 'it doesn't work.'

Alison turned towards him and let her hand slide slowly down his torso. 'How about this?' she murmured.

There was another silence and then Felix turned to face her. 'That might just do it,' he said.

Felix was slightly reassured by the fact that neither Lennie nor Phoebe seemed anxious to set a date for the wedding. Nevertheless, when he came down to breakfast on Monday morning, he was not in the best of moods.

Felix was a GP in a group practice that covered a large range of villages between Bath and Frome. He got on well with his fellow doctors but had become increasingly irritated by the energetic enthusiasm of the new practice manager. He had received an email from him the night before and was still seething. 'Do you know his latest brilliant idea?' he said, sitting down and pouring cornflakes into his bowl. 'He's given us all kitchen timers. Every time a patient comes in, we're supposed to set it for ten minutes and then, when the pinger goes, we have to usher the patient out, even if we're in the middle of telling him he has an inoperable disease that will probably kill him the day after tomorrow. Sometimes I wonder if I went into the right profession.'

Felix wondered this quite regularly, usually at breakfast time on Monday mornings. 'That's rubbish,' Alison said, trying to stop Magnus from getting in her way, which was difficult since Magnus had slower reflexes than a snail. 'Everyone knows you're the best GP they've got and *you* know you never pay any attention to ideas you don't want to pay attention to.'

She said this with some feeling. Over the years, she had done her best to smarten him up, buying him good-quality shirts and stylish ties. There was a weird sort of alchemy about Felix so that no matter what he wore, he always looked as if he had just pulled his clothes out of the laundry basket.

As if sensing her critical scrutiny, Felix made a half-hearted attempt at straightening his tie and then glanced at his watch. 'If Eva doesn't come down soon, I shall have to go without her. Thank God she finishes her job on Friday. When does she go to university?'

'Two weeks yesterday,' Alison said. 'You'll miss her when she's gone.'

Felix gave a grunt, which could have meant anything but Alison correctly interpreted it as meaning that yes, he would miss her but that he'd have his teeth pulled before he admitted it.

Eva, like her father, was never at her best in the mornings. When she eventually appeared, dressed in her Billingford Garden Centre uniform of black jeans and green overall, she said breathlessly, 'I'll do my hair and make-up in the car. See, Dad, I'm ready.' She received a piece of buttered toast and an apple from her mother and murmured, 'Thanks, Mum,' before following her father out of the door.

Having seen off her husband and daughter, Alison turned her attention to the daily challenge of getting her sons to school on time. She went through to the bottom of the stairs and called out, 'Boys! We're going in fifteen minutes.' She went back to the kitchen, opened the cutlery drawer and took out a cutting from yesterday's paper, which she placed in the middle of the table.

After two increasingly shrill exhortations to her sons, her efforts were rewarded. Harry came down, mumbled what might have been a hello and reached for the Sugar Puffs.

Alison felt the usual stab of irritation whenever she was confronted by his appearance. Harry *should* be extremely good-looking. At seventeen, his body had already sloughed off its adolescent lankiness after its recent startling growth. He had broad shoulders and a muscular torso. Like all her children, he had inherited Felix's long dark eyelashes, although it was impossible to see how long they were, since his brown hair hung over his face like a pair of moth-eaten curtains. It was equally difficult to identify Harry's nice, muscular torso since his shoulders had a tendency to slump forward like those of a gorilla in what was possibly an attempt to disguise the phenomenal growth spurt – Harry was already taller than his father. Worse, he would insist on wearing his voluminous white shirt outside his trousers.

Alison gave Harry his coffee and carelessly pushed the cutting towards him. 'I read this article and cut it out for you. I found it really interesting.' She looked hopefully at him before going to the stairs and shouting, 'Nathan! We're going in *five minutes*!'

Back in the kitchen, Harry was staring at the piece of paper as if it had been printed in Chinese. ' "Does No Ever Mean Yes?" ' He made a face. 'I don't understand it.'

'You would if you read more than the title,' Alison said. 'It's about the misunderstandings that happen when you're with a girl. Sometimes, it can be difficult to *tell*.'

'It can be difficult to tell *what*?' Harry asked.

'Well,' Alison began, 'when you're with a girl and you like her and she likes you and you're on your own—'

'I'm on my own without the girl?'

'No, of course not, you're on your own *together* and you're having a nice time—'

'Why?' asked Harry. 'What are we doing?'

'Oh Harry, for goodness sake . . .' Alison paused to take a deep breath. 'Just read the article, it's very – very thought-provoking.'

'All right,' Harry said and helped himself to more cereal.

Alison glanced at the clock, muttered, 'Where's Nathan?' and went through to the stairs again. 'Nathan!' she shouted. 'It's time to go! Now!'

She and Harry were in the car and she'd hooted twice before Nathan finally came out of the house, bare-chested, clutching his school bag, his shirt and an apple. At fifteen, Nathan might still be the shortest boy in his class but, in Alison's impartial opinion, he was just as handsome as his elder brother would be if he only looked after himself. Nathan's hair was the colour of early morning sunlight and he had dimples that appeared whenever he smiled. Since he smiled a lot, they were often in evidence. In the last six months, he had developed the infuriating habit of being unable to rise without at least three warnings from his mother but it was impossible to be cross in the face of his persistent good humour. 'Sorry I'm late,' he said, climbing into the back seat. 'I couldn't find the last page of my essay. I found it under my bed. It's good, actually. Very philosophical.'

Alison ignored her elder son's 'Yeah, right,' and having negotiated her car out of the drive and into the lane, asked Nathan what it was about.

'You wouldn't understand the science,' Nathan said kindly, 'but it's about the way human beings influence evolution. So, for example, the killing of elephants for their tusks has led to greater numbers of tuskless elephants. They can reproduce and survive better than the normal ones, you see. And talking of tuskless elephants,' Nathan turned to his brother, 'is it true you dumped Francine yesterday?'

Harry responded by turning round to throttle Nathan,

an exercise abandoned only after Alison threatened to stop the car and make the two of them walk to the bus stop. She spent the rest of the journey alternately admonishing Harry for resorting to violence and irritably telling Nathan to stop coughing in that melodramatic way since Harry hadn't had time to really hurt him anyway. When they finally arrived at their destination, Harry lurched out of the car before she had had time to lift the handbrake. Alison turned and rebuked Nathan for comparing Harry's girlfriend to a tuskless elephant.

'She isn't his girlfriend now,' Nathan said. 'He dumped her. And then I saw him talking to Nicola Casement yesterday; it was like he was glued to her.' He got out of the car, oblivious to the fact that he had just wrecked his mother's morning.

In the first week of the summer holiday, Alison had heard Harry and Francine making love. She had come home unexpectedly early after a lunch with her editor turned out to be sandwiches in the office rather than the two-course restaurant meal she had expected.

Her first response had been to bolt. Whispering to Magnus, she had fastened his lead and crept out of the house. She felt a little ashamed of her cowardice but then, what could she do? They thought she was out and they would all three be embarrassed if they discovered she wasn't. At least, she and Francine would be embarrassed; she wasn't sure about Harry.

Alison had wondered if she should have gone in and broken up the love-making but that was surely ridiculous. Both parties were over the age of consent and it did sound as if Francine was enjoying herself which was nice since at least it meant that Harry had some idea of what he was doing. Although for goodness sake, Alison, she had told herself, you should not be clapping yourself on the back because your seventeen-year-old son has apparently acquired a good sexual technique. Alison had found some condoms in his room a few months earlier but there was a great difference between having a son who *hoped* to have sex and having a son who *was having* sex.

And now here was Harry, according to Nathan, on the verge of going out with one of Nathan's classmates, a young girl of *fifteen*! The possibilities didn't bear thinking about and so, of course, Alison thought about them all the way home. She hoped he'd digested the article but strongly suspected he hadn't. And really, she should know better than to try to engage his brain before the middle of the day.

She climbed out of the car and walked round to the back of the house. She loved this time of the day, just after the frantic family exodus and before the beginning of her own carefully organized timetable. She sat down on the bench on the stone patio and gazed out across the lawn to the rich green landscape beyond. Sloping hills fell gently onto one another like hands clasped in friendship, their smooth grassy surfaces unscarred by roads or fences. Instead, they were decorated with a profusion of deciduous trees: majestic ashes, comforting beeches, elegant silver birches and magnificent oaks.

She heard the phone and ran back into the house and picked up the receiver a little breathlessly. As soon as she heard Leah's voice, she asked quickly, 'Did you have a nice time with Merrily? Did you see her husband?'

'Yes, I did.' There was a slight pause. 'Look, I can't speak for long, I'm in the office. I don't think I can come to supper with you all on Saturday. I'm not sure Jamie can have the children and I can't get a babysitter.'

'Well, that's no problem,' Alison said. 'Bring them here. They can sleep in the spare room.'

Leah sighed. 'I thought you'd say that. If you must know, I – I didn't like Merrily's husband.'

'What does *that* matter? This isn't about Merrily's husband, this is about you and me and Merrily being together again. You *have* to come. What's wrong with the man anyway?'

'Well, for a start, I think he's moved her down here against her will. She didn't seem at all happy about it. And there's something really odd. Their son doesn't want to move schools so he's staying up in London. He's gone to live with Isobel.'

'*Isobel?*' Alison gasped. 'I wouldn't let any of my children near her.'

'Perhaps she's changed,' Leah said doubtfully.

'It's a well-known fact,' Alison said, 'that bitchy girls grow up to be bitchy women. She used to love making Merrily look small. Tell me more about the husband. Why else don't you like him?'

'Well,' said Leah with uncharacteristic reticence, 'I just don't.'

'Honestly,' Alison said, 'you're as bad as Felix. And I'm sorry but I won't take no for an answer. You have to come to supper. I don't care what the husband is like. It's going to be a brilliant evening.'

Despite this confident assertion, Alison was rattled by

Leah's phone call. It was unlike Leah to take such a vague and nebulous dislike to someone. Leah usually knew exactly why she didn't like people.

Leah arrived on Saturday looking enviably slim but distinctly funereal in black trousers and black shirt. She refused Felix's offer of wine and asked for an orange juice, which was even more out of character. 'I'm driving,' she explained.

'You could leave your car here and get a taxi back,' Felix suggested.

'I don't think so,' Leah said. 'I have to catch up on some work tomorrow and I'll need a clear head.' She glanced around the kitchen. 'Where is everyone? Eva hasn't gone to Manchester yet, has she?'

Alison rolled her eyes. 'Eva's at yet another farewell party. She seems to be doing nothing *but* go to farewell parties at the moment. Nathan's gone down the road to watch a DVD with Luke, and Harry's in town. I'm glad they're not here, to tell the truth. It means we can concentrate on Merrily.'

As if on cue the doorbell went and Alison pressed her hands together. 'Here we go!' she said.

Introductions were made, coats were taken and glasses were filled. Alison had time to notice that Merrily's outfit looked like it might once have been a maternity dress and Christopher was a rather imposing man who was nearer fifty than forty. He wore a well-cut herringbone jacket, brown corduroy trousers and a good-quality roll-neck jumper. He had a mane of darkly greyish hair, good teeth and a fine pair of black eyes, which he now turned on

Alison. 'You and Leah look far too young to be friends of Merrily,' he said. 'The air down here must have rejuvenating qualities.'

'I hope so,' Leah said, 'because you look far too old to be married to Merrily.'

Alison glanced quickly at both Leah and Christopher. She couldn't believe Leah could be so breathtakingly rude, even if Christopher's remark had been unwittingly unflattering to his wife. She gave a tight little laugh and said, 'You mustn't mind Leah, she has a very wicked sense of humour!'

Fortunately, Christopher seemed unperturbed. 'So I see,' he said. He put his face close to Leah's. 'I can see I'm going to have to watch you,' he said.

'Let's go through to the sitting room,' Alison said. 'I know it's only September but I thought it would be nice to have a fire.'

Merrily was entranced first by the view out to the valley and then by the silver-framed photo on the mantelpiece. It had been taken shortly after they moved to Tucking Friary. Phoebe and Eva sat laughing at each other on either end of the garden bench. Between them was Harry, sporting a broad gap-toothed grin, holding on his lap a five-year-old Nathan, who gazed up lovingly at his elder brother.

'They all look adorable,' Merrily sighed. 'I was hoping I'd see them tonight.'

'They want to meet you too,' Alison assured her. 'There's plenty of time for that. I wouldn't exactly describe any of them as adorable these days. They were all so easy at that age. Teenagers are always difficult.'

'Tom isn't,' Merrily said. 'Perhaps that will happen later.'

'My wife,' Christopher said, 'has rose-coloured glasses when it comes to our son.'

Felix grinned. 'I'd like to borrow them,' he said. He raised his glass to Merrily and said, 'I think we should have a toast. To friends reunited!'

Everyone duly intoned, 'To friends reunited,' and Alison couldn't resist adding, 'I'm only sorry we had to wait fifteen years for it.'

Christopher sat down on the sofa and crossed his legs. 'May I speak frankly, Alison? Merrily can tell you I am not a man who likes secrets or unspoken resentments. I have always believed in honesty, however difficult that might sometimes be. I have to say I do detect a residue of bitterness or at least bewilderment in your voice. Will you allow me to respond with an explanation that might help you to understand Merrily's self-imposed exile?'

He leant forward as he spoke, his black eyes earnestly studying her face. She was rather flattered by his attention; it was a little like being courted by Gordon Brown, who had a very similar voice and an almost identical authoritative solemnity about him. She gave a gracious nod of her head and said, 'Please, do go on.'

'Thank you.' He folded his arms and spent a few moments staring down at them, presumably gathering his thoughts. 'I understand that Merrily was brought up in an isolated environment.'

'We all were,' Alison said. 'We lived on a farm in the middle of nowhere. The farmer converted three outbuildings into houses and our families all moved in at about the same time. There was no one else for miles around. That's why we became such close friends, even though we were in different years at school. Whenever my children complain we live in the sticks, I tell them they know nothing about it.'

Christopher gave a sympathetic nod. 'I'm sure it must have been difficult, particularly as you got older. However, it strikes me that you and Leah were better equipped to deal with the remoteness of your location. Merrily had a family who had little time for her and as a result she had few social skills and no self-worth. You, on the other hand, apparently had loving parents and found it easy to make friends. As for Leah, Merrily tells me she was allowed to run wild and so,' he displayed a knowing smile, 'run wild is what she did.'

'I never said that.' Merrily sounded uncomfortable. 'It was only—'

Christopher glanced sharply at his wife. 'Please don't interrupt,' he said. Ignoring his wife's murmured apology, he took a thoughtful sip of wine. 'It's interesting for me to meet Merrily's old friends. You and Leah are bright, attractive women. I can see Merrily as a teenager: shy and rather plain and—'

'Actually,' Felix protested mildly, 'she wasn't.'

Christopher regarded him with ill-concealed impatience. 'I beg your pardon?'

'Merrily may have told you she was plain,' Felix said, 'but she wasn't. I remember the first time I met them all. I shared a flat in London with Alison's brother and he invited me to his parents' home for the weekend. We arrived in time for lunch and Leah and Merrily were there. Alison was seventeen, so Merrily must have been a little younger. She had a lovely smile.' He raised a glass to Merrily. 'You still have a lovely smile.'

For the first time that evening, Leah laughed. 'Can you remember what *I* was like?'

'I certainly can,' Felix retorted. 'You were fourteen going on forty with enough eye make-up to sink a battleship and you were amazingly rude to Alison's brother.'

Leah grinned. 'I was always rude to Alison's brother. I loved being rude to Alison's brother.'

'When I met Merrily,' Christopher said, doggedly ignoring this second interruption, 'she was lonely, insecure and desperate to find a purpose to her life.' He paused impressively. 'I gave her that purpose.'

Felix broke into a sudden fit of coughing, which was only resolved by a slug of wine. Alison looked at her husband suspiciously and said hastily, 'How very interesting.'

'I don't think it's interesting,' Leah said with a fierceness that Alison felt was a little unnecessary. 'I don't think it's interesting because I don't think it's true. I don't remember Merrily being particularly insecure and lonely.'

Christopher allowed himself a little chuckle. 'I suspect you were rather preoccupied with your own very colourful private life. All I can tell you is that I could see right away that Merrily needed to cut herself off from her childhood influences. In order to repair herself, it was necessary for her to close the door on her past life and give herself up to the future.'

'Forgive me for being dense,' said Felix with a modesty that Alison knew was completely bogus, 'but by "the future" do you mean your own good self? Because if that's so—'

'Forgive me for interrupting,' Alison said, leaping to her feet and clapping her hands together. 'But I think we should go and eat. Do bring your glasses.'

She had made a variety of salads to go with her poached salmon and she hoped that by the time they had all been served they would be able to move the conversation on. Christopher, however, had other ideas.

'I don't want you to think,' he said, 'that Merrily isn't pleased to see you again. These days, she has the confidence to cope with her past. These days, she has a meaning to her life.'

Felix ignored his wife's desperate eye movement. 'And that meaning is you?'

'She helps me in my work,' Christopher said simply. He gazed round the table and said, 'I am a writer. I am Christopher Trumpet.'

This clearly revelatory statement was received with blank incomprehension by three of his listeners. Alison was instantly apologetic. 'I'm afraid we're total philistines. Felix only reads *The Lancet* and Leah and I can just about manage the odd magazine.' She darted a glance at Leah who opened her mouth and thankfully shut it again. 'Do tell me,' she added nervously, 'what sort of things do you write?'

'Most people,' Christopher said, 'would tell you I write novels. I prefer to call them spiritual explorations. I find that within the parameters of fiction, I can examine the big questions facing humanity today.'

Merrily cleared her throat. 'Christopher has written eight novels. He's translated in sixteen languages. He gets letters and emails from all over the world.'

'Well,' Alison said, 'that is certainly impressive.' She was beginning to feel quite exhausted. Leah was no help and Felix was positively dangerous. As the meal progressed, it became apparent that any attempt to have a quiet chat with Merrily was out of the question. Christopher maintained what was virtually a monologue. During the chocolate mousse, Alison managed to ask him about his latest book and immediately regretted it as he proceeded to give a long explanation in which he talked about allegories and metaphors and accessibility and tangential thinking. It made no sense to Alison whose understanding nods became increasingly random.

And then, quite suddenly, while she was clearing away the pudding plates, Christopher pushed back his chair and said, 'I'm afraid we must go. It's been a most enjoyable evening.'

Alison stared at him in astonishment. 'But we haven't had cheese yet. Can't I make you some coffee at least?'

'Merrily will give me some peppermint tea at home. The Muse is tugging at my sleeve and when the Muse strikes, I must act. I'm afraid, like a doctor, I am always on call. Now please don't get up, we can let ourselves out.'

Of course they all did get up and they all went out onto the drive to wave goodbye. Then the three of them returned to the table and Felix said, 'I need another drink.' He refilled his glass and raised it in the air. 'Here's to Christopher Trumpet, saviour of Merrily.'

'I can't believe they just left like that,' Alison said. 'Do you think he was offended by something we said? I mean, I know Leah was—'

'Actually, I don't think it's possible to offend him,' Felix said. 'The man absolutely knows he is better than the rest of us.'

'I must say,' Alison mused, 'I did find him a terrible

bore. And he was so horrid to poor Merrily. Most of the time he talked about her as if she wasn't there and I hated the way he kept banging on about how plain she was. I thought he would never stop talking. But I have to say that you two behaved very badly. Felix, you spent the first half of the evening trying to be rude to him and in the second half of the evening you just gave up the ghost. And as for you, Leah, you hardly spoke and when you did I wished you hadn't! What on earth got into you? I thought you were as pleased as I was about seeing Merrily. You made no effort at all. I can understand that you don't like Christopher – I don't either – but we owe it to Merrily to try to get close to him.' She saw Leah give a faint smile and said irritably, 'What's so funny about that?'

'I did get close to him,' Leah said. 'That's the trouble.'

'No, you didn't. What *do* you mean?'

'I mean,' said Leah, 'I slept with him.'

CHAPTER FOUR

Leah Changes Her Mind

It was quite funny – except Leah had never felt less like laughing – to see the faces of Felix and Alison, the way their reactions veered from a half-amused, yeah-right look to an oh-my-God expression.

Felix was the first to speak. 'Leah,' he said, 'one of the great pleasures of knowing you is that you never fail to surprise me.'

Alison said, 'Leah, how *could* you sleep with Merrily's husband?'

Leah could feel her face burning. 'You see, this is why I didn't want to tell you. I *knew* you'd take this high moral tone.'

Alison shook her head impatiently. 'I don't mean how could you sleep with him – well, I do mean that as well – I mean, how *could* you sleep with him? You only met him last week and—'

'If you'll give me a chance I'll tell you. First off, I had no idea he *was* Merrily's husband, because, funnily enough, if I had known, I wouldn't have slept with him. It was last Friday, the night before Merrily moved here. I was feeling a bit down. Jamie came over to collect Fred and Molly. They were all going to his parents for the weekend. When I went out to see them off, I saw he had a girlfriend in the car with him.' She stared defensively at first Alison and then Felix. 'All right, I know it was pathetic but it . . . it upset me.'

'I don't know why,' Alison said. 'I mean, we all know what Jamie's like.'

Leah looked longingly at the bottle of wine and poured herself a glass of water. 'You don't understand. Of course I know that Jamie has girlfriends. It's just that this is the first time he's taken one of them to see his parents. That means this one is serious.'

'Leah,' Alison said, 'you've been divorced for three years now . . .'

'I know, I know. It's stupid and I'm stupid and I don't need you to tell me I'm stupid.'

'Oh Leah.' Alison stood up, brought the cheese board over to her and said, 'The Stilton is good.'

It was a typical Alison olive branch and Leah fought off an urge to start crying by taking a gulp of her water and cutting a big piece of cheese. Duly fortified, she finished her confession as quickly as she could. 'After Jamie left I went down to Terry's to drown my sorrows and I met Christopher, only I didn't know he *was* Christopher, and I ended up taking him home with me.' She caught sight of Alison's shocked face and said hotly, 'It's very easy to be sensible and well behaved when you're happily married. It's not something I do on a regular basis and there's no need to look like that.'

'I'm not looking like anything and I wouldn't dream

of criticizing you,' Alison protested before immediately proceeding to do so. 'I just think it's silly. You knew nothing about the man; he could have been a psycho, or worse.'

'What could be worse than a psycho?' Leah asked.

'Well, *I* don't know – he could have been a psycho with syphilis and house-burning tendencies; *you're* the one who likes horror films. I hope he wore a condom.'

'Well, of course he did.'

'What fascinates me,' said Felix, a past master at defusing potential clashes between his wife and his wife's best friend, 'is what it was that led you to succumb to Christopher's undoubted charms. Was it his great sense of humour or his ability to listen?'

Leah gave a reluctant smile. 'It was definitely his sense of humour. And the margaritas helped. The whole thing was a big disaster. I couldn't wait to get rid of him the next morning. He was horrible.'

'Really?' Alison looked alarmed. 'What did he do?'

'Well,' Leah said, 'he made me bring him breakfast in bed.'

Felix nodded sympathetically and then sucked in his mouth and began making noises that sounded like a faulty engine being started.

'It actually isn't funny, Felix,' Alison said. 'Think about the man's behaviour this evening. Any normal man would be completely thrown by the sight of Leah.'

'I'm always thrown by the sight of Leah,' Felix agreed.

'Felix, you're being annoying. Stop it. He comes to a meal at which his wife and a woman he has recently bedded are both present and he shows absolutely no confusion or awkwardness whatsoever.' Alison cut herself a piece of cheese and looked curiously at Leah. 'What was he like when he met you with Merrily?'

Leah shrugged. 'It was like he'd never met me before. He was polite and friendly. We all chatted for a bit. He said he'd moved down to Bath a few days before Merrily in order to avoid the packing up. And then he stared straight at me and said he found Bath a very exciting place.'

'I bet he did,' Felix said.

Leah shook her head at the memory. 'It was a nightmare. I just wanted to disappear. I made my excuses as quickly as possible and fled.'

'Can you believe the hypocrisy of the man?' Alison fumed. 'Do you remember him going on about believing in honesty at all times? And he dares to tell us he was the answer to Merrily's problems.' She frowned thoughtfully. 'And that's another thing. All that stuff he told us to explain Merrily's vanishing act: it still doesn't explain why she gave up on us as well as her family. You and I were always telling her not to let them get to her. And then Christopher banged on about how unhappy she was when he met her. I don't remember her being like that.'

'I'm not so sure,' Leah said. 'That last time the three of us met up at your parents' house, she was still going on about Dennis.'

'Was he the boyfriend?' Felix asked.

Alison grimaced. 'She fell in love with him at university. He spent two years trying to decide whether to sleep with her or not and then he decided to become a monk instead.'

'I remember now,' Felix said. 'It's all so sad. The Merrily I knew might have been shy but she had a great sense of humour. I didn't see any sign of that tonight. She hardly spoke.'

'Let's face it,' Alison said. 'Christopher made it impossible for anyone to speak.'

Leah sighed, 'Felix is right, Merrily's changed. Her husband makes my skin crawl. There's no way I can go on seeing her. I have nothing in common with her now.'

'How can you say that?' Alison demanded. 'Apart from me, she's the only old friend you have. You have an entire childhood in common.'

'I know. But all that is in the past. We're different now. Trying to recover that friendship would be like raising someone from the dead. I can't do it and I'm not going to try.'

What Leah didn't say was that she didn't see how she could enjoy being with Merrily when she had – albeit inadvertently – slept with her husband. Guilt was never the best of ingredients in any relationship.

On Monday morning, Leah walked the children to school and then made her way to her office, devoutly hoping that the day's business would be interesting enough to keep her mind off Merrily. A few hours later, she would remember that hope and would remind herself that one should always be careful what one wished for.

She noticed the car at once, first because there was a double-yellow line outside her office and so cars should not be there, and secondly because it looked as if the entire contents of a house had been packed inside it. As Leah stopped to pull out her keys, the driver of the car got out. Leah glanced quickly at the woman sitting in the front passenger seat and then at the boxes and pictures and saucepans in the seat behind her.

Three days ago, this man and woman had presented Leah with a bottle of wine. Three days ago, she had left them, surrounded by packing cases, in their brand-new flat.

She had liked the Websters immediately. They were a hard-working couple in their mid-thirties, obviously happy together and thrilled about the fact that they were expecting a baby in two months. It was evident from what they said that they had been trying for some time. Robert was a barrister, with chambers in Bristol. Lizzie was part-founder of a company that specialized in producing text books for schools. They had bought an old house in Bathford that was being done up and in the meantime they needed a flat to rent.

Leah had known exactly what to offer them. One of her landlords had recently renovated a large Georgian house and converted it into flats. Leah had shown them the ground-floor one; it had access to a small courtyard garden and they'd loved it. On Friday morning she had been there to give them the keys and they had been happy and grateful. Now, Lizzie Webster sat silently in the front seat of the car, pale-faced and tense, looking as if she'd seen a ghost.

Which, apparently, she had. Robert said that in the middle of the night, Lizzie had gone to the kitchen to get some milk. She had taken a few sips and then looked up to see before her a Roman soldier. Before she could do or say anything, the soldier had *gone through* her and disappeared. Lizzie screamed and dropped her glass. Robert woke up and leapt out of bed. He found his wife standing in a pool of milk, crying hysterically.

They had spent the next few hours packing up; they had arrived outside Leah's office a half-hour ago. They were planning to visit the doctor to make sure the baby was all right before going to check in at a hotel. They wanted Leah to find them somewhere else fast.

Leah had only to look at Robert's face to know there was no point in querying his story. It didn't really matter if Lizzie had or had not seen a ghost. The point was that she and Robert believed she had and it was clear there was no way that either of them would ever step foot in that house again.

Alarmed by the sight of Lizzie's shell-shocked appearance, Leah told Robert to take her to the doctor. She would sort things out and find them alternative accommodation as soon as she could. She would deal with it.

Having waved the couple off, she went into the office and made herself an extra-strong cup of black coffee. All she had to do was ring the landlord of the Websters' flat and inform him that the ghost of a Roman soldier had apparently taken residence there and, by the way, his tenants had left and weren't coming back. Then all she had to do was find another property that was instantly available and guaranteed to be free of ghosts.

It was a terrible day. At least she was not completely alone. A year ago, she had taken on Diana Masters, a 45-year-old woman who had only, she'd told Leah humbly, been a housewife for the last fifteen years. Diana turned out to be a treasure and on days like these, when Leah had to drop everything, proved to be invaluable. Having quickly briefed her about the jobs that needed covering, Leah took a deep breath and rang the landlord. The landlord was not interested in Leah's views on Robert and Lizzie Webster. He didn't care how charming and intelligent they were. All he knew was that in the months he and his builders had been renovating the property, none of them had ever once been aware of Roman legionaries tramping through the place. All he also knew was that Leah had provided him with crazy tenants who had agreed to pay him six months' rent. As far as he was concerned, he was minded to sue the Websters and sue Leah unless she could sort something out pretty fucking fast. Leah listened to his opinions on her and the Websters and Widcombe Rentals for another twenty minutes and then promised she would not stop until she had sorted everything.

A Mr Porter had left a message on the answerphone to say he and his wife were interested in finding a flat in town in the next six months or so. He sounded pretty old and Leah did wonder if her conscience would let her suggest a haunted house to an old-age pensioner. In the light of the present circumstances, her conscience proved to be surprisingly malleable. Leah rang him and said she had a very nice place that was available right away. Would he care to see it this morning? If Mr Porter was surprised by her urgency he didn't show it. He said he and his wife relied on their daughter for transport and unfortunately she was away for a couple of days. Leah offered to pick them up immediately and take them home afterwards. When he told her they lived in Melksham, a good half-hour away from Bath, she hesitated for only a moment and said she would leave right away. After hurling more instructions at Diana, she grabbed her bag and walked swiftly home to pick up her car.

It took her some time to find their house, and when she got there she tried to remain patient while Mrs Porter looked for her bag and Mr Porter wondered whether to take his coat. On the drive to Bath, Mr Porter told her why they had decided to leave their home of eighteen years. Their daughter, their daughter's partner and their two grandchildren had moved in to live with them a few months ago. 'It's been very nice,' Mr Porter said, 'but we think it's time to leave the place to them.'

It was obvious that the attempt at cohabitation had been far from successful. Leah admired their restraint and their unselfishness and tried to be deaf to her increasingly uncomfortable conscience.

They thought the flat was perfect. They loved the position and they loved the garden. 'It's perfect,' Mrs Porter said. 'It's absolutely perfect!'

It was no use. Leah knew she had to speak up. She told them it was only fair to let them know that the previous tenants had left after apparently seeing the ghost of a Roman soldier near the fridge. Mrs Porter looked at Mr Porter, Mr Porter looked back at Mrs Porter, and Mrs Porter said, 'We'll take it! I *do* hope we see the ghost!'

When Leah got back to the office, she rang the landlord with the good news. Then she went through the properties the Websters had discarded and found out that one of them, a tiny terraced cottage in Batheaston, was still available.

That evening, Leah decided a celebration was in order

and told her children they would have a takeaway followed by a game of Monopoly. At half past six, they sat round the table contentedly eating vegetarian spring rolls, egg fried rice, roast pork chow mein and prawn crackers. Leah was in the middle of giving a highly embellished account of the ghostly flat incident when the telephone rang. Leah would have let the answerphone take it but Molly instantly jumped up. At first she had on her polite phone voice but soon she was chatting away about her favourite lessons and it was only after Leah pointed to Molly's rapidly cooling dinner that she said, 'I'll pass you to Mummy. We're eating a takeaway.'

Leah took the receiver and heard an apologetic voice say, 'Leah? I'm sorry to interrupt your meal.'

Leah swallowed hard. 'Hi, Merrily. We've nearly finished eating but actually, I can't talk for long. I have a very important engagement. I'm about to play a game of Monopoly.'

'Can I play too?' Merrily sounded genuinely excited. 'I can be with you in no time.'

As Leah proceeded to give directions, she felt her good spirits melt like chocolate in the sun. It had not occurred to her that although she'd decided to refrain from contacting Merrily, Merrily might choose to contact *her*. The whole evening was about to go very badly wrong. She couldn't think of anything worse than having a family game of Monopoly with an old friend who was no longer an old friend and who made her feel sick with guilt every time she looked at her.

There was also the added complication that she had already fobbed off Molly's queries about Merrily's disappearance with a vague explanation that Merrily had been too busy to get in touch. She had also implied that Merrily was still too busy.

Fortunately, Molly accepted Merrily's unexpected presence quite easily; and in fact, within half an hour of Merrily's arrival, Leah realized she was enjoying herself. Merrily was a very different person from the watchful, timid woman at Alison's supper party. It was immediately obvious that she was completely at home in the company of children. She declared at the beginning of the game that she just knew she was going to win, and when she landed on Fred's Mayfair for the third time her howls of rage made both children giggle. When Leah finally called time on the proceedings, Merrily declared that next time she would definitely win.

'Have you ever played Cluedo?' Molly asked.

'I am brilliant at Cluedo,' Merrily said.

'Yes,' Fred said, 'but you did tell us you were brilliant at Monopoly.'

'That's true,' Merrily conceded, 'but I'm even better at Cluedo.'

'I tell you what,' Fred said carefully. 'Let's play Monopoly next time and then you can see if you can beat me, and after *that* we'll play Cluedo.'

'I'm going to win next time,' Molly said, tugging at Fred's arm. 'I'm going to beat you next time, Fred.'

'All right, but now it's really late,' Leah said, 'and you have school in the morning, so go to bed.'

Fred got down from his chair and went to stand by Merrily. 'Do you want to know something?' he asked her. 'At night, a barn owl can see a hundred times better than a human being.'

'Gracious,' Merrily said. 'I had no idea.'

'I'll tell you something,' Molly said. 'I've written a poem about the sea. Do you want to hear it?'

'Next time,' Leah said firmly. 'Go to bed now. I'll be up in ten minutes.'

After they'd gone, Merrily smiled at Leah. 'You have two very bright children,' she said.

'They certainly liked you! You realize you are now committed to endless board games, week after week after week.'

Merrily began to gather up the property cards. 'It's so funny. I never thought of you as the maternal sort and yet here you are bringing up two terrific children on your own while running a hugely successful business. I don't know how you do it.'

'I hate to disillusion you but Widcombe Rentals is hardly setting the world alight. At the moment, it's a modest success, a very, very modest success.'

'Well, I couldn't do it. I used to be worn out after a day's teaching. I don't remember playing board games with Tom on a weekday evening. Just accept you are impressive. How do you manage for child care?'

'In term-time it's easy,' Leah said. 'Where I work is only a few minutes' walk from the primary school. One of the mothers drops the kids at my office after school and then we all go home together at five. Holidays are far more complicated. We sort of get by with a mixture of child-minders, friends, ex-husband and ex-parents-in-law. It's pretty haphazard but most of the time we seem to manage.'

'The results speak for themselves,' Merrily said. 'I've had a lovely evening. I feel so lucky that you live just down the road from us. Christopher works most nights and I'm not used to being without Tom.' She bit her lip fiercely and bent down to pick up her bag, then said, 'It's time I went home. Don't forget to tell me next time you're having a games night.'

'I won't,' Leah said. 'The children will look forward to it!'

Once Merrily had gone, Leah made a mug of tea. It was clear that Merrily loved children. It was even more obvious that she loved her son. What sort of marriage was it in which a man could make his wife leave their only child behind in London and move down to Bath for no good reason? Come to that, how had Merrily got to the point where she had *agreed* to leave her only child behind?

Leah thought back to the conversation she'd had with Alison and Felix. She had been wrong when she'd told Alison that Merrily had changed. Merrily might be cowed in the presence of her horrible husband but the old Merrily, the Merrily who had been Leah's close companion all through her childhood and teens, had been very much in evidence tonight.

It was not so surprising really. Most people behaved slightly differently with different people. The secret was to mix with the people who brought out one's *best* characteristics. This, as Leah knew only too well, was easier said than done. By the time she stopped living with Jamie, she was a jealous, insecure wreck. It had been obvious to everyone but herself that he was no good for her at all. Presumably, if she hadn't actually found him shagging his assistant in his studio, she might still be with him.

Leah sighed. It was equally obvious that Christopher

was no good for Merrily. Tonight had proved something else as well. Leah's earlier doubts about Merrily's state of mind had crystallized into certainty. Merrily was unhappy. Leah sipped her tea. It had been a terrible mistake to sleep with Merrily's husband. It would be a crime to abandon his wife.

CHAPTER FIVE

Alison Feels Sorry For Herself

Alison was ready and dressed for what she knew would be an enjoyable evening with Sally and Michael Bracewell. Harry and Nathan were out. Felix was having a shower. Eva was getting ready for her very final farewell party. And here Alison was, sitting in the garden on a perfect late September evening, drinking Elderflower Crush with the male contingent of what Felix had christened Eva's Posse.

Eva's Posse comprised her best friend, Kate, who was no doubt busy at home preparing to receive her friends; identical twins, Robbie and Ronnie; and Gordon, a boy with Byronic dark locks and a temperament that was clearly less than Byronic since his two-year flirtation with Eva had never appeared to progress to anything more interesting.

Alison had known the twins since they were eleven-year-old schoolchildren with rosy-cheeked complexions and a passion for doing word games. She still couldn't tell who was Robbie and who was Ronnie and they still had rosy-cheeked complexions. Indeed, apart from the fact that their passion for word games had long since been replaced by more pressing concerns about the worldwide inequality of wealth, their characters had remained remarkably untainted by the usual dark moods of their age group.

Gordon was a relative newcomer. Leah was convinced he was secretly in love with Eva and Leah was usually right about these things. Alison was fond of all of them and quite understood that Eva would want to spend the last evening of her holiday with them. 'What I don't understand,' she said now, 'is why you've all changed your plans at the last moment. I thought you were going into Bath. I mean, it's fine that you're going to Kate's house but I don't understand why you have to stay the night there. Eva and I are travelling up to Manchester in the morning.'

'There's a problem,' Robbie, or perhaps it was Ronnie, said. 'Kate's family have an old Labrador called Emily and Emily is about to die. They've been expecting her to die for weeks. Yesterday, the vet said it could only be a matter of days or even hours. And then this afternoon, Kate's grandfather had a stroke and Kate's parents have had to go and stay with Kate's grandmother, but they don't want Emily to be left on her own so Kate has to stay in the house. And Kate doesn't want to be on her own in case Emily *does* die so we said we'd all stay with her.' He stared thoughtfully into his Elderflower Crush and added, 'Kate's parents must be gutted.'

Alison supposed that was one way of describing how Kate's parents must currently be feeling. She tried to imagine what she'd feel if both Magnus and her father were at death's door and said, 'Well, I'm glad you're going to be there. Just don't stay up too late. Eva has a long day tomorrow. She's been packing up all day. She must be tired.'

The subject of her concern called out, 'I'm ready,' and walked across the lawn towards them. Far from looking tired, she looked lovely in a short floaty dress that revealed her long legs and her generous cleavage. She was carrying an overnight bag and her long dark hair shone in the evening sun. 'We ought to go,' she said. 'We're going to be late.'

Really, Alison thought, Eva's friends were remarkably long-suffering. None of them pointed out they'd been waiting for Eva for at least twenty minutes. They simply stood up and thanked Alison for their drinks.

'Have a good evening,' Alison said. 'And remember, Eva . . .'

'I know,' Eva said, 'I'll go to bed very early. I'll see you in the morning.'

'I'll be at Kate's house at nine,' Alison said. 'And—'

'I know. I'll be ready for you. Goodbye, Mum.'

Alison watched them go and thought what a pity it was that they were all going their separate ways. Kate and the twins were having a gap year, working for a few months in order to fund their travelling plans. Gordon was going to Cardiff University and Eva, of course, was going to Manchester.

Alison sat back in her deckchair and breathed in the scent of the nearby roses. It was pleasant to be sitting here in the evening sun. She could feel a rather delicious lethargy creeping up on her. She was tired even if Eva wasn't. She had spent the morning washing and ironing clothes, bringing suitcases down from the attic and rummaging through kitchen drawers for spare mugs and cutlery and plates and pans.

In the afternoon she had tried to help Eva with her packing, a task which required huge reservoirs of patience since Eva kept changing her mind about what she wanted to take. She was a little hurt that Eva couldn't wait to get away from Tucking Friary, which was stupid since such an attitude was only to be expected. When *she* had been Eva's age, she had been in love with Felix and couldn't wait to leave home.

A hand touched her gently on the shoulder and she jumped.

'Did I wake you?' Felix asked.

'I don't think so,' Alison said. 'Are you ready to go?'

'I am. I've just seen the Posse off. They're all packed like sardines in the twins' little car.'

'I can't believe Eva's going to university,' Alison said. 'I feel it's the end of an era.'

'I know,' Felix said. 'I might be able to start using my own computer at last.'

Alison had known Sally was inviting Jenny and Jonathon Rushton, but she had forgotten that the point of the dinner was to meet the historian from Newcastle. Alison sat next to him at dinner and warmed to him at once. He was not only extremely easy on the eye, he was also good company. He told her he had always had a passion for history and he was fascinated by what she had to tell him about Hadrian's Wall. He was delighted to be living in Bath. He'd been brought up in the city, he said, and moving back after such a long time was like coming home. He had bought a flat in Sydney Place, which was not too far from his mother's house in Forester Road. He spoke with great affection of his mother and said she kept bringing round meals, having apparently forgotten that he'd been looking after himself for almost twenty years now. Alison thought he was charming and would once have earmarked him as a definite love interest for Leah.

Her enjoyment of the evening was rather dented at the end when the Bracewells said goodbye to them. 'We're going to have to opt out of the Hadrian's Wall holiday at half-term,' Sally said. 'I know it sounds pathetic but it's the only week I can get the decorators in to do the kitchen and I really need to be there to oversee everything. We *are* sorry!'

Alison expressed her dismay but said she quite understood. Once safely out of earshot, she said to Felix, 'Can you believe that? Did you see how uncomfortable Sally was? Whenever anyone says, "I know it sounds pathetic but . . ." you know very well it's because that person knows it *is* pathetic!' She glanced across at her husband. 'Felix, are you listening to me? What are you doing?'

Felix was walking in the middle of the lane with his head craned backwards. 'I'm looking at those stars,' he said. 'I'm trying to work out if that's the Milky Way. What do *you* think?'

'I have no idea and I don't care. How much have you had to drink tonight?'

'Too much,' Felix said. 'I always drink too much when we have supper with Sally and Michael. It's the great joy of being able to walk home afterwards. What was it you were cross about?'

'I'm not cross, I'm just disappointed. I've spent a lot of time planning this holiday and now Sally and Michael are dropping out for no good reason.'

'Perhaps they never wanted to come,' Felix said. 'You were always so enthusiastic about it . . .'

'If they didn't want to come they should have told me before I started organizing it.' She shot a suspicious glance at Felix. 'Do *you* want to go?'

Felix took her hand. 'I always want to go anywhere with you,' he said.

'Right,' Alison said, pausing to catch her breath, 'now I *know* you've drunk too much.'

Eva was waiting outside Kate's house when Alison arrived the next morning and her punctuality was both unexpected and impressive. It was all the more impressive given that she looked like she'd just been resuscitated after a two-year coma. She fell asleep within minutes and remained so until they stopped at a service station for lunch. No sooner had they sat down with sandwiches and soup than she rushed to the Ladies. She returned ten minutes later, looking pale and shaken. Once they resumed their journey, she fell asleep again and remained so until they reached the Fallowfield campus. Apparently, it was the main residential part of the university and Alison thought it looked rather bleak. When she turned off the engine, Eva woke up, announced she felt much better and swore she would never go near any alcohol again.

They were told that Eva's room was on the sixth floor of the vast grey tower block that dominated the campus. The two of them filled the lift with cases and carrier bags and got out at the sixth floor. Eva's new home looked pretty bare and resembled a prison cell. It had a narrow bed, a small table and chair by the window and a notice-board that was empty save for a short list of fire regulations. Alison noticed the naked light bulb dangling by a dusty cord from the ceiling and wished she had brought a lampshade.

Twenty minutes later, Eva came back down with her mother to say goodbye. When Alison drove away, she could see Eva in the driving mirror, standing in the shadow of the tower block. She was waving furiously and looked very small and undeniably forlorn.

All in all, Alison was glad the next day was an exceptionally busy one. She had an interesting assignment this morning and felt a sense of pleasurable anticipation as she turned into a long, gravel-covered drive. She parked in front of a large rectory that was covered in ivy. It was like a Christmas present waiting to be opened.

Alison had been doing this for over five years. When the children were small, she had submitted occasional pieces to the local paper and had eventually been taken on in a freelance capacity. And then, at a Christmas office party, after drinking a few glasses of the seasonal punch, she met the editor of three local property magazines and managed to talk her way into her present occupation. Every month she visited various places newly available for sale and wrote about them in suitably enthusiastic language. It was a job that was perfectly suited to her interests, since it legitimized her nosiness about other people's homes and utilized her love of writing.

In the early days, she had found it difficult to wax lyrical about a 'modern family home' that had an 'integral garage' and was 'handily placed for the A36', meaning that the A36 virtually thundered through the sitting room. Nowadays, she found it easy to find the right phrase or paragraph. And of course, when she had an assignment like this one, it was a complete pleasure.

She walked across the crunchy gravel and knocked on the front door. She could hear the sound of footsteps and then the door opened and a teenager in grey jodhpurs and a pink shirt said, 'Hello! You must be Alison Coward. I'm Ginny. My mother's stuck in a traffic jam. Would you like to look at the garden first? By the time you've done that, she'll be here and can show you round the house. Do you want me to come round the garden with you?'

'No, I'll be fine.' Alison glanced around her. 'This is a beautiful place.'

'Isn't it? I shall be sorry to leave it. When you've finished with the garden, walk straight in and give me a shout. Can I get you a cup of coffee or tea?'

'No, thank you. I can't wait to see the garden.'

'Take as long as you like. See you later!'

The garden – all two acres of it – was superb. Alison walked across the lawn to the lake. Ducks and moorhens glided on the surface and she was sure she could see an enormous trout flicker through the greenery below.

Stopping only to take a few photographs, Alison walked past the tennis court and the row of chestnut trees and spied a narrow spring. It led directly down to the Kennet and Avon canal. The sunlight sparkled on the water and a red houseboat floated past her. A girl, with blonde hair trussed up in a ponytail, sat near the prow. She smiled and waved at Alison, who immediately waved back.

Alison walked back up the garden, past the heated swimming pool, towards the house. She pushed the door open rather gingerly and found herself in an enormous hall with a highly polished limestone floor and a stupendous flower arrangement on the table by the inglenook fireplace.

She called out a diffident 'Hello' and the girl immediately appeared on the stairs. 'What did you think of the garden?' she asked.

'I loved it,' Alison said, 'especially the lake.'

'That's my favourite part too. Apparently, monks used to fish there in the fourteenth century. Mummy should be back soon, but if you don't want to wait I'd be happy to show you around.'

The girl proved to be remarkably well informed, pointing out the eighteenth-century panelling in the dining room, the views across the northern hills of Bath from the master bedroom and the fact that the thirty-one-foot sitting room had once been a ballroom.

When the girl's mother finally appeared, apologetic and breathless, Alison was able to say with complete sincerity that she wished she had such informative guides when she visited other houses. As she drove away, she could see mother and daughter, their arms interlinked, waving and smiling at her.

Alison felt a sudden twist of pure, naked jealousy. She knew it was silly. After all, that nice girl – what was her name? Ginny? – Ginny would probably be leaving home within a year or two and her poor mother would probably feel like Alison felt now. But that didn't really help. Alison sniffed. There was Eva living in some strange northern city that probably had loads of smelly factories and coal mines and strange northern people with strange northern accents, and who would be there to make sure she got up in time and ate properly?

Just over a year ago, she reminded herself, she had felt the very same worries when Phoebe moved to London, and Phoebe was fine. Then she remembered that Phoebe was engaged to loathsome Lennie and she sniffed again.

After a brief walk with Magnus, Alison drove into Bath to see a flat in the Royal Crescent. The owner was a charming old lady who was selling up so she could go and live with her daughter and son-in-law. Her son-in-law, she said, was just like a son to her. Alison instantly imagined herself thirty years on, moving in with Phoebe and Lennie, and inwardly shuddered.

After lunch, she sat down to write up the properties she had seen in the morning. She found it easy to write effusively about the large country house and only stopped when she discovered she had used the word 'tranquil' three times. The house phone rang and she picked up the receiver quickly, hoping it might be Eva.

'Mrs Coward? It's Roger Gale.'

Roger Gale was Nathan's head of year. He was a large, rotund man with a lively sense of mischief. Today, the lively sense of mischief seemed to be absent from his voice.

'Mr Gale, how are you? I hope you had a good summer holiday.'

'I did. Thank you. Mrs Coward, I'm afraid I have some rather upsetting news. Nathan's been involved in a fight with Russell Clink.'

Alison felt her blood run cold. Russell Clink was nearly six foot tall and already looked like a professional boxer. She clutched the phone. 'Is Nathan all right?'

'Nathan's fine,' Mr Gale said. 'Nathan has a black eye and nothing else. Russell, on the other hand, has a broken nose.'

'There must be some mistake,' Alison protested. 'Nathan wouldn't hurt a fly.'

'Mrs Coward,' Mr Gale said, in a voice that was curiously sympathetic, 'I think you should know that this is not the first time Nathan has been involved in a fight.'

After Mr Gale rang off, Alison sat staring out of the window. She knew he had been surprised by her complete ignorance about Nathan's state of mind. Her youngest child, her baby, was so unhappy about the fact that he was shorter than his peers that he felt compelled to resort to fisticuffs any time any boy referred to it. Why had he not felt able to talk to her about it? Why had she not possessed any idea that her sunny-tempered Nathan was wracked with such insecurity?

The phone rang again and she picked up the receiver, half hoping that it would be Mr Gale to say he had made a mistake.

'Alison, it's Jonathon. Wasn't Sally's supper party fun? I liked that historian man, didn't you?'

Perhaps she was being hyper-sensitive, but it did seem to her that Jonathon Rushton sounded uncharacteristically nervous. 'Oh I did,' she said. 'I had a lovely chat with him about Hadrian's Wall. Isn't it a pity that the Bracewells have pulled out of our expedition? Did they tell you they can't come with us?'

'They did.' Jonathon cleared his throat. 'That's why I'm ringing. The thing is, Jenny and I have been talking about it all day and we think . . . we feel . . . well, we think that if it's just the four of us, it will be a little . . . intense.'

Alison stiffened. 'Intense?'

'Absolutely!' Jonathon said, as if he hadn't used the word himself two seconds earlier. 'That's *just* what we think. I reckon we should cancel the whole thing and then the six of us should go somewhere in a few months' time. We could have a weekend break in Paris, perhaps, or Bruges. Don't you think that would be fun?'

Alison reached for her diary. 'I'm not sure, I'll need to talk to Felix. Jonathon, I don't mean to be rude but I'm in the middle of writing an article. I'll ring the pubs I booked and cancel them. I'm sure they'll understand.'

'I'm sure they will,' Jonathon said. 'And you do see what I'm saying? Jenny and I just think . . .'

'I'm sure you're right.' Alison drew a line through her half-term entry written in capital letters: HADRIAN'S WALL EXPEDITION!!!

'I mean,' Jonathon said, 'we'd love to go on holiday with you . . .'

'I'm sure you would. We'll talk again soon. Goodbye now!'

Alison replaced the receiver. Her son had been going through hell and she had had no idea. The Rushtons had bowed out of the holiday once they discovered they'd have to spend four days with only Alison and Felix for company. There seemed to be a pattern here. Alison put her hand to her mouth. She had always thought she was a good mother with good friends. It looked like she had been mistaken on both counts.

CHAPTER SIX

Leah Reacts Badly to Some News

The second meeting of the newly established Games Society was a great success although Merrily was appalled that Fred was once again the winner. Once he and Molly had been persuaded to go to bed, Leah put the kettle on and insisted that Merrily stay for a cup of tea. 'This is the fourth time I've seen you and we still haven't caught up,' she said, putting two mugs on the table. 'I keep thinking about those things Christopher said at Alison's house. I wish we'd known how unhappy you were back then.'

Leah's kitchen was not large and it was ill-suited to anyone who might want to pace the floor while gathering thoughts. Merrily was thus forced to take a seat. Leah, eyeing her furtively while warming the teapot, noted that she vented her restless energy on her cardigan, pulling her sleeves over her hands and tying and untying them.

'The thing is,' Merrily began and then stopped and tried again. 'I mean, it wasn't quite like that.' She bit at her lower lip and stared intently at her knotted sleeves. 'I mean, now I've seen you and Alison again, I look back at that time and think, what was I doing? But the trouble was that every time I thought of getting in touch, I felt guilty about having *not* been in touch and each year it got more and more difficult to do anything.'

'I'd like to understand, that's all,' Leah said. 'I know that Christopher said—'

'He said I was unhappy. Yes. The thing is I'm not sure I was *that* unhappy. I just felt rather a failure. When I went to university I suppose I assumed that by the time I graduated, I'd be completely different. I'd be confident and clever and attractive. Instead, I was just the same. I still had bad hair, I still had no idea what I really wanted to do and I was still a virgin, even though I tried really hard not to be.' She caught Leah's eye and gave a reluctant laugh. 'Of course I know this sounds silly to someone who discovered sexual bliss with Metal Mickey years before in some romantic cornfield . . .'

Leah poured out the tea and handed a mug to Merrily. 'Do you know something? Sex with Metal Mickey was the biggest disappointment ever. A text message from Vodaphone lasts longer than sex did with Metal Mickey.'

'But you said . . . You told Alison and me it was incredible!'

'I know I did. I wanted to impress you.'

'Well, you did impress us, you big fraud! I remember you told us it was like exploding fireworks. All these years I've waited for fireworks to explode and it's all your fault.' Merrily grinned. 'I have missed you, you know.'

'I've missed you too,' Leah said. 'Tell me about meeting Christopher.' It seemed to her that the mention of his name snuffed out the laughter in Merrily's eyes, but perhaps that was fanciful.

'I met Christopher when I was doing my teaching practice. He was teaching at the school and I thought he was very charismatic and wise. He could have had anyone and he chose me. It's funny, you know: he knew he would be a successful writer and he said he needed *me* to help him. He made me feel *so* important! He asked me to put myself in his hands and I can't tell you how happy I was to do so. He said I would never find true confidence until I left my family and my past behind.' Merrily glanced quickly at Leah. 'It wasn't that I didn't want to see you and Alison again. It was more that I needed to wipe the slate clean and start again.'

'And that's presumably what you did.'

'Yes. I applied for a teaching job in Cornwall. We decided that Christopher would stop working so he could concentrate on writing. We got married and rented a cottage in Falmouth.'

'Were you happy there?'

'I was. I liked my job and then after a while I had Tom. By that time, Christopher was already on his second book. I carried on working, and a few years later I was actually offered promotion. Christopher and I talked about it but by that time he felt he needed a change. His Aunt Clemency had given him some money and so we moved to London.'

'And is that when you got in touch with your family again?'

'Yes. Christopher thought I was ready by then. My parents had moved but Isobel was still living in the same house in Regent's Park so it was easy to contact her.'

Leah raised her eyebrows. 'The last time I spoke to Isobel was when she told me I couldn't come to her wedding because I didn't know how to dress properly.

Given that the reception was in a field at the back of our house, it seemed a bit unfair.'

Merrily smiled. 'It didn't stop you turning up there. I can remember exactly what you wore: a tartan miniskirt, a black top with giant zips and a huge pink wig.'

'My mother and my stepfather didn't talk to me for a week,' Leah said. 'I have to tell you, it was worth it.'

'*And* you got into the cutting-the-cake photo. That did not go down well.'

'In my defence,' Leah said, 'I was only sixteen. The terrible truth is that I'd do the same today. What's Isobel like these days? I bet she's the best-dressed mother in London.'

'She looks fantastic,' Merrily said. 'And everything in her house sort of gleams. You should see her taps: they're like mirrors.'

'I bet they are. What about your parents? Do you see much of them?'

'They live in Berkshire now but they come and stay with Isobel and her family quite a lot. I see them occasionally. We're very polite to each other.'

'What was it like seeing them all again?'

'It wasn't as bad as I thought it would be. Mind you,' Merrily gave a slight smile, 'it could never have been as bad as I expected it to be. It helped that Isobel turned out to be a fan of Christopher's books. She's been very good to us. She even gave a party for him when his last novel came out.'

'So you're glad you got in touch with them?'

'Yes. I'd have got in touch with them earlier if I hadn't been so frightened of their reaction. And it's been interesting to see Isobel with her children. It's odd how often family patterns repeat themselves. My parents always thought Isobel was the perfect daughter and now they treat Isobel's daughter the same way. So do Isobel and her husband. To be honest, I like their younger child, Dominic, far more than I do my niece. But then, of course,' Merrily gave a mischievous smile, 'I would do. He reminds me of me.'

'I'd like to meet him,' Leah said. 'So tell me about your home in London. Where was it? What was it like?'

Merrily took a sip of her tea. 'We bought a flat in Vauxhall overlooking the Thames. I could see the river from our bedroom. I loved it. When we moved there, we decided I should do supply teaching rather than take a full-time job. I do tend to get too involved in things. That's why I'm so impressed by you. I don't know how you manage to run a business and work full-time and still bring up two small children on your own. It must have been terrible when you split up from your husband. I can't imagine how you coped.'

'Alison was amazing,' Leah said. 'She made the whole moving process so much easier. She helped me sort out schools and a job and a place to live. And for the first few months in Bath we spent nearly every weekend at Tucking Friary. Fred and Molly still worship Harry and Nathan. And then Jamie decided to relocate to Bath to be nearer the children. He's a commercial photographer and travels a lot, but he has them over to his place pretty regularly.'

'It still can't be easy.'

'It's a lot easier than it was.' Leah topped up her tea. 'Now I want to hear more about *you*. You moved to London and you got a job as a supply teacher. Was that fun?'

'No,' said Merrily, 'but I only did it for about a year

or so. Something rather unexpected happened. I was out shopping and I had my shopping list and pen in my hand, which was just as well because I saw a green Audi misjudge a corner and knock a man down. The driver didn't even stop. I wrote down the car number and I went over to the man. He'd hurt his ankle and I saw a policeman and told him what I'd seen. Anyway, the man turned out to be a record producer and he said he needed an assistant who was calm and competent and he thought I'd be perfect. And I went to work for him and . . .'

She stopped and looked up at the ceiling, which made Leah smile because that was what Merrily always used to do when trying to explain something she found difficult to articulate.

'Do you ever find this? Do you find that if someone expects something of you and assumes you can do it, you find that somehow you *can* do it? I mean, I never thought of myself like that but the funny thing was that all the time I worked for him, I *was* calm and competent.'

'The trouble with you,' Leah said, 'is that you always underestimated your abilities.'

'That's lovely of you to say so,' Merrily said. 'I don't think it's true. But I know I was good at that job. He asked me to go to Texas with him this year. There's a big music fair there.'

'Did you go?'

'No. Christopher decided he wanted to move again. His Aunt Florence had died and she left him her house down here.'

'Christopher's been very lucky with his aunts.'

'Neither of them had children and they both adored

Christopher. He had intended to sell the house but then he decided he'd like to try living down here.'

'But Tom wanted to stay in London?'

'He's happy at school, he has some lovely friends there and now he's playing in a band.' Merrily smiled. 'It's pretty cool to be only thirteen and be invited to play guitar in a band, don't you think?'

'It certainly is. So you had a brilliant job and Tom was happy at school. There was no way you could want to leave London. Why didn't you just say no?'

Merrily gazed at Leah's fridge, which was currently decorated with school letters and unpaid bills pinioned by multicoloured magnets. 'I didn't feel I could do that,' she said. 'I know you haven't heard of him but you have to believe me when I tell you Christopher is a brilliant writer. He has a huge following. People treat him like he's some sort of religious guru. You wouldn't believe some of the letters he gets. He's always said that in order to work well, he needs the right environment. For a while it was Cornwall and then it was London and now it is Bath. He's not sure how long he wants to stay. He's let out our flat to a friend for six months. He says we might go back there. That's another reason why we haven't taken Tom out of his school.'

'In the meantime how does Tom feel?'

Merrily gazed up at the ceiling again. 'Well,' she said, 'Tom knows that Christopher's career is very important.' She lowered her eyes and looked at her watch, 'And now I must go home. Thank you for another lovely evening. You must come over and see our house. What are you doing at the weekend?'

'I'm not sure,' Leah said. 'It depends on Jamie's plans really.'

'I'll ring you on Friday. Tell Fred I know I'll win next time.'

Merrily was out of the door in a matter of moments. Leah felt bad about bringing up the subject of Tom. She should have remembered he was a sensitive subject and she felt guilty for hassling Merrily. She wished she didn't feel guilty, because she had work to do and knew she would be unable to concentrate. She picked up the phone and rang Alison.

Alison sounded tired and said she was missing Eva. She perked up when Leah told her she had just seen Merrily and needed advice. Alison loved giving advice and listened attentively while Leah did her best to give a balanced summary of the conversation she'd just had. 'What I can't understand,' Leah concluded, 'is how someone as intelligent as Merrily can't see she's being duped. Look at the facts: Merrily comes home and tells Christopher she's been offered a job promotion. He reacts by making a sudden decision to up sticks and move to London. Merrily lands a job she loves and tells Christopher she's been invited to go to Texas with her nice boss. Christopher reacts by making a sudden decision to up sticks and move to Bath. Every time Merrily starts to establish any sort of independence, he reins her in. It's deeply creepy.'

'It might be,' Alison said, 'but, on the other hand, it does sound as if Merrily has been happy to *be* reined in. She could always say no.'

'She doesn't have the confidence to say no. She never did have any confidence. That's why she stayed with

Dennis the Monk for so long. Any other woman would have left him after a week.'

'I never knew what she saw in Dennis,' Alison said. 'He had the smallest chin I've ever seen and he smiled all the time, even when he had no reason to. I hate people who smile for no reason.'

'The point is that he finished what her parents began. She grew up feeling ugly and Dennis made her feel even uglier. And then she met Christopher who told her how lucky she was to have him and I bet he's gone on telling her that ever since. I reckon she's been brainwashed. You should have heard her telling me why his career had to come first. It was like some mantra she's been taught to say again and again.'

'I keep meaning to go and see her,' Alison said. 'I'll try to do it tomorrow. Oh yes, there's something else I wanted to talk to you about. It's probably nothing. Has Nathan ever told you he's worried about being shorter than his friends?'

'No, but I'd be surprised if he wasn't.'

'Why? Do you think it's a problem?'

'No, I'm sure it isn't. But he's fifteen and he's shorter than average. At that age, you want to look average. So of course he's worried. All teenagers worry about their looks. I used to worry about being too tall. He'll soon grow, and if he doesn't he'll realize it's no big deal.'

'I expect you're right. Leah, would you describe me as intense?'

'I'd never describe you as intense. Why?'

'No reason. I'll speak to you soon.'

Leah replaced the handset. Alison could be very odd

sometimes. She gathered up the mugs and took them to the sink. It was good to have Merrily back in her life. To Merrily, Leah was still the fearless teenager who did outrageous things. Of course, these days, Leah knew she was neither fearless nor outrageous, but it was nice to have a friend who thought she was.

The phone rang again and on hearing the caller starting to leave a message, Leah butted in. 'Hi, Jamie. Are you still all right for this weekend?'

'I'm busy till Saturday. I can be with you by four. Is that all right?'

'I suppose so. And you'll bring them back on Sunday evening?'

'I'm afraid I'll have to drop them back in the morning. I'm going to Taunton with Charlotte. We're going to see her parents.'

'That's nice,' Leah said.

'I'm not sure it will be,' Jamie said. 'Charlotte's pregnant.'

'Oh.' Leah reached for a chair and sat down heavily. 'That must be quite a shock. Or did you plan it?'

'It was a shock for both of us. I think Charlotte's quite excited now.'

'That's good.'

'Yes.' Jamie didn't sound too sure. 'I don't want to tell the children yet but I wanted you to know.'

'Thank you,' Leah said. 'You're probably right about Fred and Molly. It's best to wait a few weeks. I expect you and Charlotte have a lot of planning to do.'

'Yes. Well, I'll see you on Saturday.'

After Jamie rang off, Leah bit her lower lip hard. Charlotte was pregnant. Charlotte was pregnant and was going to keep the baby and Jamie was going to keep both of them. It was pretty funny that he was about to start a second family when he'd never been that keen on starting a first. Of course he'd adored both children once he had them. Presumably, he would adore this new child too.

What would Fred and Molly say? Would they be excited by the prospect of a new little baby sister or brother? Leah desperately hoped they would be but she knew it was highly unlikely.

They had been thrilled when Jamie moved down to Bath. He had bought an entire floor of a large Victorian building in Larkhall, just off the London Road. He had his studio there, two bedrooms, a small kitchen and bathroom and a big sitting room with a vast television and other essential items such as table football and a pinball machine. The children loved going there.

There was just one unfortunate by-product of Jamie's move but it was a big one. Fred and Molly had been far too young to understand the implications of their parents' separation. In that first horrible year, they had been tearful and confused. When Jamie came to Bath, Leah explained as carefully as she could that he had moved because he loved the two of them and wanted to be nearer them. Somehow, they had convinced themselves that it also meant that Daddy still loved Mummy and that at some point in the future, Mummy and Daddy would get back together. It was only now that Leah, angrily wiping her eyes, realized Mummy had hoped for that too.

CHAPTER SEVEN

Alison Visits Merrily and Finds She Has Much to Think About

Alison had been having a talk with Nathan when Leah rang. It was actually much easier to try to fathom the mysteries of Merrily's marriage than it was to explain to Nathan why he should not resort to violence when confronted by sneering giants who wanted to make him feel small by telling him he *was* small. She had tried to point out that he was bound to grow in the next few months and that even if he didn't, being a little short hadn't stopped women from flocking to Tom Cruise, Al Pacino and Dustin Hoffman. Nathan's response had been that if he was as rich as any of them he wouldn't worry about being short.

In bed that night, she voiced her worries to Felix. 'What do we do,' she asked, 'if he doesn't grow?'

'It wouldn't be the end of the world,' Felix said. 'Look at Napoleon. He did all right and he was shorter than Nathan.'

'That's the whole point,' Alison said. 'He did not do all right. He had such a big complex about being short that he ended up fighting the whole world and dying in prison.'

'Yes,' said Felix, switching off the light and rolling onto his side, away from Alison, 'but he did get to sleep with Josephine.'

Felix could be very annoying. He must know that she would lie there, worrying about their son developing Napoleonic tendencies. She switched off her light and shut her eyes. Now was not the time to rerun tonight's argument; she'd do far better to go to sleep and awake refreshed in the morning. She breathed in and then breathed slowly out again. I am not going to think about Nathan, she thought, I am going to concentrate on my breathing and think of nothing. The trouble was that as soon as she stopped worrying about Nathan, another worry zoomed to the surface. She'd rung Eva earlier in the evening and Eva had assured her that she liked the students on her floor and was going out with some of them later on, but Alison could tell she was homesick. Of course, she had only been there a couple of days and was bound to feel homesick but Alison wished Manchester wasn't quite so far away. She sighed and turned onto her side. She would ring Eva tomorrow or perhaps the day after. She turned onto her back and tried once again to concentrate on her breathing.

She opened her eyes. 'Felix,' she said, 'I spoke to Leah tonight. She doesn't think I'm intense.'

There was a brief silence and then, 'That's a relief.'

'I know you think I'm silly but I'd like to know why Jonathon thinks we're intense. It's such an odd thing to say, especially about you. You're *never* intense. Often I think you're not intense enough. They must be referring to me. They find *me* intense.'

Felix gave a deep sigh. 'It's just a word. Jonathon didn't want to go to Hadrian's Wall and he threw out the word.'

'You don't use a word like "intense" without meaning it.'

'Jonathon would never mean to insult you. Never mind any of them. We'll go on our own and we'll have a great time inspecting Roman stones and mounds.'

'Felix,' Alison said, 'you don't want to go, do you?'

Felix turned himself onto his back. 'I'm not sure it would be my first choice of holiday,' he conceded.

'I shall cancel our rooms tomorrow,' Alison said. 'I wish you'd all told me you didn't want to go in the first place.'

'I think,' Felix said tentatively, 'we were carried along by your enthusiasm.'

'Well, you'll be glad to know that my enthusiasm has gone.' She pulled the duvet up to her chin and hoped Felix felt a little ashamed.

'Alison,' Felix began and then uttered a few choice expletives at the sudden sound of the phone. He switched on his light and picked up the receiver. 'Hello . . . Hi, Phoebe . . . No, thanks to your mother I am awake and your mother is very, very awake. I'll pass you over. Goodnight.'

Alison took the phone. 'Phoebe, how lovely to hear you.'

'Dad sounds grumpy,' Phoebe said.

'He's fine. Is everything all right?'

'I had to tell you straight away. Lennie and I've been talking. We've decided there's no need for a long engagement. We want to get married in March. If we marry on the twenty-seventh, it will be exactly a year since we met. We've got enough time to organize a wedding in March, haven't we?'

'Well,' Alison said, 'I'm not sure . . .'

'And Mum, is there any chance you can come up to London one Saturday soon and help me find a wedding dress? From November, I'm going to do some voluntary work at Battersea on Saturdays, so we haven't got much time.'

'I could do the last Saturday in October. We've decided to cancel the Hadrian's Wall trip so that weekend is free.'

'That'll be great. I'm so excited! I'll give you a ring in a day or two and we can start planning things. I'll let you go to sleep now. Goodnight!'

Alison switched off the phone and passed it to Felix. As she watched him put it back on its stand, she decided she wouldn't tell him about the revised wedding plans till the morning. There was no need for both of them to have a sleepless night.

She rang Merrily in the morning. Merrily asked Alison if she felt like coming over to see the house and giving some advice about colour schemes. Alison was happy to say she could come right away. It had to be more fun than looking at wedding websites. She had no idea that marquees could be so expensive.

According to Merrily, Alison had only to look out for conifers on arriving at Widcombe Hill and she would know where to go. Alison spotted them at once and duly turned into the long drive to their left. She presumed they had been planted in order to hide the house from the road but the effect was lowering and oppressive and it was a huge shame since they blocked out the views of the city of Bath. If *she* lived here, she would get them all cut down as quickly as she could. As she got out of her car, she knew she would never want to live here. This was a grim Victorian red-brick house with mean little windows. It would make the perfect children's home or old people's home for someone who disliked children or old people.

The garden seemed as cowed by the house as she was. It comprised a large, square, moth-eaten lawn in the middle of which sat a faded grey bench. Why anyone would want to sit on the bench was a mystery since the only view to be had was the row of huge, menacing trees. Should someone turn the bench round, he or she would have a view of the house and, behind it, more huge, menacing trees.

Alison shivered and rang the bell. Perhaps, she thought hopefully, it would be more promising inside. She heard the sound of footsteps and then the door was flung open and there was Merrily, in a pair of shapeless green cords and an even more shapeless blue jersey.

'Oh it's so good to see you! Thank you for coming! Let's go through to the kitchen.' Seemingly oblivious to the darkness of the hall and the narrowness of the corridor, she maintained a steady flow of chatter. 'I'm so glad you've come. Your home is so beautiful and I don't have an idea where to start but I thought you should see the kitchen first and perhaps try to absorb the atmosphere, if you know what I mean.'

The kitchen was horrible and Alison had no wish to absorb its atmosphere. It was a joyless room that had belonged to someone who had no interest in cooking. There was a narrow work surface covered in laminated beige plastic, a small cracked sink and a cheap cooker that looked like it had been there for at least fifty years.

It probably *had* been there for fifty years. The floor was covered in hard, cold quarry tiles and the walls were a lurid crimson colour. In the middle of the room there was a small rectangular table and four spindly chairs. Above the sink, a tall, narrow window looked out onto a scruffy strip of lawn and beyond that a row of the ubiquitous conifers, blotting out the house next door along with any other sign of life.

'The thing is,' Merrily said, 'everything needs doing. I'm not sure what I can do with the kitchen but I promised Christopher I'd try. It is difficult, though.'

Alison had a mental image of her own large, beautiful kitchen with its twin Belfast sinks, its gigantic fridge, its cream-coloured dresser and its comfortable sofa. She felt a flash of pity for Merrily and said, 'Yes. It is certainly difficult.'

'Sit down,' Merrily said. 'I'll make us some coffee and then I'll show you round the house. I think it might need quite a lot doing to it.'

'I can imagine it does,' Alison said. 'Who did you say lived here? It was one of Christopher's relations?'

'His Aunt Florence moved here when she married and when her husband died she continued to live here on her own. I gather she became quite a recluse. The postman told me the other day that in the last few years the only person she spoke to was her cleaning lady who was nearly as old as she was. It sounds as if she was pretty eccentric.'

'I'm not surprised if she lived all alone in this place,' Alison said. 'Did you never meet her?'

'No,' Merrily said. 'She liked to have Christopher to herself.' She put a sugar bowl and a biscuit tin on the table. 'Would you like black or white coffee?'

'Why don't we look round the house first? I've brought paint brochures with me and I can give you the number of a very good decorator.'

'Christopher suggested I do it myself,' Merrily said. 'He says I can decorate it any way I want.'

'That's nice of him.'

'Well, it makes everything a lot simpler. The only room he's concerned with is his study and he's got that the way he wants it. I want to do Tom's room first. I'd like to get that done before he comes home for Christmas. Are you ready for the guided tour?'

'I am.' Alison stood up and said, with an enthusiasm she was far from feeling, 'Right, let's go!' She felt a little confused. She was sure Merrily had said she'd come down before the move to check on house improvements. It was horribly obvious that no improvements had been done.

The rest of the ground floor comprised a dining room, a cloakroom and a sitting room. In the cloakroom, Alison admired the quantity of coat hooks. In the dining room, she praised the generous dimensions of the dining-room table and refrained from mentioning that both it and the sideboard were grim, heavy pieces of spectacularly ugly furniture. In the sitting room, she marvelled at the high ceiling and failed to mention that the room, empty apart from a small television and two faded green armchairs, looked as if it had been despoilt by burglars who had lost interest and gone home.

With every step, Alison felt her determined smile set harder onto her face. At the top of the stairs, Merrily stopped and nodded towards a door on the right. 'That's Christopher's study,' she whispered. She gave a gentle knock, opened the door and said, 'Christopher? I've brought Alison to say hello.'

The reaction was explosive enough to make Alison jump. From within the room came a voice like an incoming tidal wave. 'What the hell do you think you are doing? How dare you interrupt me when I'm working? You are a silly, stupid woman. Get out, get out, get out!'

With flaming cheeks, Merrily quickly closed the door. Without looking at Alison, she murmured, 'I'm so sorry about that. I should never have disturbed him; he needs to have complete silence when he's working. I'll show you Tom's room next.'

Alison, following along, was stunned by Christopher's extraordinary outburst. The man was so rude! She didn't mind that he'd been so rude to *her* – though, actually, come to think of it, she did mind quite a lot, especially since she'd cooked him a very nice dinner just over a week ago – but it was unforgivable to shout at Merrily in front of her. It was obvious that Merrily was both painfully embarrassed and deeply upset. Her voice, as they entered Tom's room, was unsteady. 'I don't quite know where to start with this. It doesn't seem to be a very welcoming room at the moment.'

The last time Alison had been in a room as welcoming as this was when she'd spent three hours with Nathan in Casualty after a tree-climbing adventure had gone spectacularly wrong. But a few antique copies of *My Weekly* had brightened up that place, at least. Her eyes flitted over the blood-red walls, the eight-foot-tall chest of drawers, the small stained-glass window and the tiny white basin in the corner. There was absolutely nothing to commend this room and she didn't even try.

From downstairs, they heard the sound of the front door being slammed. Merrily whispered, 'Oh dear,' and raced to the window. Alison was quick to follow her.

They watched Christopher set off down the drive. Alison's eyes widened. Christopher looked like he'd joined the Ministry of Silly Walks. He had his elbows high in the air and pushed them backwards and forwards as if he were trying to ski down a slope with skis that were glued to the ground.

'Merrily,' Alison said, 'what *is* Christopher doing? He looks very odd.'

Merrily smiled but her eyes were strained and anxious. 'He walks like that when he's upset. He's trying to recapture his Muse.'

'Now he's nodding his head,' Alison said. 'He looks like a funny little steam engine.'

Merrily turned away. 'I'll show you the last two rooms and then we've finished.'

The master bedroom finally prompted a genuine cry of pleasure from Alison, or rather the four-poster bed did. It had heavy damask curtains and was really rather romantic. The bathroom also possessed an advantage in that it did not have crimson walls. On the other hand, the violent green colour was hardly an improvement.

As they walked back along the corridor, Alison had an idea. 'Merrily,' she said, 'since Christopher's gone out, can we take a look at his study? Do you think he would mind?'

For answer, Merrily opened the door and led the way inside. 'Well,' she said, 'what do you think?'

Alison caught her breath. She had visited many houses over the years and had seen all sorts of weird and wonderful rooms but none of them had ever surprised her as this one did. It was like stepping into a different world. It was big and beautiful and luxurious. A fire crackled in the grate. At the far end of the room, by the window, was an enormous oak desk with a green leather surface, on which sat a brass reading light. Christopher had the desk placed so he could sit with his back to the window. He could therefore admire the fire, the book-lined walls, the generous-sized wine-coloured sofa, the two standard lamps and the thick cream carpet.

'It's fabulous,' Alison murmured. 'It should be your sitting room, not a study.'

Merrily shook her head. 'Christopher needs a big room in which to write. He likes to walk around. It's lovely, isn't it? He hired an interior decorator to do it for him.'

'It's great,' Alison said. 'It must have cost a lot to do.'

'Christopher needs a comfortable room for his writing,' Merrily said. 'He's completely unmaterialistic. He doesn't mind what the rest of the house is like. He says his Muse is very exacting.'

Alison raised her eyebrows. 'I'd say his Muse is rather spoilt,' she said.

Merrily laughed. 'She's certainly very demanding. But then, Christopher's a great writer. Shall we go down? I want your honest advice about Tom's bedroom. And if you have any ideas about the rest of the house, let me know those too. Christopher's going to the States in January to visit his Aunt Clemency and that's when I thought . . .'

'You thought you'd do everything else? Listen, Merrily, you can't paint this house without professional help. It'll take you forever. I can give you the name of some reliable professionals and I'm happy to help with Tom's room but you cannot do the rest of this place on your own.'

'Right,' said Merrily, looking unhappy.

'If I were you,' Alison added, 'I'd sell most of Aunt Florence's furniture because it's horrible.'

'Right,' said Merrily, looking even more unhappy.

'As far as Tom's room is concerned,' Alison said, 'you can paint over the crimson walls with a gold-coloured paint. The crimson would give a rather good grounding to the gold. And then I'd do something fun like paint the door and window frames blue. I've brought lots of paint brochures with me. We could have a look at them now, if you like.'

'That sounds marvellous,' Merrily said. 'I knew you'd know what to do!'

Alison followed Merrily down the stairs. She might know what to do about the house – burn it down was a suggestion that came to mind – but she did *not* know what to do about Merrily. She could hardly look her in the eye and tell her she was married to a selfish, self-absorbed adulterer. And yet, she felt very strongly there was something she should do. She just didn't know what that something was.

CHAPTER EIGHT

Leah Falls Beside an Attractive Male

Leah had meant to keep the news about Charlotte's pregnancy to herself, at least until the children were told. As with so many of her resolutions, she broke it almost immediately. On Friday morning at the school playground, her friend Anthea noticed that she seemed a little down and within moments Leah found herself explaining Jamie's latest transgression.

In fact, she was glad she did since Anthea suggested a drink at Terry's Wine Bar the following evening and Leah knew that that would do her a lot more good than watching TV on her own and feeling sorry for herself. She could trust Anthea to keep quiet about the pregnancy and she could also trust Anthea to be delightfully rude about Jamie.

As if aware that he might be in trouble, Jamie arrived on time to collect the children on Saturday afternoon. He obviously *wasn't* aware, since he also hinted that he had time for a cup of tea and a chat. Leah eyed him coldly and said that actually she had a lot of paperwork to do. The truth was that at the moment she didn't trust herself to spend any time in his company without betraying her feelings about Charlotte's pregnancy. It was much better not to talk to him at all.

Having waved off Jamie and the children, she spent a satisfying hour or so in her small, pocket-sized garden, ruthlessly extracting every weed she could find. By the time she'd finished, she put a hand to her aching back and decided she deserved a long bath and a bit of pampering.

Consequently, when she walked into Terry's, her long hair shone and her skin glowed with the effects of an expensive bath scrub. She wore only jeans and a long-sleeved T-shirt but she still won an appreciative smile from Terry. He was busy mixing cocktails and Leah had an unwelcome memory of the margaritas Christopher had bought her.

Terry remembered them too. 'Are you planning to meet that pleasant senior citizen you went off with last time you were here?'

'Ha, ha, very funny,' Leah said, 'and I'd be grateful if you'd forget you ever saw me with him. Personally, I blame your margaritas. I'm meeting Anthea. Can I have a nice, small glass of wine while I'm waiting?'

The place was quite busy tonight. A group of thirty-somethings sitting under the Kate Moss poster caught her attention, or at least one of the men did because he was seriously good-looking. On the other side of the room, six women in earnest conversation were drinking champagne and Leah would have loved to know *why* they were drinking champagne since they didn't look like they were celebrating anything at all. At the end of the bar there was an elderly foursome who were far more jolly and who presumably had ordered the cocktails.

'What *are* you making?' Leah asked. 'They look pretty lethal.'

Terry brought the chopping board over to the bar and sliced a couple of lemons. 'It's called a Bolshoi Punch: vodka, rum, crème de cassis, lime juice, lemon juice and bitter lemon.' He turned and reached for a glass of wine and put it in front of her. 'Here's your drink, by the way. When I have a moment, remind me to tell you what my wife told me last night.'

Leah's phone started buzzing and she picked it up. 'Hi, Anthea,' she said. 'Where are you?'

Anthea was at home. Anthea's son had just been sick and she didn't feel she could leave him with her babysitter, who had gone distinctly queasy at the sight of said son's vomit. Leah said she quite understood and agreed they'd do drinks another time soon. Leah put her phone back in her bag and sat watching Terry handing out his Bolshoi whatever it was to the two elderly couples at the end of the bar. She wondered what it was his wife had said. Knowing Terry's wife – and Terry talked about her so much that Leah felt she *did* know her – it was yet another confession of lurid extra-marital behaviour.

She picked up her drink and quite suddenly someone jogged her arm, and most of the contents of her glass went flying onto the floor. She blinked and glanced up at her assailant. It was the good-looking man from the group by the Kate Moss poster and he stared at her in stunned dismay. 'I am so sorry,' he said. 'I don't know how that happened. Are you all right?' He reached over for a paper napkin from the steel container and tried to dab at her arm with it.

She took it from him and brushed down her sleeve and her jeans. 'Really,' she said, 'it's all right. Most of it went on the floor.'

'You must let me buy you another drink. That's the least I can do.'

'I'm fine, honestly. I was waiting for a friend and she's just rung to say she can't come so I was about to go home anyway.'

'Please let me get you a drink. If you don't, I'll feel full of guilt. It will be one of those things that wake me up at three in the morning and keep me from going to sleep again.'

'Well, I wouldn't want that.' Leah smiled. 'I'll have a small glass of white wine, please.'

Terry, who Leah knew would have been watching everything, suddenly surfaced in front of them and looked enquiringly at Leah's new friend.

'A small white wine for the lady, please, and I'd like to settle my bill at the same time.' The man passed a couple of notes to Terry and began telling Terry about the spilt wine.

Leah had time now to take a good look at him. He was a few inches taller than her, with short light brown hair that tipped slightly onto his forehead, a straight nose and a strong chin. He looked casually elegant and sophisticated in his black suit, white shirt and thin tie draped loosely round his neck. But then, when he smiled at something Terry said, his green eyes sparkled and he didn't look sophisticated at all. When he smiled, she could see exactly what he must have looked like as a little boy.

Terry handed her a new glass and she raised it up and said politely to her benefactor, 'Thank you for my drink. Aren't you going to have one too?'

He stared at her for a moment and then smiled. 'I really shouldn't, but – what the hell, I'm celebrating!' He nodded at Terry. 'Can you get me another small glass, please?'

'Certainly,' Terry said. He was loving this.

'David!'

Both Leah and the man turned. His friends were standing by the door and one of the women raised her voice and said, 'We're going on to Sam's. We're already late. Are you coming?'

'Tell Sam I'll be along soon,' the man said and raised his hand in a casual farewell before turning back to receive his wine from Terry.

'So tell me,' Leah said. 'What are you celebrating?'

'Oh.' David looked a little embarrassed. 'I've written a book. That's why I'm wearing this.' He gestured at his suit. 'I gave a talk tonight. That lot came along to give me moral support. They're old schoolfriends.'

'Have you lived here all your life?'

'No. I left to go to university and I've been in Newcastle for the last eight years. It feels a bit weird coming back to live here – like stepping back in time. I've moved into a flat near my mother, who's convinced I'm not looking after myself. She keeps bringing round casseroles.'

So, Leah thought, he wasn't married or living with anyone. 'Tell me about your book,' she said. 'Is it a novel?'

'No, it's an extremely serious history book. It's called *The Crimes of Queen Victoria*.'

'That's a great title.'

'Isn't it? My editor came up with that.'

'So,' Leah said, 'you're a published writer. I'm impressed. You should be very proud.'

'It's funny what makes us proud,' David said. 'I mean, of course I'm pleased about my books. But actually, in terms of what makes me most proud, I'd have to say that learning to ride a bicycle beat the books by a mile.'

'You're joking.'

'No, I'm not. I have a sister who's two years older than me. These days she happens to be one of my most favourite people but as a child she was probably the most evil sister you could imagine. We used to play football and French cricket with my father and she always won. We used to play card games and she always won them too. And every time she won, she produced this sort of demonic cackle that froze the blood. Then one Christmas we were both given bicycles and of course she learnt to ride hers within a few hours and I couldn't get the hang of it, and while I kept falling down she'd ride round and round me, giving her horrible laugh. And then, one morning, I could just *do* it and she came out to watch me and her mouth dropped, and I can tell you this: nothing will ever come close to how I felt at that moment.' He looked at her expectantly. 'So what's yours?'

Leah blinked. 'My what?'

'What's *your* greatest achievement?'

Leah put her head to one side and gave the matter some thought. 'I can show you,' she said. 'Watch.' She took the rest of the lemon from Terry's chopping board and put it in her mouth. Then she sucked in all the juice before extracting the husk of lemon and holding it out before her.

David stared at her with genuine admiration. 'How did you *do* that?' he demanded. 'How did you keep your face so . . . so blank?'

'Oh,' Leah said modestly, 'it's nothing much really. My stepfather used to love telling me I looked like I'd just sucked a lemon so I used up hundreds of lemons training myself to keep my face normal when I sucked them and then, one evening when he said it again, I was ready. I whipped out half a lemon and I sucked it dry and I said, "Do you mean like that?" '

'What did he say?'

'He just stared at me and said, "You are a very silly, stupid girl." '

'He doesn't sound much fun.'

Leah shrugged. 'Well, we have never got on.'

'He doesn't sound very bright either,' David said. 'Anyone who can master the art of keeping a straight face while sucking a lemon is clearly destined to go far.'

'Thank you,' Leah said. She put the piece of lemon back on the chopping board and suddenly felt an excruciating pain as the third finger of her left hand hit Terry's kitchen knife. She winced, turned over her hand and watched thick tears of blood ooze from her flesh. Her hand started swimming all over the place and then the entire bar seemed to be a jelly-like mess of beige and chrome and then everything went utterly, mercifully black.

When she came to, the man who couldn't ride a bicycle was staring at her anxiously and, behind him, Terry had a phone clamped to his ear. She was no longer sitting at the bar, she was propped up on one of Terry's leather sofas. She murmured, 'What happened?'

Terry put away his phone. 'David saved you,' he said. 'You cut your finger on my knife and then you just fell from your chair and David caught you.'

David and Terry seemed to have become very good mates all of a sudden, Leah thought woozily. She blinked a few times and said, 'I always faint at the sight of blood. I'm sorry. It's just something I do.'

'It was my fault,' Terry said. 'I shouldn't have been chopping lemons at the bar. You could probably sue me.'

'You can give me a free drink,' Leah said, 'but not tonight.' The bar was still dangerously fluid in its structure.

'Terry's ordered a taxi,' David said. 'It's just coming from the station so it will be here any moment. I'm going to see you home.'

'Really, there's no need,' Leah spoke without much conviction. 'I only live a few minutes away. I can walk home.'

'You're in no state to walk anywhere,' David said. 'And besides, I can use it to go on to my friend's house. It's all settled.'

Once they were in the taxi, it took no time at all before they were outside Leah's front door and she was too weak to protest when David insisted on escorting her into the house. 'Are you sure you'll be all right?' he asked. 'Do you want me to carry you up to your bedroom?'

She was *so* tempted to accept his offer. 'I'm fine,' she said. 'This has happened before. Can I give you some money for the taxi?'

'No, you can't. Look, I'm passing this way in the morning. I have to get a train to London. Can I call by and see how you are? Is half past eight too early?'

'Half past eight is fine. I make good coffee.'

'I'll look forward to it. Goodbye till then.'

She shut the door behind him and walked through to the kitchen, where she poured herself a large glass of water. She was glad David would be dropping by in the morning, even if it was at half past eight. He would have to take her as he found her, she thought, and immediately decided to get up at seven in order to wash her hair and do her make-up.

She should have set her alarm. It was twenty past eight and he'd be here in ten minutes. He really would have to take her as he found her. Damn. She only had time to find her slippers, put her long grey cardigan over her white cotton nightdress, run a brush through her hair and do her teeth before tearing downstairs to make the coffee.

When David arrived, he took one look at her and said, 'I won't come in. I shouldn't be disturbing you; you need to rest.'

'I shall be very cross if you *don't* come in,' Leah said. 'I did oversleep but I've made a large pot of coffee and I am fully recovered, so come in at once.'

'If you're sure.' David put down the large canvas bag he was carrying and followed Leah through to the kitchen. He wore the suit he'd been wearing last night but this time he had on a pale pink shirt with no tie.

'You're looking smart again,' Leah said. 'You make me feel even worse than I already did about oversleeping.'

'I'm going to my godson's christening,' David said. 'And then I'm going to stay the night with my sister and be as un-smart as I possibly can.'

'Is that the really evil sister?'

'She's not evil any more. She's actually rather nice.' He took a chair and, sitting down, looked up at her. 'Are you really all right?'

'I really am.' She brought a packed tray over to the table and offloaded two mugs, milk, sugar and the coffee pot. 'Do you like your coffee black or white?'

'I like it very black. It smells delicious.' He watched her pour it out and said, 'I've been thinking about last night. You had a terrible time. First, I spill your drink, and then you cut your finger and pass out. I'm so sorry.'

Leah sat down next to him. 'You might not believe this, but apart from the spilt wine and the bleeding finger and the fainting, I had a very good time.'

'So did I,' David said. 'I mean, I could do without the guilt over your wine and the terror when you fell from your chair, but otherwise it was a great evening. I can't remember when I've had one quite like it.' He took a sip of the coffee. 'That is *good.* Thank you.'

'It's the least I could do. I'm grateful to you. It was kind of you to see me home last night. Were you very late for your friends' party?'

'It wasn't really a party and I don't think they expected to see me for ages,' David said cheerfully. 'They could see I was smitten.' He caught Leah's eye and sighed. 'Now I've embarrassed you. I'm sorry.'

Leah scratched her head and gave what she hoped was a careless shrug of her shoulders. 'You haven't embarrassed me. It's just rather difficult to tell when you're being serious. Your eyes have this twinkle that is definitely suspect. In fact,' she added, almost without thinking, 'you have very nice eyes.'

'Now I'm embarrassed,' he said. He frowned at her for a moment, sighed again and then leant forward and kissed her. He smelt of fresh air and soap and coffee.

She blinked and said levelly, 'That was a surprise.'

'I can see it must have been,' David said. 'I'm afraid I always kiss people when they embarrass me.'

Leah raised an eyebrow. 'That must produce some awkward situations.'

'It does. Of course, I only get embarrassed when attractive women compliment me on my eyes.'

'Tell me honestly,' Leah said, 'how many women have complimented you on your eyes?'

David narrowed them thoughtfully. 'Well,' he said at last, 'I think you might be the first.'

Leah laughed. 'Now *I'm* embarrassed.'

'Are you?' David considered her gravely and then kissed her again.

'I take it,' Leah said a little shakily, 'that you're embarrassed that you embarrassed *me*?'

'No,' David said. 'I just wanted to kiss you.'

The sound of the doorbell made them both jump. Leah stood up at once. 'That will be my ex-husband with my children. I didn't expect them quite so early.' She went through to the hall to let them in and was greeted by a jumping daughter who immediately informed her that she'd helped her father make eggy bread for their breakfast.

Jamie and Fred followed behind with the rucksacks. All three of them stopped in their tracks when they saw David. David seemed quite oblivious to their blatant curiosity.

'Hello,' he said. 'I'm David. Forgive me for rushing off. I have a train to catch. Where's my overnight bag? Ah, here it is.' He picked it up and turned to Leah. 'Are you free on Friday? Can I take you for a drink?'

Leah felt her cheeks burn under the scrutiny of her

children and her ex-husband. 'All right,' she said and offered him a fleeting smile.

'Great,' David said. 'I'll be over at eight.' He gave a quick wave to the others and made a hasty exit, shutting the door behind him.

Molly spoke for her brother and her father. 'Who was *that*?'

Leah hugged her cardigan round her nightdress. 'It's a long story. Anthea suggested we had a drink at Terry's Wine Bar last night and I cut my finger and fainted and David was standing next to me and caught me before I fell to the floor. He came round this morning to see if I was all right and I had only just woken up . . .' She was aware she was gabbling and gave a laugh that even to her own ears sounded definitely forced. She bent down to hug her children. 'It is nice to see you!'

'Kids, I need to talk to your mother about money and stuff,' Jamie said. 'Why don't you go and unpack your bags? I won't be very long.'

Money and Stuff was one rule the children knew better than to question. Fred said, 'We'll have a game of Stratego.' This was pretty quick thinking on Fred's part since Leah usually rationed their time on computer games and she hardly ever let them play before teatime.

'Just this once,' she said and watched them run off to the sitting room before taking Jamie through to the kitchen. 'Do you want some coffee?'

'Thank you.' Jamie sat down at the table. 'Your young man seemed very nice.'

'Do you *know* how patronizing you sound?' Leah asked.

'I don't mean to be. It does occur to me that it might be

better if you get rid of your men friends before the children come home in future.'

Leah's eyes narrowed. 'I can't believe you said that.' She folded her arms tightly in front of her. 'Perhaps it's better if we both pretend you didn't say it.'

'I'm sorry.' Jamie threw up his hands in a calming gesture that was instantly irritating. 'Put it down to jealousy.'

'You lost any right to be jealous a long time ago.'

'I know. I'm sorry.'

Leah poured him a cup and set it down in front of him. 'What did you want to talk about?'

Jamie scratched his head. 'I wanted your advice.'

'Oh I get it,' Leah said. 'You're going to break the happy news to Charlotte's parents today. Well, if I were you, I'd take a big bunch of flowers.'

'It isn't that,' said Jamie, 'although Lord knows I'm not looking forward to seeing them. I want to know when you think I should tell the kids.'

Leah raised her eyebrows. 'I don't know. Perhaps they should get to know Charlotte a bit better first. Then, in a few weeks, when she begins to get bigger, you could—'

'She *is* bigger.' Jamie rubbed the back of his neck. 'The baby's due in January.'

Leah stared at him blankly and then, as the full implications dawned, she felt a rush of pure fury. She took a deep breath. 'How long have you known about this?'

Jamie shifted uncomfortably in his seat. 'She did a test after she missed her second period but—'

'And you've only *just* started thinking about telling the kids? Jamie, you're incredible! You're going to have a baby in a little over twelve weeks! In case you haven't noticed, you have two particularly bright children who are not going to be impressed by the fact you've kept this from them. I have no idea how they'll react but I do know that I'll be the one picking up the pieces. You must tell them as soon as possible. I can't believe you've left it this long.'

'Charlotte wanted to tell her parents first. Her father hasn't been well and she wanted to wait until he felt better.'

'I don't give a damn about Charlotte's father. Your children should be your first priority. You must tell them right away.'

'I can't,' Jamie said. 'I've got to drive Charlotte down to her parents in half an hour and I can't have the children next weekend as I'm going to Ireland – and before you say anything, it's work not pleasure. Leah, I'm sorry about this. I'm not exactly jumping for joy at the prospect of yet another mouth to feed.'

Leah instantly bridled. 'That's a bit rich, isn't it? I think most people would agree you pay remarkably little towards the maintenance of your children. You have a BMW, I have a clapped-out Toyota Yaris. You buy your jumpers from Joseph, I buy mine from the Oxfam shop. You have high-definition—'

'I know, I know. I wasn't getting at you, I was just saying this wasn't what I wanted.' He stared directly at Leah. 'None of this is what I wanted.'

For a moment, Leah met his gaze. *Don't go there, Leah,* she told herself savagely. *Don't go anywhere near there.* 'Well,' she said, 'you have my advice. You tell them as soon as you can. Do you want me to be there with you?'

'No,' Jamie said, 'I don't. Look, I'll do it as soon as I can. You don't need to hassle me.'

'Perhaps,' Leah suggested thoughtfully, 'it might be best to do it when you take them to your parents for half-term. Prime your mother. Mary's brilliant at this sort of thing. She'll be able to help with any fallout and there *will* be fallout. You're going to have to do a lot of reassuring. Make sure you let them know it will make no difference to your feelings for them.'

'Of course it won't,' Jamie said. 'If you really think . . .' He stopped as there was a knock on the kitchen door. He rose from his seat and went to open it.

Molly said, 'Have you finished yet? Because I forgot to ask Mummy if she fed Stephen last night.'

'Yes, I did,' Leah said. 'Jamie's leaving now so you can say goodbye to him.'

Molly put her arms round her father. 'I wish you could *stay*,' she said.

'So do I,' Jamie said, looking at Leah. 'So do I.'

In bed that night, Leah rewound the moment when Jamie's eyes had looked at her with such unusual intensity. She knew exactly what had caused it. Jamie thought she'd spent the night with David. He had never seen her with another man before this morning and the sight had aroused in him a simple Pavlovian response of jealousy, which was as automatic as it was meaningless. What hurt was the fact that after all this time she could be so pathetically affected by him that she was currently losing precious sleep time. It meant nothing, she told herself angrily, it meant nothing at all. And then there was David, who was going to take her out for a drink on Friday even though she couldn't go out with him on Friday because these days she never went out with a man unless the children were with Jamie. But she had to go out for a drink with him because she had no idea how to contact him to tell him she couldn't. And didn't she want to go out with him anyway? But Molly would almost certainly be impossible. Perhaps, just perhaps, she'd be all right for once.

It was a forlorn hope, of course. When Friday evening came round, Molly was fine over supper but her mood darkened when Leah went upstairs. When she returned to the kitchen, Molly was sitting at the table eating a yoghurt. She took one look at her mother before launching an attack. Why had she changed into her blue dress if she was only going out for a drink with a friend and why did she need to go out with him anyway? If he wanted a drink so badly why couldn't he have a drink *here*?

'First,' Leah said, 'I'm going out with David because it's quite pleasant to have adult company occasionally, and secondly, if I were to give him a drink here, you'd just sit and glower at him.'

'I wouldn't glower at him,' Molly said. 'What does glower mean anyway?'

'If you glower,' Leah said, 'you look like this.' She knit her eyebrows together and pushed her bottom lip out.

'I would never look like that,' Molly said.

Leah glanced at her watch. 'Stacey's late.'

Molly pouted. 'I don't want Stacey to come.'

Leah sighed. 'That's silly. You know you like Stacey.' She stopped at the sound of the doorbell. 'That'll be her.' Both she and Molly went out to the hall.

It was David. He wore black jeans and a green jersey over a white T-shirt. He looked nice, Leah thought. He looked really nice. He smiled at Molly and said, 'I didn't have a chance to introduce myself last time. I'm David.'

'You *did* tell me that last time,' Molly said. 'And you don't need to take Mum out. You can stay and have a drink here.'

'Molly!' Leah exclaimed and then smiled gratefully as Stacey came up the path. 'Stacey,' she said, 'how very nice to see you.'

Stacey was full of apologies for being late. Leah brushed them away. 'It's fine. Fred's on the computer playing Virtual Villagers. He can play for another fifteen minutes. Usual bedtime rules apply. Any problems, I'll have my mobile.'

'When will you come home?' Molly demanded. 'Will you come back soon?'

'I'm not sure,' Leah said. 'I won't be too long.' She grabbed her bag from under the hall table, called out, 'Goodbye, Fred,' gave Molly a quick kiss and made a fast, determined escape.

As soon as they were on the pavement, she said breathlessly, 'I'm sorry if Molly was rude. She's a little possessive, I'm afraid.'

'I did rather get that impression last Sunday. On balance, I was glad I had a train to catch.'

So he *had* noticed. 'They were just a bit surprised to see you,' Leah said. 'They're not used to seeing strange men in the house.'

'How long have you been divorced?'

'Three years. I don't think that either of the children has grasped the basic idea of divorce. Or rather, I don't think they want to grasp it. And they don't seem to mind all the women floating around Jamie but if any stray male comes anywhere near me, Molly acts like it's the end of the world.'

'That's understandable,' David said. 'You're her mother. I take it she only sees her father at weekends?'

'When he's not too busy,' Leah said sourly. She gave her head a little shake. 'I'm sorry. I shouldn't let it upset me.'

'I'd be surprised if it didn't.' He stopped as they approached the main road. 'Where are we going?'

'I thought we could go to the White Hart. We can have a civilized drink there and forget about annoying ex-husbands and difficult daughters.' She glanced up at him. 'Have you ever been tempted by matrimony?'

'I was married for a while.'

'Why did it end?'

'Well,' David said, 'she was a beautiful woman.'

'That's not a reason.'

'It was, though. Beautiful women are used to receiving lots of attention. At the time, I was teaching undergraduates while trying to write my first book. She got bored and decided she wanted out.' He glanced down at her. 'You look rather like her.'

'I'm flattered,' Leah said, 'but I know I'm not beautiful and I'm certainly not used to receiving lots of attention. There's something about having two small children that makes a man lose interest.'

'You've been meeting the wrong men,' David said.

Leah laughed. 'Tell me about it. I've spent my whole life meeting the wrong men.'

'I knew we had something in common. My sister tells me I always go for the wrong women. My relationships always end in disaster.'

'But then,' Leah mused, 'I suppose you could say that all relationships end in disaster until you find the one that doesn't.' They had reached the White Hart now and she said quickly, 'I'm buying the drinks. You paid for the taxi and I owe you.'

'Yes, but I'm still celebrating the new book,' David said, 'and you know the best tables here so you're the right one to find us a seat. Are you happy with white wine?'

Leah was more than happy with white wine and after vowing to buy the second round, she went off to bag the table by the window. While appearing to check her mobile, she allowed her eyes to settle briefly on David, who was chatting easily to the barman. He was very engaging company, she thought. She didn't know why she'd been so nervous about this evening. The memory of his mouth on hers suddenly came back to her and she knew exactly why she was nervous.

'Do you want to know something funny?' David said, approaching the table with two very full glasses of white wine and setting them down with exaggerated care. 'Here we are, sitting down to have a drink together, and I realize I don't even know your name. Who are you?'

'My name's Leah Payne and I'm delighted to meet you.' Leah held out her hand and he took it; his was warm and strong. She felt suddenly shy. She said, 'I know you're David and you write history books. Do you write history books all the time?'

'No,' David said. 'I wish I did. Unfortunately, until the great British public finds out what a brilliant writer I am, I have to do other things as well. I've taken up a post at Bristol University and I do a bit of TV.'

'Do you?' Leah was impressed. 'I like history programmes. Do you remember Simon Schama's programmes on Britain? I watched all of those.'

David sighed. 'Oh dear.'

'Don't you like Simon Schama?'

'I love Simon Schama. I'd love to *be* Simon Schama. He is a TV star. I, on the other hand, have just been taken on by an obscure educational channel in Bristol that produces history programmes for schools.'

'It's a start,' Leah said.

'It is and I'm grateful. It's one of the reasons that made me leave Newcastle.'

'It's quite a move,' Leah said. 'Do you have any regrets? Are you glad to be in Bath?'

'I am now,' David said. It was a simple statement, made in a matter-of-fact manner, but the way he held her with his eyes made her heart contract and she was almost glad that her phone diverted her attention.

It was – surprise, surprise – Molly. 'Mummy? When are you coming home?'

'Not for a bit and you should be in bed.' Leah darted an apologetic glance at David.

'Will you come home soon? I have a tummy ache.'

'Molly, you do *not*. I won't be long. I'm just having a drink.'

'I *do* have a tummy ache. Will you come home soon? I can't get to sleep.'

Leah sighed and checked her watch. 'I'll make a deal. I'll be back within the hour but only if you promise not to ring me again.'

There was a silence and then, 'I'll see you in an hour.'

'You're on. Goodnight, Molly.' Leah put down the phone and said, 'I'm sorry. This is why I usually save my social life for weekends when Jamie has the children. It's more trouble than it's worth.'

'Molly reminded me of someone,' David said thoughtfully. 'It was the way she stared at me. She looked like Damien in *The Omen* just before he kills his nanny.'

'That,' said Leah, 'is not funny.'

David looked abashed. 'You are absolutely right. She's more like Cerberus.'

'Who is Cerberus?'

'He was a two-headed dog who guarded the gates of hell.'

'Great. First, you tell me my daughter is Damien from *The Omen* and now you compare her to a dog from hell . . .'

'Only she's *far* more frightening.'

Leah grinned but felt compelled to stand up for her daughter. 'She *is* only nine.'

'I know and I do understand.'

'Thank you. I *am* sorry she sabotaged this evening.'

'We still have almost an hour,' David said. 'That's better than not seeing you at all.'

Leah smiled. 'You are a very nice man,' she said.

'Oh,' David said, 'it's easy to be nice to a woman one likes.'

She looked up at him and her heart raced. The last time she had felt like this was the evening she met Jamie. She could almost see the warning light switch on in her brain.

CHAPTER NINE

Alison Has a Momentous Moment of Madness

Ever since Alison's visit to Merrily, she had been worrying about her. She hated the fact that she couldn't tell Merrily that Christopher was unfaithful, and she hated it even more now that she knew he was a bully who made her live in a house that would give anyone nightmares. She had tried to explain her feelings to Leah and both times Leah had rung off prematurely, pleading first pressure of work and then activities with the children. This morning she would be unable to use either excuse since Jamie had taken the children down to his parents for half-term and Leah would be enjoying a peaceful Sunday on her own. Knowing Leah, she was still in bed. Alison finished basting the potatoes and reached for the phone.

In fact, Leah was not in bed for the very good reason that she was not having a peaceful weekend on her own because Jamie was not taking the children to his parents until the following Saturday. 'You forget that their half-term is a week after your boys',' Leah said. 'Molly and

Fred and I have been up for hours already. I've got them outside weeding the garden at the moment.'

'That's impressive,' Alison said.

'I'm paying them to do it. I'm sorry I didn't get back to you about Merrily. I've been a bit preoccupied lately.'

Alison began to stir the gravy. 'Anything in particular?'

Leah hesitated. 'The kids don't know yet so keep it quiet. Jamie and his girlfriend are going to have a baby.'

'Oh Leah!' Alison put down her wooden spoon. 'I'm so sorry.'

'It gets worse. The baby's due in three months.'

Alison whistled. 'I don't believe it! Jamie is hopeless! Why's he left it so late to tell Fred and Molly?'

'That's exactly what I said. It's so typical of Jamie.'

'Are you very upset?'

'I was. Mainly, I'm just cross now. He should have let the children know ages ago so they could get used to the idea.'

'Of course he should have done!' Alison thought quickly. 'Listen, why don't you come over now and have Sunday lunch with us? We've only got Harry's girlfriend coming over and I'll get Felix to pick some more beans . . .'

'Honestly, Alison, I'm all right. And I have loads of work to do here.'

'I just think you might—'

'Really, I'm fine. I've even started seeing a new man.'

'Have you? That's fantastic! What's he like?'

'He's nice. I think he's nice. I've only been out for a drink with him but I'm seeing him next week. It'll probably come to nothing. You know what I'm like.'

Alison contented herself with a simple, heartfelt, 'I do.'

'And I've been thinking about Merrily. It seems to me you have three main objections to Christopher. One, he's been unfaithful, two, he lost his temper with her, and three, he's made her live in an unpleasant house.'

Alison went over to the sofa and sat down. 'It's not quite as simple as that.'

'Oh I know we don't like him, but that's just *us*. If we take the unfaithful bit first, there could be any number of reasons for that. I mean, I went to bed with him because I was upset about Jamie. Perhaps he went to bed with me because *he* was upset about something. Perhaps it was totally out of character and he feels really bad about it. Secondly, he shouted at Merrily. That's terrible but it's not *that* terrible. You're married to Felix and Felix is lovely. I have friends whose husbands have done far worse things than shout at them. And thirdly, there's the house. I'm sure it is as horrid as you say but it's still a house near lovely fields and flowers and things. At least they're not living in some poky flat. What I'm trying to say—'

'I know what you're saying. We can't do anything about the fact that Merrily is married to a scumbag.'

'That's it. All we can do is introduce her to people and show her we care.'

'I suppose you're right,' said Alison. 'But I still wish you'd go and see the house for yourself. I know you don't want to see Christopher, but . . .'

'I will go round. Her son's there at the moment. He's come down for *his* half-term. Merrily's got all sorts of plans for him. I'll go when he's gone back to London.'

'All right.' Alison levered herself off the sofa and went

over to the Aga. 'I'd better get on with the lunch. Let me know how your romance goes.'

'I will,' Leah said. 'I'm not sure it *is* a romance yet.'

Alison put down the phone. Perhaps she *had* been overreacting. Other people's marriages were always a mystery and who was she to judge Christopher on the strength of one possibly much-regretted one-night stand and one possibly uncharacteristic bout of temper? She went back to the gravy and resumed her stirring. She ought to take up yoga or Buddhism and develop a calmer attitude. Most things worked out in the end. Nathan, for example, had been quite happy to go off on his week's geography field trip and when she'd dropped him off at school yesterday morning she had left him happily chatting to friends, and the odious Russell Clink was nowhere to be seen. Eva had rung the other day and seemed much more positive about Manchester. Phoebe might be going to marry Lennie in a worryingly short period of time but he did seem to make her happy. And as for Harry's relationship with the fifteen-year-old Nicola Casement, the very fact that he'd invited her to have Sunday lunch with his parents had to imply a degree of respectability that had been lacking in his association with the luscious if slightly large Francine.

She heard the scrunching of gravel outside and almost immediately Harry appeared in the kitchen in his blue jeans and the anti-Fascism T-shirt that Eva had given him last Christmas. 'That'll be Nicola and her father,' he said and he pushed back his hair, which, Alison noted, was newly washed. He opened the door as soon as the bell rang.

Alison had never met Nicola. Nathan had mentioned her

a few times after she won a prize in a poetry competition. Alison had imagined a sweet-faced young beauty, charmingly unaware of her attractions. In fact, she looked at least three years older than her age and her skin-tight trousers, tiny T-shirt and elaborate eye make-up suggested that she was on more than nodding terms with her sexuality.

Her father looked like an egg. He had a small oval face with a startlingly bald head, and his body seemed to flow out from his neck, reaching its climax around his girth and then dwindling into two short legs.

'Won't you come in for a drink?' Alison asked. 'My husband's in the garden. I'm sure he'd love to meet you.'

'Another time, Mrs Coward,' the egg said. 'My good wife is cooking our lunch and I am sure you are doing the same.' He fixed her with a pair of dark, beady little eyes and said with some deliberation, 'Perhaps you will walk with me to my car?'

'Yes, of course.' Alison turned to Harry and Nicola. 'Would you two go and find Felix and tell him to come in soon? Lunch won't be long.' She turned back and followed Mr Casement.

'I hope you won't mind, Mrs Coward, if I speak frankly,' Mr Casement said. 'This is not easy to say, but Nicola tells me you have two daughters so I'm sure you will understand.' He cleared his throat and stood with his hands behind his back, rocking slightly on his heels. 'My daughter has always been a very loving and affectionate child. I have nothing against your son, but boys will be boys and there's no doubt that your Harry is very *taken*.'

'I understand,' Alison said, not understanding at all. How did he know that Harry was taken? She could never tell what Harry felt about anything. Perhaps when he was away from his parents he was a different person. Perhaps he was demonstrative and chatty and charming.

'When Nicola asked me to give her a lift here, I was happy to do so, Mrs Coward. It gave me the chance to have this little talk. She is only fifteen and she can easily be swayed by other people, particularly if they are good-looking young men like your son!' He gave a little chuckle here and Alison responded with a polite chuckle of her own, though whether he was laughing at the idea that Harry might be described as good-looking or at the idea that his daughter was easily swayed was difficult to tell.

Mr Casement climbed into his car and popped his head out of the window. 'I know I can trust you with the safety of my little girl,' he said, 'and I feel so much better for having this conversation with you. I'll be along to collect her at six.'

Alison stood and watched him reverse out of the drive. She felt quite incensed. Was he asking her to keep an eye on Harry? Did he really believe that Nicola was in danger of being ravished on a Sunday afternoon? What sort of boy did he think Harry was? She walked back into the house. The trouble was that Harry probably *was* the sort of boy Mr Casement probably thought he was. She glanced at her watch. It was just after one. For the next five hours she would have to keep a very strict watch on Harry and his loving and affectionate girlfriend. It dawned on her that it was just as well that the Hadrian's Wall trip had been called off. Now was not the time to leave Harry in the house without his parents.

* * *

On Saturday, Alison went up to London to meet Phoebe. Phoebe had suggested they meet outside Topshop in Oxford Street. When Felix drove Alison to the station, she pointed out that while he might not be overjoyed about his daughter's imminent wedding, he should at least be grateful she had such inexpensive tastes.

Phoebe was waiting for her when she emerged from the underground and Alison couldn't help smiling. Only Phoebe would come out for such a serious shopping spree dressed in a pretty frock, her old army jacket and her extremely scuffed trainers. She gave Alison a hug and said, 'I know we'll find something in here.'

They didn't. Phoebe tried on a number of outfits, none of which were quite right. They almost bought a floor-length empire-line dress which had delicate green and silver embroidery on the bust. Alison thought it made Phoebe look like a Jane Austen heroine. Its fate, however, was sealed when a hugely pregnant woman tried on an identical dress and declared it was just what she needed.

Two hours and five shops later, Phoebe said a little wearily that a friend at work had told her there was a terrific shop in Notting Hill.

Alison had never been in a shop like this before. They had to ring the doorbell in order to be let in, and the two saleswomen, who were charming, were dressed in the most exquisite little black numbers. They were effusive in their praise of Phoebe's figure and complexion and hair and insisted that Alison sat down on the pink velvet sofa with a cup of tea while they helped pick out a few possibilities.

Eventually, Phoebe disappeared into the changing room while Alison sat back and chatted to the sympathetic staff about the difficulties of finding a wedding dress that didn't look too *like* a wedding dress.

Then Phoebe came out and Alison caught her breath. Phoebe looked like Phoebe had never looked before. The cap-sleeved, ivory-coloured dress had a racy cut-away at the breast that was softened by a layer of sheer fabric. It was gathered at the waist, slid over her hips like honey and dropped to just below her knees. It was, quite simply, magnificent. It gave Phoebe curves that Alison had never known her slender daughter possessed. She looked like a film star and it was obvious that she felt like one too. She stood with her shoulders back and her head held high, and her eyes shone with confidence.

She gave a little twirl. 'What do you think?' she asked.

Alison sat up straight and clapped her hands. 'It's beautiful,' she said. '*You're* beautiful.'

Phoebe swallowed hard. 'I feel beautiful,' she said. 'For the first time in my life, I feel beautiful.'

The two ladies in black agreed. One of them said Phoebe should be a model and the other said the dress fitted Phoebe perfectly and was positively *made* for her.

Phoebe stared at her reflection in the mirror. 'I love it!' she said. 'I LOVE it! I don't want to try anything else on! This is IT!' She started to laugh and then just as suddenly glanced at Alison with an anguished look. 'I bet it costs a fortune. I didn't think . . . I'll get changed.'

At this point a sensible woman would have simply nodded. While Phoebe was in the changing room, Alison asked the ladies for the price of the dress. When they told her, she blinked and tried to focus on the voice in her head that told her to get out of the place as quickly as possible.

One of the ladies said thoughtfully, 'It would be a tragedy not to get that dress. It is so right!'

The other lady sighed. 'I tell you what,' she said. 'I shouldn't do this but I can't bear it if your daughter doesn't have it. We'll take seventy-five pounds off the price. Which means,' she paused impressively, 'that you can have it for two thousand, three hundred and seventy-five pounds.'

Alison had never wanted to buy anything as much as she wanted to buy that dress. If she didn't buy it for Phoebe, she would always regret it. And, after all, it was Phoebe's wedding day and Phoebe had been so happy when she had put it on! Surely, there were times in one's life when one had to say to hell with the expense? Admittedly, Alison felt a little sick as she passed over her credit card but Phoebe was over the moon. As they walked back to the station, Phoebe kept giving little jumps, and when she said goodbye to her mother she hugged Alison hard and whispered, 'I never thought I could look like that. Thank you *so* much!'

It was only as the train made its inexorable way back to Bath that Alison began to panic. Neither she nor Felix ever paid out large sums without consulting the other. Further, in the ten years since she had persuaded a very doubtful Felix to buy the horrendously expensive house in Tucking Friary, she had been careful to practise economy in every area of household expense. She looked down at the huge pink box with the black velvet handles. What had she done? How could she explain her madness to Felix when she didn't even understand it herself? She had committed the most grotesque act of extravagance only a few hours after assuring her husband that she would do nothing of the kind. She had given way to a moment of reckless, outrageous insanity and she had an ominous feeling of doom that grew stronger with every mile. The only course of action was to tell Felix at once. He'd know what to do. Perhaps the shop would take it back. She was sure the shop would take it back.

She heard two little beeps from within her bag and pulled out her phone. Phoebe had sent her a text.

U R a perfect mother. thank U!!

She put the phone back in her bag and bit her lip fiercely. She was getting herself in a state. She would tell Felix. Felix would understand.

Her phone was buzzing. She reached into her bag for the second time and swallowed before answering. 'Hi, Felix. I was about to ring you. My train's on time. I should be in Bath in about half an hour. Are you still able to pick me up?'

'I am. Did you buy a dress for Phoebe?'

'I did,' Alison said. 'It's beautiful.'

'Good. I'll see you later.'

When she rang off, she realized her hands were shaking. There was no question that she would have to tell Felix as soon as possible. She would not be able to sleep until she'd told him. She bit her lower lip and decided she would allow herself *one* sleepless night. She would tell him tomorrow.

CHAPTER TEN

Leah Visits Merrily's Lovely Home

Leah's Saturday began well. Jamie – definitely driven by a guilty conscience this time – arrived on time and managed to give Leah a whispered assurance that he'd tell Molly and Fred about the baby in the next few days.

Having waved them off, Leah walked into town to buy her provisions for the evening. It was still only eleven when she got home and, remembering her promise to Alison, she decided to walk up the hill to see Merrily.

It was the sort of autumnal weather that Leah loved, with a bracing wind that swept her hair back and forth. The trees on the hills beyond the fields were a riot of russet-brown, deep red and rich ochre. It was a great day for a walk, which was just as well since it was a fair climb to the top of the hill and by the time she reached her destination she had taken off her jacket.

Alison had told her to look out for conifers and she found Merrily's house without difficulty. Alison had not been exaggerating; it looked like the perfect location for a horror film. As she walked up the drive and smoothed her hair, she noticed that even the wind was subdued by this place.

When Merrily opened the door, it was obvious she'd been crying. Leah said uncertainly, 'I thought I'd drop in for a few minutes. Jamie's taken the kids off to his parents for the week and I felt like some company. I should have rung first. I can always come round another time.'

'I was about to make a cup of tea,' Merrily said, 'and it's lovely to see you. I've just come back from taking Tom to the station. You're a very welcome distraction.'

Leah followed Merrily along the narrow corridor to the kitchen. 'Did you have a good half-term with him?' she asked.

'Oh it was lovely. We went to Longleat and Stourhead and the American Museum. He's quite happy. He doesn't seem to mind living with Isobel. It's just that this house seems rather big and empty now he's gone.'

Leah glanced around the kitchen. 'Merrily,' she said earnestly, 'this house *is* big and empty and I think you are very brave to live here. You deserve a medal. You deserve a whole bag of medals.'

'I don't,' Merrily said shakily, 'but I love it that you think I do. It's only that our flat in Vauxhall is so light and friendly and this house is rather dark. I know I'm being pathetic. I'm sure it has huge potential.'

'So does the London Dungeon,' Leah said. 'It doesn't mean I'd want to live there.'

'It might be better with different furniture,' Merrily said doubtfully. 'All our stuff is still in the flat and Aunt Florence's things are a little old-fashioned.'

'It would help if you cut down all those trees,' Leah said. 'At least it would lighten the place.' She watched Merrily take out tea bags and mugs. 'Does Christopher really like it here? I can't understand how anyone would want to work in this house.'

'He's happy to be out of London. The noise and pollution got him down. He says he can hear himself think now.'

'That doesn't mean you have to stay *here*, in this house. You could sell it. I'm sure it would make a brilliant prison or something.'

'Leah!' Merrily gave a guilty laugh. 'It's not as bad as all that.'

'You could sell it,' Leah repeated. 'If Christopher wants peace and quiet, there are loads of pretty villages round Bath. I could show you some of them. You'd love Freshford. And then there's Limpley Stoke and Southstoke and Combe Hay.'

'It's not as simple as that,' Merrily said. 'Christopher finds the atmosphere here conducive to his Muse, and that is hugely important. I've got a copy of his latest book here. I was looking at it only the other day.' She took a pile of papers and books from the top of the fridge and extracted a paperback. 'This is why we're here.'

What sounded like a school bell rang out from upstairs and Merrily, pausing only to put the book on the table, said, 'That will be Christopher. I won't be a moment.'

Leah watched Merrily scurry out of the room and felt a stab of anger. Even if Christopher was half as brilliant as his wife claimed he was, he had no right to treat her like a slave. She sat down at the table and began to read the blurb on the back of his book.

The Open Door *is another triumph for C. J. Trumpet in which he explores the meaning of life in a society that has lost its way. With characteristic sensitivity and insight, the author grapples with the competing forces of love and ego and . . .*

Leah rolled her eyes. She strongly suspected that Christopher had never done much grappling apart from the physical sort. In fact, she strongly suspected that he had never grappled with competing forces at all. It was pretty obvious that Christopher had long ago put his ego above all else and, worse still, had somehow brainwashed Merrily into also putting his ego above all else. She sipped her tea thoughtfully and scrutinized the book's cover. There was a photo of an open door through which could be seen a pale blue sky. Underneath was written: *Another masterpiece from C. J. Trumpet.*

Leah was, grudgingly, impressed. Perhaps it *was* a masterpiece. Perhaps she'd been wrong to judge Christopher so quickly. Who was she to dismiss Merrily's marriage when Merrily was so proud of her husband? She did not regret her bluntness about the house, though. Alison had been right: it had a cold, dank atmosphere. There was no way Merrily could be happy here.

Merrily reappeared and said, 'Leah, Christopher's so pleased you're here. Would you mind taking his tea up to him? His study's at the top of the stairs on the right. He'd love to say hello.'

I bet he would, Leah thought grimly. She stood up. She supposed that now was as good a time as any to reassure him of her discretion.

Alison had described Christopher's study but even so it was a shock. It also made her very angry. No expense had been spared here and yet, according to Alison, Merrily was expected to renovate the rest of the house in her own time and on the tightest of budgets.

Christopher looked up at her and smiled. 'Leah, how nice to see you. Could you put the tea on this little mat here?' He pointed to a coaster next to his computer.

Leah brought it over to him without speaking and set it down. She froze suddenly as she felt his hand stroke her right buttock. She stared down at him and said furiously, 'Will you please remove your hand? What sort of woman do you think I am?'

He glanced up at her. 'I know precisely what sort of woman you are,' he said. He sounded almost amused.

She did not trust herself to speak. She walked across the room and closed the door with a bang. Then she breathed very deeply before returning downstairs.

In some ways, Leah's childhood had prepared her well for adult life. In every clash between herself and her stepfather – and there had been many clashes – Leah's mother had supported her husband rather than her daughter. If Leah had never quite got used to being let down by her mother, she did at least get used to *expecting* to be let down. This was, Leah thought, a useful lesson. As far as she was concerned, the great advantage of never quite trusting people was that she never got disappointed. True, she had been utterly miserable when her marriage broke down but even then she responded quickly to Alison's bracing advice to stop moping and start a new life.

While Leah was programmed to accept the shortcomings of others, she found it far more difficult to cope with those times when she disappointed herself. She far preferred to be the victim of bad behaviour than being the instigator. When Christopher looked at her with such calm contempt and told her he knew what sort of woman she was, Leah felt like she'd been hit in the stomach. She was upset because she knew he was right. He *did* know. He knew she was the sort of woman who got drunk and had sex with strange men.

To add fuel to her self-loathing, her mind was clogged with jealousy and rage against a woman she'd never met. She had seen the back of Charlotte's head, which was enough to indicate that she was young and beautiful and spoilt and selfish, with no business to be having a baby when Jamie had two fabulous children already. She hated the fact that Fred and Molly would be upset and she hated even more the fact that her righteous maternal anger was threaded through with very unrighteous older-woman/rejected-ex-wife general nastiness and venom.

All in all, Leah thought as she walked back from Merrily's house, it was just as well that she had a meal to prepare and a dinner guest to entertain. Otherwise, she would probably drown in a mire of self-disgust. She had invited David to dinner because he had refused to let her pay towards the taxi or the drinks in the pub the other week. It was some time since she'd cooked a special meal and she was looking forward to flexing her culinary muscles.

Apart from the menu, she had not allowed herself to think too much about the evening ahead. She knew she liked David and she was pretty sure he liked her a little. She knew she wouldn't sleep with him tonight and her decision was only partly to do with the Christopher debacle.

Certainly, she was not in the market for casual sex. More to the point, she hoped that she and David might actually embark on a relationship, and if they did she felt it important to take it slowly in order to cope with any attendant problems that might come up. The fact that any attendant problems all looked remarkably like Molly was something she preferred not to think about at this stage.

At seven thirty, Leah surveyed her kitchen and felt pretty smug. The subdued lighting – ceiling light off, soft lamp by the bread bin on – the cleared work surface, and the candlelit table with paper napkins and wine glasses had all transformed the small room. The all-in-one chicken dish was simmering gently, the blueberry fool was in the fridge and she had prepared the batter for the savoury pancakes. She had showered and washed her hair and was dressed in her blue jersey dress and silver necklace. Even if David turned up early, it didn't matter. She was ready.

The house phone went and Leah knew it would be Molly. Her first thought was that Jamie had already made his confession, which was impressive given that Jamie was an expert at putting off unpleasant tasks. Her second thought was that she wished Jamie had shown a little more of his weakness for prevaricating since she would now be on the phone for hours.

It was indeed Molly but, fortunately for Leah's dinner plans, she had only rung to inform her mother that she'd cut her knee and Grandma had put a plaster on it and Grandpa had given her a peppermint for being so brave. Fred then came on to tell Leah they were playing croquet in the morning. When he finally asked Leah if she wanted to speak to his father, Leah knew that she *should* speak to him to remind him to tell the children about Charlotte. She also knew it was almost eight o'clock. She said quickly, 'Just give him and Grandma and Grandpa all my love. I miss you very much.' She rang off and felt guilty because at this precise moment she didn't miss Fred at all, she just wanted to get on and make the pancakes.

If she hadn't been feeling so guilty, what happened next would almost certainly not have happened. Preoccupied with her maternal shortcomings, she picked up the bowl of batter. The doorbell rang and, somehow, she tipped the bowl's entire contents down the front of her pretty dress.

Holding up the material to stop the batter dripping all over the floor, Leah went through to the hall, let David into the house, told him to avoid the mess in the kitchen and raced upstairs to change. Never ever, ever again would she tell herself she was a clever girl before a special dinner.

When she flew downstairs, dressed in shirt-dress and leggings, she made straight for the kitchen and said dramatically, 'This is a *disaster*! If you had seen me earlier, I was completely ready, everything was fine, and then I tipped over the pancake batter and now—' She stopped and took in first the floor and then David. 'You've done it! You've cleared up the mess.'

David pulled down the sleeves of his shirt, which he'd rolled up above his elbows. 'I hope you don't mind. I found a cloth and some cleaning stuff under your sink.'

'Of course I don't mind. I'm incredibly grateful. I'm just disappointed that our starter is ruined. Can I offer you a drink? I've some wine in the fridge.'

'I would love a drink,' David said. 'And we do have a starter. I brought you a present.' He nodded at the Tupperware box on the table. 'I'm a cheese-straw expert. For years, they were all I could cook. Why don't you sit down and let me do the wine? Fire instructions at me.'

So Leah fired instructions, and while she did she noticed that her leggings had a hole in the knee. Great, she thought. Clever Leah. She gave a long, self-pitying sigh.

David poured them both wine, opened the lid of the box and cast a shrewd glance at Leah. 'What's wrong?' he asked. 'Everything's all right now.'

'No, it isn't,' Leah said. 'I looked really nice before you came. You look very smart in your trousers and your shirt and I've got a hole in my leggings and I'm pretty sure I've got a bit of batter in my hair.'

David passed her the box. 'Have a cheese straw,' he said.

Leah took one and bit into it. 'It's very good,' she conceded.

'So it should be. I had to throw away the first lot I made.'

'I thought you were a cheese-straw expert.'

'I was. About fifteen years ago.'

'At least,' Leah said gloomily, 'you're wearing the right clothes.'

'At least,' David responded, 'you didn't have to buy new trousers.'

Leah frowned. 'What do you mean?'

'This morning, I realized I had two pairs of trousers, neither of which were good enough to wear to dinner with Leah.'

'You went out and bought some more? Just for tonight?'

'Now you're laughing at me,' David said. 'I wish I hadn't told you.'

Leah grinned. 'Have a cheese straw.'

'I will,' he said, 'in a moment.' He leant forward and kissed her very slowly.

Leah could feel her heart racing and said a little unsteadily, 'David, I am not going to sleep with you tonight.'

'That's fine,' he said. 'I can't do tonight either. Tomorrow is fine, but not tonight.'

She knew he was teasing her but couldn't resist asking, 'Why can't you do tonight?'

'I'm doing a talk on Bristol radio in the morning,' he said. 'There's a new campaign aimed at raising the profile of history in primary schools. I've been asked to get involved. So tonight I must go home early in order to have a clear head in the morning.'

'Well, in that case,' Leah said briskly, hiding a disappointment she had no right to feel, 'we'd better get on and have supper.'

And actually, by the time she'd finished her first glass of wine, she was glad they'd sorted out the sex business so effortlessly. It meant she could enjoy the meal and enjoy David's company. They talked about his books and his TV work and he told her about his mother, who, after two unhappy years, had apparently transformed herself into a very merry widow.

After supper, they had coffee on the sofa in the sitting room and then David said he ought to go if he wanted to prepare for his interview in the morning. Leah suggested they could conduct a fake interview now if he liked and David said that was an excellent idea.

Leah said gravely, 'Good morning, Mr Morrison.'

David sat back and rested his arm along the back of the sofa. 'Good morning, Miz Payne.'

'Tell me, Mr Morrison,' Leah said, 'what made you wish to join this campaign to promote history in schools?'

'It's very simple, Miz Payne. The number of students studying history at A level is dropping every year. I believe it to be one of the most important subjects we can study and yet under our national curriculum it's been edged onto the sidelines.'

'Of course,' Leah said, trying to ignore the fact that David's left hand had found its way inside the top of her shirt-dress, 'the national curriculum is a contentious issue.'

'I like your choice of word, Miz Payne.'

'I'd like you to be a little less patronizing, Mr Morrison.'

'I apologize. I'm a little distracted at the moment and spoke without thinking.'

David's hand conducted an interesting pincer movement and Leah felt a little shaft of pleasure. 'Perhaps,' she said unsteadily, 'you should remove your left hand from its place inside my bra.'

'I'm sorry,' David said. 'It's carrying out an exploratory manoeuvre.'

She felt David's other hand gently prise her knees apart, and said, 'Now what are you doing?'

David sighed. 'My right hand wants to join in.'

'David,' Leah breathed, 'this is not at all . . . sensible.'

'You're right,' David said. 'We should go upstairs.'

'I mean,' Leah said, making one last valiant effort to uphold her earlier resolution, 'I thought you wanted to go home tonight.'

'I lied,' David said.

* * *

Leah tried very hard not to make a sound because she knew how thin the walls were. It was difficult *not* to make a sound. Sex was a little like playing the piano: some people could create a cacophony of discord and others could produce quite heavenly harmonies. David was an expert. David could light up the Albert Hall, let alone Leah's bedroom. For a man who'd never slept with her before, he seemed to know his way round her body remarkably well, and when she finally came, letting out a euphoric expletive, the shame over Christopher and the bitterness over Jamie seemed to melt and disappear in a fire of straightforward, purifying ecstasy. She discovered she was now at the wrong end of the bed and when she found her way back to her pillows and sank against them, David leant over to kiss her and said gently, 'Sleep well, Leah Payne.' And she knew, she absolutely knew that she would.

The next morning, she found herself confessing her recent shameful sexual encounter with Christopher, although she concealed the even more shameful fact that he had turned out to be an old friend's husband. She tried, stumblingly, to explain that she had promised herself she would never again have a one-night stand. When he didn't say anything, she glanced up at him, fearing she would read contempt in his eyes. In fact, he was staring thoughtfully at her and finally asked, 'When do your children come home?'

'Friday,' she said, remembering guiltily that she hadn't thought of them at all since she'd dropped the batter on her dress.

'So we have another five nights,' David said, and Leah forgot them all over again.

* * *

The next few days at work were spent in a fever of impatience and tedium. Leah couldn't wait to get home. They didn't go out in the evenings. They cooked together and watched a bit of television. Neither of them talked about the immediate future. It was as if their time together existed in a parallel universe, a delightful bubble in which nothing was important but the nightly exploration of each other's bodies.

And then, on Friday, the bubble burst. Jamie rang at six to tell Leah they'd be late since he was stopping at a service station to give the children some tea. When they finally arrived, Leah could tell at once that something was very wrong. Usually, when the children came home from a holiday with their grandparents, they were eager to tell their mother every detail of their time in Winchester. Tonight, they came into the house with their rucksacks in their hands and said hardly a word. Meanwhile, Jamie had the rictus smile of a man who was trying very hard to convince those around him that he was not, after all, standing up to his neck in hot water.

Leah said briskly, 'You two, go and get ready for bed. I'll bring you up some hot drinks in a little while. I want to walk your father to his car.'

'Goodbye, you two,' Jamie said with exaggerated heartiness. 'I'll speak to you very soon.'

Leah grabbed her keys and ushered Jamie out of the front door. 'So,' she said, once they were safely outside, 'why do the children look as if they've been force-fed cold Irish stew?'

Jamie raised his jacket collar. 'We had some pizzas. I told them Charlotte was pregnant and they seemed to be all right about it. So I told them she'd be moving in with me quite soon and Molly started crying. She wouldn't stop. The couple on the next table looked at me as if I were Jack the Ripper.' He shook his head. 'I've had a hell of a time.'

'You left it till today? You left it till the journey home?' Leah asked incredulously. 'And why did you have to say that Charlotte was moving in with you? Couldn't you have let them get used to the first bombshell at least before you handed them another?'

Jamie ran his fingers through his hair. 'I told you: they seemed to be fine. And then Molly started doing this big drama-queen number.'

'What did she say?'

'I don't know – she was going on in that hysterical way she has. I told them both that none of this would affect *them* and that—'

'Well, that's a stupid thing to say, for a start. Of course it will affect them. From now on they have to share you with Charlotte and a baby. Of course they're going to be upset. I thought you were going to tell them earlier in the week. We agreed your mother would be able to help.'

'I haven't been there for most of the time. I've got a hell of a lot of work on and I'm under a lot of pressure at the moment and – don't look at me like that, Leah, I did my best and . . . Look, I have to go. I'll ring you later to see how they are. I just want you to know that this is *not* a good time for me!'

Leah watched him get into his car and then she turned on her heel and went back into the house. She could hear the children moving around and stood for a moment at the bottom of the stairs before making their drinks. She took Fred's through first and told him she'd be back in a minute, and then she went on into Molly's room.

Molly was in bed, reading *The Magic Finger*. This was a bad sign. Molly had read the story so often that she knew it by heart and these days only brought it out when she was ill or seriously upset.

Leah sat down on the bed beside her and handed her the mug.

Molly took a sip and put it on her bedside table. 'I don't want to go to Daddy's house next weekend,' she said.

'Well, actually,' Leah said, 'I've been thinking about that and it makes sense for you to be here at home. You have the Guy Fawkes party on Saturday and it's silly to go to your father when the party's only just round the corner from our house.'

'I don't want to go to Daddy's house ever again.'

'You don't mean that.'

'Yes, I do. Charlotte will be there all the time and they'll be doing baby things.'

Leah reached out to stroke her daughter's hair. 'Listen, Molly, the baby's not going to be born for weeks and weeks, and even when the baby does come you'll always be Daddy's lovely Molly. He'd be devastated if you didn't go and stay with him.'

'So why is he having a new baby? He doesn't need one. He has Fred and me.'

'I know, but Charlotte would like a baby of her own and he loves Charlotte and wants her to be happy. He adores you and Fred, and that will never change however many babies they have.'

Molly cast a startled glance at her mother. 'Are they going to have other babies? How many babies are they going to have?'

'I don't know. Perhaps they'll only have one. What's important is that new babies won't stop your father loving you and Fred.'

'I don't like babies,' Molly said.

Leah smiled. 'You were a baby once, you know.'

'Yes, but I didn't know I was. Was I a nice baby?'

'You were a beautiful baby and you had the most gorgeous baby smell. Everyone noticed it. And you were so sweet. Every time I picked you up, you'd press your face into my shoulder. And even before you could talk, you'd make these funny noises and they sounded so clever, as though you were really making sense if only we could understand you. You made us laugh so much!'

'I bet the new baby won't be like that.'

'Of course the new baby won't be like that. No one will ever be like that. You, Molly Payne, are quite unique!'

'What does "unique" mean?'

'It means there is no one else in the world like you. Did you have a lovely holiday with Grandma and Grandpa?'

'Grandpa taught us how to play Fishes and Grandma made us a chocolate-button cake yesterday. I put the buttons on *and* I made the icing.'

'You're a lucky girl. Grandma makes the best cakes in the world. Goodnight, Molly.'

When Leah went into Fred's room, she thought he must be asleep. She whispered, 'Fred?' and could detect a slight movement under the duvet. She went round to the other side of the bed and gently pulled the duvet down a little. 'Oh Fred!' she sighed.

Her son swallowed hard and bit his lip. His eyes were red and his face was puffy. 'I'm not crying,' he said.

'It doesn't matter if you are.' Leah sat down beside him. 'Is this about the new baby?'

Fred nodded.

'It is a bit of a shock, isn't it?'

'I like Charlotte,' Fred said, 'but Dad's home won't be the same now she's going to be there all the time. And when the baby comes he'll need his own room and Molly and I will have to share it with him, and the house will be his home and Dad's home and Charlotte's home but it won't be our home.'

'I think Jamie would be very sad if he knew you thought that.'

'It's true, though.'

'And anyway, you have a pretty nice home already!' She smiled but Fred wouldn't meet her eyes. 'Fred,' she urged, 'come on. Talk to me.'

Fred sat up and reached for the mug on his bedside table. He took a sip of it and said, 'Dad said things never stay the same. You might meet someone soon and you might have a baby and then this won't be our proper home either and . . .' He sniffed and quickly took another sip of milk.

'Listen,' Leah said. 'Let's just suppose I did one day meet someone else. Do you really think I'd simply install him here without consulting you and Molly? This is your home as much as it's mine and it always will be – unless of course we win the lottery and then I think we'll go and live in some swanky house in the Royal Crescent!'

'If we win the lottery,' Fred said, 'can we have a dog?'

'If we win the lottery,' Leah said, 'we'll have three dogs.'

'Actually,' Fred said, 'one will be enough.'

'Oh Fred!' Leah gave him a hug. 'I do love you! Now, you listen to me. *Some* things never stay the same but there are other things that *don't* change. For the rest of our lives, Jamie and I will always, always love you. That's all that matters.' She leant forward and kissed him. 'Now, no more thinking! Drink your milk and go to sleep.'

Leah went downstairs and poured herself a glass of wine. She couldn't remember when she had been so angry with Jamie. It was unbelievably crass to decide to tell Fred and Molly about the baby at the end of a holiday on a Friday night in some roadside cafe. It was unbelievably stupid to get Charlotte pregnant in the first place. Leah shut her eyes for a moment in a useless attempt to delay the next obvious conclusion. This was her fault as much as Jamie's. She should have rung him days ago to make sure he told the children early in the week while their grandmother was on hand to explain the situation in the best possible way. She should have rung him on Monday and if necessary she should have gone on ringing him until he'd done what he was supposed to do. She didn't ring him because when she was at work she was thinking of David and when she was not at work she was *with* David. She didn't ring him and she had let her children down.

She could feel the tears welling up in her eyes and shut them again tightly before angrily rubbing them with her hand. If she thought about this any more she would give herself a migraine and that wouldn't help anyone. She would watch something silly on the television and think about it tomorrow. She would let the answerphone deal with any possible calls from Jamie because if she talked to him this evening she would explode.

There was only one job she had to do first. This was another job she should have tackled days ago. She picked up the phone and rang Alison who had to be prised away from her television and wanted to know why she couldn't talk to Leah in the morning.

'I won't keep you a minute,' Leah promised. 'I need to meet you for lunch very soon.'

'All right,' Alison said. 'Is something wrong?'

'It's Merrily,' Leah said. 'We need to talk about Merrily.'

CHAPTER ELEVEN

Alison Decides to Pull Merrily Out of the Darkness

In an attempt to evade disaster, Alison bought four lottery tickets on Tuesday, which surprisingly failed to land her a million pounds or even ten. She had tried to tell Felix the truth about Phoebe's dress three times in the last twelve days. On the first, he had a headache and she didn't want to make it worse. On the second, he was in such a good mood that she didn't want to spoil it. And on the third, another bright idea from the practice manager made him far too angry to be able to receive further bad news.

This week was squaring up to be one of titanic awfulness. The charming heating engineer rang her on Tuesday morning to tell her that the part required to restore the boiler to its previous efficiency was now discontinued and he was sending her a quote for the cost of fitting a new boiler.

This ominous news failed to dent Felix's good humour when he came back from work. Michael Bracewell, he told Alison, had rung him to suggest that their families take a joint villa in Paxos next year. Alison's initial response was that it would have to be a very big villa to house both families and would – gulp – be pretty expensive. Felix pointed out that for three years now they had spent their summer holidays in his aunt's damp cottage in even damper Devon and they deserved a bit of sun for once. He said that she was quite right to worry about the cost, what with Phoebe's wedding coming up, but he had no worries on that score. 'I know what you're like,' he said. 'You won't spend a penny you don't need to.'

Alison did consider the humiliating possibility of returning the dress to the nice ladies in the shop. That idea died a death after a phone call from Phoebe on Wednesday in which she revealed that whenever she had a bad time at work she had only to think of her wedding dress and she was instantly happy. Rather sweetly, she revealed that, given the expense of the dress, she and Lennie were intent on drastically reducing the guest list. In the light of such self-sacrifice, there was no way Alison could suggest the return of the dress.

She did wonder if she could sell her entire wardrobe on eBay, but it wasn't as if she had hordes of designer outfits, indeed it wasn't as if she had even one designer outfit. In the end she decided she would preface her confession to Felix with a summary of the money-saving schemes she had devised for the wedding and segue into a simple and straightforward justification for the one and only expense. She would tell him tomorrow, she thought. Or possibly on Friday.

By the time she went off to her Pilates lesson on Thursday, she'd decided it would definitely not be this evening. Today was a write-off. She had visited two horrible houses and both of them would require every ounce of creativity that she currently did not have to make them seem even remotely saleable. She had made a casserole for supper that she had disastrously over-salted due to the fact that she was sprinkling salt into it while trying to work out how best to approach Felix. Then Felix had rung to say he had forgotten he had a partners' meeting and would therefore be late. This was bad because he would be too tired to cope with any horrid revelations. On the other hand, it turned out to be good because it meant that he missed the irritating argument she had with Nathan over supper. Nathan wanted her to know that she was the *only* mother who had refused to let her child go to Sam Hardy's party on Saturday. Alison protested that the mother of his friend Jake had now withdrawn her permission too. Nathan then felt it necessary to reveal that Alison was the *only* mother to ring before a party to make sure parents were going to be on hand and that Jake was furious with *him* for having a mother who had seen fit to tell *his* mother that Sam's parents were not going to be around. In fact, Nathan felt compelled to point out that his mother was doing a very good job of ensuring he would soon have no friends at all, and by the way did she know she'd put too much salt in the casserole?

All in all, Alison was quite glad to go to Pilates, except that after Pilates Sally came up to her and asked her what she thought about Paxos. Sally had been too busy for dog walks in the last few weeks – she was organizing a big new exhibition in Bristol – and Alison had had neither the chance nor the inclination to tell her about Phoebe's wedding dress. Now she said brusquely that she and Felix hadn't had a chance to talk about it yet. She then left the village hall quickly without talking to anyone else. As she walked along the lane, she realized that Sally probably thought she was still smarting from the Hadrian's Wall debacle. Well, Alison thought, she didn't care. Now that she came to think about it, the whole wedding dress disaster was Sally's fault anyway. If Sally hadn't dropped out of the Hadrian's Wall holiday, then Jonathon and Jenny Rushton wouldn't have dropped out either and they would all have gone to Hadrian's Wall and she wouldn't have gone shopping with Phoebe and bought the sodding wedding dress.

The house was unusually quiet when she got home. The only member of the family in the kitchen was Magnus, who stretched his limbs before padding over to brush her knees with his body. 'Hello, funny face,' she said, patting his flanks. 'Where is everyone and how are *you*?' She gave him another pat and noticed that today's post was no longer on the table. She heard Felix calling her and went through to the study.

'Hello,' she said. 'It's very quiet here. Are the boys still at the village fireworks do?'

Felix nodded and took off his glasses. 'They'll be back soon. Magnus hasn't barked for at least twenty minutes. How was Pilates?'

'It was quite relaxing tonight despite the bangs from the village green. I nearly fell asleep during one of the exercises. Would you like a cup of tea?'

'Not yet. Sit down for a minute. We need to talk about money.'

Alison sat down on the two-seater sofa, her eye caught

by the small pile of opened envelopes on the desk. 'Has the boiler quote come?'

Felix grimaced. 'The good news is that the new boiler will be eco-friendly. The bad news is that he's given us an estimate of three thousand, five hundred and forty-four pounds and fifty-three pence.'

Alison sat back against the cushions and blew out her cheeks. 'Oh hell!'

'I know. I suppose we have to go for it.'

'I think so. Mr Burns is always reliable. If he says this is what we need to spend, you can be sure he's right. And we need to do it soon. It takes about five hours to run a bath at the moment.'

'Give him a ring tomorrow, then. And while we're talking about money, we need to let the Bracewells know about Paxos. It's probably crazy, given this latest bill, but I think we should go for it. Eva rang while you were out and I described the place to her and she said she'd love to come, and the boys are really keen too. I told Michael I'd give him a ring tomorrow.'

Alison felt her mouth go dry. 'Felix,' she said, 'there's something I have to tell you. It's about Phoebe's dress. It was quite expensive. It was actually very expensive. It was very, very expensive.' She took a deep breath. 'It was two thousand, three hundred and seventy-five pounds.'

Felix didn't say anything. He looked at her as if she were mad.

Alison cleared her throat. 'What you are looking at is the one and only major expense of your daughter's forth-coming wedding. Everything else is going to be incredibly cheap. I know this *isn't*, but that's because it is, quite simply, the most perfect wedding dress you could ever wish for and the lady in the shop gave us a seventy-five-pound discount . . .'

Felix stared at her as if she were a *Doctor Who* monster whose language he was unable to comprehend. 'How much did you say it was?' he asked faintly.

'It was two thousand, three hundred and seventy-five pounds and I know it seems an awful lot but—'

'It doesn't *seem* an awful lot. It *is* an awful lot. I didn't even know a dress *could* cost that much money.'

'I know and I'm terribly sorry. But if you'd seen Phoebe's face when she put it on, you'd understand. She said she'd never felt beautiful before. She was almost crying she was so happy. I've given a lot of thought to this wedding. We don't need to have a marquee. I only have to pay twenty-five pounds to hire the village hall and it's quite big enough, it allows for one hundred and ten people. I can save a fortune on caterers if I do most of the food myself and I don't need a new outfit, my green suit will do perfectly well. So, all in all, it will be a very economical wedding apart from the dress, and Felix, she looks so lovely in it, it will make you cry when you see her.'

'I'm sure it will. I know it will. At the moment I feel like bawling my head off. None of this makes any sense. We knew when we bought this house that we'd have to make sacrifices in other areas. And we have done. *You* have done. You've been brilliant. This is so unlike you.'

'We went to this shop. We'd been to so many. Phoebe tried it on and it was just perfect. I got caught up in the moment and Phoebe was so radiant. Felix, I am really sorry. If it's any consolation, I've been dreading telling you about it.'

'That isn't any consolation at all.'

'I know. I—'

The phone rang and Felix reached across for the handset. 'Hello? . . . Oh hi, Sally . . . Yes, she's just got back . . . No, it's a lovely idea but . . . I know, but we've decided we can't have a holiday next year, not with Phoebe's wedding in the spring . . . No, of course not . . .We'd love to do it some other time . . . Absolutely . . . Right . . . Right . . . Goodbye now.' He put down the phone and swivelled his chair round towards his desk.

'Felix,' Alison said, 'you have every right to be upset.'

'I don't have time to be upset. I need to go through our accounts to see how we're going to pay for a new boiler now that I've apparently spent two thousand, three hundred and seventy-five pounds on a dress.'

'Would you like a cup of tea?'

'I'd prefer a coffee. Can you make it very black and very strong?'

Alison stood up and bit her lip. She returned to the kitchen and filled the kettle. She felt overcome with guilt and remorse. It had been *she* who'd persuaded Felix to buy their beautiful big house with its amazing views over the valley and its vast kitchen. It had been she who'd persuaded him to take on the crippling mortgage, even though she knew he had a tendency to worry about money. He'd only agreed because he trusted her to manage their finances. And now she'd forfeited that trust. She went over to Magnus, knelt down by his basket and buried her face in his fur.

* * *

It was good to drive to Widcombe the next day and think about something other than Felix's shocked expression. When Alison entered the Ring O' Bells, Leah was not there, and knowing that Leah's lunch hour would be exactly that she ordered a savoury platter for the two of them, a jug of water and two glasses of Chablis.

Leah arrived at the same time as the Chablis, looking every inch the businesswoman in grey skirt, pink top and tailored black jacket. 'I shouldn't drink any wine,' she said. 'I have to work this afternoon.'

'And I have to drive,' Alison said. 'It's only one glass and you can drink loads of water if it makes you feel more virtuous.'

Leah took off her jacket and adopted a quizzical expression. 'Am I right in thinking that you are – to use your mother's favourite phrase – a little out of sorts?'

Alison sighed. 'I told Felix last night how much I spent on Phoebe's wedding dress. He wasn't very happy.'

Leah draped her jacket over the back of her chair and sat down. 'How much was it?'

Alison winced. 'Two thousand, three hundred and seventy-five pounds.'

'I happen to know,' said Leah, 'that Paula Jackson spent five thousand pounds on *her* daughter's wedding dress.'

'Really?' Alison breathed.

'So tell Felix he should count himself lucky. Cheers!'

'Cheers!' Alison said. She squared her shoulders. 'Now let's get down to business. Tell me about Merrily.'

'I went to see her the other week.'

'What do you think of the house? Isn't it terrible?'

'It is hideous. You could spend a fortune on it and it would still be hideous.'

'I don't know,' said Alison. 'If you gave me a hundred grand I could make it look quite reasonable.'

'In the meantime, Merrily has to live there. When I saw her, she'd been crying. She obviously hated putting Tom on the train back to London. Then Christopher rang this bell and Merrily almost ran upstairs to see what he wanted. When she came down, she said Christopher wanted me to take him a cup of tea. So I took one up and entered his study, and it's beautiful and there's a fire in the grate—'

'And we all know who would have lit it,' Alison interjected.

Leah gave an angry shake of her head. 'The more I think of it, the more Merrily seems like Cinderella trapped in a house with her Ugly Husband. Anyway, I go to his desk and suddenly I feel this hand stroking my bottom. I ask him to remove it and I ask him to tell me what sort of a woman he thinks I am . . . and do you know what he says?'

'No,' said Alison. 'What did he say?'

'He says he knows very well what sort of a woman I am and then he just smiles. What do you think of *that*?'

Alison was tempted to point out that Christopher's comment was not altogether surprising, given Leah's reckless behaviour the first time she met him. However, Leah had just given her some very welcome news about Paula Jackson's daughter and she had little hesitation in responding with, 'That's appalling!'

'I know it's appalling, but it's also deeply significant. It is conclusive proof that Christopher didn't go to bed with me because of some unknown, deeply sensitive trauma. He went to bed with me because he likes going to bed with other women and he made it quite clear he'd be ready to go to bed with me again.'

'The man's an ogre,' Alison said. 'But I don't see what we can do. We can't tell Merrily he sleeps around because Merrily would want to know how we know and I'd love to see you explain that one. And besides, she adores him.'

'That's no reason not to do anything. Jennifer Aniston loved Brad Pitt, Eva Braun loved Hitler, Mrs Stalin probably loved Mr Stalin.'

'I think Mrs Stalin killed herself. I don't see the point of your argument.'

'What I'm saying is that love can sometimes hide a multitude of sins. Sometimes,' Leah warmed to her theme, 'love can be a well-disguised trapdoor. What we need to do is pull Merrily out of the darkness and show her the light.'

'That's very poetic,' Alison said, 'but supposing Merrily wants to stay in the darkness?'

Leah was prevented from replying by the arrival of the waitress with a large plate of cold meats, mozzarella, tomatoes and artichokes. As soon as the waitress had gone, Leah said gravely, 'Merrily has always been vulnerable. She's never been any good at standing up for herself. You only have to look at her to see that Christopher has been a terrible influence on her. She's too thin, her hair is a mess, she wears no make-up, her clothes look like they've come from the tip and even if they have to live on a tight budget . . .'

'I don't think they do,' Alison said, pausing only to swallow a piece of salami. 'If there's one thing I know about, it's interior design and those lights and that sofa in his study are *not* cheap. Merrily could have had a new kitchen for the price of that sofa.'

'And night after night,' Leah said, 'Merrily rattles

around that great dank house while Christopher sits cosily by the fire in his study.'

'So we agree that Merrily needs our help,' Alison said. 'The question is: what can we do?'

Leah stared thoughtfully into her wine. 'We could break up her marriage.'

Alison frowned and then slowly nodded her head. 'Of course! That's it! That's what we have to do.'

'Alison,' Leah said. 'I was joking.'

'I'm not. We're her best friends. Who's going to save her if we don't? We could spend months trying to make her feel better about herself but in the end, if she stays with him, he'll always drag her down.'

Even as Alison spoke, she was aware of the enormity of her suggestion. She truly believed that Merrily could find no self-respect until and unless she left Christopher. She also knew that, despite that belief, a part of her would be relieved if Leah decided to draw back from the brink.

Leah had a gulp of wine and then pushed her hair back. 'All right,' she said. 'Let's do it.'

CHAPTER TWELVE

Leah's Visitor Leaves Her With Much to Think About

On Saturday, Leah took the children to their fireworks party at half past five. They had been told to dress up as scary people. Fred looked like an incredibly cool zombie and Molly made a slightly less convincing vampire since she insisted on wearing her hair in a ponytail. Once home, Leah cast a critical eye over the kitchen and decided it would do. In the sitting room, she puffed up the cushions and moved Fred's homework from the old tea chest that doubled up as a coffee table. She glanced at her watch and went upstairs. She changed into her black trousers and her silk blouse and reapplied her make-up. She surveyed her reflection in her bedroom mirror and undid the top three buttons of her blouse. She spent a few minutes doing up her top three buttons and then undoing her top three buttons before finally deciding to leave only the top two undone. She sprayed herself liberally – too liberally? – with perfume and went downstairs. In the sitting room, she turned on the fire and the standard lamp. She went through to the kitchen and decided it might be a good idea to open the bottle of white burgundy and see if it was all right. It was definitely all right. She sighed and looked at her watch. She had told David to come at quarter past six. She had warned him she had to join the children's party at seven. She hoped he'd come soon because the way things were going she wouldn't be seeing too much of him in the future.

The doorbell answered her wish. Taking a deep breath, she went through to the hall and opened the door. 'David,' she said, 'you're late.'

He wore his new trousers and a grey polo-neck shirt and looked far too gorgeous to be the author of a book on Queen Victoria – not that Leah had ever met any other authors of books on Queen Victoria. He followed her through to the kitchen and deposited a bottle of wine on the table. 'I'm sorry,' he said. 'I only got back from Newcastle an hour ago.'

'I forgot you weren't coming back till today.' She poured him out a glass of wine and picked up her own. 'How was the book tour?'

'I'm glad to be home. I love teaching students and the TV is fun but I really hate selling myself. The trouble with being a writer is that you spend hours in a room with only a computer for company. You're not really equipped to persuade strangers that they need to buy your book. At one talk I gave, this woman stood up and asked me why I thought we needed yet another book about Queen Victoria and I started rambling on about a fresh pair of eyes and new research and all the time I was thinking, "She's right, why *do* we need another book about Queen Victoria?" Do you ever get that feeling when you're talking away to someone and another voice inside you is providing a running commentary about how boring you are?'

'All the time,' Leah assured him. She felt bad that she'd been short with him. She raised her glass to him and said, 'Here's to the success of *The Crimes of Queen Victoria*.'

'Thank you,' David said. 'I did get some great news this morning.'

'Let's go through to the sitting room,' Leah said, 'and you can tell me all about it.'

He sat on the sofa and looked appreciatively round the room, his eyes finally settling on the glass decanter on the mantelpiece. 'That's beautiful,' he said. 'I haven't noticed it before. It looks seriously old.'

'It *is* seriously old. I fell in love with it the moment I saw it. It belonged to my mother-in-law and she gave it to me for a birthday present. It belonged to her grandfather. I tried to give it back to her when Jamie and I got divorced but she wouldn't hear of it. I'd never dare use it but I love the idea that previous generations sat at table passing it round.'

David grinned. 'I like the fact that right next to it you have such a very modern piece of pottery.'

'I think it's pretty good,' Leah said. 'Fred made it at school. It's supposed to be a vase but it wobbles if you put anything in it so, like the decanter, it's just there for decoration.' She looked at him expectantly. 'Go on, then: tell me your good news.'

'My agent has found an American publisher for my book.'

'Well done! Does that mean you have to go round the States giving lecture tours?'

'I wish,' David said, 'but I very much doubt that will happen. Tell me about *you*. You sounded rather distracted when I rang you on Monday.'

'I know,' Leah said. 'I meant to ring you back but this week has been pretty dire. I had to placate a client whose plumbing has gone on the blink, I tried to persuade my bookkeeper not to retire just yet and I've been worrying about a very nice friend who's married to a complete tosser.'

'Why is he a tosser?'

'He thinks he's God's gift to the world, especially to women. He's very unpleasant to my friend. He's a writer, like you, and whenever he gets the Muse he says—'

'Whenever he gets the what?'

'The Muse. He says whenever the Muse approaches him he has to drop everything and write. It's all rather too convenient, if you ask me. Do you have to wait for the Muse to come along before you write?'

'If I did, I'd never write a word. What sort of stuff does he write?'

'He writes books with boring titles. I haven't actually read any of them. I looked him up on Google the other night. Apparently, he's an expert on the human psyche.'

'I've never been quite sure,' David said, 'what the human psyche actually *is*.'

'I'm sure my friend's husband would tell you. He's happy to talk about his books for hours. Personally, I'd rather read *The Crimes of Queen Victoria*. Do you know that you are the first historian I have ever met?'

'You make me sound like an endangered species.'

'If that's the case, I will treat you with great care and attention.'

'That sounds promising. I've been thinking about this American deal. I really feel it deserves a celebration – perhaps dinner next weekend.'

'That would be nice,' Leah said wistfully. 'I'd love to do that.' She had a gulp of her wine. 'The trouble is that the timing is lousy. This is why I wanted to see you. I didn't want to tell you over the phone. I'm afraid I've got some rather bad news. My ex-husband's girlfriend is pregnant and the children are all over the place. Molly flatly refuses to go and stay with him and the girlfriend, and even Fred is making excuses. They're terrified that everything's about to change all over again. The one thing I can't do at the moment is go out on the town with some new man. For the moment at least, they're not ready to—'

'To see their mother start dating again?'

'That's it,' Leah said. 'Obviously, I have to put the children first. I have no idea how long they're going to refuse to stay with Jamie. And the worst thing I can do is tell them I've met someone new. Which means that for the time being I can't see you. Everything's such a mess . . .'

Her voice died away. David wasn't looking at her. He was staring over her shoulder as if he was watching someone else. What froze her blood was the expression in his eyes. The customary sparkle had gone. There was no warmth, no affection, no anything. She said quickly, 'Of course, you must feel free to bail out. The immediate future doesn't look much fun, I'm afraid.'

'No,' David said. He frowned and put his left hand to his forehead. 'Leah, I'm sorry but I'm going to have to go. I've got this headache and I think I just need to go home and lie down.'

Leah put her glass down on the tea chest. 'Of course. You must let me drive you back.'

'That won't be necessary. I knew I was late so I drove down. My car's outside.' He stood up and gave her his glass. He'd barely touched his wine. 'Thank you for the drink.'

She saw him to the hall and opened the door. 'Are you sure you're all right to drive?'

'Yes. Thank you. I'll see you soon.'

She knew she wouldn't. She'd seen it in his eyes. Oh, he liked her, but not enough to cope with an indefinite period of abstinence and the constant company of two unhappy children. She couldn't blame him. A man would have to be a saint to say he'd want to hang around.

It was, she supposed, shutting the door behind him, all rather predictable. It had happened to her before and it was more than likely that it would happen again. If Alison were here, she would tell Leah she had brought it on herself by indulging the children, which was why she wouldn't be ringing Alison any time soon with a detailed account of what had just happened.

The trouble was that, somewhere along the line, Leah had thrown away the rule book where David was concerned. Somehow, she had allowed herself to believe that David could be trusted, David was special. Somehow, in an absurdly short period of time, she had allowed herself to fall in love with him. She had even thought he might be in love with her. She swallowed. If there was one thing she knew about men, it was that she didn't know anything about men. Whatever he had or had not felt, one thing was crystal clear: he definitely wasn't interested in her now.

* * *

She had a phone call from Jamie on Tuesday evening. He began by saying that he thought she should keep the children with her at the weekend as Charlotte was moving in on Saturday and things might be a little chaotic. Leah said that was just as well since neither Molly nor Fred wanted to go round there anyway. Jamie then launched into a long justification of his actions, which he somehow concluded by suggesting that Leah was responsible for their unexpectedly negative reaction to his news. Leah said she couldn't quite understand how she could be held responsible for the fact that he knew nothing about diplomacy, kindness, sensitivity and sheer common sense, let alone birth control. She ended by saying that perhaps for the time being the children should not be pushed into visiting their father, and by the way she hoped he had started buying nappies and baby wipes.

She was quite pleased by that final salvo. She put down the phone and picked up her post. There was an official A4 brown envelope but the address was in Alison's not very official handwriting. She pulled out two sheets of paper and sat down with them at the kitchen table. No one, she thought, could accuse Alison of letting the grass grow beneath her feet. She began to read.

CAMPAIGN FOR LIBERATION OF MERRILY

AIM: To liberate Merrily from Christopher.

SUGGESTED STRATEGIES:
1: Boost Merrily's confidence.
2: Destroy Merrily's confidence in Christopher.

POSSIBLE FURTHER STRATEGIES:
3: Play on Merrily's guilt about leaving her son in London – tricky as could be counterproductive, see Strategy One.
4: Leah to seduce Christopher again – tricky as Leah might be unwilling and could lead to problems between Leah and Merrily.

METHODOLOGY FOR STRATEGY ONE:
1: Improve Merrily's appearance. We need to change her haircut, her clothes, suggest make-up and improved deportment since she has a tendency to hunch her shoulders.

Tact and subtlety will be necessary.

Can Leah suggest joint haircut and joint shopping trip?
2: Expand Merrily's social circle. We need to introduce her to interesting women with independent minds who have relationships of healthy equality with their husbands.

We could also suggest areas of employment with the aim of getting Merrily out of her house.

Alison could introduce Merrily to suitable friends.

Alison can research employment opportunities.

METHODOLOGY FOR STRATEGY TWO:
1: Throw doubt over Christopher's brilliance as a writer. In order to do this, we need to read some of Christopher's books. If they ARE brilliant we can still find something negative about them. Even Shakespeare had his off days.
2: Throw doubt on Christopher's qualities as a husband. Not difficult.

Alison will research lives of other writers. While writers may be odd, some of them at least must lead normal lives.

Merrily needs to see that Christopher's fanatical adherence to his Muse is self-indulgent and silly.

Alison and Leah need to indicate with TACT and SUBTLETY that they think Christopher is a selfish pig.

Leah needs to let Merrily know that despite her single status she is able to lead a fulfilled and happy life. Perhaps Leah could introduce Merrily to some of her more sensible single friends.

POSSIBLE METHODOLOGY FOR POSSIBLE STRATEGY THREE:
Alison could explain to Merrily that teenagers needed a mother's guidance and that, without such guidance, Tom could fall into drugs, drink, depravity etc., etc.

Alison is not sure about this strategy since it could make Merrily depressed, but feels she could do it in such a way as to avoid this outcome.

POSSIBLE METHODOLOGY FOR POSSIBLE STRATEGY FOUR:
Leah could seduce Christopher again but only if she is happy to do this. Christopher might come to behave with undue recklessness, thus alienating Merrily.

Alison is not sure if this would work as she does not think Christopher would want to leave Merrily for Leah.

Alison and Leah could engineer some alternative marital crisis leading to unacceptable behaviour by Christopher and consequent end of marriage.

CONCLUSION:
Alison welcomes Leah's suggestions.

Leah spent the next few minutes inserting red exclamation marks in sundry parts of the margin. Then she picked up the phone and rang Alison. She got Felix, who sounded pleased to hear her. Leah, however, was in no mood for niceties. 'Can you get Alison?' she asked. 'I need to talk to her about her campaign statement.'

'She's right here,' said Felix.

Leah heard a short interchange between husband and wife and then Alison came to the phone and said, 'Hello, Leah, how nice to hear you,' followed by a much softer, 'I haven't *told* Felix about the campaign.'

'Why not?' Leah asked.

'He wouldn't approve of it. So tell me: have you read CLOM?'

'What is clom?'

'CLOM,' said Alison, 'is the Campaign for the Liberation of Merrily.'

'Yes, I have,' said Leah, 'and there are a few points I'd like to raise.'

'Hang on, I'm just finding my folder . . . Here it is. Fire ahead.'

'For a start,' Leah said, 'you suggest I seduce Christopher *again*. I didn't seduce him in the first place and I'd like you to strike that from the record.'

'You and I are the only ones who are going to read this.'

'I don't care, it's not true, so delete it, and while you're at it you can delete the whole suggestion because I would rather eat porridge for a year than seduce Christopher.'

'Actually,' Alison said, 'porridge is very good for you.'

'Well, Christopher *isn't*. Moving on to the introducing friends bit, how come you're the only one who knows women with interesting minds? I know lots of women with interesting minds.'

'Good,' said Alison, 'you can introduce them to Merrily.'

'And I also take objection to the word "despite". You say that *despite* my single status I can still lead a happy life. You imply that single women can't lead happy lives, which is not only patronizing but also completely untrue.'

'You're right,' Alison said. 'I take that back. I'm sure you lead a very happy life.'

'Well, actually,' Leah admitted, 'I don't. I'm certainly not able to rhapsodize about the joys of single motherhood at the moment.'

'Why? What's happened?'

'Jamie was completely inept when it came to telling the children about the new baby. I don't know what he said but they're both terrified I'm going to meet someone and start having my own new baby. Bang goes my social life for the foreseeable future.'

There was a meaningful pause from Alison. 'Leah,' she said, 'I know I've said this before and perhaps now is not the time to say it again, but on the other hand perhaps it *is* a good time to let the children know you are entitled to a social life of your own. There are some good men out there if you give them half a chance. What's happened about that nice man you were dating?'

'It's over before it began. He's made it very clear he doesn't want to get involved in my domestic misfortunes. I'd rather not talk about it.'

'Oh Leah!'

'Oh Alison! I'm fine. I'll have a think about the haircut idea. I'll speak to you soon.'

Leah put the phone down. She wished Alison hadn't brought up the subject of David. She had been trying so hard not to think about him. It was quite simple: he didn't want to see her. 'Well, David Morrison,' she said defiantly, 'it's *your* loss.'

CHAPTER THIRTEEN

Alison Activates CLOM

There were times when Alison wished Felix was the sort of man who ranted and raved, lost his temper and said terrible things about which he would then feel huge pangs of remorse. Unfortunately, Felix didn't do anger. He hadn't even mentioned Phoebe's wedding dress in the last few days. She almost wanted him to. Instead, he was quiet and preoccupied and took Magnus for longer walks than usual. Her three younger children showed no such restraint. Alison felt duty bound to explain to them that Greece had been sacrificed for the sake of Phoebe's wedding dress.

She rang Eva, who was speechless for at least half a second before expressing her views on the questionable morality of spending so much money on an item of clothing when said money could have fed an entire village in Zimbabwe for a year. She then said she hoped her mother realized that it would only be fair if she spent the same amount on her when *she* got married, which Alison couldn't help feeling rather went against the earlier morality diatribe.

Nathan and Harry couldn't believe anyone could think one dress was worth an entire holiday and Nathan also wanted to know why there was enough money to spend thousands of pounds on a stupid dress but not enough to buy him a computer he could have in his own bedroom, which would probably make all the difference between him getting brilliant exam results and terrible exam results. Alison could think of no good answer to this and it got to the point where she hated walking past Phoebe's room and seeing the pink box sticking out from under the bed.

And then on Tuesday, after an unsettling phone call from Leah, who sounded unusually dejected, she had another phone call that continued to trouble her throughout the next day and into the evening.

Phoebe rang to say she would not be coming home for Christmas. A friend of Lennie was getting married in Thailand and Lennie and Phoebe were going to the wedding. Alison assured her daughter she quite understood. Alison did not understand. Phoebe had never even *met* Lennie's friend in Thailand. This was to be the last Christmas ever when the family would have Phoebe to themselves and there was no reason why it was necessary for Phoebe to accompany Lennie. Alison said none of this to Phoebe. It was obvious to her that Phoebe was trying very hard to convince herself that she was excited about spending Christmas abroad. It would be unfair to undermine these efforts. It would also run the risk of alienating her future son-in-law. Alison suspected that there would be many future occasions when she would be tempted to run the risk of alienating Lennie.

But it was not easy to be silent. Tact had never been a quality that came naturally to Alison and Phoebe's news was particularly hard to swallow. Of all the children, it was Phoebe who loved Christmas the most. It was Phoebe who woke her siblings so they could open their stockings all together on the parental bed. It was Phoebe who sorted the presents into heaps on the sitting-room floor and it was Phoebe who organized the washing-up after Christmas lunch. Christmas without Phoebe would be like roast beef without Yorkshire pudding and Christmas without Phoebe was evidence of the fact that Alison's life was undergoing a metamorphosis. She was, she felt, standing in the doorway of a new era, one which, despite her best efforts, offered nothing but gloom and decay.

She sighed and finished smoothing the potato over her shepherd's pie. The phone rang and Alison was relieved to find it was her mother, who was exactly the right person to talk to when she was floundering in a mire of existential angst. Alison spent the next few minutes unburdening her soul, telling her about the wedding dress and Phoebe's plans for Christmas.

'Well, to begin with,' Alison's mother said, 'I adore Felix but he does have an irrational streak where his finances are concerned. He was convinced you'd all be bankrupt within a year of moving to Tucking Friary and yet you're still there. You just have to give him time to see that he can actually afford to give his daughter a beautiful wedding dress. And as for Christmas without Phoebe, it will be different, certainly, but it means you'll have more time to concentrate on the other three. With Eva in Manchester this term, that can't be a bad outcome.'

'I suppose so,' Alison said. 'I wish you and Dad could come to us this year.'

'We came to you last Christmas. It's your brother's turn. He's already asked me if I'd cook the Christmas meal.'

'I bet he has,' Alison said. She was fond of her sister-in-law but cooking was definitely not one of her attributes.

'You'll be fine,' her mother assured her. 'I remember the first time we had Christmas without your brother. I was dreading it. And yet we had a lovely time. I remember Leah came round in the evening and we all played charades. How *is* Leah?'

'Don't get me started,' Alison said. 'Jamie's girlfriend is pregnant. Fred and Molly are distraught. Leah's given up on a new romance in order to concentrate on them. She's not very good at the moment.'

'It must be difficult for her. I blame Sylvia.'

'Mum, you can't blame Leah's mother every time something goes wrong in Leah's life.'

'I certainly can,' Alison's mother said. 'Sylvia's never been there for her.'

Magnus padded over to greet Felix as he came through the door and Alison nodded a greeting at him before returning to her phone call. 'There comes a time,' she said, 'when Leah has to take responsibility for her own actions. Mum, I've got to go, Felix has come back. I'll talk to you soon.' She put down the phone and gave Felix an ingratiating smile. 'How are *you*?'

Felix took off his mac. 'What were you saying about Leah?' he asked.

Alison sighed. 'I was talking to Mum about her. Jamie's done it again. He made a complete mess of telling the kids about the baby and it's Leah who pays the price. Because of him, she's got it into her head that she has to go on living like a nun for the rest of her life.'

'I wouldn't say,' Felix said mildly, 'that Leah lives a particularly nun-like life.'

'You know what I mean. She adored Jamie and he let her down. She's indulged Molly's possessiveness because she's afraid of falling in love and being hurt again. And now, just as she was beginning to test the water, Jamie goes and delivers another right hook. I feel so angry.'

'I know,' Felix nodded sympathetically. 'I feel angry too.' He glanced hopefully at his wife. 'I also feel hungry.'

The main subject over supper was the forthcoming production of a new little Jamie baby. Harry recalled with a smirk that Jamie had once given him a man-to-man piece of advice, warning him never to have children since they always ruined things. Felix muttered something about Schadenfreude and said it was pretty funny that Jamie of all people would be shortly plunging back into the world of smelly nappies and broken nights. Alison said there was nothing funny about it and added for Harry's benefit that it only went to show that irresponsible sex always led to trouble. The effect of this sombre pronouncement was rather spoilt by Nathan who added 'Amen' in a sepulchral voice. For some reason Harry found this very funny and started laughing and then Nathan did too, and he intoned 'Amen' again, which made Harry laugh even more. Alison was pleased to see that fraternal harmony had been restored although it was annoying to realize it had been achieved at her expense. Nathan asked his father what he thought of irresponsible sex and Felix responded with a hasty, 'Oh I'm against it,' which didn't fool Alison for a moment. She decided she had had quite enough of all three of them and announced that she would be happy to do the washing-up on her own tonight. Felix went off to fall asleep in front of the news while the boys decided to refresh their brains with a horrible game called Doom, which Alison's gentle sister-in-law had inexplicably given them many Christmases ago.

Alison set about loading the dishwasher while wondering if she should give Leah a call. She hated having conversations that raised interesting questions without providing interesting answers. She would very much like to know more about why the promising new man had turned out not to be promising. The trouble was that, for nearly a year now, Leah and Alison had had an unspoken rule that they would avoid the subject of Leah and Men. This was because nearly a year ago Alison had expressed herself perhaps a little too forcefully after Leah had allowed Molly to derail yet another potential new relationship. Alison had assured Leah that her sentiments had nothing to do with the fact that *she* had introduced the poor man to her, even though, as she'd felt compelled to point out, this was the third man she had introduced to Leah and she was beginning to feel like some handmaiden, preparing men for human sacrifice on the altar of the great goddess Molly. Alison had also felt it was important to point out that Leah wasn't doing Molly any favours by letting her dictate the conditions of her mother's social life. The resulting argument had been eventually resolved by a mutual agreement to disagree. Alison had forsworn introducing any more men to Leah and she was sadly aware that Leah would probably refrain from discussing affairs of the heart with her for some time to come. Given that Leah had recently slept with Merrily's husband without even knowing that he *was* Merrily's husband, it was not unlikely that Leah was performing her own version of irresponsible sex, which was all very sad.

Alison closed the dishwasher and decided that there was no point in worrying about Leah while Leah was so unwilling to heed her good advice. Besides, she had a campaign to run and she might as well start it right away.

She dropped in on her target the very next morning. Merrily welcomed her in but was obviously busy, being dressed in paint-splattered overalls.

'I was just passing,' Alison said. 'I'll only stay for a moment.'

'I'm painting Tom's room,' Merrily said, 'but I'd welcome the break.'

The opportunity was too good to miss. 'How *is* your son?' Alison asked. 'I'm so looking forward to meeting him.'

'He's very well,' Merrily said. 'Come on through.'

There was a small painting in the hall that Alison had failed to notice last time. It depicted the top half of a woman in a high-necked purple dress. She had her hair parted in the middle and looked like she had indigestion. Alison wondered if it was Aunt Florence.

The kitchen was as hideous as ever. Alison sat down on one of the chairs and asked brightly, 'How old is Tom? I know you did tell me.'

'He's thirteen,' Merrily said.

'It's funny about children,' Alison said. 'When they're babies they're utterly dependent on you and then when they get older, you assume they need you less but it's really not true. I've been having a worrying time with Nathan lately.'

Merrily was washing her hands in the sink but she turned to give Alison an anxious glance. 'He's your youngest, isn't he?'

'Yes. He's a lovely boy. He's never given me any trouble. He has a wonderful temperament; he always sees the funny side of things. He's a brilliant mimic. But a few weeks ago I had a call from his teacher, who told me Nathan's been involved in fights with other boys. I've always been able to talk to my children and I can tell you that in the last few weeks Nathan and I have done a lot of talking. It turns out that Nathan is worried about his height. He's a little shorter than his friends at the moment and every time he gets taunted he feels he has to lash out.'

'Poor Nathan,' Merrily said. 'I'm glad I'm not that age any more. I know I had a whole army of neuroses.'

Alison was not at all convinced that Merrily did not still have her army marching behind her but she nodded in agreement and said, 'I think now that we've talked things through, he feels a little better. I always feel sorry for teenagers at boarding school. They're far from their parents and sometimes,' she cast a sideways look at her friend, 'they do need desperately to speak to them.'

Merrily was staring at the ceiling in that way she had when she was thinking deeply. Perhaps, Alison thought, there was no need to say any more.

'Have you thought about a guitar?' Merrily asked.

Alison blinked. 'I beg your pardon?'

'It could be ideal for Nathan. I bought one for Tom a couple of years ago and I've never regretted it. Last year, he played "Wake Up Little Susie" in the school Christmas concert and he got the best applause of the evening. He and his friends have even formed a band now. What can be more glamorous than a boy who plays a guitar? And sometimes, if Tom's worried about something, he'll go to his room and play his guitar for an hour or so and it calms him down. You should get Nathan a guitar.'

'Do you think so?' Alison frowned. 'He can play the piano. He got up to grade four. Would he need to have guitar lessons?'

'Tom learnt from a book. You can sound really good if you know a few chords.'

'Well,' Alison said, 'it's a thought. I'll go and have a look at the shop in Argyll Street.'

'You should do that,' Merrily said. 'Now let's have that tea.'

When Alison drove home, she couldn't help feeling that her first step in the campaign had been unsuccessful. She had not convinced Merrily of the need to put Tom before Christopher. In fact, she had probably made her feel quite complacent about Tom since she now knew he was not a burgeoning psychopath like Nathan.

As she turned into Parsley Lane, she wondered if she had not after all been hard on herself. She might not have succeeded with Strategy Three but by enabling Merrily to give her advice about Nathan, she had boosted her self-esteem, thus going some way to achieving Strategy One. And actually, Merrily's advice had been rather good. A guitar might be just the thing for Nathan.

CHAPTER FOURTEEN

Leah Makes a Flurry of Phone Calls

Diana had popped out of the office for a few minutes and returned with a package and a shy smile on her face. 'Do you have time for me to show you something?'

'I do,' Leah said. 'I had a phone call while you were out. One of our clients wants to keep a donkey in his flat. He assured me it was a very well-trained donkey. Sometimes this job makes me think the whole world is mad. So I certainly have time for you because at the moment you offer the only proof that there is some sanity somewhere.'

'You wouldn't say that if you'd seen me at the weekend,' Diana said. 'We had a bird fly into our kitchen and I was screaming hysterically. Did you ever see that film about birds taking over the world? It gave me a lifelong phobia.' She took a framed photo out of its thick padded envelope and held it up. 'What do you think?'

Leah had always thought of Diana Masters as an attractive woman. She'd met Diana's husband, Simon, a couple of times and found him to be a cheerful, balding man with twinkly eyes and a big chin. In the photograph, the two of them looked fantastic. Diana's shoulder-length hair was swept back from her shoulders, revealing an elegant neck that was only enhanced by the silver lace top she wore. Simon was dressed in a pinstripe suit and looked almost suave.

'Wow,' Leah said. 'You both look so glamorous!'

'We had it taken for our silver wedding anniversary. I had my hair done and we spent ages deciding what to wear. We've missed Emma so much since she went to university. We've felt really flat and old and this has been very good for us. It's made us feel *less* flat and old.'

'If I look this good in ten years' time,' Leah said, 'I shall be a happy woman.'

'It's amazing what a good photo can do,' Diana said. She caught Leah's eye and said uncertainly, 'Why are you looking at me like that? What did I say?'

'Diana,' Leah said solemnly, 'you have just given me the most brilliant idea and I love you.'

Leah had been uncomfortably aware that her contribution to the Merrily campaign had been thus far non-existent. Alison had drawn up the battle plan and had visited Merrily only yesterday. She had started the self-esteem project, she told Leah, by asking Merrily for advice about some minor problem with Nathan. This was particularly impressive since Alison was much better at giving advice than taking it; it must have been hard for her.

The trouble was that Leah had been unable to find any way of suggesting haircuts and new clothes to Merrily without sounding at best patronizing, and at worst insulting. Now Diana had shown her the way.

In the evening, she made a flurry of phone calls. The first was to Jamie, who sounded understandably wary.

'Hello,' he said. 'What have I done wrong now?'

'Nothing,' Leah said. 'I want your help. Do you remember me telling you about my old friend Merrily?'

'Of course I do. Molly told me she's living in Bath now.'

'She is and she has a brute of a husband who delights in making her feel as ugly as sin. And so, of course, I immediately thought of you.'

'Leah,' Jamie sounded hurt. 'I was *never* a brute.'

'No, you don't understand. You are an expert when it comes to making a woman feel good and you're the master when it comes to making a woman look good. So I thought if I could tell Merrily I'd like a photo of her and me and Alison, you could do it and . . . I know you're busy tomorrow. What are you doing next Saturday?'

Jamie sighed. 'We're going to Charlotte's parents. It's her mother's birthday.'

'Perhaps we can do it some other time. I thought I could bring Molly and Fred along. If we can get them to help you with the photo it might smooth relations between you.'

'I'll do it,' Jamie said. 'Next Saturday will be fine. I don't mind missing Charlotte's mother's birthday if it will help the kids.'

'That's very kind of you,' Leah said, although she knew Jamie too well to believe he actually wanted to go to Charlotte's mother's birthday celebrations. 'And remember, your job is to make Merrily feel and look fantastic. I know you'll be wonderful.'

'Well,' said Jamie modestly, 'I'll do my best.'

It was amazing, Leah thought, what a little flattery could do.

Next on the agenda was Merrily. 'Hi,' Leah said. 'I want you to do me a very big favour.' She proceeded to tell Merrily about the entire Jamie/children/baby disaster and finished by saying, 'I can't get the children to go and stay with their father and then I came up with this brilliant idea. I'm telling them I want to have a photo of you and me and Alison. Jamie says he can do it next Saturday afternoon. It's a perfect excuse to take the kids over and get them talking to him again.'

'I'm happy to do it if it will help,' Merrily said. 'Mind you, I hate having my photo taken. I always look like a horse.'

'That's rubbish. The thing is that in order to show Fred and Molly this is not just a ruse to take them over to Jamie, we need to do the thing properly. I'm going to ring Stacey in a minute. She babysits for me and she's the best hairdresser I know. If you come over next Saturday, say at ten, she'll be able to make us both look beautiful—'

'Leah,' Merrily protested, 'I do not do beautiful.'

'You will do next week. What are you doing tomorrow?'

'I'm still painting Tom's room. It seems to be taking forever.'

'Can you take time off? Why don't you come out with me and the kids? I'll take you to our favourite charity shop and we'll see if we can find some clothes for the shoot. Will Christopher mind if I borrow you?'

'Oh no,' Merrily said. 'He'll be working all day.'

'Does he *never* stop writing?'

'Not when he's nearing the end of a book. Once he finishes it, he takes time off for book tours and lectures.'

'Well, I'm glad he's busy at the moment because I need your help here. I'll see you in the morning.'

Next on the agenda was Alison, who was impressed with Leah's plan but less pleased about giving up the following Saturday since it would mean missing the Tucking Friary Autumn Fayre.

'I'm sorry,' Leah said, 'but it was you who started all this and if we're going to do it properly, we have to make sacrifices.'

'Tell me, Leah,' Alison said, 'what sacrifices have *you* made so far?'

'I had to be nice to Jamie,' Leah said.

Fortunately, both Fred and Molly had inherited their mother's love of charity shops and were quite happy to look through the books and toys while Leah and Merrily rifled through the clothes. Leah found a pale green jersey dress and persuaded Merrily to try it on.

Merrily came halfway out of the changing room and said doubtfully, 'It's quite clingy.'

'With a figure like yours,' Leah said confidently, 'clingy is good.'

'You don't think it's a little too feminine for me?'

'You *are* feminine. Stand tall, put your shoulders back and tell me you do not look fabulous.'

'It does feel comfortable,' Merrily conceded. 'Do you really like it?'

'I really do. You're not used to wearing things like this, that's all. It will be perfect for the photo.' She held up a blue sleeveless linen shift dress and a short turquoise cardigan. 'What do you think of these?'

'I think they'd look lovely on you.'

'They'd be better on you. Try them on!'

Merrily glanced over at Fred and Molly and said, 'Shouldn't we go? Those two must be so bored.'

'No, they're not. And besides, they owe me. I'm taking them to yet another fireworks party tonight, which is incredibly noble of me as I hate loud bangs. Now go and try those things on.'

When Merrily came out, even *she* had to admit she looked good. Merrily, Leah thought, was a perfect illustration of the importance of clothes. In her baggy jumpers and shapeless jeans, she hunched her shoulders and pulled her sleeves over her hands as if she were trying to obliterate herself. In the blue dress and little cardigan, she exuded, if not confidence, at least a dawning understanding that she was not completely hideous.

A week later, Merrily sat on a stool in the kitchen, her hair wet and her face a picture of embarrassment.

Stacey, her own hair a riot of blonde and pink highlights, stared intensely at Merrily's face. 'Right,' she said at last. 'I know what to do.'

'I'll nip out and get some stuff for lunch,' Leah said. She glanced at Molly, who was drawing a picture at the table. 'Do you want to come?'

'I'll keep Merrily company,' Molly said graciously.

'Thank you,' Merrily said with what Leah could see was genuine gratitude. Stacey, with her bright pink trousers, black leather waistcoat and ten strings of beads, clearly terrified her.

Fred volunteered to go with his mother and they had a very satisfactory expedition, choosing cheeses and bread and pâté. When they came back, Molly rushed to the hall and said, 'Stacey's just finished. Come and see!'

It was magic. Stacey had given Merrily a light fringe and cut inches off her hair so that it now fell smoothly over her ears. The difference it made was, as Leah said, unbelievable. 'Stacey, you're so good,' she said. 'Merrily, have you *seen* yourself?'

Merrily nodded. Her face was a little pink and she whispered, 'I like it!'

Afterwards, Leah would remember that afternoon as the happiest occasion they had had as a family since the break-up. For a start, Jamie was in his element, doing what Jamie did best, and his easy authority helped erase the memory of his recent disastrous car journey with his offspring. They had always loved helping him with his work and after the first few minutes, he had them moving props around and changing lights.

Also, he was terrific with Merrily. It helped, of course, that for once she was not ashamed of her appearance and it helped even more that Alison was so visibly impressed by her transformation. But even so, Jamie was perfect. He introduced himself by saying, 'Merrily, I've heard so much about you.'

'I've heard a lot about you,' Merrily said.

Jamie smiled. 'I wish I could tell you to disregard every word of it but I'm afraid it's all probably true. I hope you don't mind if I tell you that you have the perfect face for a camera.'

'Do I?' Merrily asked. She sounded as if she was unsure whether she had just received a compliment or not.

'Your eyes are wide apart, you have a well-defined profile. This is going to be easy. All three of you are so distinctive-looking. Let's start by putting blonde Alison in the middle, with the two brunettes on either side. Let's have some fun!'

And fun they had. Jamie took hundreds of photos and finished by printing out three copies of one of them. 'You can have them to take home,' he said. 'I'll go over them all later and decide which ones are the best.'

The three women looked down at their photos. Merrily sat in the middle with Leah on her left and Alison on her right. The three of them looked as if they were sharing some delightful secret joke, an effect achieved by the fact that at the moment it was taken, Fred had wrapped a pink feather boa round his head.

'Jamie,' Merrily said, 'this is the only photo with me in it that I've ever liked. Leah *said* you were good and she's right.'

Jamie gave a self-deprecatory shrug which fooled no one. 'I'm only as good as my material.'

'That's definitely not true,' Merrily said. 'I must be getting home now, but thank you for a wonderful afternoon.'

Leah smiled and impulsively moved forward to kiss Jamie's cheek. 'You're the best,' she said. She turned to Molly and Fred. 'Are you ready to go?'

Jamie nodded enquiringly at the children. 'If you like,' he said, 'you can stay on with me for an hour or so and help me choose the best photos. I could even take some of you two before I take you home.'

Neither of them hesitated. For now at least, Daddy was back to being the hero; and for now at least, Leah felt he deserved to be.

They had all driven over in Alison's car; Alison now suggested that she drive Leah and Merrily back to Merrily's house first to see what Christopher thought of the picture. 'Of course, he hasn't seen your new look,' she said. 'I can't wait to see his face.' While Merrily made her farewells to Molly and Fred, Alison whispered to Leah, 'Now remember, be nice to Christopher. He mustn't think we don't like him. Tact and subtlety are our watchwords.'

'I'll try to remember,' Leah said. She was in too good a mood to be irritated by Alison's apparent conviction that she could not be trusted to behave with discretion.

The three friends drove home in huge good humour and Merrily said at least twice that Jamie was a genius.

As Merrily opened the front door, Christopher came down the stairs and smiled benignly at them all. 'That's excellent timing,' he said. 'I was about to make a cup of tea.' He looked a little intently at Merrily's hair but did not comment on her appearance.

'We've had great fun this afternoon,' Alison said. 'And we have a splendid photo to prove it. Show him, Merrily.'

Merrily carefully took the photo from its envelope and handed it over.

Christopher stared at it for a few moments. 'The man is very good at his job,' he said graciously. He beamed at Merrily. 'Your nose doesn't look as big as it usually does.'

Leah wanted to kill him. She stepped forward but Alison was there before her. In a trembling voice, Alison said, 'I always thought writers were supposed to be observant, Christopher. Merrily does not have a big nose. To be honest, Merrily's nose is a lot shorter than *your* nose. Your wife looks stunning in that photo and anyone but you could see that.' She glanced at Leah and said in her grandest voice, 'Come along, Leah, I'll take you home.'

Pausing only to throw a nervous smile at Merrily, Leah followed Alison out into the darkness. She felt like a second-in-command who's just seen her leader slaying the enemy. She had to stop herself from cheering.

CHAPTER FIFTEEN

Alison is Worried by Some Startling News

'MUM! Nathan won't get out of my room!'

In a parallel world, Alison would have shouted up at the ceiling: 'Harry, you are seventeen years old. If your brother's annoying you, you deal with him.' But then, of course, in the parallel world Alison would be overcome with guilt since, if Harry were given permission to deal with Nathan, Nathan would probably end up in Casualty.

Alison sighed and then shouted up at the ceiling, 'Nathan, get out of Harry's room!'

There were times, she thought, chopping basil furiously, when she wished Harry's room was not directly above the kitchen. There were times – if she were really honest, there weren't times, it was most of the time these days – when she felt she was losing control of her family. She was aware that the day's events had conspired to give her what was probably a jaundiced view of her life. On her morning walk with Magnus, she had caught her anorak on a piece of barbed wire and torn it. On her way home, she had a breathless phone call from Nathan to tell her it was a matter of life and death: he'd thought it was Tuesday and had found out it was actually Wednesday and he'd left his homework on his desk in his bedroom and would she please be the best mother in the world and bring it in, now, this minute, please, please, please?

She was therefore late for her appointment to view a spectacularly hideous house, matched only by the hideousness of its soon-to-be-divorced occupants, who were extremely unpleasant about her being fifteen minutes late for them. She had driven home in a furious mood only to find that Magnus had been sick all over the kitchen floor, a consequence of his determination to eat any and every disgusting item that came his way on his morning walk.

The postman had brought her two quotes from the only caterers in the area who weren't already booked up for the weekend of Phoebe's wedding. Both quotes were shockingly expensive and, given Felix's current belief that they were destined to hit the bankruptcy courts, there was no way she could have an intelligent conversation with him about the best way of feeding their guests at their daughter's wedding. Worryingly, he appeared to have taken her at her word when she'd said she could do the catering herself.

Sally Bracewell had dropped by in the afternoon with a copy of the Tucking Friary Reading Group's latest book, *Jude the Obscure*. It had been kind of Sally to lend it to her but in her present state of mind she wasn't at all sure she wanted to immerse herself in what Sally admitted was the most depressing novel she had ever read. As it was, she was having a hard enough time ploughing through a book by Christopher called *A Clear Day*. Christopher's book was not clear at all. At first, she thought it was about a woman living in Mongolia and it was only after she read three whole chapters that she discovered that Mongolia was supposed to be a metaphor for something and that actually the woman lived in Ireland.

'MUM! Harry's trying to murder me!'

Alison rolled her eyes and put down her knife. 'Harry,' she shouted up at the ceiling, 'stop trying to murder Nathan and—' She broke off to answer the phone. It was Leah. Alison had left a message on her answerphone, asking her to supper along with Christopher and Merrily.

'I'm sorry,' Leah said now, 'but I can't sit down and share a meal with that man, especially after his behaviour on Saturday. I don't even know how you could bear to invite him.'

'That's easy. I want to get him out of Merrily's life. Have you forgotten we're running a ruthless campaign here? We have to show Merrily that Christopher is a monster. I don't think it even occurs to her that his behaviour is unacceptable. I invite them to supper. I emphasize the fact that Felix is a great and caring doctor who is also a great and caring husband and Merrily can see up close that Christopher compares very badly.'

'Well, you don't need me for that. Anyway, I did some good campaigning work yesterday evening. Merrily came over to play Cluedo with me and the kids. She helped Fred with his homework too.'

'I hope it wasn't his maths homework. I remember spending ages trying to explain long division to Merrily when we were children. I don't think she ever did understand.'

'It was English. Fred had to write a poem about butterflies. Merrily was great. After the kids went to bed she asked me why I'd left Jamie – I can see he's completely charmed her – and I told her he'd been unfaithful once too often and it was much easier being a single mother than being an unhappily married wife and mother. How was that?'

'That was good,' Alison said gravely, 'but I still think you're a coward not to come to supper with—' She could hear Nathan shouting again. 'Leah, I've got to go. Civil war has broken out upstairs.'

She put down the phone and looked up as Felix came in. Felix gave one last shake of his umbrella before shutting the door and offering her a weary smile. She paused to acknowledge the sounds of muffled shouts and thumps from the ceiling. 'Hi, Felix,' she said. 'Supper's nearly ready. Welcome back to our happy home.'

'I'll get out of these clothes,' Felix said, 'and I'll say hello to my darling boys.'

As soon as he'd gone, Alison concealed the catering estimates underneath the local paper. There was no point in showing Felix the quotes since in his present mood he would insist that the wedding guests would be perfectly happy with crisps and peanuts. And actually, if Alison was really honest, now was not a good time for her to discuss wedding plans with Felix since at this precise moment she was finding it difficult to summon any enthusiasm at all for the entire project.

The phone interrupted any further conjecture. Alison picked up the handset and was delighted to hear her younger daughter say, 'Hi, Mum.'

'Eva!' Alison exclaimed. 'How lovely to hear you! How *are* you? I haven't heard from you for ages!'

'I know. I'm sorry.'

'Well, it's lovely to hear you now! What have you been doing lately?'

'Writing an essay. I went for a walk today.'

'Did you? That's good. What's the weather like up there?'

'It's raining.'

'It's doing the same here. What else have you been doing?'

'I've been sick twice,' Eva said. 'And I did a pregnancy test.'

Alison felt her heart lurch. She sat down at the table, clutching the phone as if it were a lifeboat.

'Mum?' Eva said. 'Did you hear me? I did a pregnancy test.'

'I heard you.' Alison's mouth felt as dry as parchment. She licked her lips. 'What was the result?' She already knew the answer. If it had been negative, Eva would never have mentioned it.

Eva's voice sounded uncharacteristically scared and small. 'It's positive.'

Alison bit her lip and twisted her right leg tightly round her left one. 'Are you sure you read the instructions right? It's easy to—'

'I did it properly,' Eva said. 'I should have had my period a month ago. I never miss my period. And I feel sick. I feel sick all the time.'

'Right,' Alison said, 'I see.' She was sure there were sensible responses to this sort of situation and she was aware that she was flailing impotently, like someone who's forgotten how to swim. 'I didn't know . . .' She began again, 'I didn't know you'd been seeing anyone.'

'I haven't been,' Eva said. 'I'm not.'

'So,' Alison said, 'who's the father?'

There was a pause. 'I don't know.'

'How can you not know?' Alison put a hand to her mouth and then slowly removed it as her brain tried to process Eva's answer. 'Eva, were you raped? Were you unconscious at the time? Look, you need to—'

'Mum, I wasn't raped and I wasn't unconscious.'

Alison bit her lip. This was no time for judgement or recrimination. She struggled to keep her voice calm. 'Eva, if you had sex with some stranger you need to get tested for—'

'They weren't strangers.'

'*They?*' Alison's mind had turned into a giant cinema screen depicting a drug-fuelled orgy in some seedy basement room where her own little Eva was passed around by a crowd of leering students who wore tight leather trousers and black T-shirts emblazoned with skulls and crossbones. She should never have let Eva go to Manchester. She shut her eyes for a moment and cleared her throat. 'How many men have you had sex with?'

'Mum!' For a moment Eva sounded like her usual self. 'Only two.'

'I see. Well, if they weren't wearing condoms you still need to get tested for things like HIV. You need to talk to Felix about all that. But I do know that if you want to know who the father is, a DNA test would soon tell you.'

'That's the whole point,' Eva said. 'A DNA test wouldn't help at all.'

'Eva,' Alison walked over to the fridge and took out the bottle of wine that Felix had opened last night, 'I know you're upset but—'

'A DNA test wouldn't be able to identify the father. I've already checked that out. A DNA test wouldn't work on identical twins.'

Alison filled a glass with wine. 'Identical twins?' she queried. 'Why are we talking about identical twins?'

'I had sex with Robbie and Ronnie.'

Alison's mind was desperately trying to catch up. 'You had sex with Robbie *and* Ronnie? I don't understand. When did you have sex with Robbie and Ronnie?'

'It was the night before I went to university. Do you remember I went to Kate's house? Her parents were away and it was a weird evening because Kate was upset about her grandfather and the dog and we all drank too much and we got talking about sex, and I said I didn't want to go to university as a virgin and then the others said they didn't want to be virgins either, so we drew lots and Kate got Gordon and I got Robbie, which didn't seem fair on Ronnie so I said I'd do it with both of them, and now I'm pregnant and,' Eva began to cry, 'I don't know what to do.'

Alison's mind was racing with various possible scenarios: a pregnant Eva dropping out of university, an even more pregnant Eva standing shell-shocked between the two possible fathers, a not-very-maternal Eva trying desperately to pacify a crying baby, a sweet five-year-old mini-Eva looking up at the fresh-faced twins and asking them, 'Which of you is my daddy?'

Alison pushed back her hair, had a gulp of wine and said, 'Eva, don't worry, we'll sort this out.'

'How?' Eva sobbed. 'How do I sort this out? I'm so scared.'

'Eva – Eva, darling, don't cry. We must talk to Felix. He can give you all the medical information you need. It's really very simple. What we – what *you* – have to decide is whether you want to keep the baby or not.'

There was a long silence and then Eva said, 'That's not simple at all.'

'You're right,' Alison said humbly. 'It isn't.'

'Mum,' Eva said, 'if you were me, what would you do?'

'Well,' Alison began and then stopped. It had been a long time since Eva had asked her opinion about anything and she really wanted to give her a sensible, balanced, helpful answer. She couldn't do it. The truth was that she had absolutely no idea.

CHAPTER SIXTEEN

Leah Sometimes Has Regrets (Especially Where Men Are Involved)

Christopher had put on a lot of weight since his last visit to her bedroom. Leah lay naked on the sheets like a sacrificial virgin. As Christopher climbed onto the bed and prepared to lower himself into her, his belly rippled with the exertion, his rolls of fat shaking, like washing in the wind.

Leah gulped. Behind Christopher, she could see Alison slowly opening the door of the wardrobe, mouthing the words, 'Act as if you like it.' Leah shut her eyes and then opened them again. Above her, Christopher's face was red with excitement. Slowly, inexorably, he bore down upon her and then, at the moment of entry, Merrily burst into the room brandishing the Monopoly set and screaming, 'I hate you, I hate you!'

'Merrily,' Leah cried, 'I'm doing this for you!' Then, with every ounce of determination, she forced herself into consciousness. She opened her eyes. She was alone in her bedroom, which, thank the Lord, had no wardrobe. There was no Alison, no Merrily and, best of all, no Christopher.

For a few moments she savoured the glorious knowledge that she was not about to have sex with him and then she rolled over onto her side, murmuring, 'Bloody Alison.'

The next morning was as chaotic as mornings could be when sick children were involved. Molly had flu. Leah had already taken off one day to look after her and couldn't take another. Jamie, somewhat unwillingly, had agreed to take her since he was working from home. As Leah dropped Fred off at school, he reminded her that there was a special History Fayre in the afternoon and he wouldn't need picking up until quarter past five. It was just as well, Leah thought grimly as she drove Molly across town, that Fred had a better memory than she had.

She deposited a very hot Molly with Jamie and told him he'd have to hang on to her until five thirty. She then climbed back into the car and drove back to Widcombe. It was not a restful journey. She spent the first half worrying about Molly and the second half thinking about Merrily and Alison's stupid CLOM.

She had read once that it was impossible to sleep without dreaming. Leah usually forgot all her dreams as soon as she woke up. A few of them stuck to her like burrs on a jumper. Today, she had to keep reminding herself that Merrily knew nothing about her night with Christopher and that there was no way Christopher would ever enter her bedroom – or her – again.

In the afternoon she showed a young couple round a flat in Combe Down. It had been on her books for some time and she was anxious to let it as soon as possible. She was telling them about the local shops when her mobile rang. She apologized and murmured, 'Hello, Jamie.'

It was obvious that Jamie was not in the mood for social niceties. 'Your daughter is having hysterics,' he said. 'You have to collect her now.'

Leah, aware of Mr and Mrs Browning's eyes on her, spoke in a calm, gentle voice. 'I'm sorry to hear that. At the moment I'm with some clients and—'

'Get rid of them.' Jamie's voice sounded as brittle as a toothpick. 'I am due at a photo shoot at the Ashmolean Museum in Oxford at eight. I should have left by now. Your daughter refuses to be left alone with Charlotte, who is extremely upset. If you don't come at once, my career will be on the line and Charlotte may very well have a miscarriage.'

'Why is Charlotte looking after her?' Leah asked in a furious whisper. 'You never told me you had a job on tonight.'

'I forgot. And then when I remembered I thought it would be a good opportunity for Molly to get to know Charlotte. Charlotte came back from work especially early. She's very upset.'

Leah directed a weak smile at the Brownings and said, 'I'll do my best to get over to Larkhall as soon as possible . . .'

'That's not good enough. Get over here now.'

'All right.' Leah put her phone back in her bag. 'I'm so sorry,' she said. 'We have a family crisis and I have to leave at once. I do apologize for the inconvenience. I can send you an email tonight with more information about Combe Down and the flat.'

The Brownings were nice people. They had both taken time off work to visit the flat and they couldn't have been nicer about the fact that their visit was so drastically curtailed. Leah wanted to hug them both.

Driving from Combe Down to Larkhall in the rush hour was about as much fun as climbing Mount Everest in wellington boots. Leah arrived at Jamie's place at quarter past five. They had obviously been looking out for her because the door opened before she had a chance to shout into the entryphone. Jamie handed a mutinous-looking Molly over without saying a word. Leah took Molly's hand and said, 'We have to be quick. I'm horribly late for Fred.'

At first, Leah was too busy manoeuvring her way back onto the London Road to say anything at all to her daughter and her daughter showed no desire to say anything to *her*. Once she'd fought her way back into the traffic and seen that the cars were as slow as snails on sleeping tablets, she muttered furiously, 'Fuck!'

Her mobile rang on its handset and Leah pushed a button. Fred's voice, calm if a little concerned, filled the car. 'Hi, Mum. Miss Simmons wants to know if you've forgotten to pick me up.'

'Tell Miss Simmons that I haven't forgotten and I'm stuck in traffic but will be there as soon as I can.'

'Fred,' Molly called out from the back. 'Mum's just said the F word.'

'Tell Miss Simmons,' Leah said, 'I'm very sorry and I won't be long.' She switched off the phone and glanced at Molly in her driving mirror. 'Molly, I know you're ill but how could you be so horrible to Charlotte? She came back early just to look after you. There is never any excuse for unnecessary rudeness. And now your father is late for a very important job and I had to leave a client and now I'm late for Fred, and it's all because of you. I know this situation is difficult for you but it's difficult for all of us.'

Molly folded her arms and dug her chin into her chest. 'I don't want to stay with Charlotte. I don't want to be friends with Charlotte. Daddy was supposed to look after me.'

'You only had to stay with her for a half-hour or so. In this world, you do sometimes have to do things you don't want to do and . . . Fuck!' Leah slammed her foot on the brake as the driver in front decided a little late that he would not, after all, jump the lights.

'Mum,' Molly said. 'That's the second time you've said the F word.'

They arrived at the school at ten to six and Leah leapt out of the car and ran into the reception area. Her heart, already overdosed on adrenalin, performed an impressive double flip at the sight awaiting her. Fred was sitting on one of the chairs and he was talking to the man who was currently keeping her awake most nights.

'Fred, I'm so sorry . . . The traffic was appalling.' She glanced at David. 'Were you involved in the history afternoon? Have you been waiting with Fred here? I'm so sorry—'

'We were having an interesting conversation,' David said. 'He has the makings of an excellent historian.'

And now here was Miss Simmons, new to the school this term, a pretty young woman whom Leah had instantly liked and who was now touching David's arm in a proprietorial way, causing Leah to instantly revise her opinion of her.

'Hello, Mrs Payne. Fred's been fine, haven't you, Fred? I told him I was sure you *hadn't* forgotten him. If you don't mind, David and I have things to discuss so we'd better get on . . .'

'Of course,' Leah said quickly. 'I'm sorry to have put you both out.'

David stood up and smiled at Fred. 'Goodbye,' he said. He followed the odious Miss Simmons down the corridor, giving Leah a slight hello-goodbye-don't-I-know-you-from-somewhere sort of smile.

Leah took Fred's hand and walked out of the school. She felt grateful for the cold night air on her flaming cheeks. 'I didn't know David Morrison was going to be here today,' she said.

'He gave us a talk,' Fred said. 'He told us that history is really important. He said it shows us that people keep on making the same mistakes and that we should learn our history so we can be more careful.'

'That sounds like good advice,' Leah said. She opened the door of the car and, studiously ignoring Molly, put on her seat belt.

Fred climbed into the back, blissfully unaware of the large thundercloud currently swamping his mother and sister. 'He told us about Afghanistan. He said the British fought there a long time ago and they had to retreat and it was very cold and only one man out of forty thousand survived and he was an army surgeon. Miss Simmons said she hoped David would come and talk to us again.'

Leah ground her teeth. 'I bet she does,' she said.

* * *

Later that evening, she pulled out her phone. She still had David's number. She also had a perfect excuse for ringing him. 'I wanted to thank you for waiting with Fred, blah, blah, blah.' But she wasn't sure she could bear to hear his voice sounding polite but uncomfortable. He had given no indication this afternoon that he was pleased to see her. He had given every indication that he was keen to talk to Miss Simmons. They were probably, even now, exchanging sweet nothings about a nineteenth-century military campaign in Afghanistan.

She wished she could stop thinking about him. This afternoon only confirmed the dismal fact that he was not even slightly interested in her and it was therefore quite pointless to recall those glorious few nights when the children had been in Winchester and David had been with her. What was the point in remembering their love-making or the way his eyes had looked at her when she made him laugh? All those memories were based on the false assumption that he had really cared for her. They meant nothing.

What was real was the smile he had given her at Fred's school. It had held no warmth at all. It had been impersonal and polite and the memory of it continued to linger in her mind like a bad smell.

At least Friday morning was easier than Thursday's had been since Stacey was able to come over and look after Molly. Today, Leah thought, she would throw herself into her work and ignore the heavy depression that covered her like a rash.

She was on the phone, having a tedious and highly technical conversation with one of her maintenance men, when a young woman came into her office. The girl was jaw-droppingly beautiful. She had long, shiny blonde hair, enormous blue eyes and a mouth that would make Angelina Jolie feel envious. The short leather jacket and grey jeans she wore only emphasized her radiant femininity and her youth. She was also pregnant and as Leah heard the woman give her name to Diana, she knew she should have guessed at once who she was.

The children had implied that Charlotte was as old as Jamie. She should have realized that to them anyone over the age of eighteen was past it. As it was, she could be only a few years on from that. Leah got off the phone as quickly as she could and stood up. 'You must be Charlotte. Can I offer you a cup of tea or coffee?'

'No, thank you.' The girl gave an apologetic smile. 'If I have a drink, I'll just want to go to the loo. I want to go to the loo all the time at the moment. I've got an appointment with the dentist this morning and I thought you wouldn't mind if I came in and had a quick word with you first. I wanted to speak to you about your daughter.'

'Right.' Leah glanced across at her assistant. 'Diana, can you man the phones for a bit? I'll take Charlotte into the other room.' It was actually more of a cupboard than a room and as she ushered Charlotte in, she apologized for the lack of space. 'At least we can be private here. Won't you sit down?' She gestured to the only comfortable chair and perched on the small wooden stool by the window.

'Thank you.' The girl took her seat and put her bag on the floor. She took a deep breath. 'I'm here to say sorry. I'm crap with children. Jimbo told me you were late for Fred because you had to pick up Molly. Jimbo said you were pretty mad.'

Leah blinked. It took her a moment to realize that Charlotte was referring to Jamie. 'I don't understand. It wasn't your fault I was late for Fred.'

'Yes, it was. If Molly had let me look after her, you wouldn't have been late. I'm crap with children. I don't know how to talk to them, especially clever ones like Fred and Molly. This whole . . . thing –' she gesticulated at her tummy – 'it's all so weird. Has Jimbo told you how we met? I met him at a party in Bristol. I work for a company that sells organic beauty products and we were celebrating the success of a publicity campaign. Jimbo was there because he'd done the photos. It was *such* a boring party, I could only keep awake by pouring champagne down my throat and then I met Jimbo and suddenly it wasn't boring any more. He came back to my flat and – I have to tell you I can't remember any of this, it's what Jimbo told me later – Jimbo said to me, "Are you all right?" and apparently I said, "I am so all right," and so he went ahead and bang, I get pregnant. After that, of course, we always used condoms and I never even thought I might be pregnant – my periods are always all over the place and I didn't look pregnant and I wasn't sick or anything – and so when I finally found out it was too late to do anything. Then Jimbo suggested I move in with him and I'd already met the children and they're so bright but I didn't know what to say to them and I could tell Fred didn't know what to say to me either and Molly won't even look at me and I don't know what to do because I really want to get on with them, do you know what I mean?'

'Well, yes, I do.'

'My mother always had this idea that there is The (

and when you find him you'll know at once. She and Dad knew straight away. They're amazing together. It's like they can read each other's minds. Now my sister and I've left home, they're like lovebirds together. Dad says Mum could have had anyone but she chose him. I'm not like Mum. I mean, I don't have any trouble getting men but they always get bored with me. I think I've just got that sort of personality. But I really love Jimbo and I want to make it work with him and that means making it work with Fred and Molly, and I don't know how to do it. I know I'm talking too much, I always do when I'm nervous but I can't help it, you're obviously really bright and so are your children and so is Jimbo and I'm not. Anyway,' Charlotte stood up, 'I'm interrupting your work, I must let you get on. I just wanted to say sorry.'

Charlotte had been talking in such a breathless, unstoppable rush that Leah was taken aback by her sudden silence. She smiled up at the younger woman. 'Fred and Molly *are* clever. I don't know where their brains come from, to be honest. Jamie can take photos and I've learnt how to run a business that rents flats to people. So could you. So could most people. And about the children: it's not that Molly and Fred don't like you, it's only that they feel threatened by the new baby. They worry that Jamie won't be interested in them any longer. They need masses of reassurance and that must come from Jamie rather than you. I am well aware that Molly can be utterly poisonous when she wants to be and you have my deepest sympathy. She'll come round in time. I will talk to her but she's pretty stubborn. I wish I could be more helpful. You just have to

'Actually,' Charlotte said, 'you've been very helpful. They seem so self-confident, it didn't occur to me they might be jealous of the baby.' She took Leah's hand and shook it warmly. 'I mustn't take up any more of your time. Thank you.' She hoisted her bag onto her shoulder. 'It's been nice to meet you.'

'It's been very nice to meet *you*,' Leah said. 'And as for those men who got bored with you, it's nothing to do with your personality. It's everything to do with *their* personalities. You just chose rotten men. Believe me, I'm an expert.'

Charlotte's eyes brimmed with tears. 'Oh,' she said, 'you are so kind! Thank you!' She flashed a smile, waved a hand and went out of the door, shutting it firmly behind her.

Leah sat looking at the closed door. Charlotte called Jamie Jimbo. Charlotte was young and Charlotte was beautiful. Nevertheless, Leah liked her. She wished she didn't since it meant she could no longer indulge her inner bitch. She would have to work hard to persuade Molly to accept her father's right to move on and have a new relationship. This would be less difficult if she hadn't so recently sabotaged any chance of forging a decent relationship with the first man to interest her properly since Jamie. For a moment Leah's inner bitch was as close to bursting out as the monster in *Alien*. But Charlotte was a sweet woman who would very likely discover in time that Jamie was as rotten as all the previous men in her life. She deserved all the help Leah could give her.

CHAPTER SEVENTEEN

When Alison Decides That Eva Needs a Break, She Breaks a Recent Resolution

Alison had waited till after supper to tell Felix. The boys, fortunately, had gone off to the television to watch a Bond film. Alison sat in the kitchen with Felix while he rang Eva. She listened while he calmly, quietly demystified the processes of termination and pregnancy, laying out the options like the good doctor he was. Then he handed the phone to Alison and she asked Eva if she'd like her to come up to Manchester on Saturday, just for the night. Eva whispered, 'Yes, please,' and then said, 'I'm sorry, I'm so sorry,' and then Alison started crying and Felix took the phone and said, 'Eva, all you need to know is that we will support you whatever you decide. Now go to sleep and don't worry.' And when he finally rang off, he took Alison's hands in his and they looked at each other and said nothing at all.

And now here she was, on the train to Manchester. She had been in such a state that she'd left behind her washbag, her hairbrush and, worst of all, her mobile. She had remembered to bring her Christopher Trumpet paperback but had not been able to read it on the train.

Her mind was far too busy racing with different visions of Eva's future. If Eva had an abortion, she would be able to carry on with her life at university. But would she? Would she regret it for the rest of her life if she pursued that course? Would she blame her parents for not stopping her? Felix was convinced that all they should do was set out the various possibilities and let Eva make up her own mind. Alison wasn't at all convinced that Eva *wanted* to be left to make up her own mind. If she didn't have an abortion, what then? She could do what the teenage girl did in that film, *Juno*, and give away her baby for adoption. Eva could make some childless couple eternally happy. But how would Eva cope with the knowledge that somewhere in the world there was a child with loads of little Coward genes who didn't know that Eva was his or her mother? Fleetingly, Alison let herself think how *she* would feel knowing that somewhere in the world there was a little grandchild growing up who didn't know that *she* was his or her grandmother. Alison gulped and told herself sternly that this was not about *her*.

There was another possibility, of course. Eva could keep the baby, she could drop out of university and live with her parents and her baby. But Eva had long since grown out of living at home. During the last few years she had been in a perpetual state of irritation. She was irritated by the distance of the village from Bath and the slowness and rarity of the buses to and from Bath. She was irritated that her parents were always so interested in what she was doing and where she was doing it. She was irritated that Alison worried about her diets, her lack of sleep and her tendency to have nothing but coffee for breakfast. In fact,

Eva found her mother, and to a lesser extent her father, very irritating most of the time. When Alison tried to imagine Eva living at home with her baby and her parents, she couldn't help thinking that Eva would go mad with boredom and frustration.

By the time Alison got off the train, she felt quite exhausted. She saw Eva before Eva saw her and had time to notice that Eva's complexion was too pale. Alison called out, 'Eva!' and her daughter ran up and hugged her tightly.

They had a late lunch in a little Italian place and Alison was glad to see that Eva ate all her lasagne even though she hardly drew breath throughout the meal. Felix's straightforward breakdown of the termination procedure had lessened her terror of the practicalities of abortion. However, last night she had had a long talk with Becky, her next-door neighbour in her hall of residence. Becky had had an abortion in the middle of her gap year and had regretted it ever since.

Eva was now in a state of emotional paralysis. She kept saying, 'On the one hand . . .' and then, 'On the other hand . . .' and Alison kept nodding and wishing Felix was here with all his medical knowledge and his common sense. At one point, Eva's eyes filled with tears. 'Isn't it ironic?' she said. 'I gave Phoebe a hard time for getting engaged. I thought she was throwing her life away. And now I'm doing that big time. I've wrecked everything.'

Alison took a deep breath. 'Eva, there's something I have to tell you,' she said. 'I've never told you before because I – well, I suppose I was embarrassed. But now I think you have a right to know.' She swallowed. 'The thing is—'

'If you're trying to tell me you had to get married, Phoebe and I guessed that years ago.'

'You did?' Alison was shocked.

'It was pretty obvious. You get married at eighteen and have a baby seven months later.'

Alison took a sip of her coffee and tried to recover her composure. 'The point is that I know exactly what you're going through.'

'No, you don't,' Eva said. 'You and Dad loved each other and you always knew you wanted to marry him and have loads of children. I don't want to marry anyone and I certainly don't want to marry Robbie and Ronnie.'

'Robbie *or* Ronnie,' Alison murmured.

'Whatever. I don't want to have a baby either. I'm not like you at all. I'm just not sure I can bear the thought of . . . of un-making a baby.'

In the afternoon, they walked round Manchester. Alison was astonished. Manchester had beautiful Victorian buildings and an impressively futuristic theatre. It had *better* shops than Bath, it even had Harvey Nichols! Given that it had been two southerners who had impregnated her daughter rather than some random Mancunian, Alison decided that it was time to revise her opinion of the north.

Eva pointed out the penthouse flats where all the footballers lived and then they went to the Selfridges food hall, which Alison thought was just like Aladdin's cave. Alison bought a chicken pie, various salads, a carton of soup and a strawberry tart for their supper. Manchester, she told Eva, was not at all like she'd thought it was. Eva said that she adored Manchester; she loved the city so much she couldn't bear the thought of leaving it.

They had tea in a place that Eva particularly liked and Eva revealed she'd talked to the twins. They'd been shocked, of course, but Eva said they'd do anything they could to help. Alison said she could just imagine them taking it in turns to burp the baby. Eva's mouth quivered and just for a moment she smiled.

In the evening, they ate supper in Eva's room and talked about adoption. As far as Eva was concerned, the big advantage was that she wouldn't have to miss university. She could have the baby near the end of the summer term, give it away to some nice deserving people and be back in Manchester for the beginning of the second year.

Alison hesitated. 'I'm not saying that's a bad idea,' she said carefully, 'but you might find it difficult getting work and exams done when you're near the end of your pregnancy. You can't guarantee exactly what's going to happen.'

'I know it will be difficult,' Eva said. 'I don't need you to tell me that, I'm not stupid. Whatever I decide is going to be difficult, everything's difficult.'

Perhaps it was fortunate that three of Eva's friends called in at that moment. They were going up to the next floor to see a couple of boys and wondered if Eva would like to come along. Alison said quickly, 'Why don't you go, Eva? To be honest, I'd quite like to go to bed.'

She was rewarded with a smile and an 'Are you sure?' and knew she had made the right decision.

Eva's friend, Becky, had gone to see her parents in Bradford for the night and had volunteered her room to Alison. Alison was grateful, though she couldn't help thinking that she might have been a lot more comfortable in a B and B. Becky's narrow bed was hard and uncomfortable and someone who had to be deaf was playing music next door. Alison felt like a sad old woman and wished she had her mobile with her so she could ring Felix.

She slept fitfully through the night and woke to see pale rays of sunlight edging through the skimpy tangerine-coloured curtains.

Eva knocked on her door and Alison got out of bed to let her in. Perhaps Eva felt guilty about going out the night before or perhaps she felt better for a good night's sleep. Anyway, she was far more expansive than she had been. 'You know the girls who came round last night? We're all going to share a flat next year. Georgie – she's the one with the blonde hair – she's a great cook. She can only cook three things but they're really good. Cassie comes from Leeds. She and her boyfriend have been together since they were fourteen. They keep breaking up but they can't bear it if the other goes out with someone else. Jess is from York and she's clever, she's cleverer than anyone I've ever met. I do love it here, Mum. I can't bear the thought of dropping out. And even if I came back after a year, it wouldn't be the same. All my friends would be in the year above me. Perhaps I should have an abortion. I don't know. I wish I did know.'

'I had an idea in the night,' Alison said. 'It's only an idea and you might say it's silly but I think it's a definite possibility.'

'Mum,' Eva said, 'I have considered every single possibility.'

'I don't think you've thought of this one,' Alison said. She took a deep breath. 'You could have the baby and let me and Felix bring him or her up.'

'Yeah, right.' Eva grimaced. 'That would be *so* weird.'

'I don't see why,' Alison said. 'It used to happen all the time. John Lennon was brought up by his aunt. Jack Nicholson was brought up by his grandmother.'

'Who's Jack Nicholson?'

'He's an actor. You must have heard of him. In fact, I remember you seeing *The Shining* years ago on television. He's quite old now but . . . Anyway, that's not important. The point is that Felix and I could do it. Of course your baby would always know you were his or her mother but I'm just pointing out that grandparents are quite capable of looking after small children. I'm still very young. Many women nowadays don't even have their babies till they get to my age. Look at Margaret who works for your father. She's two years older than me and she's only recently had her first baby.'

Eva raised her eyebrows. 'Dad says she's a wreck. He says she falls asleep every time she comes to work. He says she looks like a zombie.'

'Your father loves to exaggerate. She doesn't look anything like a zombie. And anyway, first babies are always exhausting. What I'm trying to say is that I'm not too old to bring up a baby and I've had more experience than most. I just want you to realize it's a sensible suggestion and I hope you'll consider it.'

'I will,' Eva said. 'Thank you.'

On the train home in the afternoon, Alison tried to work out how she would sell the idea to Felix. 'Felix, do you remember telling me you were worried you were becoming a grumpy old man before your time? I have the perfect solution for you! I can tell you what will keep you eternally young . . .'

No, that wouldn't work because Felix was absolutely right. Margaret looked a hundred years older since she'd had her baby. Felix would never buy the eternal youth angle.

She could appeal to his paternal instincts. 'Felix, there is something you can agree to do that will make Eva the happiest girl in the world . . .' The trouble was she could all too easily imagine Felix challenging that statement. How did Alison *know* it would make Eva happy? Eva might find it impossible to leave the baby in the hands of her parents. She might end up living at home and then Felix would have to put up with baby smells, baby noises *and* Eva's unpredictable temper.

But actually, Alison was sure that Eva would be happy to let Alison bring up the baby. It was the perfect solution. Alison knew about babies, Alison loved babies and Alison knew she would *adore* Eva's baby. Felix would come round. As soon as he saw the baby he would come round. He'd been horrified when Alison discovered she was pregnant with Nathan and yet he'd loved Nathan from the moment he saw him.

Of course they would have to make some changes at home. Felix would have to build a fence round the pond and they'd have to redecorate the spare room and turn it into a proper nursery. It occurred to Alison that, just for the moment, she would not mention her idea to Felix. She knew she had decided after the wedding-dress fiasco that she would never keep secrets from him again. But if she told him her idea right away he might raise objections, and there was no point in having what might turn out to be a difficult conversation until and unless she knew the difficult conversation was necessary.

* * *

The next morning was one of those rare occasions when Alison awoke positively fizzing with energy. She had found a solution and she knew it was right. She awoke her bewildered husband with a kiss and she chatted to her sons all the way to school. After breakfast, she dealt with the overflowing laundry basket, made the Christmas pudding, took Magnus for a bracing walk and received two phone calls, one from Phoebe and one from Leah. In the first, she assured a slightly dejected Phoebe that they would all miss her at Christmas but they knew she would have a wonderful time in Thailand. In the second, she agreed with Leah that they needed to discuss the progress of the Merrily campaign and suggested that she visit Leah on Friday evening since Felix would be at a partner's farewell dinner in Bath and would be able to pick her up at the end of the evening. This reminded her that the Merrily campaign was another secret she was keeping from Felix and she inwardly vowed that she would delay the implementation of her No Secrecy resolution until the new year.

After a quick lunch of biscuits and cheese, she changed into her grey dress and black shoes, snatched her coat and bag, said goodbye to Magnus and ran out to the car. She had an appointment to see a Georgian terrace in Bath after which she hoped to do some Christmas shopping.

The house was just off the London Road and Alison was pleasantly surprised to find a parking place without difficulty. It was an interesting fact, she thought, that when one was in a good mood, good luck seemed to follow one.

More good luck awaited her at her destination. The door was opened by a man who was probably a few years younger than her. He wore jeans and an unbuttoned denim shirt over a black T-shirt. He had dark hair and warm brown eyes that were focused exclusively on Alison.

'You must be Mrs Coward,' he said.

Alison held out her hand. 'Please call me Alison.'

The man took her hand and shook it firmly. 'Only if you call me Adam,' he said and smiled.

Adam was gorgeous.

He helped her off with her coat and asked her if she preferred to go round properties on her own. He would, he assured her, be very happy to provide her with a guided tour. Alison said she would love to have the tour if he didn't mind her stopping to take photos. Adam said he didn't mind at all.

The house was an interesting combination of traditional period elegance and contemporary sophistication. The kitchen had classic Georgian cornicing, a lofty ceiling and an original fireplace, alongside grey units and black granite surfaces. Upstairs, the sitting room had three generous Georgian windows complete with shutters but was complemented with a slick, black, hole-in-the-wall-style fireplace. Best of all was the master bedroom on the top floor.

'Oh wow,' Alison breathed, 'I love it. It's going to be such fun to write about this. If you don't mind my saying so, this is the sexiest bedroom I've ever seen.'

Adam laughed. 'I don't mind you saying that at all.'

It was enormous, the same size as the sitting room, with similar windows and a high ceiling. The carpet was a sea of cream, the off-white walls were empty apart from a huge, ornate mirror and the eye was irresistibly drawn to the vast four-poster bed planted in the middle of the room.

Alison sighed. 'I'd feel pretty good if I woke up here every morning.'

'I'd feel very good,' Adam said, 'if you woke up here every morning.' He put a hand to his head and stared at her with almost comical horror. 'What have I *said*? I am so sorry! That was appallingly rude. I have this tendency to think aloud. I am so sorry.'

Alison laughed and shook her hair back from her face. 'Please don't apologize,' she said. 'I think it was a very flattering comment.'

'You are very kind,' Adam said. 'Will you allow me to make amends by offering you coffee? I do make very good coffee.'

Adam *did* make good coffee. Alison had never seen anyone take more care over two individual drinks. He ground the beans before putting them in the filtered jug. He heated the milk and then whipped it into a profusion of bubbles. He opened a bar of chocolate, grated a few pieces and sprinkled the flakes onto the finished product. Finally, he watched anxiously as Alison raised her large white china cup to her lips.

Alison plunged her mouth into the dappled froth and then, raising her eyes, noted that Adam was smiling. She looked enquiringly at him.

He leant forward and gently brushed his index finger across the side of her mouth, collecting a stray speck of froth. It was a peculiarly intimate gesture and she was grateful for his laughing comment, 'You see the perils of drinking cappuccino . . .' because it immediately punctured the awkwardness she'd felt when he touched her mouth with his finger, an awkwardness almost wholly caused by a powerful surge of excitement.

'So,' she said, seeking refuge in her professional role, 'there's nothing else I need to see. Have I seen everywhere?'

'Well,' Adam said, 'we rent out a self-contained flat downstairs. The trouble is that the woman we rent it out to is away. I have a key but I can't find it. I'll have another look for it after you've gone.'

'Don't worry too much,' Alison said. 'I can just mention the flat's existence in my article; that will be enough.' She took out a business card from her bag. 'That's got my mobile number and my email address. If you think there's anything further I need to know, you can always get in touch.' She took another sip of her drink. 'This is an *excellent* cup of coffee. You've spoilt me.'

'I'd like to spoil you,' Adam said and almost immediately hit his forehead with his hand. 'Sorry, sorry, sorry! I've done it again! Forget I said that! Change the subject, Adam! Tell me about your job. What's the best house you've ever visited?'

Alison told him and they continued to chat about houses and prices and the readership of magazines like her own until she glanced at her watch. 'I must go,' she said. 'I had no idea it was so late. I've only paid for an hour's parking.'

'There are times,' Adam said with quiet deliberation, 'when I feel quite fierce about traffic wardens.'

Alison laughed. 'I've had a lovely time. Thank you so much.'

As she walked back along the street, she nodded a smile at each passer-by. It had been a long time since she had been openly admired by a good-looking man and she felt literally buoyant, as if she could float away on a tide of confidence and goodwill.

It was only when she was almost home that she remembered she had intended to do some Christmas shopping. Well, she would write up the house instead. The boys had an inter-house competition at school and didn't require collection till half past five. At the very least she should be able to get a first draft completed.

Back at the house, Magnus greeted her with his customary enthusiasm. She put down her bag, took off her coat and knelt down to stroke his ears. 'Hello, Magnus,' she began. 'Who's a lovely—' and then stopped as the house phone rang. She stood up, went over to the dresser and picked up the receiver.

'Mum?' It was Eva. 'I've just been on the phone to Dad.'

An explosion of sobs came through the receiver with Alison pleading impotently, 'Eva? Eva? What is it? . . . Are you all right? . . . What's happened?'

'I'm all right,' Eva said at last. 'I'm really all right! I had my period this morning and it was very heavy and felt weird and Dad says it was a miscarriage. He says it's quite common in the early stages of pregnancy; it often happens to girls who don't even know they've been pregnant. He says there's nothing to worry about. He says he'll talk to you this evening. Mum, I'm so happy. I feel like I've been freed from a life sentence. I can go ahead with the flat next year and I can stay at Manchester and I have to go because I must ring the twins but I wanted to thank you for being so brilliant and I wanted to say –' there followed another few sobs – 'I've never been so happy in my life.'

'Oh Eva, that's wonderful. Take it easy for the next few days, won't you? And ring me very soon and let me know how you are. I am very, very happy for you.'

'Thank you. I love you. I'll talk soon.'

Alison put down the receiver and turned and leant back against the dresser. For a few minutes she didn't move, she simply stood and stared at the old sofa on the opposite wall and tried to take in what Eva had said. There was not going to be a baby. *She* wasn't going to be a grandmother. She wouldn't need to make a nursery and Felix wouldn't need to build a fence round the pond. It was fantastic to hear the relief and the joy in Eva's voice. It was outrageous that she should feel so sad when her daughter was so happy.

She was aware that she was crying but felt too numb to wipe away her tears. Eventually, a sound from her bag roused her and she went across the room to pull out her mobile and read the waiting text message.

Key found. Lunch here on Friday? At one? Yes or no? Love, Adam.

Alison looked at the message for a long time and then texted back one word.

Yes.

CHAPTER EIGHTEEN

Alison's Lunch Doesn't Pass Without Incident

Alison made Felix a cooked breakfast on Friday morning. Felix was pleased, if a little wary. He asked what he'd done to deserve it and Alison gave an awkward laugh and told him she just felt like cooking a breakfast for him.

Driven from their beds by the smell of bacon, the boys both came down unexpectedly early and she had to make them a cooked breakfast too. So for once she was able to drive them to school on time and now here she was, walking Magnus through the woods, trying to rid herself of the guilt that clung like dog pooh on a boot.

Why *should* she feel guilty? All she was going to do was have a light lunch with a vendor while checking out his self-contained apartment.

The fact that the vendor was an extremely attractive man who had intimated he found *her* extremely attractive was neither here nor there. Nor was the fact that the prospect of the lunch filled her with a combined sensation of anticipation and dread. That simply showed what a sad woman she had become. She only ever had lunches with other middle-aged women like herself. Leah probably had lunches with attractive men all the time. Adam had wanted her to see his flat and had rather sweetly invited her to have lunch with him at the same time. Why should she feel guilty about accepting his suggestion?

Alison picked up a stick to help her push back the undergrowth and called to Magnus, who had gone careering off after a squirrel. She wished she could work out why she felt – not guilty, that was too strong – but a little unsure about her lunch-time engagement. She had not told Felix and until recently she had told Felix everything she was doing, even if Felix wasn't particularly interested. But then again there was no sinister reason why she *hadn't* mentioned this lunch. They had been preoccupied by Eva's news and last night she had gone to bed early in a vain attempt to finish Christopher's dreary novel. Felix told her this morning that he'd found her asleep with the book on her face. He said he'd picked it up and read the first paragraph and that was quite enough. Life was definitely too short, he said, to read anything by Christopher Trumpet. Then he smiled and asked for some more bacon. He had been in a good mood ever since Eva's phone call on Monday and the fact that she knew that she should be and wasn't made her feel both guilty and irritable. And somehow, because she was irritated with Felix for failing to understand how she felt, it seemed somehow fair that she didn't tell him about her appointment with Adam. She knew perfectly well that she was being irrational. It was not Felix's fault that he was as pleased as his daughter was to discover there was to be no baby. She was the unnatural parent in this situation.

Alison thrashed a nearby clump of stinging nettles with

her stick, called Magnus again and pulled his lead from the pocket of her anorak. She should stop trying to analyse everything. She was in a bit of a depression and as a result she was looking at everything in a negative way, and that included the forthcoming lunch. She would come home afterwards and wonder what on earth she had been worrying about. This evening, she would go round to Leah and the two of them would have a good laugh about her assignation with a dreamboat.

Back at home, Alison resolutely banned from her mind any further attempts at introspection. Did it matter that she was having such difficulty in deciding what to wear today or that she washed her hair and sprayed her throat with her best perfume? No, it did not. She had had a traumatic week and it would do her good to get out and chat to someone new who seemed to appreciate her.

At ten to one she parked the car and checked her face in the driving mirror. She got out of the car, and after deciding her coat was unnecessary she took it off and threw it into the back seat. She wore her grey sleeveless dress with a cropped pink cardigan and low-heeled shoes. She had dismissed her high heels on the grounds that she didn't want to look as if she had made *too* much of an effort; and besides, she didn't want to tower over Adam, who, she was pretty sure, was only an inch or so taller than her.

As she walked down the street towards Adam's house, she did wish her heart wasn't beating quite so fast since it rather suggested that her heart didn't understand that there was nothing wrong in what she was doing. When she arrived at the house, she found herself hesitating in front of the brass knocker. But then Adam opened the door. He said he'd seen her from the window and was so pleased she was here: wouldn't she come in out of the cold?

He wore dark blue chinos, matching navy blue jersey and a crisp white shirt. He looked as gorgeous as she'd remembered. He gave her a light kiss on the cheek and she caught the lemony scent of his cologne. He told her he'd thought about buying in the food but had made the quiche himself.

The meal was laid out on the table along with napkins and wine glasses. He took from the fridge a bottle of wine. 'I bought a rather serious Chardonnay. I hope you like it.'

'I shouldn't really,' Alison said. 'I'm driving.'

'One glass won't hurt. I'll be sure to make you a large coffee before you go.'

She watched him open the bottle and pour them both glasses before passing one of them to her. 'Thank you,' she said, taking a sip and sitting down at the table.

'I do appreciate you taking the time out to come,' he said, returning the bottle to the fridge. 'I'm sure you must be busy.'

'Things aren't too bad at the moment and anyway it's very nice to be sitting here with you in this lovely house.' Alison shook her hair back from her face. 'Do you ever have the feeling you want to step outside your life for a moment or two and do something out of the ordinary?'

'Oh I do,' he assured her. 'I get that feeling quite often these days. May I ask what's been happening in your life to make you feel like that right now?'

She shrugged. 'You wouldn't want to know. It's all too silly.'

'I *would* like to know. Please tell me and while you tell me, help yourself to all this. I meant to make all sorts of complicated salads but it took so long to make the pastry I only had time to do something simple.'

'I didn't want you to go to any trouble,' Alison said, cutting into the quiche and carefully easing a portion onto her plate. 'This looks terrific.'

'I hope so.' Adam sat down next to her and fixed her with a purposeful eye. 'Now tell me what's been going on in your life.'

So she did. She wasn't sure what prompted her to unburden herself but his eyes looked at her with such sympathy and concern that somehow she knew he would understand. She told him about Eva's pregnancy and her own response to it and she told him about Eva's miscarriage and her own response to that and the fact that she couldn't express her feelings to Felix or Eva because they would have thought she was crazy.

'And they'd be right,' she said. 'I can see that. As far as Eva's concerned, she has had a reprieve from what must have seemed like a life sentence. She can move into a flat next year with her friends and continue doing her degree and then start a career. Why can't I be like Felix and celebrate that? I feel so selfish and self-absorbed.' She took another sip of her wine. 'I told you it was silly.'

Adam passed her the bowl of green salad. 'I don't think it's silly at all. It's obvious that you're a fantastic mother. You've gone through one hell of a drama. I suspect it's a lot easier for your husband. I'm guessing his job is important to him?'

Alison gave a weary nod. 'Oh, it is. Don't get me wrong, I don't grudge him his work. I know he's a very good doctor and I respect that but—'

'It makes it difficult for you to talk to him about your feelings at the moment? I'm sure it is. You've been the one to bring up the children and keep the family together. Like the good mother you are, you thought of a solution to your daughter's problem. I bet you've spent hours and hours and hours thinking about it.'

'You're right, but that's not the point.'

'I think it's precisely the point. You're used to putting your family first. You spent a huge amount of time working out how you could look after your daughter's baby for her and now you don't have to. Your husband and your daughter have already moved on and you can't and you feel guilty. You do feel guilty, don't you?'

Alison nodded.

'You can learn from this,' Adam said. 'You need to start thinking about yourself a bit more. You have as much right to an independent life as do your husband and children. There's a life beyond your family. There are experiences beyond your family. You are an extremely attractive and fascinating woman.' He stopped and gave a rueful laugh. 'I'm sorry. I have a habit of speaking my mind. You must tell me if I'm speaking out of turn.'

'You're being very helpful,' Alison assured him.

'I do feel,' Adam said, 'that you need to stop submerging yourself in family concerns. Your children are grown and no longer need you. That is a cause for celebration not commiseration. You are free. There is so much to discover. Look at you and me. We met for the first time on Monday and already I feel as if I know you. I don't understand it but I feel we're kindred spirits, you and I.' He laughed. 'I know that sounds ridiculously clichéd but I mean it.'

'I think it sounds lovely.' Alison smiled at him. 'You are a kind man.'

'Kindness has nothing to do with it,' Adam said, looking at her intently. He glanced suddenly at her plate. 'You've hardly touched my quiche. Is the pastry that bad?'

'It's very good. I've been talking too much to eat. In fact, I've been talking far too much about myself and now I'd like to hear about *you*. Why are you selling this beautiful house, for instance?'

'That's easy.' Adam drained his glass and went to the fridge to refill it. 'Penny and I moved in here six years ago. She's a make-up artist. At the time, she was struggling. It didn't seem to matter since we planned to have a family and I was happy to support her. And then her career took off; she had to spend more time in London, we shelved the family plans for a year and then another year and then another year after that. A few months ago she told me she'd met someone else. I should have seen it coming. She's younger than me and she's not exactly the maternal type, if you know what I mean. If I'm honest I was always the one who wanted to have babies. I can't really blame her.' He gave a small shrug. 'Of course I say all this to you and I sound so rational and understanding, but actually I feel pretty bleak a lot of the time. For so long I've been planning a future for the two of us and now it's only me. Cue the violins. I do sound sorry for myself, don't I?'

'Well, that's completely understandable,' Alison said. 'If I were you, I'd be feeling just the same. But if I can speak as an impartial outsider, I have to tell you that I know things will get better for you. Can I speak frankly? You're good-looking and you're charming . . . I would bet any amount of money that you won't be on your own for long!'

Adam gave a sad smile. 'You're very kind.'

Alison laughed. 'What was it you said? Kindness has nothing to do with it!'

Adam leant forward and kissed her gently on the mouth. 'Thank you,' he said. 'Thank you for making me feel better.'

Alison was rather taken aback. She said uncertainly, 'That's quite all right.'

Adam glanced at her plate. 'Are you really going to leave my quiche?'

'I'm sorry,' Alison said. 'I'm just not hungry today. I don't know why.'

'I do,' Adam said. 'Your mind is on other things. Shall we go upstairs now?'

'I'm sorry?' Alison asked.

Adam put a hand on her knee. 'I thought we might revisit that bedroom you liked so much.' The hand on her knee began teasing back the hem of her dress. 'Do you want to know something? I woke up this morning and imagined you lying on my bed.'

Alison was hypnotized by the fingers of his hand, which were crawling up her thigh with the slow and steady persistence of an earwig on a tree trunk. She swallowed and then clamped her hand on top of his. 'Do you want to *have sex* with me?'

For a moment, Adam looked disconcerted and then he smiled. 'I don't want to have sex,' he assured her, 'I want to make love.'

'Well, I don't want to do either,' Alison said, 'at least

not with you.' She pushed back her chair and stood up. 'Is that why you asked me to lunch? You thought I'd go to bed with you?'

Adam's smile wavered and then disappeared. 'If I may say so,' he said, 'you made it pretty obvious you wanted it.'

'I did not,' Alison said hotly. 'I can't believe you just said that.'

'You couldn't have made it any clearer. So I made a quiche and I bought an extremely expensive bottle of wine—'

'Which you drank!' Alison cried. 'I had one tiny glass. And anyway,' she added, picking up her bag from the floor, 'it jolly well is *not* an expensive bottle of wine. It's on a special offer from Sainsbury's at four pounds ninety-nine. I know that because I bought the very same brand only the other day – in fact, I bought six of them for the very good reason,' her voice was rising dangerously now, 'that if you buy six of them you can get another ten per cent off as well.' She stormed out of the kitchen towards the front door and her grand exit was marred only by her inability to open it.

Adam came up behind her. 'Alison,' he said, 'I'm disappointed. We're two unhappy, confused people. Why don't we go upstairs and make each other happy? I promise you, if you let me, I can make all your problems disappear.'

Alison finally managed to open the door. 'I don't *have* any problems,' she said, 'but I would do if I went upstairs with you.' She shot out onto the pavement and began to walk off. 'And by the way,' she shouted, turning abruptly, 'your pastry had way too much flour.'

CHAPTER NINETEEN

Leah Analyses Why the Rite of Seduction is Not Always Quite Right

'I don't understand,' Molly persisted, 'why we can't come home on Sunday morning.'

Leah pulled up at the traffic lights and switched on the windscreen wipers. She disliked driving in the dark, she hated driving in the dark when it was raining and she utterly loathed driving in the dark when it was raining while she was trying to have a reasonable discussion with her daughter.

'You haven't stayed with your father for ages,' she said. 'It's only fair he should have you for the whole weekend.'

'He's seeing us tonight and all day tomorrow *and* on Sunday morning. Why can't we come home for Sunday lunch?'

'The thing is,' Fred said, joining in the debate for the first time, 'we don't get Sunday lunch with Dad. He doesn't know how to cook it.'

Encouraged by her brother's unsolicited support, Molly's voice acquired a wistful note. 'And we do love Sunday lunch.'

'I've already explained,' Leah said, moving on as the lights changed colour, 'that Charlotte is leaving her friends and coming home in time for lunch on Sunday so that she can see you. She knows very well that the only reason you're happy to stay with Jamie this weekend is because she won't be there for most of the time. If you were leaving just as she came back it would be rude and hurtful. She's very keen to get to know you better. She likes you.'

'Well, I don't like *her*,' Molly said.

'She's a nice woman. I know. I've talked to her. And she's going to be the mother of your half-sister or half-brother.'

'I don't want a half-sister or half-brother,' Molly said.

'And anyway,' Leah said, 'I won't have time to cook a proper lunch on Sunday because I'll be going to the Harrisons for a drink and –' she glanced at her driving mirror as she realized she had a trump card to play – 'if I collected you both on Sunday morning, you'd have to come with me.'

There was a thoughtful silence in the back of the car. Leah knew very well that Molly and Fred found Richard Harrison boring and Tanya Harrison irritating. For the rest of the short journey, Leah was left in peace with her thoughts, or rather her one thought: she would have saved herself a lot of bother if she had remembered about the Harrison invitation as soon as Molly started her onslaught.

Arriving at Jamie's building, she accompanied the children to the door and watched Molly shout into the entryphone, 'Dad! We're here!'

They heard Jamie call, 'I'm coming,' and Molly whispered to her mother, 'If you decide not to go to the Harrisons on Sunday, let us know and we'll come home.'

'Molly, you are going to have lunch with Jamie and Charlotte on Sunday and you are going to be nice to Charlotte and—'

The door opened and Leah adopted a brisk cheerfulness. 'Here we are! I'm delivering two very hungry children to your door! You did say you'd give them supper?'

Jamie smiled. 'I've got a takeaway in the kitchen. The prawn crackers are on the table.'

'Goodbye, Mum,' Molly said, giving Leah's waist a quick embrace and raising her head to whisper dramatically, 'Don't forget!' before flying off in pursuit of the prawn crackers.

Fred said, 'See you on Sunday,' and gave Leah a quick, fervent hug before chasing after his sister.

Jamie put his hands in his pockets and said a little awkwardly, 'Thanks for talking to Charlotte last week. She likes you.'

'I like her too,' Leah said. 'I'm glad she dropped by.'

'Yes.' Jamie gave her one of his more inscrutable glances. 'Do you have to rush off? There's enough Chinese, if you'd like to join us.'

'Thanks,' Leah said, 'but Alison's coming over to supper. Goodbye, Jamie.'

She walked quickly back to the car. She hated these handover occasions, particularly when Jamie acted as if he wanted her to come in, even more particularly when Fred showed that he wanted her to come in too.

Back at home, she made a spinach and blue cheese sauce and put together a salad. She was glad Alison was coming round: hopefully, she would dispel the stubborn depression that had settled on her spirits like snow. Leah opened a bottle of wine and poured herself a glass. On an impulse, she picked up her notepad and began to write.

SECOND MEETING OF CLOM

1: Merrily's confidence boosted by haircut, clothes and photo but constant vigilance is necessary in light of Christopher's attitude.

2: How do we dent Merrily's confidence in Christopher? We made clear our distaste for his nose remark. Should we continue to show our dislike of the man?

OR . . .

Should we be nice to Christopher? If Merrily sees Christopher respond to Leah's undoubted beauty, she will lose yet more confidence. If, however, Merrily sees him respond to the wiles of both Leah and Alison, she might be forced to see that he is simply a randy old goat who would sleep with anyone.

Leah heard the doorbell ring and paused only to add with a flourish:

Leah welcomes Alison's suggestions.

She went out to the hall to let in her friend. She was a little surprised by Alison's appearance. Her blonde hair was tied back in a severe ponytail and she wore a check shirt and old jeans. Leah herself was dressed informally in leggings and a baggy jumper but it was unlike Alison to go anywhere without making a modicum of effort.

She settled Alison at the kitchen table and offered her a glass of wine.

'I'd better not,' Alison said. 'I'm driving.'

'I thought you were getting Felix to pick you up.'

'Well, I'm going to pick *him* up now.' Alison looked a little uncomfortable. 'It seemed a bit mean not to let him drink tonight. He's at this farewell party in town and there'll be lots of booze.' She hesitated. 'Give me half a glass.'

Leah poured the wine, and after putting water on for the spaghetti she sat down opposite Alison. 'Diana has lent me a Sandra Bullock DVD. We can watch it after supper, if you like.'

'That would be nice,' Alison said. 'I could do with cheering up.'

'I was hoping you'd cheer *me* up,' Leah said. 'What's wrong with you?'

'What's wrong with *you*?'

'I didn't tell you,' Leah said. 'I had a visit from Charlotte last week.'

'What did she want? Is she pretty?'

'She is beautiful. I mean, she is really, really beautiful: long blonde hair, big blue eyes, perfect skin. Even her bump is beautiful.'

'Oh Leah!' Alison said. 'I'm so sorry.'

'I don't mind about that – well, I do, it's not the greatest feeling in the world to know that you could never look that good even if you were ten years younger – but she's nice too, which is even worse. I can see she really loves

Jamie, she wants to love his children and she doesn't know how to cope with Molly. Which I can understand, because I'm Molly's mother and I don't know how to cope with Molly.' Leah stood up abruptly. 'I've forgotten our starter: very naughty crisps and very lovely hummus.' She took the latter out of the fridge and reached into the larder-cupboard for the crisps.

'I shouldn't,' Alison said. 'I'm trying to lose weight.'

'You don't need to lose weight,' Leah said. 'And it's Friday, after all. Now, what was I saying?'

'You said you didn't know how to cope with Molly.'

'I remember,' Leah nodded. 'The thing is that talking to Charlotte made me see how everything we do has these unforeseen consequences. I couldn't cope with Jamie's affairs. So I left him and I screwed up the kids and they hate that we're apart and they're terrified I'll meet someone else and that's why Molly gets so jealous – and I know you think I indulge Molly but it's my fault she's like that. I left Jamie and now he's gone off with Charlotte, who's a lovely girl and deserves better than Jamie, and he'll screw her up and he'll screw the new baby up and if I hadn't left Jamie none of this would have happened. We'd still be a family unit.'

'Leah,' Alison said, dipping a crisp in the hummus, 'for an intelligent woman, you do sometimes spout a great deal of rubbish. Have you forgotten what you were like when you were married to Jamie? You adored him. I've never met anyone who tried so hard to make a marriage work. You turned a blind eye so often I'm surprised you didn't develop a permanent squint. You worked overtime to make excuses for him: Jamie's so handsome, he can't help it if women flirt with him, Jamie has to go out a lot, in his job he needs to network, it's difficult for Jamie, he was never sure he wanted children . . .'

'It *was* difficult for Jamie; he found the idea of being a father very scary.'

'Jamie's problem was that he never wanted to grow up and take responsibility for anyone else. He was very happy to have Molly and Fred once they were born, so long as you did all the work. He made you miserable! Admit it!'

'Some of the time he did,' Leah conceded.

'If you hadn't left Jamie when you did, you'd have become a total wreck. Yes, it's been difficult for the children, but things weren't easy for them anyway. They could sense things weren't right. You forget what you were like. You were crying a lot, you got those headaches. Of course you had to leave him. And who's to say that if you hadn't left him, he wouldn't have met Charlotte and got her pregnant and wanted to leave you anyway? There are some men – and Jamie is one of them – who are genetically incapable of being monogamous. You were never going to change that.'

'You might be right,' Leah said. 'I just feel a bit of a failure at the moment.' She got up to put the spaghetti in the boiling water. 'You're very lucky, you know. I wish my life was as straightforward as yours.'

'Leah,' Alison said, reaching for another crisp, 'you have no idea.' She pulled at her shirt. 'I've been doing penance all afternoon: my kitchen is now immaculate and I'm abstaining from alcohol so my husband can drink tonight.' She took a deep breath. 'I went out to lunch today. I had lunch with a man.'

Leah grinned. 'You sound like you've committed a major sin.'

Alison stared mournfully at Leah. 'I'm not sure I didn't. He was very attractive.'

'Was he single?'

Alison nodded.

'You should introduce me,' Leah said. 'Alison?' She paused and gave an incredulous laugh. 'Are you telling me you had some sort of secret assignation?'

'No! It wasn't secret. He was selling his house and he invited me to lunch so I could see more of his property for my article. It wasn't secret. I mean, I didn't tell Felix, but it wasn't secret.'

'Well, in that case, then,' Leah said, 'what's the problem?'

Alison shrugged her shoulders. 'If you really want to know, I made a complete idiot of myself. It was awful. It was excruciating. He thought I wanted to go to bed with him.'

Leah laughed. 'You wicked woman!'

'It's not funny, Leah. If you're not going to listen seriously—'

'I'm sorry.' Leah couldn't remember a time when she'd seen Alison look so miserable. 'Tell me everything.'

'It was fine at first. He was very attentive and seemed so kind and concerned and I just started telling him *everything*.'

'I don't understand,' Leah said. 'Am I missing something here?'

Alison took another crisp. 'You really shouldn't have put these out,' she said. She fixed Leah with weary eyes. 'Eva rang me last week to tell me she was pregnant. I went up to Manchester to see her. She was in a terrible state. She didn't know what to do.' Alison pulled off her hair scrunchy and shook her hair free. 'And then on Monday she had a miscarriage. It wasn't traumatic or painful. She just started bleeding like she had a bad period.'

'What a relief. At least there's no need for poor Eva to think about terminations and things. At least it's all sorted now.'

'Yes. It all seems rather unreal. One minute I have an unmarried teenage daughter who's pregnant and the next . . .'

'You were an unmarried pregnant teenager for a while. These things happen. In your case you were born to have hundreds of children. I'm surprised you stopped at Nathan.'

'Felix had a vasectomy.'

'So he did. The point is, Eva's not like you. She'd have found it far more difficult. It sounds like you all had a lucky escape.'

'I suppose. One way or another, it's been a difficult time. I'm not trying to justify what I did with Adam—'

'What *did* you do with Adam?'

'I didn't do anything with him. I *did* tell him about Eva and he seemed so sympathetic and interested and then he told me he was selling his house because his girlfriend had left him and then he asked me – quite casually, as if he was asking if I'd like some tea – he asked me if I'd like to go upstairs.'

'He didn't waste any time! What did you say?'

'Well, really, Leah, what do you think I said? I said no, of course. But it was what he said afterwards that hurt.

He made me feel as if I were to blame, as if I were the one who'd led him on. He said I'd admired his bedroom.'

'*Did* you admire his bedroom?'

'Yes, but I often admire people's bedrooms and it is a beautiful bedroom: it has a cream woollen carpet, a fantastic four-poster right in the middle of the room. Anyone would love it. All I said was that I'd love to wake up in a room like that. I didn't mean I wanted to wake up in the room with *him*!'

'Yes, but he's not to know that your idea of nirvana is a day in Ikea. All he can see is that he's showing you his bedroom and you go weak at the knees.'

'It's my job to inspect his bedroom! I have to write about his bedroom!'

'I know, but men are very good at seeing what they want to see. Personally, I wouldn't waste time thinking about him. Either he's rotten at seducing women – I mean, you'd think he'd realize that women usually need a bit of time and subtlety before they're ready to commit adultery – or he's so attractive, he doesn't usually have to put in the ground work.'

'Leah,' Alison said, 'do you know how cynical you sound? Are you saying that if he had shown more time and subtlety I *would* have gone to bed with him?'

'I'm not saying *you* would have succumbed, I'm saying that some women might well have been tempted. The point is that he's obviously an arrogant idiot and I don't understand why you're so upset. You did nothing to be ashamed of.'

'No.' Alison looked unconvinced. She picked up Leah's notepad. 'What's this?'

'You can read it while I drain the spaghetti.'

Alison looked at Leah. 'There was a moment in the kitchen when – I mean, it was only for a moment but . . .'

'You wanted to have sex with him? So what? I spend my time fantasizing about having sex with unsuitable men; it doesn't mean I'm actually going to do anything about it.'

'Well, in your case it probably does,' Alison said matter-of-factly. 'And it's all right for you because you're single and you've slept with hundreds of men and—'

'Alison, I have not!'

'But what you forget is that I have only ever slept with Felix! Phoebe's only nineteen and to my certain knowledge she's already slept with three men. At least Felix got to sleep with a few women before he met me.'

'It's not the quantity that counts,' Leah said, 'it's the quality. Do you enjoy sex with Felix?'

'Yes, of course, but . . .'

'There's no of course about it. I have had sex that has been so boring I've slept through it. If you're still having a good time in bed with Felix after a lifetime of regular bonking then, believe me, you are a lucky woman.'

'I know I am. It's this business with Eva.' Alison reached for another crisp and dipped it into the hummus. 'I feel all over the place at the moment.'

'I'm not surprised. What about the would-have-been father? Is he still on the scene?'

Alison frowned and then stared intently at Leah. 'If I tell you something,' she said, 'you must promise not to tell a soul. And by the way, Harry and Nathan don't even know that Eva was pregnant, so you must never say anything in front of them.'

'I won't say anything to anyone,' Leah assured her. She had hoped to be diverted from her own worries tonight and, boy, was she being diverted. As she glanced at Alison's miserable face the thought occurred to her, not for the first time, that one should be careful what one wished for.

Alison gave a heavy sigh. 'You know her friends Robbie and Ronnie? The night before she went to university, she slept with them both. Apparently, they all wanted to get rid of their virginity before they sallied out into the world.'

'Wow.' Leah put the lettuce in the salad shaker and twisted the handle vigorously. 'Did she go to bed with both of them at the same time?'

'Really, Leah, how do I know?' Alison looked aghast. 'I don't want to think about it. It's bad enough that she felt she had to sleep with one of them, let alone both of them. I blame myself. I told her the facts of life years ago and thought that was enough. I should have talked to her about sex and peer pressure and love and things but she's never really had a proper boyfriend so I didn't think it was necessary. I let her down.'

'She's eighteen,' Leah said. 'You can't control what she does. You have to accept she's going to make mistakes. We all do.'

Alison took a tissue from her trouser pocket and blew her nose. 'I don't feel I have control over anyone, least of all my family. I've spent my entire adult life bringing up four children and I'm beginning to feel I don't know any of them. And I certainly don't know Adam. There I am, sitting having lunch with him, and he tells me it's time to have new experiences and I'm nodding away at him, thinking how wise he is, and the only experience he can come up with is for me to go and have some rumpy-pumpy on his bed with him – Leah, it is *not* funny.'

'I'm sorry,' Leah grinned. 'I can *see* you hanging on to his every word. He must have thought he had you in the bag!'

'It only goes to show,' said Alison sadly, 'that I don't understand people.'

It was clear that Alison's confidence had been badly dented. Leah gave her hand a reassuring squeeze. 'I think you're being far too hard on yourself. You made a mistake about Adam because you were preoccupied with Eva. It's totally understandable that you're all over the place at the moment.' She nodded at the notebook. 'Have a look at that instead while I serve out the spaghetti. I've made a few more additions to your CLOM manifesto.'

Alison picked up the notepad and Leah turned her attention to her saucepan. She couldn't resist glancing at Alison to see the effect of her deliberately provocative suggestions. In fact, Alison was staring thoughtfully across the room at Stephen in his place above the fridge.

'I suppose,' she said slowly, 'it might be a good idea if we both encourage Christopher.'

'It would be rather a volte-face from both of us, and especially me,' Leah pointed out. 'Last time I was on my own with him, I was very angry with him.'

'I don't think that matters,' Alison said. 'You can easily make him think you like him really. And if I flatter him as well we might be able to induce some cringe-making behaviour from him and, if that happens, Merrily will see what sort of man he really is. It could work.'

'It's worth trying,' Leah said. 'But, at the same time, we need to indicate to Merrily that we don't rate him.'

Alison sighed. 'This is not going to be easy. I've invited them both to supper next week. Are you sure you won't come?'

'Definitely not. And anyway we can't both fall on Christopher at the same time. It would simply confuse him. You can do the big seduction bit on your own.'

'That's all very well,' said Alison, 'but I also have to show Merrily how much better Felix is than Christopher while making Christopher think I think he's gorgeous while making Merrily think I think he's pretty tedious and meanwhile I have to keep Felix in the dark because he'd refuse to let me interfere otherwise.' She sighed. 'It's going to be a very exhausting evening.'

CHAPTER TWENTY

Leah Attends an Exceptional Party

By the time she went to bed on Saturday night, Leah thought she could justifiably feel satisfied with her contribution to the new campaign. It had certainly been an interesting day and Alison would be impressed by the skill with which she had negotiated the opportunities that had presented themselves to her.

She had dropped in on Merrily late in the morning. Merrily was in her painting overalls, eager to show her what she'd been doing in her son's bedroom. 'I hope you like it,' she said. 'I reckon I'll have finished it by bedtime.'

'I'll stay and help, if you like,' Leah said. 'You don't need to feed me, I've only just had breakfast.'

'Have a bit of bread and cheese at least,' Merrily said. 'It's all on the table.'

They were joined by Christopher, who was in a playful mood. When Leah told them she'd drunk far too much wine the night before, he fixed her with a meaningful smile and said, 'You should be careful with alcohol when you're out on the town. Strange things can befall attractive women when they drink alcohol, Leah. You never know what might happen!'

Leah dredged up a smile from somewhere and said, 'That's very true but I'd hardly call an evening at home with only Alison for company a night out on the town.'

He was incapable of complimenting women without patronizing them and the fact that he was so blatantly referring to their night together made her itch to slap him. Mindful of the need for cunning dissimulation, Leah managed an additional simper and changed the subject by asking him how his work was going. Christopher announced with a sad little sigh that he was having problems with motivation. 'I shall be working right through till midnight,' he said. 'A writer's life can be a lonely one.'

'It certainly can,' Leah said and nodded thoughtfully as if struck by the immensity of Christopher's task. 'But at least Merrily needn't be lonely too.' She turned to Merrily and smiled. 'Why don't you come out with me this evening? I'm going to the cinema with a girlfriend. You'll like Anthea, she's a teacher, like you.'

'Merrily,' Christopher said with a hint of reproof, 'is no longer a teacher.'

'It sounds fun,' said Merrily, glancing anxiously at her husband. 'But it's not fair on Christopher. He'll need some dinner.'

'We can get it ready for him before we go,' Leah said. She gave Christopher her warmest smile. 'You won't mind that, will you? I'm sure you wouldn't want to keep Merrily from having fun?'

'Well,' Christopher said, 'if Merrily feels she can enjoy herself while I'm working hard, then of course I don't mind.'

'I'll do my best to make sure she does,' Leah said briskly.

'And don't forget: she and I are going to be working hard on your son's bedroom all afternoon.'

'Perhaps, Leah,' Christopher said, '*you* would like to bring my tea at three o'clock?'

After lunch, the two women went up to Tom's bedroom and Leah was sincere in her admiration. Merrily had almost finished it and the room was virtually unrecognizable. The ceiling was now a gleaming white and the crimson walls were replaced by a smooth golden veneer. The window frame, skirting board and door had been given a white undercoat and, as Leah said, all that was left to do was the fun part with the blue topcoat. Merrily said she'd tackle the window frame and Leah suggested that she start on the door.

While they painted, Merrily talked about Tom: his ease with people, his prowess on the guitar, his enthusiasm for football. She said she couldn't wait to introduce him to Alison and Leah; Alison had invited him along to her Christmas party and they would be able to see how good-looking he was. Merrily was almost like her old self, talking in a breathless rush, words tumbling over themselves in her efforts to communicate her thoughts. Tom was so clever too, she said. Had she mentioned that he wanted to be a doctor, like Alison's husband and brother? 'And oh,' she laughed, 'did you know that I used to have a gigantic crush on Alison's brother? I loved him for years!'

'You wouldn't nowadays,' Leah said. 'He's fat and bald and incredibly pompous. He talks at people as if they're his medical students. His poor wife is never allowed to speak. You had a lucky escape there.'

'It's funny how some people change,' said Merrily. 'It

makes you wonder whether they'd always be like that or whether it's the things that happened to them. I thought I'd change when I married Christopher. I certainly wanted to.'

'But you didn't?' Leah prompted.

Merrily smiled. 'Not really. That's not Christopher's fault. If you're not happy with yourself, you can't blame anyone else. It's up to you to do something about it.'

It was perhaps just as well that Christopher's bell rang at that moment since Leah was tempted to throw caution to the winds and tell her exactly what she could do. Instead, Merrily said, 'Oh dear, Christopher wants his tea,' and Leah put down her paintbrush and said she'd go and get it for him.

Knocking on Christopher's door, she was struck once more by the contrast between his study – warm, cosy, well lit and well furnished – and the rest of the house. She said as much to Christopher and he said complacently, 'It *is* nice, isn't it? It used to be the sitting room, you know. I need to be comfortable when I work.' He beckoned her over. 'Put the tea on my desk, will you?'

It was after she had put it on the coaster next to his computer that she felt his hand stroke her thigh. This time, she looked down at him with a smile that would have impressed Alison. 'Christopher,' she said, 'you are a very naughty man, you know.'

'Leah,' he murmured, 'I could be a lot naughtier if you'd let me.' He took her hand and guided it down between his legs. 'Tell me you're not as tempted as I am.'

Leah would have loved to let him know exactly what she was tempted to do. However, she could almost feel Alison hovering by her side, muttering, 'Tact and subtlety,' and contented herself with another sickly smile. All credit to him, she thought, his member was certainly ready for action. She issued a wistful sigh, and moving gently out of range she said, 'Oh Christopher, I am *very* tempted but I think we should restrain ourselves, don't you?'

'You could always send Merrily out with your friend this evening,' he said. 'And you could come over here.'

'I could,' Leah said, 'but I think my friend Anthea would find it rather odd if I wasn't there. And I can't imagine what I'd say to Merrily.' She gave him a light, little laugh and walked out of the room. For a man who was supposed to hold the key to the human psyche, he was incredibly dense. Alternatively, Leah supposed, she might be an exceptionally good actress. Either way, Christopher had shown himself to be conceited, amoral, disgusting, lecherous and outrageous. And that was being kind to him. He didn't deserve to live in the same house as Merrily, let alone be married to her. And if Leah had her way, he soon wouldn't be.

The film in the evening was a rather gory thriller and Merrily seemed to spend most of it with her hands covering her eyes. Afterwards, Anthea and Leah felt in need of a drink and they persuaded Merrily that she needed one too.

Anthea, like most of Leah's girlfriends, was single. She had not been single for very long and she was soon on her favourite subject: the dastardly nature of her ex-husband. Since his many crimes – refusal to lift a duster, unreasonable demands on her time, inability to appreciate his children – were mere trifles compared to those of Christopher,

Leah felt the evening had given Merrily much food for thought. She and Leah shared a cab home and when Leah said goodbye and suggested another girls' night out soon, Merrily agreed with enthusiasm.

On Sunday morning, Leah woke with the pleasurable complacency of one who has performed well. She reached for her book and decided she deserved an extra half-hour in bed. There were moments when not having children at the weekends was a positive bonus.

The Harrison party was at twelve. When Leah had a final check in the mirror she decided she was satisfied with her appearance – grey overgrown-jersey dress, which was in fact just an overgrown jersey, her favourite leather belt, black tights and high-heeled ankle boots. It was a pity, she thought, resolutely casting David from her mind, that there would be no one there she wished to impress.

The party was in full swing when she arrived. There was something not quite right and Leah couldn't work out what it was. All the usual suspects were there. Leah flitted between the doctors from Number Seven, Amanda Johnson from Number Three with her loud laugh and the husband whose name Leah could never remember, and old Mr Carter with his bow tie and mustard-coloured waistcoat. As usual, Richard Harrison was an assiduous host, passing round cheese straws and smoked-salmon sandwiches. As usual, Tanya Harrison held court by the fire, smoking furiously and gesticulating wildly.

Leah had always found Richard rather attractive. He was a big bear of a man and made her feel pleasantly fragile and feminine. She could see why the children found him dull. He liked to talk about politics and the community and had twice been a local councillor. He didn't have a great sense of humour but he had a self-deprecatory way of referring to himself which was all the more endearing given that he had a highly successful probate business.

As for Tanya, there was something almost heroic about her persistent depiction of herself as the put-upon wife when everyone knew that she micromanaged every spare moment of Richard's time. Today, for example, just like every year, she stayed rooted to her position in front of the fire, regularly checking on Richard to make sure he was doing a non-stop circuit with wine and canapés.

And yet today there was something definitely not quite right. There was a febrile atmosphere in the room as if everyone was waiting for something to happen.

And then it did. Tanya clapped her hands and called out for silence. 'First of all,' she said, 'I'd like to thank you for coming to our party today. Amanda has just told me that she always regards our annual get-together as the starting gun for Christmas and I hope you all feel suitably festive.' She gave a complacent smile as her audience responded with the expected affirmative cheers, and then took a last drag of her cigarette before throwing it into the fire. 'Secondly, Richard and I have something to tell you and I do hope you will find it as exciting as we do. Richard and I have decided to end our marriage!'

Tanya made this revelation in a tone of huge enthusiasm and she glanced round the room expectantly, as if she hoped for an ovation. 'I know you will all feel this is distressing but, actually,' she paused for dramatic effect, 'it isn't! I do believe that every marriage has a natural shelf-life and that most long-term marriages are held together by convention rather than by love.' Her eyes fell on the Appletons, a sweet old couple who responded to Tanya's attention with startled confusion. 'Richard and I are not people to be governed by convention. Some of you might condemn us for splitting up when our girls are still young. But at their boarding school most of their friends are children of divorced parents so divorce is not a concept that frightens them. I know that when I tell them what is happening they will both understand and respect our decision. Richard and I face a challenging future. I am moving to Bristol to be with my new partner. Some of you have met Graham Cox and I know you will all wish me well. As for Richard, he is setting out on a fabulous new path as a single man, ready to embrace any new experience he encounters. So,' Tanya gave a little laugh, 'there you are! Enjoy the rest of the party and be as happy for us as we are. Thank you!'

Leah glanced across at Richard. He stood by the door to the kitchen, a bowl of cheese balls in his hands. He looked utterly, utterly miserable.

There was a shocked silence in the room and then, as people resumed their now hushed and stilted conversations, Leah slipped across to Richard and put a hand on his arm. 'Richard,' she said, 'I am so sorry.'

It was awful. He looked at her with stricken eyes and opened his mouth to speak and then shut it again. She said, 'Look, I'm going now. But any time, any time at all that you feel you need a friend, come over and we'll down a bottle of wine together.'

He looked down at the half-empty bowl and then swallowed hard. 'Dear Leah,' he said. 'You are very kind. If you'll excuse me, I think I'd better fill this bowl.'

She watched him dive into the kitchen and then looked across at Tanya, who was now talking with great gusto to the doctors. Leah took a deep breath and walked over to her hostess.

'Leah, how lovely to see you,' Tanya beamed. 'What do you think of our news?'

'I know you believe in being honest,' Leah said, 'so I'll tell you. I think it stinks. I think what you've done just now is cruel and stupid and insensitive and I can't bear to stay here a moment longer. I'd like to wish you happiness in your new life – well, actually, I wouldn't, Tanya, and I very much doubt you will be happy with Graham Cox and I'm pretty sure he won't be happy with *you*. I'm sorry if I've been rude but that's what happens when one believes in being honest.' Without waiting for a response, she turned on her heel, walked out of the room and out of the house.

Almost as soon as she left, she regretted her explosion of temper. Back at home, she set about making a bacon sandwich for her lunch. Had she been unfair to Tanya? Had Tanya really believed her conduct was the best way to announce a marital split? If so, she would have to be stupid and Tanya might be many things but stupid she was not. On the other hand, perhaps she *was*. She had, after all, chosen Graham Cox over Richard.

The Harrisons had invited Leah to dinner a few months ago. Graham Cox was one of the guests and Leah had thought Tanya was trying to set them up together. Graham was a thin, bespectacled man who brushed his few remaining hairs across his scalp. He had views on everything and expected rapt attention from one and all while he pronounced them. Leah couldn't imagine what Tanya could see in him. Perhaps he was a tiger in bed, in which case he would be a particularly unattractive tiger.

After lunch, she sat down and did some paperwork. The events of the morning had given her an energy she rarely felt on Sunday afternoons and by four she decided she deserved a cup of tea.

She heard children's voices outside and went to the door, saying, 'Hello there! You're back early!'

Jamie stood on the doorstep with his arms on the shoulders of his children. 'I suddenly felt like buying some doughnuts,' Jamie said, 'so we thought we'd come back here for tea.' There was a slightly forced gaiety in his tone from which Leah deduced that all was not well. 'I'll put the kettle on, shall I? Kids, you can get out the plates.'

Leah felt almost sorry for him. He had always enjoyed such effortless authority with his offspring. It must be frustrating to find that he couldn't control their feelings towards his girlfriend.

Once tea and doughnuts were on the table, he visibly relaxed. Leah talked about the film she'd seen the night before and gave a lively account of the plot, adding smugly that Merrily had been unable to cope with at least two of the murders on the screen.

'I could never work out why you liked films like that,' Jamie said. 'I recall one visit to the cinema where you nearly pulled my arm off, you were so terrified.'

Leah laughed. 'I know. But, if you remember, the girl in front of us was far worse than me. She actually screamed at one point.'

Jamie chuckled. 'That was more frightening than the

film.' He glanced appreciatively at Leah. 'You're looking very lovely today.'

A blob of jam had fallen from Leah's doughnut onto the plate. She scooped it up with her finger and licked it. 'I've been to a drinks party.'

Molly made a face. 'Mum went to the Harrisons.'

'They live in Widcombe Crescent,' Leah said. She nodded at the children. 'We might be seeing a lot more of Richard soon. He's going to need all our help. It was a very weird party. The hostess gave a speech and announced to us all that she and the host were getting divorced.'

'That sounds embarrassing,' Jamie said. 'What did the host have to say?'

Leah shook her head at the memory. 'It was horrible. Poor Richard looked so miserable. I couldn't bear to stay. I'm afraid I was very rude to Tanya.'

'What did you say?' Molly asked, moving onto her father's lap.

'I can't quite remember. But I don't think I'll be on her Christmas card list this year.'

'I wish I'd been there.' Jamie smiled. 'You always look great when you're angry.'

'Mummy always looks great all the time,' Molly said piously. 'And she doesn't have a big stomach either.'

Behind her, Jamie kept his face carefully neutral but drew a hand slowly across his throat. Leah's mouth quivered but she said gravely, 'Thank you, Molly.'

'We were talking about Christmas at lunch,' Jamie said, 'and Charlotte had a brilliant idea. She suggested we all have Christmas together. And then I had a brilliant idea too. Why don't we all go down to Mum and Dad on

Christmas morning? Charlotte says she'll drive us since she's off alcohol.'

Leah stared at her ex-husband. So much for the doughnuts. She ought to have known that Jamie never did anything spontaneously. 'Well,' she said, 'I need to think about that. Why don't I ring you from work later this week?'

Jamie didn't blink. 'Well,' he said, 'I think that as this involves Fred and Molly, we might as well sort it out with them now.'

'Well,' said Leah in a voice that was as sweet and as hard as a sugar cube, 'I think it also involves your parents, so . . .'

'No problem,' said Jamie, 'I rang them before we came here. They said they'd love to have us all stay for a couple of days.'

Leah gazed at him with acute dislike. 'Well—' she began.

'Why does Charlotte have to come?' Molly asked, vacating her father's lap and taking up a position by the door.

Jamie's face hardened. 'Do you know something, Molly? I am deeply ashamed of your behaviour towards Charlotte. It's time you accepted that she's part of this family. She's bent over backwards to be kind to you. She's not feeling well and every time you're rude to her, she feels worse. If you *knew* how unhappy you make her—'

'Tell Charlotte,' Leah said quickly, 'I think it's a great idea. I'm sure we'll all have a lovely time at Winchester together.'

The resounding silence that greeted this optimistic assessment was broken by Molly, who asked in a dignified voice if she and Fred could go and play on the computer.

After they'd gone, Jamie gave a weary sigh. 'Thanks, Leah,' he said.

'I'm doing this for Charlotte not for you,' Leah retorted. 'And in future it might help if you discuss your plans with me beforehand instead of springing them on me in front of the children.'

'Agreed,' Jamie said. He reached across to take her hand. 'I'm sorry. You were always too good for me, you know.'

She looked him straight in the eye and said, 'I know.'

It was a defining moment. They both knew he had finally lost the power to hurt her. For years to come, he would probably irritate her, enrage her, even at times endear himself to her, but he would never again be able to hurt her. That this was probably due to the fact that a feckless historian had lodged himself in her heart was something she preferred not to consider.

Once Jamie left, it took an exhausting argument with Molly, a difficult conversation with Fred and a few games of Boggle with both of them to restore the equilibrium. In the circumstances, it was not surprising that she felt like collapsing after the children had gone to bed.

First, she had one important task to perform. She rang Alison and gave a faithful account of the events of the day before. 'Christopher's conceit is boundless,' she said. 'I don't think you'll need to flirt with him next week. You can't very well do that in front of Merrily anyway. What you *can* do is flatter him. Flatter him outrageously. The man's like a whale. He'll swallow any compliment you throw at him. We need to show Merrily that her genius of a husband is actually quite ridiculous. I'm beginning to think that ridicule is the key.'

'I'll do my best,' Alison said. 'But I have to tell you I am already having sleepless nights about next Friday. It's going to be such hard work.'

'I know it will be,' Leah agreed. 'All you have to remember is that we're doing this for Merrily because we have to get her away from Christopher. What you do next week might very well be crucial.'

'Right,' Alison said drily. 'No pressure, then.'

Leah grinned. 'None at all,' she said. 'Goodnight and sleep well.'

CHAPTER TWENTY-ONE

Alison's Party Goes With a Bang

Without the campaign, Alison would be looking forward to having Christopher and Merrily to dinner. Without the campaign, she would be able to chat to Merrily and make Felix look after the odious Christopher. But Leah had rung two days ago to remind Alison to let her know of any developments. It was possible, of course, that Leah had only been teasing her, but even so it had been an uncomfortable reminder that Friday evening was a matter of duty rather than pleasure. It was all very well for Leah to go on about everything *she* had done. It was easy for Leah; she didn't have a husband who had to be cajoled into playing his part, a particularly tricky task since he had no idea he was *supposed* to be part of anything.

Alison slept badly on Thursday night and throughout the following day she was on edge and apprehensive. Her brain went into overdrive, practising ever more strangulated conversations for the evening's dinner.

At eight o'clock, she stood in her kitchen like a gunfighter waiting for her opponent. She had Stilton and broccoli soup simmering on the Aga, a pork casserole inside the Aga and a lemon cheesecake in the fridge. She wore a coffee-coloured dress with a plunging neckline and had covered herself with perfume. She hoped she hadn't overdone it.

Nathan was at the cinema and Harry was out with Nicola. Everything was ready. Alison went through to the sitting room, where Felix was building up the fire. She felt a rush of affection for him and said, 'I love you, Felix.'

He stood up and dusted ash from his trousers. 'I love you too,' he said, 'even if you do insist on having a dinner party on a Friday evening.'

'It's not a dinner party,' she said, 'we're simply having old friends to supper.'

'If Christopher's an old friend,' Felix grunted, 'I fear for our social life.'

'You know what I mean,' Alison said. 'Do you fancy a glass of wine?'

'That's a good idea,' Felix said. 'I think the best way to approach this evening is to get pleasantly plastered.'

'Well, I'm not sure about that,' said Alison uncertainly; but actually, it might not be a bad idea since Felix invariably fell asleep when he drank too much and a sleeping Felix might be a lot easier than a conscious Felix.

There was a knock at the door and Alison said, with a doggedly determined enthusiasm, 'Here we go!'

Christopher's eyes went straight to her chest, which she supposed was a good thing. Merrily took off her Gestapo mac to reveal an elegant figure in a blue shift dress and a turquoise cardigan.

'Merrily,' Alison exclaimed with genuine delight, 'you look fabulous!'

'It's all down to Leah,' Merrily said. 'She took me to her favourite charity shop. The whole outfit was less than twenty pounds.' She stopped to glance nervously at Christopher. 'Leah said it was a real bargain.'

'Leah's right,' Alison said. 'You look amazing. Christopher, doesn't she look lovely?'

Christopher bestowed an indulgent smile on his wife. 'Merrily lost what looks she had some time ago,' he said, 'but it is a pretty dress.'

'If Merrily's lost her looks,' Felix said, coming forward to take their coats, 'then I'm a banana.' He kissed Merrily on the cheek. 'How nice to see you.'

'I think we need a drink,' Alison said with feeling, taking a bottle from the fridge and handing it to her husband, who had rather pointedly failed to greet Christopher.

Fortunately, Christopher had no idea that he had aroused Felix's anger. He was in a benevolent mood. He had had an excellent day, he said, the Muse had been sitting on his shoulder, urging him onwards, and he had written an entire chapter. A writer's life was a curious one, he explained. Every day was different and a single, random reflection could ignite pages of peerless thoughts.

'I'm sure you're right,' Alison said. She cleared her throat. 'It must be so difficult to be a writer. Anthony Trollope's mother was a writer and she used to get up at four every morning so she could do her writing before the family woke up. Her son wrote many of his novels while working full-time for the post office. T. S. Eliot worked for Lloyds Bank. Most writers do have to fit in their writing when they can. They have to make room for their daily responsibilities.'

'I don't,' Christopher said. 'That's why I have Merrily.'

Perhaps, Alison thought, it was just as well that Leah wasn't here. 'Let's go through to the sitting room,' she said.

Christopher settled himself into the armchair by the fire. 'The writing process,' he said, 'is extraordinary. It can be as physically exhausting as any wrestling match. And, of course, there are times of doubt when I question the entire validity of what I am doing. But then I will get an email, like the one I received just before we came here, and at once the entire struggle is worthwhile.'

He looked expectantly around him. Merrily was gazing into the fire and Felix looked as if he had lost the will to live, so Alison said, 'Do tell us what the email said.'

'It was from a woman in Missouri.' Christopher gave a modest smile. 'It was very short and very simple. She had read my latest book, she said, and it had saved her life.'

'Felix saved someone's life last year,' Alison said. 'He was called out to help a child who'd swallowed a toy and was choking. Felix had to pull out a knife and make a hole in the child's windpipe.' She pointed dramatically at her throat.

'Oh how horrible,' gasped Merrily, looking at Felix with awe. 'Weren't you frightened?'

'Yes,' said Felix, 'I was terrified. I've never had to do it before and I rather hope I never have to do it again.'

'You wouldn't believe some of the things Felix tells me,' Alison said. 'Last year, he had a patient he'd sent to a consultant. The consultant said she'd have to have a colostomy. Felix wasn't convinced and arranged to send her to another consultant and he said the same thing.

But Felix still wasn't happy and sent her to another one who discovered it was some extremely unusual condition that could easily be treated with simple medication. Felix makes life-changing decisions every day of his life.'

'I really don't,' Felix said, shifting uncomfortably in his chair. 'I spend most of my time trying to persuade patients they don't need antibiotics for what amounts to a mild attack of flu. Most of my job is extremely pedestrian.'

'I think you're far too modest,' Merrily said. 'There must be times when a good doctor can change lives and it's quite obvious you're a good doctor.'

'You know, Felix,' Christopher said thoughtfully, 'in a funny sort of way, you and I perform the same function. You repair bodies and I repair souls.'

There was a brief silence while the company digested this thought and then Alison said brightly, 'I'll just go and check on the supper.'

Alison was aware that as the meal progressed she drank too much. This was because it proved very stressful to orchestrate the conversation in a way suited to her particular agenda. Following on from her successful depiction of Felix as a saintly doctor, she did try to get across his equally holy virtues as an all-purpose help-mate. Felix, however, was visibly and vocally surprised by her lavish praise and confided in his guests that only last week Alison had berated him for his lack of enthusiasm for all things domestic. This irritated Alison so much that she very nearly brought up the reason for her earlier diatribe: the fact that on a totally work-free weekend, he had still managed to avoid putting together the Ikea bookcase that had now been languishing in the spare room for six whole months.

Just in time she remembered that Felix was supposed to be the perfect husband and instead gave a glittering laugh and said Felix had never been able to take a compliment.

By the time they returned to the sitting room for coffee, she realized she had not yet got round to one of the evening's tasks, namely, a subtle undermining of Christopher's virtues as an author. She hastily told Christopher she had read one of his books. Christopher immediately started droning on about its inner meaning, and by the time she was able to get a word in to tell him – and more importantly tell Merrily – that she found it impossible to work out what was going on, she discovered that not only Felix, but also Merrily – who had matched her, glass for glass – was fast asleep. Christopher proceeded to enlighten Alison about the complexities of the human soul, and was still enlightening her an hour later when Nathan and Harry returned from Bath.

At this point, both Merrily and Felix woke up and encouraged the boys to join the party. Christopher suggested to Alison that the two of them should adjourn to the kitchen to continue their fascinating discussion. Alison spent the next hour nodding mutely while Christopher talked. She could hear frequent bursts of laughter from the other room and tried not to resent the fact that the rest of the party were obviously having a good time. Occasionally, Harry and Nathan would come through to collect beers and then disappear back to the sitting room.

Eventually, at one in the morning, Christopher pressed Alison's hand and confided that he couldn't remember when he had had such an entertaining time. The trouble with Merrily, he said, was that she was not only intellectually unable to follow his line of thought but she was also rather too keen on her alcohol, which was why in his own house he tried not to encourage it. For his own part, he only ever drank in moderation since he found that it dulled his intellect. Alison, who by this time felt as if she'd been repeatedly driven over by a steamroller, said she couldn't agree more.

Alison was quite happy to be too busy to think about the campaign in the next few days. Leah had been unsympathetic about her ordeal and had seemed to find it rather funny. Felix had been equally annoying, saying what a good time he had had with Merrily and the children once Alison had taken Christopher off to the kitchen. Alison said loftily that it shouldn't surprise her that he had failed to think even once about the fact that she might be having a miserable time stuck in the kitchen with Christopher; he did, after all, have a tendency not to think about his wife. Annoyingly, Felix only grinned and said that he'd distinctly heard her tell Merrily what a thoughtful man he was.

Fortunately, she *was* too busy to dwell on these injustices. She had Christmas stockings to prepare, groceries to buy, Christmas trees to decorate and the party to organize. Best of all, she had Eva home for the holidays – and what an Eva! Her long, dark hair glowed with health, her complexion was clear and she radiated energy. She had found herself a holiday job with a wine bar in Bath, perfect for her as it meant she didn't need to start work till eleven. She had a two-thousand-word essay to do and intended to get up early every day in order to take Magnus for a walk before settling down to her writing. It was great to be home – 'That won't last,' murmured Felix – and she had loads of Christmas shopping to do.

Eva's enthusiasm was infectious and helped to lessen the sadness caused by Phoebe's absence. As Alison prepared the house for her annual Christmas Eve party, she felt full of the Christmas spirit.

Unlike poor Leah, who rang on the morning of Christmas Eve. She spoke in a mangled, husky croak and announced she had bronchitis and would not be able to come over this evening. She wished Alison a happy Christmas and reminded her to look after Merrily at the party, which was annoying since of course she would look after Merrily.

No sooner had Leah rung off than Merrily rang to say that she and Tom were looking forward to the party but that – and here Merrily sounded uncomfortable – Christopher would be unable to come because of his Muse. Alison said with total honesty that she didn't care at all about Christopher, she was simply looking forward to meeting Tom and seeing Merrily again. 'I love my Christmas parties,' she said, 'they always put me in a good mood.'

She felt momentarily inclined to revise that view when the doorbell rang at six and their first guests arrived. Standing on the doorstep, looking sheepish, were the would-have-been fathers of her would-have-been grandchild. Alison just stared at them until Felix nudged her – Felix told her later she had looked like a goldfish – and she said stiffly, 'Hello, Robbie, hello, Ronnie. What a surprise to see you here.'

'I invited them, Mum. You don't mind, do you?' Eva said airily, and it was perhaps fortunate for Eva and Robbie and Ronnie *and* Alison that at that moment the Rushtons turned up.

Within half an hour the kitchen was heaving with people and Felix was directing guests through to the dining room and sitting room. Most of the people there were old friends and neighbours but there were a few new faces, amongst them the lovely historian she'd met at Sally's house, who told her he couldn't stay too long. 'My sister and her family came down tonight. They're staying with my mother, and when I left they were all trying to get the children to bed. To be honest, I was glad to get away.'

He really was very good-looking and, unlike Christopher, he never went on about his books. It was a rule, Alison thought, that all writers should follow.

'Come and meet my daughter, Eva,' she said. 'I'm sure I told you she's doing history at Manchester. She'd love to meet a real live professional historian.'

Eva was talking to a dark-haired boy and an attractive woman in a green jersey dress. It took Alison a couple of moments before she realized the attractive woman was Merrily. She even wore mascara and a touch of eye-shadow. She smiled proudly at Alison and said, 'Alison, this is Tom.'

'It's very nice to meet you,' Tom said, 'and I love your dog.' Tom had inherited his father's eyes but apparently nothing else since he was quite charming and had a delightful smile.

'I have to watch Magnus at these parties,' Alison told him. 'Last year he ate an entire plate of sausage rolls.' She put a hand on David's arm. 'Now I want to introduce you all to David Morrison, a professional historian who's recently moved down here from Newcastle and—'

'David, it *is* you,' Merrily said with obvious delight. She beamed at Alison. 'David and I were in the same year at university, but he had long hair then. He went out with my flatmate for a couple of months. She was madly in love with him.'

'In that case,' David said, 'she was very clever at hiding her feelings.' He looked as pleased to see Merrily as Merrily was to see him.

Alison saw Jenny Rushton waving at her from across the room and said brightly, 'I'm glad I brought you both together again. I'll see you later. Eva, make sure Tom has something to drink.'

Alison made her way across the room to Jenny, who wanted to know about Eva's love life. She said she had never seen Eva look so beautiful and that it had to be down to a new man. Alison was happy to agree that Eva looked fantastic but was even happier to add that it was Manchester rather than a man that was responsible.

She was enjoying herself now. She had a pleasant conversation with the vicar, who for once did not try to persuade her to come to church, and she had a long chat with Sally's daughter, Naomi. She was pleased to see that Tom was now talking to Nathan. He was actually showing him a card trick. She didn't even mind about Robbie and Ronnie any more, particularly since they were talking with Eva to the Bracewells. And there, over in the corner, David Morrison and Merrily were conversing like the two old friends they apparently were.

It was only much later, after she'd said goodbye to the Rushtons, that she noticed that David and Merrily were *still* talking to each other. They hadn't moved from their place by the standard lamp. David was listening intently and Merrily was talking away like a woman who hadn't spent the last fifteen years being ground down by an unpleasant bully. Alison was suddenly struck by an amazing thought and she wished Leah could be there to share it. It seemed to her that the campaign was just about to take a fascinating new direction.

CHAPTER TWENTY-TWO

Leah is as Sick as a Dog Who's Eaten Too Many Eggs on a Slow Boat to China

If she wasn't feeling so sorry for herself, Leah would be feeling sorry for Charlotte, who was trailing behind Jamie with an anxious smile on her face, only to be ignored by Molly and – worse still – be given a formal little nod from Fred.

'Right,' Leah said with as much energy as she could muster. 'I think we've remembered everything. There are the presents.' She handed a bulging carrier bag to Jamie. 'Everything else is in their rucksacks. I know you'll all have a wonderful time . . .'

'I want to stay with *you*,' Molly said.

'If you did, you'd be very bored,' Leah said. 'As soon as you've gone, I'm going back to bed and I'm going to stay there for the next forty-eight hours.' She smiled at Charlotte. 'You're looking well,' she said, which in comparison with her own appearance was the understatement of the year.

'Thanks,' said Charlotte. 'I feel like an elephant these days. I'm so sorry you can't come with us.'

'So am *I*,' said Molly pointedly.

'Leah will be much better with some peace and quiet,' Jamie said briskly. 'I think it's time we left her so she can get to bed.'

'I do hope you're better soon,' Charlotte said. She put a beautifully wrapped present on the table. 'This is from Jimbo and me,' she said.

'Goodbye, Mum.' Molly gave her mother an extravagant hug. 'I shall miss you *all the time*.'

'I'll miss you too,' Leah said. She disengaged Molly gently and gave her son a light kiss. 'Give me a ring this evening, won't you?'

'Of course we will,' Jamie said. 'All right, guys, let's go! Come along! Goodbye, Leah. Happy Christmas.'

Leah watched the party troop down the path. Charlotte, at the front, glanced back first at Leah and then at the children, her nervous smile looking more uncertain with every step. Leah stood in the doorway and waved till the car disappeared round the corner. She went back into the kitchen and realized this was the first Christmas Day she had ever spent on her own. Stop it, Leah, she told herself; it wasn't as if you wanted to be crammed in a car behind Jamie and Charlotte. She picked up the phone and sat down at the table.

'Mary? It's Leah. Happy Christmas. I thought you'd like to know they've just left.'

'Oh Leah, thank you! Now tell me: how are *you*?' The voice of her former mother-in-law was warm and sympathetic and made Leah want to cry.

'I'm not too bad,' Leah said and promptly broke into a fit of coughing.

'Do you have a temperature?'

'I think so. We've had an exciting morning. The children were up at six to open their stockings. I'm going back to bed now.'

'Very sensible, dear, and try to drink lots of fluids throughout the day. I'm so sorry. We were looking forward to seeing you. It seems far too long since you came down here. I know that –' the voice was uncharacteristically hesitant – 'I do know that you're busy and we don't want to push you, but we do miss you.'

It dawned on Leah that while *she* had been thinking that her ex-in-laws no longer wanted to see her, they had been thinking that she no longer wanted to see *them*. She should have known better. Mary had, after all, gone out of her way during the divorce proceedings to express her affection for Leah. She said quickly, 'I'd love to see you. I'll ring you in the new year and we'll fix a date.'

'That would be lovely. Now get back to bed and get better!'

'I will do. Send my love to John.' Leah rang off and sniffed hard. In her present state of mind, the slightest indication of sympathy for her plight could induce a flood of tears and in the case of her ex-mother-in-law, who had always been more like a mother than her own mother . . .

'Damn,' she murmured. She ought to ring her mother for their requisite exchange of colourless seasonal greetings. 'Not yet,' she said firmly. She filled a tankard with water and went back upstairs to bed.

She had a sip of water and put the tankard down by the phone before sinking back against the pillows. Her forehead was burning, so was her throat. She should stop feeling sorry for herself. She was lucky not to have the children with her when she felt like this. Things could only get better.

She drifted into a light sleep and was woken by her telephone. She struggled up onto her elbow and reached across for it.

'Leah? I'm ringing to find out how you are and to wish you happy Christmas!' It was Alison, sounding impossibly loud and healthy and happy.

Leah pushed back her hair. 'Happy Christmas. Say happy Christmas to Felix and Eva and Harry and Nathan.'

'They're not here at the moment. Felix has dragged them all out for a walk.'

'Really? How did he manage to get them out of bed?'

'Well, it is half past one,' Alison said. 'And anyway it's a family tradition. They always have a walk before we have champagne and prezzies and Christmas lunch.'

'I remember,' Leah said. Two Christmases ago, she had agreed to let Jamie take the children to Winchester and she had gone to Alison's, where she was enveloped in a sea of warmth, good humour, hot punch, roast turkey and party games. It had, against all her expectations, been a lovely Christmas.

'Poor Leah,' Alison said. 'Are you feeling *very* ill? It's rotten luck. However, I have some amazing news that will make you feel much better.'

'I could do with cheering up,' Leah admitted.

'Our party last night,' Alison said in a voice pregnant with expectation, 'was a great success.'

'Did Merrily enjoy it? Did she wear the green dress?'

'She certainly did,' Alison said. 'I would never have

believed that she could look so attractive. And her son was *so* nice. You must make sure you meet him before he goes back to London.'

'I will, if I can beat this stupid bronchitis.'

'You will never guess what happened last night. I'll give you a clue: Merrily and Tom arrived without Christopher. Go on now, guess!'

Leah sighed. 'I don't know. Christopher's left her? Christopher's had a heart attack?'

'No such luck. He had his Muse with him so he couldn't come. Merrily and Tom came on their own and – get this – they were two of the last guests to leave!'

'That's promising,' Leah said. 'They obviously enjoyed themselves.'

'They did,' Alison said. 'Can you guess why?'

Leah's thought processes were currently mired in treacle. 'I don't know,' she said. 'Did Tom get off with Eva?'

'Of course he didn't, he's only thirteen, but he did get on very well with Nathan. And Eva's looking lovely at the moment. However, I want to talk about Merrily because Merrily had a particularly good time. Merrily,' Alison paused for dramatic effect, 'met a man!'

That was one possibility Leah had never considered. 'No!' she breathed, sitting up in bed and rearranging her pillows. 'Tell me!'

'I knew that would perk you up,' Alison said. 'And when I say she met a man, I don't mean she met your usual Tucking Friary overweight, over-the-hill, over-everything sort of man. This one is good-looking, he's not married – well, not any more, at any rate – he has a great body, fab cheekbones, lovely eyes. He's bright and good company; he's a real alpha male.'

'How did this paragon come to be at your party?'

'I met him at Sally's home a few months ago. He's a friend of Sally's friend. We hit it off right away. We talked about history all evening.'

'Since when were you interested in history?'

'I'm very interested in history, especially when I'm talking to a professional historian.'

It couldn't be. Of course it couldn't be. Leah tried to swallow and winced as her throat contracted in pain.

'Leah?' Alison prompted. 'Are you still there?'

'It's only that my throat hurts when I talk. So tell me more about this man. What do you mean when you say he's a professional historian? Is he a teacher?'

'He used to teach at Newcastle University but now he writes books, and apparently he even does the odd bit of television. He has a lovely smile.'

'I don't suppose,' Leah paused to clear her throat, 'that you're talking about David Morrison?'

'Yes, I am! Have you heard of him?'

'Well, actually,' Leah said, 'I've met him.'

There was a long pause and then Alison said, 'Please tell me you didn't sleep with him. Leah? Oh Leah, you *did* sleep with him. Do you have to sleep with every man you meet?'

'That is grossly unfair,' Leah croaked, pausing to take a gulp of water from her glass. 'You seem to think I spend all my free time picking up men in bars, and before you mention Christopher, that was a one-off and a pretty horrible one-off at that.'

'Well, where did you meet David?' Alison asked.

'I met him in a bar,' Leah admitted, adding quickly, 'but I didn't take him home and sleep with him. He asked me out and I thought – well, I thought it might lead somewhere and . . . and then it didn't.'

'Oh Lord,' Alison said. 'Was he the man you were seeing when Jamie's girlfriend got pregnant?'

'Yes. The children were upset and David couldn't cope. I quite understood. It wasn't as if it were serious or anything.'

'Well, I don't mean to be rude,' Alison said, 'but a man would have to be pretty special to be able to cope with Molly.'

'I suppose he would. Tell me about him and Merrily.'

'Are you sure you don't mind?'

'I don't give a damn. I'm just curious.'

'All right, then.' Alison was obviously bursting to tell Leah about them. 'It turned out they were at university together. Merrily's flatmate at the time had been in love with him. I could tell right away they were pleased to see each other. The two of them spent the entire evening talking to each other and Merrily – well, she sparkled, Leah. I'm not sure I've seen anything like it since she won the School Prize for Best Effort.'

'It seems rather unlikely,' Leah said. 'I mean she adores Christopher. And she's so shy . . .'

'She wasn't shy last night! Every time I looked at her – and I looked at her quite a lot – every time she was talking and laughing, and so was he. The chemistry was bouncing off them like head lice! When he arrived, he told me he couldn't stay long but in fact he left at the same time as Merrily. And I'll tell you something else: I overheard him suggesting to Merrily that they should get together quite soon. Something happened last night and everything is different and—'

She was interrupted by a cacophony of voices and Leah heard her say, 'I'm on the phone to Leah.' Various voices shouted out, 'Happy Christmas, Leah!' and Leah smiled weakly.

'I'd better go,' Alison told her. 'It's time for the champagne and prezzies. Ring me when you're better and we'll have a good talk. Happy Christmas!'

'Fat chance,' Leah thought as she put the phone down on its base. She lay back and pushed her hair from her forehead, which was damp and clammy. Of course, Alison was prone to hyperbole. Of course, Merrily loved her husband. The very idea that she'd abruptly transfer her affections to a man who was so utterly different from Christopher was absurd.

Leah could feel the jealousy unfurl like a ball of string. She was pretty certain that Alison's vision of gymnastic sexual atoms was wishful thinking. Nevertheless, David and Merrily had spent an evening chatting and laughing and finding each other so interesting that they had no wish to talk to anyone else. What had they talked about? Why had he found her conversation so riveting? He obviously *had* found it riveting since he wanted to see her again. Whether he fancied Merrily or not, he wanted to be friends with her. He wanted to be friends with Merrily and he didn't want to be friends with Leah.

There had been no point in giving Alison a description of the miserable details of her last evening with David. If she had done, Alison would have simply pulled out her old, well-worn lecture about Leah sabotaging any chance of a love life by being overprotective towards her children. And even supposing that David *had* been interested, his interest had to be pretty lukewarm if he couldn't even be bothered to wait for a few weeks until Fred and Molly were a little less traumatized by the whole baby saga.

There was a poetic justice in the fact that David liked Merrily. Actually, it would serve Leah right if Merrily went off with him. At least then she might be able to stop feeling so guilty about spending a horrible night with Merrily's horrible husband. Leah had a gulp of her water. Her future lay before her like the sea at Chesil Beach on a particularly gloomy day. In a few years, Fred would go and live in New York or Seattle and become a brilliant scientist and marry an American woman who would give him American children Leah would never get to see. Molly would go to London and have some glittering career and a fabulous love life and eventually have children whom Leah would occasionally get to see if she was lucky. And meanwhile she would carry on running her business and go home at night to a simple supper of cheese salad or sardines on toast or stale bread and post-sell-by-date hummus. Sometimes she'd go and visit Alison and Felix or Merrily and David and perhaps they'd take it in turns to invite poor old Leah to spend Christmas with them.

Leah welcomed the hot tears falling down her face. If Alison hadn't rung, she'd have been able to sleep her way through the worst Christmas Day in living memory. Since she couldn't do that, she might as well give herself up to self-pity.

The trouble with crying was that it made her eyes hurt and her throat feel like sandpaper. She got out of bed and put on her dressing gown. Her dressing gown had been a birthday present from Jamie in the dying days of their marriage. It was bulky and comfortable and sexless and should have told Leah something had been very wrong.

She staggered down to the kitchen and poured herself a glass of milk. She took it to the table and picked up Charlotte's present. That it *was* Charlotte's present rather than Jamie's she didn't doubt for a minute. She untied the red ribbon and carefully unwrapped the tartan paper. Inside was a leather-bound diary in which she would be able to relate all the dull details of her dull life in the forthcoming dull year. But it was kind of Charlotte to think of her and made her wish she'd spent more time on the pedestrian gifts she'd bought for the children to give to Charlotte.

She put it down, went through to the sitting room and switched on the lights of the Christmas tree. Then she put on the television and watched the familiar figure of James Stewart tell Donna Reed that he wanted to explore the world. She had seen *It's A Wonderful Life* many times before but she didn't care.

She had got to the point when James Stewart was about to throw himself over a bridge – a sentiment with which she had total sympathy – when she heard the doorbell. Perhaps, she thought, it was her guardian angel, like Clarence in the film, ready to tell her how great her life really was. She stood up and walked through to the hall.

Richard Harrison stood on the doorstep, his hands clutching a dusty bottle of wine. 'Leah,' he said, 'happy Christmas.'

'Thank you,' she said. 'Happy Christmas to you.'

'I was walking past your house,' he said. 'I saw you watching television through the window and I thought: Leah's on her own and so am I. So I went back home and got the wine I'd been saving for our silver wedding anniversary – it's a bottle of Château Lafite – and I thought: I'll go and see if she'd like to share it with me. But I can see you're not well and you probably don't feel like drinking wine or having company and—'

'Richard,' Leah said with heartfelt sincerity, 'I would love to share your bottle of Château Lafite and I would love to have your company. Come on in.'

CHAPTER TWENTY-THREE

Alison Has One Surprise After the Other in Quick Succession

The great joy of throwing a party on Christmas Eve was that one could feel quite justified in spending the rest of Christmas solely in the company of one's family. It was, of course, sad that Phoebe wasn't there but Eva was a star, taking on her sister's mantle with surprising success, waking the boys on Christmas morning and dragging them into their parents' bedroom so they could all open their stockings together. She even got her brothers washing up after Christmas lunch so that Alison could have a pleasant snooze on the sofa with Felix while apparently watching *The Sound of Music*.

The pregnancy episode, traumatic though it had been, seemed to have left Eva with a new maturity and motivation. Throughout the rest of the Christmas holiday, she did her job at the wine bar, made time for academic work and kept her promise to take Magnus out for his daily walk. Best of all, there was a definite sea change in her relationship with her sister. She had confided in Alison that she'd rung Phoebe once the crisis was over to apologize for her lukewarm reception to the engagement and to confess her own recent mistake. Phoebe had been generous in her response.

And then, joy of joys, Phoebe came back from Thailand for a flying visit before New Year and they had a second Christmas, with chicken instead of turkey. Phoebe joined Eva on a walk with Magnus, teased Harry about Nicola and grimaced at Nathan's attempts to play his guitar. Alison was beginning to regret taking Merrily's advice, particularly since Nathan had, as Merrily predicted, taken to playing it in his room at night, with horrible consequences for all the family. It was marvellous to see Phoebe and yet, throughout her brief visit, Alison felt something was wrong.

In bed with Felix, she tried to articulate her concerns. 'She's told us so little about Thailand,' she said. 'And she's hardly mentioned Lennie. She's marrying him in three months. She should be bubbling with excitement. Have you noticed how every time I try to mention the wedding, she tries to change the subject?'

'No,' said Felix. 'But that might be because I try to change the subject every time you mention the wedding.' Noticing his wife's worried frown, he added, 'She's just got back from Thailand. She's probably jet-lagged and tired. If I spent a holiday with Lennie I'd be tired too.'

'Something's wrong,' Alison insisted. 'I can feel it in my bones.'

Felix yawned and switched off the light. 'I think you're worrying unnecessarily,' he said. 'You do have a tendency to worry unnecessarily.'

Alison knew this was true but it didn't stop her worrying. At least she had the CLOM campaign to take her mind off her daughter. She rang Merrily on New Year's Day and Merrily suggested she come to lunch once Tom had returned to London and Eva to Manchester. She mentioned that Christopher would be in Florida on a visit to his Aunt Clemency and Alison assured her she'd be happy to have Merrily to herself.

The chosen date was the last day of the boys' school holiday and Alison had to make an extended detour to drop Harry off at a friend's house. Harry promised his mother that he and Scott were going to spend the day revising, the veracity of which Alison strongly doubted since Harry's friend didn't just have attention-deficit syndrome, he had attention-bankruptcy syndrome. She finally arrived at Merrily's house just after one.

It took a while for Merrily to answer the door, and when she did she was a little breathless. 'Hello, Alison!' she said. She looked surprised to see her. 'I'm sorry I took so long to answer the door, I was upstairs.' She made no attempt to invite Alison into the house.

'Have I got the date wrong?' Alison asked. 'Were you expecting me for lunch today?'

'So that's why you're here!' Merrily's brow cleared. 'I'm so sorry, I've got it down for tomorrow. I'd invite you in now, but . . . I've nothing in the house and I have to go out anyway and I'm running late.'

'I'm sure it's my fault,' Alison said. 'This is always happening to me. I don't listen properly, I suppose. Anyway, it doesn't matter; I have a clear day tomorrow so it's no problem. I'd better let you get on.'

'Right,' Merrily said. 'Goodbye now,' and without further ado she closed the door.

Alison walked back to the car, her mind in overdrive. She was pretty certain that Merrily wasn't rushing out to visit the doctor or the dentist or the supermarket. Merrily was wearing her green dress and Merrily was wearing perfume *and* make-up and she'd obviously washed her hair. Merrily was meeting someone and Alison had a pretty good idea who it was.

On her way home, she stopped off at the farm shop and spent a pleasant time stocking up with ice cream, fruit juice, home-made apple pies and meat for the freezer. In the car park on her way out she bumped into Jenny Rushton, who was on her way in.

'I was going to ring you,' Jenny said. 'I've been talking to Sally and we wondered whether you'd had any thoughts about decorating the hall for the wedding party. If you haven't organized anything yet, we'd love to do it. We're so fond of Phoebe and we'd like to be involved.'

'Well,' Alison said, 'that would be very kind. Thank you, Jenny.'

She drove home, feeling both heartened and chastened by the encounter. It had been kind of Jenny to make such an offer. Perhaps it was time to put the Hadrian's Wall fiasco behind her.

The house was quiet when she came home. She had expected to find Nathan eating his usual three bowls of cornflakes but the table was bare. She greeted Magnus, put her purchases on the table and went through to the sitting room. Still there was no sign of Nathan. She presumed he had gone over to see Luke. She went upstairs and stopped on the landing. She could hear a soft giggle coming from his room. Mystified, she went in.

For a moment, she caught sight of two faces above the duvet smiling at each other with what looked remarkably like post-coital bliss. The two faces caught sight of her and then the female face abruptly disappeared under the duvet.

'Nathan,' Alison burst out, 'what are you doing in bed with Nicola?' It was a remarkably stupid question since it was quite obvious what Nathan had been doing with Nicola.

Alison had to wait till bedtime for her argument with Felix. 'It's your fault,' she told him. 'Nathan's never been the same since you gave him the sex talk.'

Felix looked up from his book. 'That was two years ago and you *told* me to give him the sex talk.'

Alison finished brushing her hair and got into bed beside him. 'I didn't tell you to tell him you had sex for the first time at fourteen. He's been dying to have sex ever since.'

'Show me a teenage boy who isn't dying to have sex. And anyway,' Felix said, 'that was your fault.'

'How do you work that out?'

'You told me to tell him the facts of life. Tell him everything, you said; answer all his questions, you said; be fearless, you said. So he asked me how old I was the first time I had sex and I told him. What was I supposed to do – lie? Of course I know that's what you did to me . . .'

'I never lied to you! When did I lie to you?'

'The first time we had sex, you implied beforehand you weren't a virgin.'

'Implying is not the same as lying and anyway don't change the subject. And when you told Nathan the facts of life—'

'And that's another thing,' said Felix, obviously deciding that attack was the best form of defence, 'why did I have to tell Nathan? Why didn't you do it? Sally Bracewell told *her* children.'

'Sally told her children because Michael's an emotional retentive who likes Sally to do the talking for him on anything that's even mildly uncomfortable. You're Nathan's father. Fathers are supposed to talk to their sons about sex. So what are you going to say to Nathan now?'

Felix looked startled. 'I didn't know I had to talk to Nathan about anything. What have *you* said to Nathan?'

'Nathan's made damn sure I haven't had the chance to say anything. Nicola fled from the house before I could say anything to her, and then, very conveniently, Luke rang to ask me where Nathan was since he was expected to lunch, and so Nathan said he had to go straight out and then he didn't come back till supper, and by that time Harry was back. And meanwhile poor Harry has no idea what's happened. He'd be devastated if he found out. He's been ticking off the days until Nicola's sixteenth birthday.'

'I happen to know,' Felix said, 'that Harry has been trying to get rid of Nicola for weeks.'

'Is this your famous intuition speaking? What possible indication has he given you to make you think such a thing?'

'Well,' Felix shrugged, 'he told me.'

Alison's eyes widened. 'He told you? When did he tell you?'

Felix put his book on his bedside table and took off his reading glasses. 'It was a week or so ago, I think. You were at your book club or Pilates. You were out doing something anyway. We had a beer or two and he told me.'

'Oh,' Alison said. 'He never told *me*. I've obviously been wasting my time worrying about him. It would be nice if just occasionally you kept me informed as to the state of mind of our children.' She switched off the light. 'Goodnight, Felix.'

'Alison,' Felix said, reaching out to switch off his light. 'You're upset and you shouldn't be. Harry knew you thought Nicola was too young for him. I suspect he was too proud to let you know you were right. To be honest, I think he'd have dumped her much earlier if it weren't for the fact that he knew you wanted him to do just that.'

'I see. So it *is* my fault.'

'It's nobody's fault.'

'Felix, your son has had sex with a minor!'

'Yes, but she's had sex with a minor too. At least Nathan wore a condom.'

'So Nathan *has* talked to you about it?'

'No, not really. I asked him if he wore a condom and he said he did.'

'Well, I suppose that's something at least.' Alison sat up to bash her pillows into shape and turned her back on her husband.

When Merrily opened her door the next day, she looked so exactly like the old Merrily that Alison felt momentarily confused. The make-up had gone and Merrily wore her old, shapeless cords and what looked like one of her son's cast-off school sweatshirts. One thing was sure: there were to be no meetings with sexy historians today.

'Merrily,' Alison said, 'I've brought you some organic

apple juice from our local shop. It's quite my favourite tipple at the moment! Happy New Year again!'

'Come in,' Merrily said. 'I'm so sorry about the mix-up yesterday.'

Alison followed Merrily through to the kitchen. It was true that the house was hideous but Merrily could have brightened up the hall table with a few flowers. Perhaps the family budget didn't extend to flowers. 'I expected to find paint cans everywhere,' Alison said. 'I thought you were going to use Christopher's absence to start painting the hall.'

'I was.' Merrily looked definitely guilty.

It appeared that Merrily had found more interesting things to do. Alison tried to imagine her lying in the arms of David, but it was difficult to imagine her lying in the arms of anyone at the moment, let alone a handsome hunk like David.

'I suppose,' Merrily said, 'it was such hard work doing Tom's room that I felt in need of a break.' She avoided Alison's eye while she said this and now she busied herself, taking out glasses and opening the apple juice. 'Tell me all the news of your lovely family. How are they?'

'I'm not sure they're lovely at all,' Alison said candidly. 'To tell you the truth, I'm rather upset. After I left you yesterday, I went home and found Nathan in bed with Harry's girlfriend.'

When Alison had rung Leah last night with the news of Nathan's behaviour, Leah had burst out laughing. Merrily's response – unlike Leah's – was perfect: sympathetic, properly shocked and obviously fascinated. 'Oh poor you,' she said. 'How upsetting for you! And how terrible for poor Harry.'

'Well, to be fair,' Alison said, 'Felix says that Harry's gone off her, and at least Nathan promised Felix he'd used a condom, but I'm still appalled. I mean, Nathan's my baby – he's only fifteen.'

'He's a teenager,' Merrily said. 'Sex is very important to teenage boys.' She opened the fridge and began taking various dishes out. She turned to smile at Alison. 'That's a rather obvious statement, isn't it? I suppose sex is rather important to men too.'

'I'm not sure that's true,' Alison said judiciously. 'I remember reading an article about Leonard Cohen. He could have slept with every woman in the world if he'd wanted and yet he chose to spend at least five years in a monastery. Of course, he did sleep with loads of women before that, so perhaps he was tired. Not that Nathan bears any similarity to Leonard Cohen. The fact is that Nathan is far too young to be sexually active.'

'I'm not sure he is really,' Merrily said, laying out green salad, fresh bread, smoked mackerel and tomatoes. 'I often wonder whether I wouldn't have been happier at university if I'd been . . . sexually active, before I went there.'

'Well, as to that . . .' Alison began and then stopped, deciding that if she told Merrily of Eva's recent experience, Merrily would assume with some justification that all her children were sexually obsessed. 'Merrily,' she said abruptly, 'what a feast you have prepared. I told you I only expected bread and cheese.'

'I know,' Merrily said, 'but I was in town yesterday and I felt guilty about your wasted car journey.'

'Oh that's all right,' Alison said. She suspected Merrily felt guilty about a lot more than a wasted car journey. She watched her hostess carefully. 'Did you have a productive time in town?'

'What? Oh yes, yes I did. I had chores, you know . . .'

Merrily's face had gone bright red. Alison felt it was kinder to look away. She took a sip of her juice. 'I've been reading another of your husband's novels,' she said.

'Really?' Merrily asked. 'Are you enjoying it?'

'Well,' Alison said and took a deep breath. 'I know you'll take this the right way so I have to confess I don't like it. I'm sure it's deep and clever but I don't understand who's doing what to who. There was one chapter where I couldn't tell whether the couple were dancing or having sex, and no one ever seems to have any money problems or house-maintenance problems, and no one ever makes any jokes. People keep looking at frost on leaves and how do they have the time? I hate to say this but I'm finding it a little dull and I keep falling asleep. Of course I know lots of people must like his books and you do as well . . .'

The words were uttered so quietly that Alison could barely catch them. 'I don't.'

'What did you say?'

'I don't like them.' Each word seemed to be pulled out of Merrily's mouth by brute force. 'I thought it was just me. I thought I wasn't clever enough to understand them.'

Alison rolled her eyes. 'If you don't mind me saying, that's so typical of you. You have *always* underrated yourself. I mean, it is possible that we're both too stupid to understand Christopher's prose, but I have to say I think it's the author who's the problem here rather than the reader.'

'I don't know,' Merrily said. 'He has thousands of

readers who'd disagree with you. Now, do sit down and tuck in.' She passed Alison the plate of smoked mackerel. 'You know, I never thanked you properly for the party on Christmas Eve. I meant to send you a card. Tom and I enjoyed ourselves so much. Your children were so kind to him.'

'They liked him very much. So did I. And wasn't it funny that you and David Morrison knew each other?' Alison threw Merrily a sly glance. 'It really is a small world.'

'I know. It's been wonderful to meet up with him again.'

'I've only met him a couple of times,' Alison said carefully, 'but I find him very easy to talk to. He's not at all conceited. I mean, you'd think that someone with his looks and brains would be full of himself, wouldn't you?'

'He was like that at university,' Merrily said. 'He's ridiculously modest. He gave me a copy of his latest book yesterday. I read two chapters last night and I find it quite gripping. He makes Queen Victoria seem so *real*. That's silly, of course, because she *was* real – but somehow David makes you feel he's really got her. Do you know what I mean?'

Alison nodded and was about to say she had also read the book but Merrily was away again, talking now about Victoria's difficult childhood, and her face was lit up and full of energy. And while Alison continued to nod and smile, she was thinking that the make-up and the dress had definitely been for David and that her friend was definitely infatuated.

She rang Leah in the evening with an account of her lunch. 'We have reached a turning-point,' she concluded. 'When I ranted on about Christopher's book, she looked like I'd shown her the light. I honestly think that's the first time in her life she's allowed herself to consider the possibility that Christopher's not as brilliant as he thinks he is.'

'So we're getting somewhere?'

'The whole lunch was interesting,' Alison said. 'We'd been talking about Nathan.'

'Oh Alison,' Leah said, 'you mustn't worry about Nathan. What teenage boy wouldn't go to bed with a pretty girl if he had the chance?'

'Well, actually,' Alison said, 'Merrily agreed with me that it was all very shocking. What I'm trying to tell you is that she went on to make all sorts of weird comments about sex.'

'What sort of weird comments?'

'They were the sort you make when you have sex on your mind. She said she wished she'd had sex before she went to university. And there's something else. I went over to see her yesterday – I got the wrong date for our lunch together – and she couldn't wait to get rid of me. She said she was going out and she was all dressed up; she'd made a real effort. I'm convinced she had sex with David yesterday. Today, she hadn't made any effort at all.'

'That doesn't mean she had sex. If anything, it means the opposite. If she had had a wonderful, passionate encounter with David yesterday, you'd expect her to look fantastically radiant today. Wouldn't you?'

'Not necessarily. She might be exhausted after a very late night and be too tired to concentrate on her appearance today. You weren't there, Leah. She told me David had given her a copy of his book and she went on and on and on about how brilliant it was and how brilliant David was. Something has definitely happened. I know what I know.'

'Well,' Leah said, 'perhaps you're right. Look, I'd love to go on discussing this but my supper will get cold. I'll talk to you soon.'

The phone went dead. Alison looked at her watch and wondered why Leah was eating supper at half past ten at night.

CHAPTER TWENTY-FOUR

Leah Finds Honey Can Inspire Joy and Anxiety

As soon as she'd rung off, Leah hit her forehead. Why in hell had she told Alison she was eating supper? At half past ten! She knew very well that Alison would worry about this and be compelled to ring her tomorrow and give her a half-hour lecture on the perils of late-night meals. Leah closed down her laptop and gave a deep sigh. It had been melodramatic in the extreme to react to Alison's comment with such panic-stricken jealousy. Had she stayed on the phone she would probably have found that Alison's comment had no basis in anything even bordering on factual evidence. This absurd fixation on David had to stop now. She was a 35-year-old working mother, not a love-struck teenager. She had barely talked to him in at least two months. She had no right to be jealous of Merrily. In fact, she should be praying that Merrily was having a wonderful time with him because if anyone deserved to have a wonderful time, it was Merrily.

She stood up and pushed her hair back. It was time for bed. She'd had one of those manic days at work when the phone never stopped ringing and at least half her rental properties seemed to be in need of structural renovation. She would go to bed and from tomorrow morning she would refuse to let her mind go anywhere near the admittedly desirable shape of David Morrison.

She supposed she was still recovering from the bronchitis. At the moment she seemed to have lost all her enthusiasm for just about everything, especially work. Throughout the next day, she kept looking at the clock and it was a relief to go home in the afternoon.

'I've bought us doughnuts for tea,' she told the children. 'We won't have supper till seven. I've invited Richard to join us.' She caught the look that passed between her children and said, 'What's wrong? I thought you felt sorry for Richard? You know how unhappy he is.'

'I do feel sorry for him,' Fred said. 'He's just a bit . . . He asks me questions while I'm eating. It's quite tiring sometimes.'

'It's only because he's interested in your views. He misses his children and he likes talking to you two. He's going through a hard time. His wife has broken his heart and it's up to his friends to rally round.'

Molly looked unimpressed. 'I bet we're doing more rallying than his other friends.'

This was undoubtedly true but Leah didn't mind. She found Richard's company restful and undemanding and she knew he was lonely. He was a good, kind man – far too kind, in Leah's opinion. She thought it was appalling that Tanya had insisted on taking their daughters away with her and her hideous lover over the Christmas break. Now the girls were back at boarding school. It was all grossly unfair.

It was also very good for Leah to spend time with a man

who had so much cause to be bitter and yet displayed so little bitterness. She wished she could be as magnanimous as he was. It was a pleasure to make an extra-large sausage casserole.

He arrived promptly at seven and, kissing her cheek, handed over an expensive-looking bottle of Merlot.

'Richard,' she protested, 'you don't have to bring me something every time you come. It's not as if you get haute cuisine when you come here.'

'I get your company and your time,' Richard said. 'That's worth a lot.'

'You're very sweet. Open the bottle and get us both a glass. I'll call the kids. They're starving, as usual.'

The children were watching television. At the sound of the word 'Supper', Molly and Fred sprang from the sofa like two Jacks in their boxes. She was pleased to see them both greet Richard politely and Molly even went as far as to sit next to him at the table.

'I was on the phone to my girls last night,' Richard said. 'I told them I was coming here and they sent their love to you. Jasmin says she saw a ghost the other night.'

Finally, he had said something that interested them. 'What did it look like?' Fred asked.

'Well,' Richard said, 'it's only fair to say Jasmin may well have dreamt it but she's sure she didn't.' He paused to look at his audience. He was obviously enjoying the fact that he had their undivided attention. 'Jasmin says she woke up, and when she went across to close the window she saw a woman in a long dress on the road outside. Jasmin swears she saw the figure disappear through the wall of the house opposite. The next morning, she went across to the house and could see from the discoloration of the bricks that there had once been a door in the place where the woman had disappeared.'

The phone rang and everyone jumped. Leah picked up the handset.

'Leah?' Jamie sounded dazed yet urgent, elated yet exhausted. 'She's had it!'

'She's had what? Oh my God, she's had the baby?'

'This afternoon, at twelve minutes past four. She had a terrible time. She'd been at it since yesterday lunchtime. At one point near the end I thought she was going to pull my hands off.'

'You were with her?' The question was out before she could think about it. Now was not the time to remember that Jamie had steadfastly refused to attend 'the whole labour thing' with her on the definitely dodgy grounds that he'd never want to have sex with her again.

'I was there all the way. She was so frightened. When the baby came out, it was incredible. Honestly, Leah, you can have no idea what it was like.'

'I think I might have,' said Leah. 'How's the baby? Is everything all right?'

'She's a little girl, she's beautiful and we're going to call her Honey. She and Charlotte have to stay in the hospital for a couple of nights. Will you bring the kids to see her tomorrow evening? If you come around six, I'll make sure I'm there. Just go straight to the maternity wing at the RUH and ask at reception. I'd better go; I have loads of calls to make. See you all tomorrow.'

Leah put the handset back on its base and smiled at the children. 'Did you get any of that?'

'Charlotte's had a baby?' Fred suggested.

'She has and everything's fine. You have a new baby sister called Honey and your dad can't wait to introduce her to you both. He wants me to take you to the RUH tomorrow. What do you think of the name?'

'I think it's very silly,' Molly said. She turned to Richard. 'Will you carry on telling me about the ghost?'

After supper and a fifteen-minute negotiation, Leah agreed to let her children play Bubble Trouble on the computer on condition that they would take themselves off to bed the moment she yelled at them. They agreed and disappeared before she could change her mind.

'That was tiring,' Leah said. 'How about one more glass of wine?'

Richard was already on his feet. 'Let's wash up first,' he said. 'Then we can feel virtuous while we drink.'

They worked well together. Richard rinsed plates and washed pans while Leah loaded the dishwasher and cleared the table. He was a relaxing companion. He talked when he wanted to talk but he wasn't afraid of silences. He was also very good at washing up.

'Right,' Leah said, after despatching her children upstairs, 'let's sit down. I make no apology for pouring a large glass for myself.' She passed the bottle to Richard. 'It's so odd to think that Jamie has another child.'

'It must be difficult for you. Does it hurt a lot?'

'Funnily enough, it doesn't. I thought it would. I do have these twinges of petty jealousy. How come he's so considerate to Charlotte when he never was to me? Is he more excited about the new baby than he was about our two? But it doesn't hurt me, not deep down. Somewhere along the line I seem to have got over him at last.'

'How long is it since you broke up?'

'Three years.' Leah directed a sympathetic smile in Richard's direction. 'So you see? I'm walking proof that things do get easier.'

'It's slightly different for you,' Richard said. 'I mean, Jamie didn't *want* to leave you.'

'No, he wanted to go on shagging other women while I cooked and cleaned for him, with the odd bit of sex thrown in.'

'But that's what I'm saying. At least he still *wanted* to have sex with you.'

'That doesn't mean anything,' Leah said. 'Jamie would have sex with a female gorilla if there was no one else available. And what you have to remember is that just because one woman has ceased to find you attractive, it doesn't follow that she is representative of women in general.' She watched Richard give a disbelieving shrug. 'Richard,' she assured him, 'I have *always* found you attractive.'

He looked up at that and flashed her a delighted grin, which made him look ten years younger. 'Is that true?' he asked. 'Do you promise me you're not just saying that? Do you really mean that?'

She laughed. 'I *swear* I mean that.'

'Well.' Richard had a sip of his wine. 'Well,' he said again, and then, 'Of course you know that I have always fancied you.'

'I thought you might do,' Leah said, 'in a vague sort of way.'

'There was nothing vague about it,' Richard said.

Their eyes met and then Leah smiled. 'Listen to us,' she said. 'What a ridiculous conversation we're having!'

'I'll tell you something,' Richard said. 'It's the best conversation I've had for a very long time.'

In her lunch hour the next day, Leah bought a tiny, exquisitely embroidered dress for the new baby and a large bottle of Jo Malone bath oil for Charlotte. She wondered what the new parents were doing now. Was Jamie tenderly wiping Charlotte's brow with a wet flannel or rocking his precious baby in his arms? She wished she wasn't such a cow. At least being a cow was better than being a wet idiot about David.

At half past five, she drove the children to the hospital and promised them a takeaway afterwards in the hope that the prospect might boost their spirits. Fred was nervous and tried to make conversation about events at school but his heart wasn't in it. Molly looked out of the window and said nothing. Leah prayed that Jamie would have the sense not to look too ecstatic in the presence of his older children.

As usual with the RUH, any attempt to park within a mile of the place was almost impossible. After fruitlessly driving round the entire campus at least three times, they finally found a place over by the psychiatric unit and hurried towards the maternity ward.

'Come on, kids,' she said, walking briskly along the corridor. 'We're late.'

The bad news was that the first sight to greet them was that of Jamie with the baby in his arms. The good news was that Jamie passed Honey to Charlotte as soon as he saw them so that he could hold out his arms to his older children. 'Hey!' he cried. 'I've been waiting to see you all day.'

'Hello,' said Charlotte. She had no make-up and she looked exhausted but beautiful in a fragile, fragrant sort of way. Perhaps that had been Leah's problem. She could never look fragile and fragrant.

'Charlotte, how are you?' Leah went over to kiss Charlotte. 'Am I allowed to see your daughter?'

'Of course.' Charlotte lowered the top folds of the baby blanket and revealed a round little face with the complexion of a rose petal and the tiniest of noses.

'Oh,' Leah whispered, stroking the baby's face. 'Well done, Charlotte, oh so well done!'

'Do you want to hold her, guys?' Jamie asked. 'Fred, have a go.'

Fred shot a glance of near-panic at Leah but sat down on the chair, as directed by his father. Jamie picked up the baby and took her to Fred. 'It's easy,' he promised. 'She's light as a feather. Hold out your arms. That's right. Now: Honey, this is your big brother, Fred. Say hello to him.'

Fred looked at the baby and suddenly smiled. 'She's got hold of my finger,' he said. 'She's opened her eyes and got hold of my finger and she's holding it really tight!'

Jamie laughed and so did Charlotte. Leah looked across the bed at Molly, who was standing to one side of her father. Her face was expressionless but her eyes showed she was implacable. Honey might have won her brother but she hadn't won Molly.

CHAPTER TWENTY-FIVE

Alison Finds Men Are Difficult to Understand

'All right, Molly,' Alison said. 'Tell Leah to ring me later.' She put her mobile back in her bag and walked furiously back up the street, cutting a swathe through the Saturday shoppers. It was too bad, she thought, it was really too bad. It was Leah who'd suggested they meet for lunch in town and she must know how difficult it would be for Alison to find a parking place in Bath on a Saturday morning; now she'd got Molly to ring at the last moment and let her down. There was no excuse for such behaviour. It might be difficult to cope with the existence of a new Jamie baby but she'd had a week to adjust to the idea. It didn't justify such thoughtless self-indulgence and it made Alison jolly fed up.

Alison was aware that these days she seemed to be fed up with rather a lot of things, but even a saint would be cross about this. So now here she was in Bath and she supposed she might as well go—

She stopped suddenly, her eyes widening at the sight of two familiar figures sitting in the window of Caffè Nero.

David was talking earnestly and Merrily was listening, nodding gravely. They were obviously having a serious conversation and Alison decided it would be quite inappropriate to go in and interrupt them. She was about to move on when she noticed a man walking down the street in her direction. It took her a moment to register that he was her hateful would-be seducer from a couple of months ago. She was pretty sure he hadn't yet seen her but it was essential to take evasive action, and if that meant barging in on Merrily's tête-à-tête then that was what she was going to do.

She swerved into Caffè Nero, walked over to the window table and said, in what even she recognized was a mad-manic-soprano-type voice, 'Hello, Merrily! Hello, David! I saw you in the window and thought I'd say hello! I'm supposed to be meeting Leah but she stood me up and I am *so* angry with her.' She stopped abruptly, worried that she sounded a little unhinged. She knew she was in the way, despite the fact that David and Merrily were far too polite to show any signs of discomfiture at her unexpected appearance.

'Alison, how nice to see you.' David stood up and directed her to a chair that, mercifully, meant she could sit with her back to the window. 'Can I get you a coffee?'

'Oh David, I'd love one. Can I have a small espresso?'

'No trouble. I won't be a minute.'

'What a nice man he is,' Alison breathed, putting down her bag and wondering desperately if the horrible Adam was still hovering around outside. 'I'm sorry to barge in on you like this, Merrily. I'm in a bit of a state and it's all very silly . . .'

Merrily gave an encouraging smile. She was wearing a quite reasonable blue jersey and her hair looked nice. 'Why are you so cross with Leah?'

'Don't get me wrong,' Alison said, taking off her coat and pushing back her hair. 'I have every sympathy with Leah and I know she's had a hard time in some ways, but she makes things so difficult for herself and she gets so ridiculously touchy where her children are concerned. Jamie's girlfriend had a little girl last week, I expect she told you.'

'She did. I rang her a few days ago. I haven't seen her for ages. First, she had bronchitis and then I had Tom at home. When I rang her, she said she was trying to catch up on all her work. She sounded exhausted.'

'I'm sure she is and I do feel sorry for her. I know the children are finding it difficult to cope with the new baby, or rather – surprise, surprise – Molly is finding it difficult. And I hate to say this, but I do feel strongly there is no excuse for—' She stopped as David came back with the coffee. 'Oh David, thank you so much, this is just what I need!'

'Alison's telling me why our friend, Leah, stood her up,' Merrily said. 'At least, I think that's what she's telling me.'

Alison turned to David. 'I was supposed to be meeting Leah, in town. The traffic into Bath was horrendous. It always is bad on Saturdays and I had to park in the Waitrose car park. I walked all the way down to the noodle bar to meet her and then I got a phone call from Molly – who's Leah's daughter – and she told me Leah was having to take her over to her friend's house in Corsham and wouldn't be able to meet me for lunch. The trouble with Leah is that she's far too soft with her children, especially Molly. The children were supposed to be with their father. He was going to drive Molly over to see her friend. Molly's refused to go to her father's because of the baby. If I were Leah, I would put my foot down and tell Molly she just has to stop being so silly. But of course Leah won't do this; she has a geisha mentality where those children are concerned. I've told her so too many times and now she won't let me tell her any more. Her entire life revolves round those children and one day they'll leave her and she'll be sad and lonely and I'll have to say to her, "Leah," I'll say, "I'm sorry but I warned you this would happen and you brought it all on yourself." ' Alison took a deep breath and then drank all her coffee in one. 'I blame the mother.'

David looked mystified. 'Which mother?' he asked.

Alison glanced at Merrily for help. 'Do you remember Leah's mother, Merrily?'

Merrily nodded. 'She was small and slim and pretty. She always got my name wrong. I spent so much time at Leah's house, in fact I spent years at Leah's house, and she never stopped calling me Mary.'

Alison nodded significantly. 'That's because she wasn't interested in us. She wasn't interested in Leah either. Now, Leah's mother really *was* the original geisha. Her sole purpose in life has been to please Leah's stepfather. They live out on one of those Greek islands now and ring Leah once a year.'

'They sound appalling,' David said.

'They are. My mother has always got incensed about Leah's mother. Leah is passionate about putting her own children before anyone else, which I can understand, given her upbringing, but she does take it too far.'

'Does she?' David asked. 'What does she do?'

'She indulges Molly, for a start. Since the divorce, Molly's become more and more possessive. I've introduced Leah to men who've been very keen to see her but as soon as Molly gets upset, Leah backs away. It's not good for Leah and it's certainly not good for Molly. Sometimes, too much attention can be just as bad as too little.'

'I don't know,' David said. 'It must be difficult to get the balance right.'

And it was then that Alison remembered that the man who was currently staring so thoughtfully into his coffee cup was the same man who'd slept with Leah and walked away from her and her difficult children. This was rapidly turning out to be one of the worst mornings of Alison's life. She blinked hard and tried to concentrate on Merrily, who was making a forceful defence on Molly's behalf.

'I think Molly's terrific,' she said. 'It's sometimes very difficult to remember she's only nine. She's fearsomely bright. So is Fred.'

'Don't get me wrong. I'm fond of them both,' Alison said. She reached down for her bag, feeling that the best course of action was to leave before she said anything else. 'I'm a little frazzled at the moment.' She smiled uneasily at David. 'My daughter, Phoebe, is getting married in a few weeks and I'm rather too aware of all that's still to be done.'

'Was she at your party?' David asked. 'I don't remember meeting her.'

'She was away in Thailand with her fiancé over Christmas. She's far too young to get married, but there you are. You must both come to the wedding! I'll send you invitations! It's going to be very simple. That's what Phoebe wants. Anyway . . .' Alison pushed back her chair, grabbed her coat and stood up. 'I have loads to do so I must love you and leave you. I feel much better now that I've sounded off! I apologize if I went on. David, thanks again for the coffee and Merrily, we must get together *properly* soon. Goodbye!'

As she scurried out of the coffee bar, she felt quite limp. None of this would have happened if she hadn't been blown off course by the sight of that wretched Casanova man. It was definitely time to go home. She got back to her car and found that if she'd arrived five minutes earlier she would only have had to pay for one hour's parking. She had a jolly good mind to tell Leah how much she'd had to pay on the car park. Then she remembered that she'd just been criticizing Leah's daughter in front of Leah's former lover. This would not have happened, she thought angrily, if Leah had kept their lunch appointment.

Her mood was not improved when she got home. Apart from Magnus, the house was empty. She rang Felix on his mobile and told him Leah had stood her up.

'The boys and I are in town,' Felix said. 'We thought we'd have a bite to eat before the match starts. We're in the Adventure Cafe. Why don't you join us?' She could hear Harry's laugh in the background and Felix sounded particularly good-humoured, which for some reason made Alison feel even worse.

'I don't think so,' she said shortly. 'I've only just driven home. If I'd known you were coming into town early, I'd . . . Well, never mind, I'll see you later.'

She put down the phone and tried not to mind that her

husband was obviously having a good time with his sons. Of course she was glad they were close. Of course she was delighted the boys could talk to their father about personal matters. It was just rather sad that they couldn't talk to their mother as well. There had been a time, not so long ago, when the boys had come to her rather than to Felix. If things went wrong at school, or if they fell and hurt themselves, they had come to *her*. These days, she had no idea what they thought about anything. Nathan's head of year had rung her a couple of days ago to say that Nathan had made an excellent start to the term and that, although it was early days, all his teachers agreed there was a new maturity about him, a realization that fisticuffs was not the answer, which was most gratifying to see.

Felix's response had been one word: Nicola. Felix's one-word response had been accompanied by an easy smile that implied the problem of Nathan's apparent insecurity about his lack of height had now been solved, which was all very well but there was no way she could make her husband see that this wasn't the sort of solution she'd had in mind. Stranger still, Harry seemed to be quite unconcerned that his younger brother was now seeing his ex-girlfriend. In fact, Harry seemed to be getting on rather well with his brother at the moment. Sometimes, Alison thought, it was very difficult to share a house with three men. Sometimes, she felt very much the odd man out. She supposed it was because she was a woman.

She tried to address herself to the tasks at hand and couldn't for the life of her think what they might be. 'Sod it,' she said to Magnus. 'Let's go for a walk.'

She had a phone call from Eva when she got back. Eva

and her friends had been to see a flat for the second time and really, really liked it and the rent was really, really cheap and they were all going out tonight to celebrate. 'And by the way, Mum, I rang Phoebe and asked her if I could invite Kate and Gordon and the twins to her wedding and she said I could.'

'Well, you should have asked me first,' Alison said. 'This wedding is getting completely out of hand.' Then she remembered that only this morning she had invited Merrily and David. 'I suppose it's all right,' she said. 'How *is* Phoebe? I never seem able to get hold of her.'

'Oh she's all right,' Eva said without any indication of interest. 'I'd better go, Mum. I'll see you later.'

This was Eva's current way of signing off. It was an extremely irritating way of signing off since not only was she not going to see Alison later, she had no intention of seeing Alison later.

She had a justifiably contrite phone call from Leah at four. Alison had meant to maintain an ice-cold and dignified tone but the desire to tell Leah about David and Merrily was too much for her and so she forgave Leah before proceeding to explain why Something was definitely Going On.

'I know that,' Leah said. 'I saw them too.'

'You did?' Alison sat down on the sofa and curled her legs up under her. 'When?'

'I dropped Molly at Corsham and on the way back I drove through Batheaston. I saw them go into a house. The funny thing is it's one of my properties. Do you remember me telling you about that couple who had to relocate after a Roman soldier popped up in the kitchen?'

'I do. Wasn't she about to give birth?'

'She was. She did. She had a little boy. I sent them flowers.'

'What were they doing? You must ring them up.'

'I must ring *who* up?'

'You must ring up your clients.'

'Oh right, and what do I say? "Hi, Lizzie and Robert, I saw my friend Merrily, and her friend David, going into your house. Will you please tell me what they were doing there?" '

'I suppose you can't,' Alison said regretfully. 'Perhaps we can find a subtle way of engineering the conversation next time we see Merrily. I could say that I think Batheaston is a very pleasant village and you can say that you like Batheaston too and I can say, "Do you know anyone in Batheaston, Merrily?" and she would say—'

'Alison, you *know* it never works when you start engineering conversations.'

'Well, I'll think of something,' Alison said. 'Actually, I wanted to talk to you about our next move. Christopher comes back from the States next Sunday. I made a note of the date. I think we both need to go and see Merrily before he comes back.'

There was a long pause and then Leah said, 'Why?'

'I think the time has come to talk to Merrily about David,' Alison said. 'We can't really proceed with the campaign until we know what's happening between the two of them. For all we know, she might be in love with David while feeling guilty about Christopher. In which case, it will be our duty to tell her she has nothing to be guilty about. What do you say?'

There was another long pause and then, 'All right.'

CHAPTER TWENTY-SIX

Leah Senses That Things Might Not Go Well

Leah stood waiting outside the Theatre Royal. She was glad she'd got here early. She needed time to calm herself. This was the first time in goodness knew how long that Molly had agreed to stay with Jamie for the weekend and behave herself, and it had taken days of persuasion to bring it about. Leah had only persevered because she was convinced that if she indulged Molly's refusal to accept the existence of her half-sister, her position would soon become too entrenched for her to climb down without losing her dignity. She had driven the children over just half an hour ago and Molly had flounced through Jamie's front door without even looking at her mother.

A hand touched her arm and a voice said, 'Leah?'

Leah jumped, and when she saw whose hand it was so did her heart. 'David!' she said. 'I didn't see you.'

He smiled. 'You didn't look as if you were seeing anything.'

'Oh.' She gave a nervous laugh. 'I was thinking of Molly. I am beginning to think I spend far too much time thinking about Molly.'

'How is she?'

'She . . . She's a little difficult at the moment. I've just dropped her off at her father's apartment and she acted like I'd thrown her into a snake pit. Tell me, how are *you*? Fred gave me a glowing report of your talk at his school.'

'I wish all my audiences were as much fun as Fred and his friends. You look well. It's nice to see you.'

'It's nice to see *you*. You're looking very smart.'

'You're very kind. I've had this suit for twenty years. My mother wants me to burn it. I don't think my producer liked it either. I've been in Bristol recording a programme for the education channel. He told me to wear something different next time.' He paused. 'I'm sorry you're having a bad time with Molly.'

'It will pass,' Leah said. 'Things are getting—'

'Leah, I'm so sorry I'm late.' Richard came puffing up to her and planted a kiss on her cheek. 'I've come straight from work and . . .' He took in David and offered an apologetic smile. 'Hello. I'm sorry to interrupt so rudely. I was so intent on getting to Leah that I didn't notice she was talking to you.'

'Please don't apologize,' David said. 'I have to go anyway. Goodbye, Leah.'

He was gone before she could say anything, and besides, what could she have said? She felt a sickening lurch of disappointment and it was with difficulty that she managed to smile at Richard. 'Well,' she said, 'I suppose we'd better go and take our seats.'

It was what had once been regarded as a risqué play, about a girl who wavers between her stuffy husband and her dashing young lover. Leah could see that one was supposed to cheer when she chose the lover but, unfortunately, he had a tendency to spit when he got excited and he bore a distinct resemblance to the Hollywood actor Matthew McConaughey, which, in Leah's opinion, was not a good resemblance to share. She kept her eyes fixed earnestly on the stage and tried to prevent her mind devising alternative conversations to the unsatisfactory one she'd had earlier with David.

What *would* she have said if Richard hadn't turned up when he did? 'I hear you're seeing a friend of mine.' That would have sounded terrible; it would have been a blatant indicator that she was desperate to know what was going on in his private life. 'It's so nice to see you. I've missed you a lot.' That would have been an unforgivable thing to say in the circumstances. Of course it would only be unforgivable if he was definitely seeing Merrily, and it was, after all, still possible that Alison was wrong.

Fortunately, Richard seemed quite happy to talk for both of them on the way back home. She nodded fervently while he praised Maugham's talent as a storyteller, she agreed about the man's refreshingly cynical attitude towards relationships and she laughed when Richard suggested he might be a little happier if he were a little more like Maugham and a little less like Mills and Boon in his own life.

As they reached her front door, Leah said, 'Would you like a coffee or a glass of wine?'

'I don't think so,' Richard said. He tightened the scarf round his neck. 'I hope you don't mind if I ask you a rather impertinent question. That man outside the theatre this evening: am I right in thinking you are fond of him?'

She hadn't fooled him for a moment. She said, 'We went out on a couple of dates. It didn't work out. He's seeing someone else now.'

'I see.' He took her hands in his. 'Leah,' he said, 'you have made these last few weeks so much easier for me. I fear I am in danger of becoming a little too . . . dependent on your friendship. You do understand when I say that I think it's best if, for a while, I don't see so much of you?'

She nodded. She couldn't speak.

He squeezed her hands and then turned and walked away. Leah watched his retreating back and bit her lip. He was such a nice man. She didn't deserve him. And he certainly didn't deserve *her*.

At twelve the next morning she rang Molly and said, 'Hi, Moll, how are things going?'

A polite voice said she was rather busy at the moment but would try to ring when she had more time. Leah deduced that this was Molly's way of telling her she hadn't been forgiven, and sighed. If she were absolutely honest, she had partly rung Molly in order to provide herself with a diversion from other matters. It was difficult to stop replaying those brief few moments she had had with David. He had appeared to be genuinely pleased to see her. He had been so nice. He had looked so desirable. She wished Alison hadn't arranged for them to go to Merrily's house this evening. She wasn't sure she could bear it if *Merrily* started talking about how desirable he was. Leah stood up and did what she always did when she wanted to close down her mind: she decided to clean the house.

She was vacuuming the stairs when Molly rang at four.

'Mum?' Molly enquired. 'I can talk to you now.'

'That's very decent of you,' Leah said.

'I'm taking you out into the studio.' Leah heard the sound of a door slamming and then a few moments later, 'Mum? Are you there?'

'As a matter of fact,' Leah said, 'I am.'

'Some things have been happening here,' Molly said. 'I've decided it's time we're all nicer to Charlotte.'

Not for the first time in her short life, Molly deprived her mother of the power of speech.

'Mum, do you know where I was when you rang? I was with Charlotte and I'll tell you *why* I was with Charlotte. Dad and Fred went to the market and Dad told me to stay and look after Charlotte and I went to my room to get my jumper and I heard Charlotte crying.'

'Oh poor Charlotte! What did you do?'

'I didn't do anything. I stood behind her door and waited for her to stop. Only, she didn't stop and then Honey started crying too and I couldn't bear to listen to them any more and so I went into the bedroom. Charlotte cried even more when she saw me and she said she was a rotten mother and her nipples hurt and she wished she hadn't had a baby because she didn't know how to look after it and it was probably going to starve to death because it wouldn't take any milk, and then she cried even more and so did Honey and their faces were both so red I thought they both might die.'

'Poor Charlotte. Did you—'

'I knew I had to do something. And then I remembered how Melissa's mother fed Melissa's baby brother last year and I told Charlotte she should put more pillows under the baby. I told her I'd help and I got the pillows and eventually Charlotte managed to feed Honey and she stopped crying.'

'Oh Molly, well done.'

'She told me I was a guardian angel and asked me if I'd hold Honey for her while she blew her nose. I rocked Honey to sleep and Charlotte asked me how I did it and I told her she just had to relax. Charlotte asked me not to tell Dad because he'd think she was being stupid. Then I put Honey in her cot and told Charlotte to go to sleep and I went away and decided what I was going to do next.'

'Wow,' Leah said faintly.

'When Dad came back, I told him he had to ask Charlotte to marry him. He was quite surprised.'

'I bet he was.'

'I told him it wasn't fair to get Charlotte pregnant and not marry her and that if he did, I'd help with Honey as often as I could because Charlotte didn't seem to know very much about babies. Dad said he'd think about it and I said, "Well, don't think about it too long. I'll ask you again this evening." And that's what I'm going to do.'

'Wow,' said Leah again.

'I'd better go and see if Charlotte wants me to help her again. I expect she does. I'll see you tomorrow. You don't need to come till after tea, if you like.'

'Right,' said Leah. 'What about—' But Molly had already rung off.

Leah put down the phone and sat looking blankly at the notice-board. Her mouth began to twitch. She could just imagine Molly happily ordering everyone around. Oh Jamie, Leah thought, your life will never be your own again.

* * *

Alison arrived at seven, armed with an overnight bag and two bottles of wine.

'Are you planning an all-night session?' Leah asked. 'I'm bringing a bottle as well.'

'I just think,' Alison said, 'that it might be easier to talk about David and Christopher if we're all a bit merry first.'

'I can see us now,' Leah said, 'laughing our socks off while we tell Merrily what we think of her husband. Can we have a quick drink before we go? I'm rapidly going off this whole plan.'

'We can't stop now,' Alison said. She put her car keys in her jacket pocket. 'Perhaps a small glass *would* be a good idea. We are walking there, after all.'

They went through to the kitchen and Leah took a bottle from the fridge. 'Tell me again,' she said, 'exactly what we are going to do.'

Alison sat down at the table and pressed the palms of her hands together. 'It's very simple. We find out what's going on with her and David. David is the catalyst. If they *are* seeing each other, we give our full support and let her know why we're against Christopher.'

'Hang on a minute,' Leah said. 'I am not going to tell Merrily I slept with her husband.'

'You don't have to. At the very worst, we need only say that he came on to you. And if it turns out that nothing is happening between her and David, we can say we wish it *were* and explain why.'

'You don't think she might tell us to mind our own business?'

'Leah,' Alison said gravely, 'the three of us share a childhood. Merrily knows us well enough to understand that we are interfering – and I'm not ashamed to say we *are* interfering – because we care about her and want to see her happy. We've done very well so far. We've shown her how to make the best of herself, we've won an admission from her that she doesn't really like her husband's books, we've even introduced her to a writer who can actually write.'

'Alison, you're such a fraud. You have no idea whether David can write.'

'Actually,' Alison said stiffly, 'that's not true. Sally Bracewell gave me his book for Christmas.'

'Have you read it?'

'Have *you* read it?'

'No,' Leah said. 'I did think about buying it . . . but then I didn't.'

'Well, I *have* read it. It's a lot more entertaining than Christopher's stuff.'

'Anything would be more entertaining than Christopher's stuff. The fact remains that I still don't see how we're going to advance these . . . objectives, without upsetting Merrily.'

'That,' said Alison, 'is why I've brought two bottles.'

'I have to tell you,' Leah said, 'I have an unhappy feeling about this.'

'Just drink your wine and don't worry. You know how tactful I am.'

'I do,' Leah said. 'That's why I have a bad feeling.'

Alison stood up and drained her glass. 'Right. If we stay here any longer, we'll lose our nerve. Come on, Leah. And put your coat on, it's cold outside.'

It occurred to Leah that Alison had been telling her to

come on for most of her life and it was about time that she stopped, but she did as she was told and took another bottle from the fridge for Merrily.

'Don't say anything about anything important at first,' said Alison as they walked up the hill. 'And remember: be relaxed.'

'How can I be relaxed when you keep telling me to be relaxed? If it makes you feel any better, I'll leave the entire agenda to you. Besides, if we drink my bottle and your two, we'll all be flat on the floor in no time, so we won't have to worry.'

'That's a very good point,' said Alison as they turned into Merrily's drive. 'Make sure you don't drink *too* much.'

Sometimes, Leah thought, Alison could be quite incredibly annoying.

'And keep in mind,' Alison whispered as they approached the front door, 'just what we've managed to do so far. Thanks to us, Merrily is attractive!'

It was perhaps a pity that when Merrily opened the door she looked pretty much like the Merrily they had met way back in September. The Alice band was in evidence again as were the cords; the only real evidence of sartorial effort was an oversized wooden chain that looked quite out of place on Merrily's heavily patterned sweater. 'Hi, you two,' she said. 'Heavens, you've brought so much wine!'

Alison handed over her bottles and took off her coat. 'We thought we might as well go to town,' she said. 'I'm staying the night with Leah so I don't have to drive back.'

'And I have something to celebrate,' Leah said, 'so I think we should get stuck in!'

Merrily might not have made much effort with her

appearance but she had done her best with the kitchen. In place of the brutal strip-lighting, she had placed candles on the table and work surface. There were Christmas napkins in place ('I know it's not Christmas now, but they're all I have'), and three glasses sat expectantly on the table.

'So,' Merrily said, opening Leah's offering: a bottle of Prosecco, which had been chilling happily in Leah's fridge all day. 'What are we celebrating?'

Leah ignored a slightly anxious expression from Alison. 'Well,' she said, 'I think something rather momentous has happened.' To her left, Alison began to fidget in her chair. 'And I feel duty-bound to say something.' Alison was flashing furious glances at her. 'I have had a breakthrough with Molly.'

Alison let out an audible sigh of relief.

'Why?' asked Merrily. 'What's happened?'

'She rang me today from Jamie's house. She caught poor Charlotte crying – classic post-natal blues. Anyway, according to Molly, she has now taught Charlotte how to breast-feed, how to wind a baby, how to make a baby go to sleep and how to be the perfect mother, and the net result is that she is now sold on both new mother and new baby. So I would like to make a toast to Molly and Charlotte.'

'To Molly and Charlotte,' Merrily said, downing in one gulp at least half her glass of Prosecco. 'I think Molly's fantastic. She has this amazing confidence in her own abilities.'

Leah nodded. 'She's like all of us. She wants to be needed. When Fred was born, I was worried she'd be jealous, but as soon as she realized I needed her help it was brilliant. I still remember her, at the age of twenty-three months, taking Fred from me after I'd fed him, putting him over her shoulder and patting his back for ages until he produced his burp. I think that Charlotte, quite unwittingly, has found the perfect way to endear herself to Molly.'

'I wish I'd had a Molly when Tom was a baby,' Merrily said. 'He had this period of projectile vomiting and I was convinced he was about to die. For a while I seemed to be ringing the health clinic every day.'

Leah laughed. 'I just rang Alison. She always knew what I should do.'

'I'm not sure I did,' Alison admitted. 'But at least I thought I did. I always wanted loads of children and as soon as Phoebe was born I felt motherhood was what I was born to do.'

'You were lucky,' Merrily said. She stood up and started serving out the soup. 'You were even luckier that Felix felt the same way.'

'To be perfectly honest,' Alison said, 'I think he'd have happily stopped at two and once Nathan was born he put his foot down.'

'I don't blame him,' Leah said. 'The way you were going, you'd have ended up with your own football team.'

'I'd have liked more children,' Merrily said. 'I always felt bad that Tom was an only child.'

Leah took a sip of her soup. She had actually begun to relax and enjoy herself. The Prosecco was going down very well and Merrily, who'd looked rather strained on their arrival, had seemed to brighten up as they talked about Molly. Leah rather hoped that Alison had forgotten the purpose of the evening. Unfortunately, Merrily's remark had obviously reminded her.

'Did you try to persuade Christopher to let you have another?' she asked.

'Yes, of course.' Merrily shrugged. 'He reminded me I'd agreed to have just the one.' She paused. 'When I married Christopher, I knew that what he wanted would always take precedence over anything I might want.'

Leah exchanged a startled glance with Alison. There was an unmistakable edge to Merrily's voice that neither of them had heard before.

'Well,' Leah said, attempting to lighten the atmosphere, 'I'm not sure I'd be able to enter into a marriage on that basis.'

'No,' Merrily said. 'It's not been easy.'

Once again, Leah's eyes met those of Alison and she knew that Alison felt as much out of her depth as she did. The CLOM campaign had suddenly hit the brick wall of bruising reality. It was all very well to make jolly plans to break up Merrily's marriage but it was difficult to know how to proceed in the face of Merrily's bleak little comment.

'This soup is very good,' Leah said.

Merrily seemed grateful for the change of subject and proceeded to give a list of the ingredients before asking, 'Do you want any more or shall I bring on my risotto?'

'I *love* risotto,' Alison said with a little too much enthusiasm. 'Shall I open the red wine?'

For a while, the conversation drifted onto the safer territory of recipes and TV chefs and then Leah saw Alison square her shoulders and knew with a sinking heart that Alison was not giving up on the CLOM agenda. Leah knew she was drinking too much but she didn't care. She picked up her wine and took a large gulp.

'It was good to see David with you last week,' Alison told Merrily. 'I like him more every time I meet him.'

'He's in a very good mood at the moment,' Merrily said. 'His book sales are going really well.'

'I've met David,' Leah said, disregarding a painful kick from under the table – really, what did Alison *think* she was going to say? 'He came to speak at the children's school and was kind enough to wait with Fred when I was late picking him up. Fred liked him a lot.'

'I'm glad,' Merrily said. 'You must tell Fred he'll be able to see him again at Phoebe's wedding. Alison invited us both to it.' She glanced at Alison. 'How are the wedding preparations going?'

'I've found a caterer at last,' Alison said. 'She's called Alberta and she's lovely. She understands exactly what I want and she's given me a very reasonable estimate. Even Felix is happy with it. I still can't believe this wedding's going to happen. Phoebe's so young. Of course, she's older than I was when I married Felix.' She nodded at Merrily. 'And you weren't much older when you married Christopher.'

Merrily began clearing away the plates. 'I suppose that's true.'

'I must say,' Alison sighed, 'there are times when I feel a little short-changed. I'm not saying I *regret* marrying Felix . . .'

'I should think not,' Leah said indignantly. 'Felix is fantastic.'

'Yes, of course he is, but I do sometimes wish I'd slept with more than one man in my life.' She directed a sharp glance at Merrily. 'How about you?'

'Me?' Merrily took another gulp from her glass. 'Well, I suppose I'm like you. It might have been . . . useful, to get more experience.'

'I mean,' Alison said, 'Leah has slept with legions of men.'

'I have *not*,' Leah said.

'I do often think,' Merrily said with huge seriousness, 'that if I'd had a bit of experience I might have been better at sex.' She swallowed. 'I'm not very good at sex.'

'I'm not surprised,' Leah said stoutly. 'You're married to someone who doesn't know how to do it.'

There was a sudden, horrible silence.

Leah scratched her head furiously. 'I mean,' she added, 'that Christopher doesn't *look* as if he knows how to do it.'

'Leah can always tell,' Alison put in quickly. 'Leah knows *all* about sex.'

There was another excruciating silence, broken finally by Merrily. 'Do you know what's so funny about meeting you two again after all this time?' she asked. 'You haven't really changed at all. All these years later, Leah, and you still scratch your head when you tell a lie.'

CHAPTER TWENTY-SEVEN

Alison and Leah Discover Unhappiness is a Guilty Conscience

Alison had never in her life seen Leah look so dumbstruck. She watched Leah's complexion turn dull red and wished she could say something, anything, but it was as if she were trapped behind a glass wall and could only look on like some impotent ghost. Strangely, Merrily looked quite calm. She had put the plates to one side and sat with her elbows on the table. 'I knew Christopher liked you. I could see that the first time he saw you. I'm so naive. It never occurred to me that you'd sleep with him.'

'Merrily,' Leah said, 'it was nothing like that. I wouldn't . . . I didn't . . .' She glanced towards the door as if contemplating escape and then rested her hands on the table. 'I swear this is the truth. I didn't know Christopher was your husband. It was before you moved down here. I was drinking at a bar. I picked him up and I took him home. We spent the night together and in the morning he left. I didn't even know his name. He wasn't bothered about seeing me again and I certainly didn't want to see *him*. That's the honest truth.'

Merrily kept her eyes fixed on Leah's face and finally gave a little nod. 'I believe you.' She turned to Alison. 'And when did *you* find out about this?'

Alison jumped. It hadn't occurred to her that she would also receive a cross-examination. 'It was the night you and Christopher came to supper with Leah. Leah told us after you'd left. I was horrified, of course, but so was Leah. She would *never* have done what she did if she'd known who he was. Merrily, I'm so sorry.'

'I'm sure you are,' said Merrily. 'Of course I could see that neither of you liked him. I'm not quite as stupid as the two of you think I am. It just never occurred to me why.'

'We never thought you were stupid,' Alison said quickly. She looked earnestly at Merrily. 'I can see you're upset and I totally understand why you might be angry with us. But you must see we've been in an impossible position. We hadn't seen you for fifteen years and then as soon as we did see you again we discovered your husband was unfaithful. What were we supposed to do? We didn't feel we could say anything. Now you *do* know, I might as well be completely honest. It wasn't just because of – of that – that we disliked him. He was cruel and rude and bullying to you and we hated him for pretending to be so good for you when in fact he was anything but, and it was infuriating to see you thinking he was so wonderful when of course we knew he wasn't.' She could see by the brief flicker of Merrily's eyes that she had used the wrong words. She wished Merrily would cry or shout or get angry. She had no idea how to talk to this still, cold stranger and she had a creeping suspicion that she was digging ever deeper holes for herself.

Merrily stared impassively at Alison. 'Do you remember

I told you this house belonged to Christopher's Aunt Florence? I had tea with her old cleaning lady a little while ago. A neighbour told me she lived in a home in Winsley and I thought it would be nice to go and say hello. She was pleased to see me. She's a little confused and she couldn't quite understand what my connection was to her old employer. Anyway,' Merrily paused to take a sip of her wine, 'she told me Aunt Florence didn't have any nephews or nieces. She said that Aunt Florence— I must stop calling her that. She told me that Florence had had a lover. She'd had a lover for twenty years. He was much younger than she was. He was a writer and he used to come and stay with her twice a year, every year. She told me his name was Christopher and Florence left him her house and all of her money. Apparently, she had rather a lot of money.'

Merrily's voice was hypnotic. Every terrible fact was pronounced in the same soft, measured tone and when she paused, as she did now, Alison could only continue to stare into those unblinking hazel eyes. Merrily removed her elbows from the table and folded her arms in front of her.

'She also told me that Florence had no sisters, not even one called Clemency so I'm not sure who Christopher is seeing in Florida at the moment. Perhaps I will ask him when he comes back tomorrow. What I'm trying to say is that I've known for the last two weeks that Christopher has been unfaithful. I almost convinced myself that he'd been in the grip of some grand passion. I almost felt sorry for him. All Leah has done is to show me that the reality is far duller than that. Christopher just likes to sleep with women who make themselves available. I suppose it's more than possible that he liked Florence's money as much as he liked Florence.'

She reached for the bottle in front of her and filled her glass.

'Would you like to know why I deliberately lost touch with the two of you as well as my family? I didn't want to see you again. I didn't want to see either of you. You were kind to me when we were children. You both looked out for me and advised me and told me what to do. Alison, you were always so sure of everything, you always knew exactly what to do and how to do it. And Leah, you were two years younger than me and yet I always felt like your younger sister. You were so bright and smart and the boys all loved you; you had an answer for everything; you didn't care if you were popular, which meant, of course, that you always were. And I knew it was kind of you to be nice to me but I also knew it made you feel so much better about yourselves to have a friend who was plain and charmless and clueless.'

'Merrily, that is simply not true—'

'I'm very sorry, Alison, but would you mind if I finish? When I met Christopher, he told me I'd been surrounded by bad influences. He was right. It wasn't Christopher who told me to give up my family and two best friends. I wanted to give you up. I didn't like the way you made me feel.'

Merrily stopped and raised her glass to her lips. Neither Alison nor Leah dared speak; they stared at her as if she had changed into some strange alien being. Merrily put down her glass and cupped both her hands round it.

'I still don't like the way you make me feel. There's you, Alison, with your perfect husband and your four lovely children and your lovely home. There's you, Leah, with your glamorous ex-husband and your fantastic sex life and your successful career and your clever son and daughter. I would be truly happy for you both if I didn't have this constant feeling that you were comparing yourselves to poor deluded Merrily with her adulterous husband and her ugly house and her only son who doesn't even live with her most of the time. So I do hope you'll forgive me for being rude but I'd like you to go. I don't want to hear you tell me how actually you've always admired me. I want you to leave and I want you to leave now. If you sincerely have my best interests at heart, you will walk out of here. I'd be grateful if you'd take the unopened bottle with you. The way I feel at the moment I might be tempted to drink it and that wouldn't do me any good.' She pushed back her chair and stood up.

'Merrily,' Alison began again but she felt a restraining hand on her arm from Leah.

It was awful. She and Leah shuffled out of the house like criminals going down to the cells. Merrily opened the door for them and then shut it as soon as they had stepped over the threshold. Alison and Leah walked down the drive in silence and it was only once they had reached the road that Alison said, 'I have never felt so *horrible* in my life.'

Leah didn't say anything. She sniffed and then she sniffed again.

Alison glanced at her. In the moonlight she could see a solitary tear glisten on Leah's cheek. 'It's my fault,' Alison said. 'This is all my fault.'

'No, it isn't. You didn't sleep with Christopher. You didn't tell Merrily you slept with Christopher.'

'I was the one who insisted we play God and wreck Merrily's marriage.'

'I was just as keen as you were.'

Alison wished Merrily hadn't insisted on returning the wine. It only emphasized the point that they'd been playing the part of bountiful, all-giving friends. It was clear that in Merrily's eyes they were every bit as patronizing as they'd always accused Christopher of being.

A car drove down the hill at a crazy speed, with headlights full on. Alison flinched. For a moment, she thought it might be Merrily out to mow them down. She said uncertainly, 'The thing is – we should remember this – Merrily had already found out that Christopher was unfaithful. Can you imagine that his aunts weren't his aunts? I always thought they sounded too good to be true.'

'None of that matters,' Leah said. 'What matters is that we've only made things worse.'

'Leah,' Alison said, 'I'm trying to make us feel better.'

'I don't want to feel better. I don't deserve to feel better.'

Alison bit her lip. It was cold and dark and it was beginning to rain. She wished she could wipe out the entire evening and start again.

It was only when they got back to Leah's house that Leah finally seemed to come to life. 'I might regret it in the morning,' she said, 'but I don't care. I need another drink.'

Alison helped Leah collect glasses and the bottle from the fridge and followed her through to the sitting room. Leah turned on the gas fire and Alison poured out the wine. Leah sat down on the floor, her back resting against the armchair. 'Cheers,' she said.

Alison sat down on the sofa and cupped her glass in her hands. 'Merrily was so angry with us. I've never seen her like that before. She virtually implied that we only helped her in order to make ourselves feel better.'

'Perhaps we did,' Leah said.

'I've been thinking,' Alison said. She gazed at the bluish flames that had sprung into life in the grate. 'Merrily thinks I think my life is perfect. I'm going to go and see her. I'm going to tell her the truth.'

Leah gave a twisted smile. 'That's what got us into this mess.'

'No.' Alison shook her head fiercely. 'I'm going to tell her the real truth. And the real truth is that my life isn't perfect at all and it never has been. My husband had to marry me because I was pregnant and I kept having babies because I love having babies even though I *knew* Felix thought we couldn't afford them. And then, when he finally had a vasectomy and thought he could relax a little, I made him buy a huge house with a horrendous mortgage that continues to eat up our money, and now my babies are older and they're much closer to Felix than they are to me and I have a daughter who's about to make a disastrous marriage and I have another daughter who nearly had a disastrous pregnancy and I nearly had an affair because I was jealous that Felix didn't mind about not being a grandfather, and on top of all that –' Alison swallowed a sob – 'I have friends who don't want to go on holiday with me.'

'Alison, what *are* you talking about?'

Alison began to cry. She had wanted to cry ever since they left Merrily's house and it was a relief to let the tears fall. 'I want Merrily to know that I know that I'm not perfect at all. I'm going to tell Merrily that. Perhaps I'll go and tell her now.'

'She wouldn't want to know – not tonight at any rate. We've all drunk too much tonight.'

Alison stared long and hard into the fire. 'I don't like myself very much,' she said.

'Neither do I,' Leah said. 'Neither do I.'

Alison awoke at ten the next morning and dressed quickly. She was glad there was no sign of life from Leah's room. She couldn't face seeing her at the moment. She left a brief note on the table and drove home.

In the kitchen, Felix and Nathan were eating an extremely messy concoction of potatoes, eggs, tomatoes and mushrooms. Alison felt a little heave of the stomach and said faintly that she rather thought she'd go to bed.

'We'll take Magnus out,' Felix said. 'You do look terribly pale. Did you overdo the booze last night?'

Alison nodded and said she certainly had.

'It's your age,' Nathan said helpfully. 'You shouldn't drink too much at your age.'

'Thank you, Nathan.' Alison raised a feeble hand at her family and tottered upstairs. She took off her clothes, curled up under the duvet and fell into sleep.

She was woken by the noise of a fire engine, which in fact turned out to be the phone. Her first thought was that it was Merrily and she reached out to answer it before any other member of the family might get there.

'Mum?' It was Phoebe.

'Phoebe. Hello, Phoebe. How are you?'

'I'm not very happy,' Phoebe said and burst into tears.

Twenty minutes later, Felix came up with a mug of tea. 'I heard the phone go so I thought you'd be awake.' He passed her the mug. 'How are you feeling? Do you want any lunch?'

'The tea is perfect. Felix, that was Phoebe on the phone.'

Felix sat down on the bed. 'How is she?'

'She was crying. She wants to cancel the wedding.'

'Hallelujah! She's seen the light at last. Did she—'

'I talked to her,' Alison said, 'and I think I've persuaded her to give him a chance.'

'I don't understand,' said Felix. 'You've persuaded your daughter to give Lennie a chance?'

Alison nodded.

'This would be the same Lennie who you and I think is a waste of space?'

Alison nodded slowly. 'Yes.'

'This is the same Lennie,' Felix continued inexorably, 'who is the last man on the planet we would want for a son-in-law?'

'The point is,' Alison said, 'Phoebe doesn't see him like that.'

'I see.'

'No, Felix, you don't. You don't like him and I don't like him but our views aren't important. What's important is that Phoebe loves him.'

'She might do,' Felix conceded, 'but if she was crying down the phone, it would appear that he doesn't seem to make her very happy.'

'Felix,' Alison said, 'if I tell you why she was crying – if I tell you what Phoebe's just told me – will you promise you won't get angry?'

'Did Lennie sleep with another woman?'

'No.'

'Has he hit her?'

'Do you really think I'd persuade her to give him a chance if he had?'

'Then I won't get angry.'

'All right.' Alison sighed. 'It turns out that Phoebe did not have a good Christmas in Thailand. It turns out that she and Lennie went there with some of Lennie's friends. She was the only girl, which was difficult. Two nights after they got there, they all went out on the town for a sort of stag do. Phoebe hadn't wanted to go but Lennie persuaded her. They had quite a few drinks and ended up in some bar that according to Phoebe was full of transvestites. One of them came up to their group and started flirting with them. Phoebe said he – she – no, *he* was quite beautiful with a blonde wig and a pink sparkly dress. Anyway he – she – *he* started coming on to Phoebe in an over-the-top sort of way and ended up groping her breasts.'

'He did *what*?'

'You said you wouldn't get angry.'

'What did Lennie do?'

'Well, that was the point. Lennie didn't do anything. He and his friends thought it was funny. They laughed. I expect they were drunk.'

'Good God.' Felix caught Alison's eye and said grimly, 'All right, all right. Carry on.'

'Phoebe was upset but she didn't say anything because

she didn't want them to think she was oversensitive. She never did say anything to Lennie about it but she was upset, she was very upset and it spoilt the whole holiday for her. And then, three nights ago, she was clearing out their bedroom and she found two tickets to Thailand. Lennie is in charge of the honeymoon and he's consistently refused to tell her where they are going. When she found that their romantic destination is to be a return trip to Thailand and more groping transvestites, she decided he was not the man she thought he was.'

'Thank heavens for that,' Felix said. 'The man's a boorish, insensitive oaf lacking anything even vaguely resembling gentlemanly behaviour. Phoebe should leave him at once.'

'She has done,' Alison said. 'She walked out there and then. She's camping on a girlfriend's floor. She told me she wished she hadn't given up her old flat. She's refusing to answer any of his calls.'

'Good for her.'

'No, Felix, it's not good. She's miserable. She needs to hear what he has to say. She needs to tell him how she feels. Then – if she's still not satisfied – I'll be the first, believe me, I'll be the very first to tear up all the wedding plans. For all we know, he might have a perfectly reasonable explanation.'

'Pigs might fly. I suppose Phoebe is going to take your advice?'

'She says she'll talk to him, yes.'

Felix glanced at her curiously. 'I must say you surprise me. It's not like you to be so . . . so . . .'

Alison looked at him suspiciously. 'Reasonable?'

'Impartial,' Felix said. 'It's just not like you.'

'The fact is,' Alison said slowly, 'I've been a terrible person lately.'

'Really?' Felix raised an eyebrow. 'I can't say I've noticed.'

'I have, though.' Alison bit her lip.

Felix cocked his head to one side. 'Do you want to talk about it?'

'Yes,' said Alison. 'I think I do.'

CHAPTER TWENTY-EIGHT

Leah Finds That Christopher is a Little Under the Weather

The phone had rung three or four times throughout the day and each time Leah had hoped and feared that it might be Merrily. Now it went again and she picked it up with the familiar mixture of dread and anticipation.

'Hi, Leah.' It was Alison. 'Thanks for having me last night. How's your hangover?'

'I slept most of the morning. How about you?'

'I did too, once I got home. Look, I'm at the station. I thought as I'm so near, I might as well drop by, if you're free.'

'What are you doing there?'

'Harry's been in London for the weekend. Felix was going to collect him but he had to see a patient so I've come instead. The train's been delayed by half an hour. Are you about to collect Molly and Fred from Jamie's?'

'They can wait a bit. Come on over and we can have a post-mortem about . . . Hang on.' She raised her head. 'Someone's rung the bell. Do you think it might be Merrily?' She went through to the hall and opened the door.

Christopher pushed his way in before she could even think of shutting him out. 'Where is she?' he yelled. 'You stupid little slut, where is she?' He slapped her hard across the face and she gave an involuntary scream, letting go of the phone, which fell uselessly to the floor.

'Christopher,' she gasped, 'will you please calm down? Christopher, you're hurting me.'

He had her left wrist now and yanked her through to the sitting room before hurling her onto the sofa. 'Now listen,' he said, 'listen very carefully because I'm tired and I don't want to repeat myself.' He bent down and craned his face towards her. 'Do you understand?'

'Yes,' she whispered. 'I do. I do understand.'

'Well done.' He straightened his back. 'I returned from the States today. I couldn't get Merrily on the phone so I had to take a taxi home. When I enter my house, there is a very nasty smell. It's a mixture of old food and alcohol. I go into the kitchen. It's a mess, Leah, it's a disgusting mess. There are dirty plates on the table. In the sink there are filthy saucepans. There are dirty glasses. And among this depressing detritus of filth, I find a note from my wife. Do you want to know what it says, Leah?' He bent down and shouted in her face, 'DO YOU WANT TO KNOW WHAT IT SAYS?'

'Yes,' Leah nodded. 'Yes, I do.'

'It says, "I know about Leah and I'm leaving you." I have been married to my wife for almost fifteen years and she takes eight words to tell me she's leaving me. Did I tell you that I've flown in from the States? So my brain's a little weary but I can just about work out that Merrily must know about you because you told her. I made a mistake about you, Leah. I always knew you were a slut but I didn't think you were a vindictive slut.'

'Christopher, I didn't mean to tell her. It was a mistake.'

'That's an original excuse, Leah: you didn't mean to tell her. I'm sure you didn't. I'm sure it just slipped out. Now, what I want you to do is tell me where my wife has gone and then I can bring her home. So,' Christopher cupped a hand to his left ear, 'I'm waiting. Tell me where she's gone.'

'I don't know. I swear that's the truth.'

Christopher's eyes travelled across the mantelpiece. He selected the small blue vase, and raising his hand he allowed it to smash onto the tiled fireplace below. He smiled. 'Try again.'

'This is madness. I was there last night and we talked, but . . .'

Christopher picked up the glass decanter. 'This is nice,' he said. 'It looks like it might be worth something too.'

'Please,' Leah gasped. 'Don't break that, please don't break that!'

Christopher held it up with both hands and looked enquiringly at her before shaking his head. 'Oh dear,' he said. 'I can't hear you telling me what I need to know. That's a pity.'

Leah jumped as the decanter fell into the grate, tiny shards of glass flying out like confetti.

'Christopher,' Leah pleaded, 'stop this. I know you're upset but you have to believe me. Merrily was angry with me last night. I was the last person in the world she would want to confide in. I swear I had no idea she intended to leave you. It's not my fault.'

'I think you've forgotten my wife's note, Leah. Let me tell you again what it said: I know about Leah and I'm leaving you. Perhaps I'm being stupid but that does suggest to me a case of cause and effect. She knows about *Leah* and she is therefore leaving *me.*' He picked up the carriage clock. 'This looks quite sturdy. It probably won't break if I throw it down. Shall we see what will happen if I throw it at your window?'

From behind Leah, a voice, steely and strong and fearless, rang out. 'Put that down, Christopher. I have a weapon and I'm not afraid to use it.'

Slowly, Leah turned her head. There in the doorway stood Alison, pointing Felix's Healthy Eating umbrella straight in the direction of Christopher's heart.

By the time Leah got to Jamie's house, it was nearer seven than six but no one seemed to notice. Fortunately, no one seemed to notice the pink swelling on the side of her face either. She was struck by her ex-husband's general demeanour. He looked as if he had been zapped by an unidentified flying object. Charlotte wafted in and out of the sitting room with sparkling eyes and a phone clamped to her ear, Fred sat on the sofa eating a piece of toast and Honey lay happily on a changing mat surrounded by nappies, baby lotion and sundry balls of cotton wool.

Molly, who had ushered her mother into this picture of domestic bliss, proceeded to give her an update of the day's events. 'Daddy's asked Charlotte to marry him and we're going to have the engagement party quite soon and Dad's just changed Honey's nappy and Charlotte wants us to go on honeymoon with them at Easter and it's all very exciting, isn't it, Dad?'

Jamie nodded. He looked as excited as a man who's fallen into quicksand.

'How terribly romantic,' Leah said. 'Have you talked to your future in-laws yet?'

'I thought,' Jamie said, 'I'd save that pleasure for later.'

Throughout the next week, Leah hoped Merrily might ring. Alison was worried that Christopher might make a return visit but Leah felt certain that a man of such self-importance would have no wish to return to a house from which he'd been evicted by a woman with an umbrella. She was far more worried that Merrily might try to harm herself.

Alison rang her mother and gave her a heavily edited version of the events leading up to Merrily's sudden departure. She asked her mother to ring Isobel and find out if she knew anything. Her mother rang back within the hour.

'I rang Isobel,' she said. 'It was rather embarrassing. I pretended I wanted her parents' new address and I knew she must be thinking it was odd that it was only now, nine years since they moved, that I wanted to speak to them again. Anyway, she gave me their number, which means that now I shall have to ring them. And what I'm supposed to say to them I do not know.'

'Never mind about *them*,' Alison said. 'Did you ask Isobel about Merrily?'

'I asked her how Merrily was and she said she was living in Bath with her husband and that *she* was looking after her nephew. So then I asked her about *him* and then after that I felt I'd better ask about her own children and—'

'Did she sound odd?' Alison asked. 'Did she sound even a little out of sorts?'

'As far as I remember,' Alison's mother said a little acidly, 'there was never a time when Isobel *didn't* sound out of sorts. I didn't get the feeling she was trying to hide anything.'

So that was that. There didn't seem anything else Alison or Leah could do. By the end of the second week, Leah reached the dismal conclusion that, for the second time in her life, Merrily had chosen to cut herself off from her childhood friends. She did suggest to Alison that she ring David. Alison had already thought of that. She had left a message on his phone but he hadn't rung back. According to Sally, he had gone away to perform in a couple of literary festivals. They had reached a dead end.

CHAPTER TWENTY-NINE

The CLOM is Concluded: Merrily is Liberated

Alison rang Leah at work. 'Did you get the text from Merrily? Can you go?'

'I've already rung Jamie. He's happy to have the children. What about you? The wedding's only a couple of weeks away.'

'I wouldn't miss this for the world. I'll book our train tickets.'

'Thanks. I feel a little like we're about to face the firing squad.'

'Don't be silly,' Alison said. 'It won't be that bad.' She hesitated and then added a little less certainly, 'I'm sure she'll be fine.'

Alison's shaky confidence was particularly unstable when Leah met her at the station on a cold Saturday morning.

'You don't think I'm underdressed, do you?' Alison asked. 'On the one hand, we're meeting in a restaurant in Notting Hill so I wanted to look smart; but on the other hand, I didn't want to make Merrily feel dowdy.' She opened her coat. 'Do you think this is all right?'

Leah surveyed the pink skirt, black shoes and grey jersey shirt. 'You look great,' she said. 'But I doubt if Merrily will care what we're wearing.'

'I suppose you're right,' said Alison. 'It's ridiculous to be so nervous.'

Leah sighed. 'It's not ridiculous at all.' It was no coincidence that she herself had chosen to wear her black trousers and black top.

On the train they sat and chatted about the forthcoming wedding. Nathan, Alison said, had already grabbed the job of master of ceremonies.

'How's Phoebe?' Leah asked. 'No more last-minute nerves?'

'No, she's happy. I'm beginning to warm to Lennie. He wrote me a very sweet letter to say how grateful he was for my help.'

'I should think so. If it weren't for you there wouldn't be a wedding.'

'Phoebe would have come round.'

'I'm not so sure. I still don't understand why Lennie wants to take her back to Thailand for their honeymoon.'

'He loves the place. He wants her to love it too. He knew he'd got it wrong first time around. He was too embarrassed to say anything but he knew he'd let her down. He's taking her to a different part of the country this time. None of his friends will be there and he's not taking her to any dodgy nightclubs.' She glanced out of the window and then back at Leah. 'You know you asked me for Isobel's address? Did you send off your letter to Merrily?'

'Yes. I addressed it care of Tom Trumpet. Even if she's

not staying with Isobel, she must be in touch with her son. It wasn't much of a letter by the time I sent it off. I tried to correct her delusions about my fantastically exciting life. I didn't expect a reply. I just wanted her to know that she didn't have exclusive rights to feeling a failure.'

'I wrote to her too,' Alison said. 'I said more or less the same thing.' She paused to catch Leah's eye. 'Why are you smiling? I'm serious.'

'I know you are but it's so silly. No one who knows you would ever describe you as a failure.'

'Well, I feel I am,' Alison said. 'You know why I think that. I told you.'

'I assumed your brain was addled by alcohol. If you think you're a failure because your children don't talk to you, then just about every mother of adolescent children in the country will feel that too. If you feel you're a failure because you were attracted for two seconds by some slime-ball, then just about every wife in the country would say, "Been there, felt that." It's impossible to take you seriously.'

'Well, I'm sorry,' Alison said, 'but I do take it seriously. These days, I am a humbled woman.'

'You didn't look very humble when you frogmarched Christopher out of my house.'

'That was different. I heard him hitting you before you dropped the phone. I have never driven so fast in my life. I was very angry.'

'I could see that,' Leah said. 'I almost felt sorry for Christopher.'

'No, you didn't.'

'You're right,' Leah said. 'I didn't.'

* * *

The restaurant was a sea of chrome and glass in which elegant waitresses and handsome young waiters glided round the tables with the grace of dolphins.

A well-endowed woman with a fabulously husky voice and a simple but well-cut grey suit showed them to their table. Alison looked after her as she walked away and murmured to Leah, 'I love that suit she's wearing. I wonder . . . Oh my God!'

Leah looked up. A woman was walking towards them. She had brown hair that seemed to bounce as she moved. She wore pink-heeled shoes and a little black dress that exposed enviably long legs. A grey silk scarf was draped loosely over her shoulders. She looked stylish and confident and utterly at home.

'Merrily?' Alison breathed. 'Is it really you?'

Merrily laughed. 'I did want to impress you.' She took a seat between the two women. 'Thank you for coming.'

And now one of the waiters came over with champagne, another held a tray with three flutes, and yet another came bearing olives and nuts and menus. Glasses were filled, waiters were thanked and Merrily said, 'We should have a toast. What shall it be?'

'I think,' Leah said, 'it should be to the liberation of Merrily. You do look liberated.'

Merrily nodded. 'I like that! To my liberation.' She raised her glass, clicked it gently against those of her friends and took a gulp. 'I'm developing a taste for this. Now, I have a great deal to say. First of all, I want to thank you for your letters. They did make me laugh.'

Alison set her glass down. 'Mine wasn't meant to make you laugh.'

'I know, but it's ridiculous to say Felix doesn't love you.'

'Oh Alison!' Leah said.

Merrily turned to Leah. 'And it's ridiculous to say you've ruined your children by leaving Jamie.'

'Oh Leah!' Alison said.

'But I did find them useful,' Merrily said. 'They helped me to see that my own insecurities have been a sort of self-indulgence. And I don't want to be self-indulgent any more.' She picked up her menu. 'May I suggest we choose what we want now, so we can get on and talk? Have anything you like. This is all on me.'

Alison and Leah exchanged fleeting glances before obediently studying their menus and making their choices. After Merrily had given their order to the waiter, she sat back in her chair and cleared her throat.

'I have an apology to make,' she said, 'I want to say sorry about the last time we were all together. I was angry with Christopher and I was angry with myself, and I took it out on you two. I said some cruel things and I regret them. They weren't even true. When I met Christopher, he did persuade me at first that I needed to break away from my family and friends. What he never knew was that I had second thoughts. I wrote to my mother and told her I was sorry. I said I wanted to see her again; I said I wanted to see you two again as well. She wrote back and said she didn't want to see *me*. She also informed me that Alison's mother had told her that you were both glad to see the back of me.'

'And you *believed* her?' Alison demanded incredulously. 'How could you think we'd say that? How could you think my *mother* would say anything like that?'

'I know,' Merrily said. 'It was stupid. At the time it seemed quite plausible, probably because I disliked myself intensely and found it very easy to think that you might too. I promise I know you are my friends and I don't want to lose you again.'

'Merrily,' Leah said, 'you had every right . . . I felt so bad . . .'

Merrily's eyes twinkled. 'I love what you said about Christopher. I love that he's bad in bed. I had no idea. That's what happens if you don't sleep around, don't you think, Alison?'

'Well, actually,' Alison prevaricated, 'I'm not sure I do but—'

'I'm joking,' Merrily said. 'You see how far I've come? I never thought I'd be able to joke about sex.'

'Merrily,' Leah said, 'will you please put us out of our misery and tell us what you've been doing since we last saw you?'

Merrily gave a little sigh. 'There's so much to tell you. It all started that night you both came round. After you left, David rang. The poor man just wanted to tell me he couldn't meet me on the Tuesday and instead he got me weeping down the phone and telling him everything . . .'

'When you say you told him everything,' Leah asked carefully, 'do you mean you told him . . . everything?'

'Oh I did!' Merrily laughed. 'I told him you'd slept with Christopher, I told him Aunt Florence slept with Christopher and I told him Aunt Clemency was almost certainly sleeping with Christopher. You know, I keep forgetting they aren't his aunts. David just listened and listened and at last I stopped crying and he told me what to do.'

'What *did* you do?' Alison asked.

'He drove me up to London the very next morning. He said his sister would give me sanctuary. It's such a wonderful word, don't you think? Sanctuary! His sister is lovely! She and her husband have two small children and a dog and they live in Clerkenwell. I stayed with them for a fortnight. The irony is that she's a marriage guidance counsellor, which is funny given that I'd decided to leave Christopher. And that's something else you should know. I'd been thinking of leaving Christopher for some time. I do admit that Leah's revelation was the deciding factor. When I found out about Aunt Florence, I wasn't sure *what* to do. I actually wondered if he'd been madly in love with her. I almost felt sorry for him. Of course, Leah's revelation changed all that. But I'd been angry for ages about having to leave London and Tom, and I was angry with myself for agreeing to it . . .' She stopped as the waiters approached with their first course.

Alison had been trying to absorb the full meaning of Merrily's narration. 'Do you mean,' she asked as soon as the waiters had gone, 'that you meant to leave Christopher from the moment you came to Bath?'

'It sort of grew,' Merrily said. 'And then I met David again and things suddenly took a rather surprising turn. The first thing he did was to ask me about my writing and—'

'*Your* writing?' Leah queried.

Merrily smiled. 'When we were at university, David and I both entered a competition in the student newspaper. We had to write about a day in our student life and I won the competition. It was nothing really, we only had to write seven hundred words, but David was very kind about my entry and he didn't forget it. When he asked me at your party, I found myself telling him about my book and—'

Alison put up a hand. 'You're going too fast. What book are you talking about?'

'Of course, you don't know!' Aware of her friends' complete attention, Merrily took her time before continuing. She had another sip of her champagne and followed it with a spoonful of her soup. 'I've written a book,' she said. 'I got the idea when I was teaching English. I mean, children have to know about adjectives and verbs and semi-colons but it's difficult to make things like that interesting. So I thought if I could write a novel that teenagers might like and combine it with exercises on punctuation and sentence structures, then I could sugar the whole educational pill. So I wrote a story about three girls. Alison is blonde and pretty and very organised, Leah is a bit of a rebel and Merrily thinks she's plain and boring and has trouble attracting the boys.'

'We're in a book!' Alison beamed. 'What happens to us?'

'You can read it when it comes out. It's going to be published!' She reached over for the champagne and replenished all their glasses. 'I owe it all to David. He read it and showed it to a friend of his called Lizzie Webster. She publishes text books. She loved it and showed it to someone else. It's going to be published as a proper novel, but Lizzie's also going to sell it as a guide for teachers. I have a book deal, you know. I'm going to write another one!'

'Merrily,' Leah said, 'I feel as if we don't know you at all. You've written a book! You have a book deal! You are incredible!'

'It was David who did it. If he hadn't been so keen I'm not sure I'd have had the confidence to send it off anywhere.'

'I bet you would have done.' Leah hesitated. 'Why didn't you tell Alison and me about it?'

'It's that old insecurity thing. I always thought you two were brighter than me.'

'For goodness sake!' Alison said. '*You* were the one who went to university!'

'I didn't want to show my book to either of you. I couldn't bear the fact that it might be bad. I knew you'd be kind and supportive and say the right things . . . And then there was Christopher. I saw the way he looked at you, Leah.'

'I'd forgotten about Christopher,' Alison said. 'Have you talked to him yet?'

'I've been staying with Isobel for the last two weeks. She's actually been incredibly supportive. Christopher came and had lunch with us last week. Isobel left me alone with him and told me to yell if I needed her. I didn't need her. I told him I wanted a divorce and I wanted to move back into our Vauxhall flat with Tom.' She paused. 'Christopher has a reputation as a writer of some . . . spirituality. The last thing he wants is to be exposed as a man who's made a lot of money from rich elderly women. As a result, he's decided to make me a very generous financial settlement. You could say he's paying for this lunch.'

Alison gasped. 'Are you saying he's a sort of gigolo? Has he seen lots of women?'

'I only know about Florence and Clemency but I'm sure there are others. That last night in Bath, I went through his bank statements and they made interesting reading. Tom and I are moving back home in a fortnight. I'm afraid I won't be able to come to Phoebe's wedding but Tom and I will be sure to drink to her health.'

'Merrily,' Leah said heavily, 'I just want to tell you I . . . I hate myself for what happened with Christopher. I'm—'

'Oh Leah!' Merrily reached across to put a hand on Leah's arm. 'I am so glad you slept with him!'

On the train home to Bath, Alison and Leah were unusually silent. 'I can't get over the fact,' Alison said at last, 'that our entire campaign was unnecessary. We didn't need to liberate Merrily. She did it all by herself.'

'Oh I don't know,' Leah said. 'You introduced her to David.'

'I suppose. And you slept with Christopher.'

'Thanks for reminding me.'

'I'm serious. It was only once Merrily knew he slept with you that she realized he'd sleep with anyone.'

'Do you know something, Alison?' Leah said. 'You really know how to make a person feel good.' She hesitated. 'I noticed you didn't ask Merrily about her relationship with David.'

'I noticed you didn't either,' Alison said, then sighed. 'If I've learnt anything at all from this whole CLOM business, it's that Merrily doesn't want us interfering in her personal affairs. And anyway, it's obvious they're a couple. You only have to see how happy she is. There was a glow about Merrily today. It was the glow of a woman in love.'

'It was the glow of a woman who's got a book deal.'

'You're so cynical. I'm happy for David as well as Merrily. He deserves to have a good woman after everything he's been through.'

Leah raised her eyebrows. 'He's not the only person in the world to get divorced.'

'It's not just that. Don't you know why he left Newcastle and moved to Bath? He was madly in love with some woman. Her husband had left her and she had two small children. David wanted them all to move in with him and then she suddenly told him she had to stop seeing him. She said she realized her children weren't ready for her to start dating again and that she was—'

'What did you say? What did you say she said? How do you know all this?' Leah sat bolt upright, her eyes fixed furiously on Alison's face.

'Sally Bracewell's best friend is a close friend of David and she told Sally and Sally told me. She said he was devastated but accepted it for the sake of her children. And then he discovered it was all just an excuse. It wasn't true at all. She'd simply met some rich property developer and wanted to dump David.'

Leah pushed her hair back with both her hands. 'Oh my God!' she said. 'It all makes sense now!'

'What are you talking about?' Alison demanded. 'What makes sense?'

Leah took a deep, shuddering breath. 'David and I had started seeing each other and then the baby thing blew up. David came round and I told him I couldn't see him for a while because the children couldn't cope with me having a new relationship. I thought he'd understand but he just said he had a headache, and then he went and he never rang me again . . .' Leah's voice tailed away and she bit her lip fiercely. 'It's possible, isn't it, that he thought I was simply trying to get rid of him?'

'It's more than possible,' Alison said. 'It must have been weird for him, hearing the same excuse all over again.'

'It wasn't an excuse!' Leah wailed. Her eyes widened. 'And I've just thought of something else. Merrily says she told David I slept with her husband. Back when I was seeing David, I told him I had a horrible one-night stand. So now he thinks I had *two* one-night stands with seedy older men in bars. Not only does he think I'm a lying bitch, he thinks I'm an evil slag as well! Oh God. Oh God!'

'Now Leah, calm down,' Alison urged. 'If I can be the voice of reason here, I will agree that he probably believes you weren't interested in him. But the fact remains that only a month or so later, he fell for Merrily. So he can't have been *that* serious about you. Does that make you feel better?'

Leah gave a long miserable sigh. 'Not really,' she said. 'But thanks anyway.'

CHAPTER THIRTY

Postscript

Alison gazed at Phoebe and felt a flash of pride. It was true – everyone was saying so – Phoebe had to be the most beautiful bride *ever*. Adjectives, most of which had never been used about her before, were now being freely scattered: Phoebe looks so chic . . . Phoebe looks so sophisticated . . . She has a perfect figure . . . She looks so glamorous. Best of all, Phoebe looks so happy.

As for the village hall, it had been transformed into a fairy-tale chamber. Sally and Jenny had excelled themselves. And Alberta what's-her-name was proving to be a total treasure. There had been sandwiches for everyone on arrival at the hall, and the wedding cake, a gossamer confection of silver and pink, had already been photographed by most of the guests. It sat, in dignified splendour, on a platter surrounded by a sea of miniature meringues and heart-shaped biscuits.

She could see Harry coming towards her, hand in hand with his new girlfriend. According to Nathan, Harry had met her while out clubbing and within ten minutes they had, in Nathan's poetic terminology, been eating each other.

'Mum,' Harry said, 'Ginny wanted to say hello.'

Ginny had blonde hair, blue eyes and a very short, very tight, silver sequined dress. She gave Alison an engaging smile and said, 'I think we've met before, Mrs Coward. You came round to see our house a few months ago. My mother was late and I showed you round. Do you remember?'

'I certainly do,' Alison said. 'It was such a beautiful place! It's very nice to see you again.'

'We'd better get a drink,' Harry said, pulling at his girlfriend's hand.

Alison watched them walk off. She couldn't help noting that Harry was clutching Ginny's bottom with his right hand and Ginny was clutching Harry's bottom with her left hand. How extraordinary it was to think that a nice girl like Ginny had been eating Harry in a nightclub. It only went to show that appearances could be very deceptive.

She sipped her champagne and glanced around the room. She could see Nathan talking to her parents, and over on the other side she saw Felix chatting earnestly to Leah. She wondered what they were talking about. Felix, she thought idly, looked extremely handsome in his suit. It was rather a pity he would only wear it for weddings and funerals.

'I hope you're bursting with pride,' Leah was saying to Felix. 'I've never seen Phoebe look so beautiful. I can't believe she's a married lady now.'

'You can blame Alison for that,' Felix growled.

'Whatever you might think of Lennie,' Leah said, 'it's quite clear he loves Phoebe. His eyes follow her wherever she goes. And look at Phoebe. I've never seen her look so lovely.'

'Well, Alison seems to think he'll make her happy. She's usually right about these things.'

'You might tell her that occasionally,' Leah said. 'I think she feels a little lost at the moment. She's not sure you and the children need her very much these days. It'll pass, of course, but you might just bear it in mind.'

'I will,' Felix said. He looked rather nonplussed. 'I can't think why she'd think that.'

Leah hesitated. 'Felix, do you mind if I ask you a question? Do you ever regret moving to Tucking Friary?'

'That's an odd question. No, of course I don't. Why do you ask?'

'It's only that I know Alison worries that she made you buy it. And there's something else. Are you aware that she's always felt bad about the fact that you *had* to marry her?'

Felix looked at her in genuine astonishment. 'That's ridiculous,' he said. 'I never had to do anything.'

They both jumped at the sound of Alison's voice. 'Hello, you two,' she said. 'You're looking very guilty. What have you been talking about?'

'I was saying,' Felix said smoothly, 'that you look extremely pretty today. I've always liked that suit on you.'

'Thank you! Felix, it's nearly time for the speeches. Will you go and round up Nathan? And if you see Alberta, ask her to make sure everyone has some champagne in their glasses.'

'Will do,' Felix said. He looked down at his own empty glass and set off.

Alison took Leah's arm. 'Come and talk to my parents. They've been longing to catch up with you.'

Leah hadn't seen Alison's parents for over a year but they seemed as ageless as ever. They were full of questions about Fred and Molly. Alison's mother remembered that the last time they'd seen them, Fred had won a maths prize and Molly had lost a tooth. Not for the first time, Leah wished that her own mother would show half the interest in her grandchildren that Alison's parents displayed towards them.

There was a sudden hammering from the platform and Nathan shouted, 'Pray silence for the best man.'

The best comment that could be made about the best man's speech was that it was relatively short. He began by launching into a joke involving Lennie and a donkey, but lost his nerve before the punchline and instead began a feverish description of the bridesmaid's beauty. Eva, a patently unwilling recipient of his attentions, shouted out, 'I already told you, I'm not Phoebe's bridesmaid,' at which point the best man seemed to lose the will to live and simply concluded that he hoped everyone was happy.

Nathan leapt up before the best man had even stepped off the platform and called out, 'Pray silence for the groom!'

The bridegroom, Leah thought, looked rather stylish in a tight-fitting green velvet suit and the narrowest of emerald green ties. She could see Felix standing with his eyes fixed on some distant spot on the horizon. It was a look she had seen on Felix's face on sundry social occasions when Felix no longer felt like listening to whoever was speaking to him. But actually, Lennie spoke rather well, so Leah hoped he *was* listening.

Lennie thanked his parents-in-law for the wedding party, he thanked his own parents for their support and he thanked Phoebe for agreeing to marry him, confessing that the scariest moment of his life had been the pause before she said yes.

And now Nathan was saying, 'Pray silence for the bride's father!'

Felix walked to the centre of the platform, took his notes from his pocket, put on his glasses and cleared his throat. 'It's a great pleasure to have you all here,' he said. 'And it's an even greater pleasure to stand here and talk about Phoebe. I am aware that I must be disciplined because I could talk about her for hours. I could tell you how beautiful she is, but of course you can see that for yourselves. I could tell you how gentle and compassionate she is, but most of you know that too. When other teenagers were playing computer games she was mucking out kennels in the rescue home at Claverton and even now, when she has a full-time job with an animal charity, she still finds time for voluntary work at Battersea Dogs' Home. But there is a lot more to Phoebe than compassion and beauty and I thought I owed it to Lennie to tell him about a particular childhood incident.'

Felix stopped and smiled as the beautiful bride could be heard calling out, 'Oh Dad, no!'

'I think,' Felix continued inexorably, 'Phoebe was eight at the time. We lived in a cottage outside Beckington. Alison's parents had kindly agreed to look after the children so Alison and I could have a weekend away together. Off we went, and when we returned on Sunday night we could see at once that something traumatic had happened.

Apparently, all went well until Saturday lunchtime, when they discovered that Phoebe had disappeared. You can imagine how they felt. They searched high and low, they knocked on neighbouring doors, they tried not to panic and then, just as they were about to call the police, the vicar drove up with the missing Phoebe. He'd been driving back from Frome when he spotted her walking along the road. She must have walked at least two miles. The vicar scooped her up and brought her straight back home, and I suspect Phoebe quickly realized she was in trouble.'

Felix paused and winked at Phoebe. 'Eventually, she came up with an explanation. She told her grandparents she'd been playing in the garden when an old man with a white beard had appeared and given her . . .' Felix paused for dramatic effect, 'a letter. On it was written in decidedly shaky capital letters: "Go to the sweetshop and get some sweets or you will die." Phoebe was so convincing that she might well have been believed if only the piece of paper had not been so obviously torn from her diary. This, Lennie, is the sort of girl you have married. Underestimate her at your peril.'

Felix took a sip of champagne and waited for the laughter to die down. 'On a serious note,' he said, 'I have to say I am not happy about this marriage. If I hadn't felt like this before, I most definitely felt it at Christmas, because at Christmas Phoebe was in Thailand with Lennie and I realized that for the rest of my life I was going to have to share her. She is a remarkably special person, Lennie, and I hope you understand that. She has her flaws: she won't always tell you when she's upset and she won't always tell you *why* she's upset. She can also be pretty stubborn at times. But she's one of the kindest people you will ever meet and I say that without any hint of partiality. She's also a lot more like her mother than she thinks she is and if I tell you a bit about my life with her mother, you'll have some idea of what's in store for you.'

Felix put his notes back in his pocket and took off his glasses. 'I've been married to Alison for a good twenty years. She continues to delight, infuriate and surprise me as much as she ever did. There are days when I drive back from work feeling depressed about the patients I've been unable to help. And on those days, I know that when I get to our lovely home in Tucking Friary, Alison will be there and I will feel better at once. Alison has brought up our children with patience and love and the results speak for themselves. As for me, I couldn't imagine a life without her. So, there you are, Lennie. If you are half as happy as I am, you will be a very lucky man.'

There was a momentary silence, followed by thunderous applause. Alison's mother stared in awe at her son-in-law. 'That was beautiful,' she whispered to Leah. 'I have *never* heard Felix talk like that before.'

'I don't think Alison has either,' Leah said. 'Look at her.'

Alison was standing at the left of the platform. She was looking at Felix with shining eyes and seemed quite unaware that tears were falling down her cheeks.

Leah could feel her own eyes well up and she knew that Alison's mother was similarly afflicted. Perhaps it was just as well that Nathan was made of harder stuff. Once again, he stepped onto the platform and called for attention. 'All right, everyone, that's the end of the speeches. Some pizzas and stuff will be coming out soon and then the band will start playing. In the meantime, please raise your glasses to the bride and groom.'

Leah raised her glass and then froze with it poised in mid-air. David Morrison was in the hall. For a moment their eyes locked, and she couldn't help herself: she smiled across at him. And he smiled back. She knew he was with Merrily. Alison said he was with Merrily and Alison was almost certainly right. But if Alison was wrong – and there was a faint possibility she *might* be wrong – then Leah would be making the worst mistake of her life if she didn't make sure Alison was wrong.

'Excuse me a moment,' she murmured to Alison's mother. Then, with a beating heart, she threaded her way through the guests. She stopped abruptly when she saw Sally Bracewell go up to David. She caught sight of Eva's friend, Gordon, leaning against the wall in the corner of the hall and made straight for him instead. It struck her that he looked as lost as she felt. He held a glass in one hand and a half-empty bottle of champagne in the other. Leah drained the rest of her glass and went over to him.

'Hello, Gordon,' she said. 'Are you keeping that champagne for yourself?'

He blinked, smiled sheepishly and filled her glass. 'I'm sorry,' he said. 'You caught me out. I was supposed to be passing it round.'

Leah had always liked Gordon, partly because he had no idea how good-looking he was and partly because he had the very good sense to be nuts about Eva. 'Gordon,' she said, 'would you like me to give you some advice? I seem to be making a habit of it at the moment.'

Gordon looked a little surprised. 'Feel free,' he said politely.

'I do feel free,' Leah said. 'I've made a spectacular mess of my private life and if I'd followed the advice I'm about to give you, I'm pretty sure I'd be a lot happier now. If you know what you want, you should go straight for it. If you don't ask, you won't get. If I were you, I'd go over to Eva and I'd tell her you have something to say. And then,' Leah paused to take a sip of her drink, 'I'd go and say it.' She smiled benignly at him.

'Leah?' The voice made her nerve ends contract and it took an effort to turn and meet his eyes.

'David, how nice to see you,' she said. She noticed that poor Gordon, who was obviously horribly embarrassed by her words of wisdom, uttered something unintelligible before taking his chance to flee.

'I hope I didn't frighten him away,' David said.

Leah laughed unsteadily. 'I think I've done that already,' she said. 'Did you get here in time for Felix's speech?'

'I did. He's a lucky man.'

'Alison's a lucky woman. A good man is hard to find.'

'A good woman is even harder.'

She looked up at him. She wished he wasn't so good-looking. It was all very well to be happy for Merrily but it would help if David wasn't standing quite so close to her. She said, 'I expect Merrily told you we saw her a fortnight ago. It's marvellous news about her book. She says she owes it all to you.'

'That's very kind of her but it's almost certainly not true. She's a very funny and perceptive writer and she's going to be a huge success.' He glanced around. 'Are Fred and Molly here?'

'No,' Leah said lightly, 'I'm on my own this weekend. They're attending the engagement party of their father.'

'Did you have to bribe Molly very heavily?'

'Actually, I didn't. A miracle has happened. She's fallen in love with her new half-sister. It helps that her step-mother-to-be is an extremely nice woman.'

'That must make life easier for you.'

'It certainly does.' She smiled. 'I didn't think I'd see you tonight. I'm sorry Merrily can't be here.'

'She's charged me with delivering a wedding present to the happy couple. They do look very happy.'

'Don't they? I love—'

'Leah, you gorgeous creature, I've been looking for you everywhere!'

It was Alison's bloody brother and she could cheerfully have killed him. She smiled wearily up at him and said, 'Hello, Ian, can I introduce you to—'

But David had gone.

In what seemed like the next two thousand years, Leah discovered that there was nothing more time-stretchingly dull than conducting a fake-flirtatious conversation with a man for whom one has never felt the slightest attraction. She batted Ian's increasingly heavy-handed compliments like a professional tennis player on centre court with a ten-year-old. She watched impotently as David chatted first to Felix and then to Phoebe.

After finally extricating herself from Ian, Leah made her way towards David, who was now talking to Alison.

And now she was stopped by Jenny bloody Rushton, who wanted to know what she thought of the decorations.

She wanted to say she couldn't care less about them, but instead she said politely they were really quite superb.

And suddenly, David was next to her.

'David,' Jenny beamed. 'I didn't know you were going to be here tonight. How lovely to see you.'

'It's good to see you,' David said, 'but I'm afraid I'm going to have to take Leah from you as I have something very particular to ask her. I'll see you later.' Then, carefully steering Leah away, he led her to two chairs in the corner.

'You do realize,' Leah murmured, 'that Jenny will be dying to know what it is you want to ask me.' She could feel her heart racing. 'As a matter of interest, what *is* it you want to ask me?'

'I said the first thing that came into my head,' David said. 'I just wanted to get you to myself for a while.'

He had positioned his chair so that he could look straight at her and his green eyes had that old sparkle that made her heart flip.

For heaven's sake, Leah, she warned herself, remember Merrily. She swallowed and said desperately, 'How is Merrily?'

'She's well. I've just been talking to Alison. I gather you and she both assumed we were . . .'

'Having a relationship?' Leah finished his sentence for him and tried not to look as if his answer was just about the most important thing she had to hear.

'Yes,' David said. 'Those are the words I was looking for.'

Leah thought she might explode. 'So?' she prompted. 'Are you?'

'She's an amazing woman,' David said. 'And she has a huge talent. You'll love her book.'

'I'm sure I will,' Leah said. 'So, are you?'

David beamed. 'Am I what?'

She wanted to hit him. 'Are you . . . having a relationship with her?'

'Leah,' David said. 'What on earth gave you that idea?'

Leah was now 98 per cent certain that they weren't, which meant that she was 98 per cent happier than she'd been a few moments previously. 'At Alison's Christmas Eve party,' she said carefully, 'Alison saw you and Merrily talking together. She said the chemistry was literally bouncing off the two of you.'

'It was history,' David said, 'not chemistry.'

'I don't understand.'

'At the party she told me about her book. We got talking about it and then I had this idea for a book that could help with literacy while also encouraging a love of history. She loved the idea. It was fantastic. She knew exactly the sort of thing I was talking about. We were so excited, we didn't talk to anyone else for the rest of the evening.'

'Alison noticed,' Leah said.

'We decided to see if we could work on it together. We met quite a lot after that.'

'We noticed that too,' Leah said.

'Leah,' David said, 'the last thing Merrily wants is another man in her life at the moment. She's only just got rid of her husband. She's thrilled to be moving back into her old flat with Tom. She's on the verge of a very promising new career. She's quite happy as she is.'

'I'm glad,' Leah said.

'You're glad that Merrily's happy or you're glad she's not having a relationship with me?'

'I'm glad that Merrily's happy,' Leah said primly. A terrible thought occurred to her. 'Are you . . . are you seeing anyone else?'

'I'm not. I seem to be hung up on this woman who dumped me back in November.'

'David,' Leah said urgently, 'I did *not* dump you. I was trying to ask you to wait for a few weeks until the children were more settled about Jamie's baby news. And then you just went off and *left* me. And then Alison said you and Merrily had got together and I've been jealous as hell. I've even dreamt about you both.'

'That's funny,' David said. 'I dreamt about you and the man who kissed you outside the theatre.'

Leah blinked. 'Richard? He's a neighbour. He lives round the corner from me. His wife left him in December and he's nursing a broken heart.'

'For a man with a broken heart, he looked very pleased to see you.' He gave a sudden grin. 'Some time, we ought to compare our dreams. In *my* dream, you and Richard were having sex on your kitchen table.'

'In my fantasy, you and Merrily were just kissing.'

'That's a pretty feeble fantasy.'

'You should have seen the way you kissed her.' She looked down at her hand in his. 'Do you remember me telling you about a one-night stand I had?'

David nodded. 'I presume that was with Merrily's husband.'

She reddened. 'I didn't know – I'd hate you to think—'

'Listen,' David said. 'We all make mistakes.'

She looked up at him. 'Why didn't you get in touch with me?'

He clasped her hand a little more tightly. 'I didn't think you wanted to see me. I was beginning to think I might be mistaken, but I decided that I wasn't when I saw you with the kitchen-table man. And then, when I came into the hall this evening, you smiled and I thought that perhaps I was wrong.'

'David,' Leah said. 'I can't believe you thought I didn't want to see you again. I've missed you so much.'

'I missed you more.' He reached forward to touch her face and then he kissed her. It was a very long kiss and at the end of it, Leah felt quite weak with desire. She remembered belatedly where they were and murmured, 'You do know that everyone will be looking at us?'

'I expect they are.' David tried, unsuccessfully, to look concerned. 'The way I see it, we have two options. The first is that we stay here where we will remain the centre of attention, which is sad because it's Phoebe's wedding and *she* should be the centre of attention. The second is that I drive you home and we make the most of the fact that for tonight at least your children are with their father, because it looks as if I'm going to spend all my free time in the next few months trying to persuade your offspring to put up with me. What do you want to do?'

Leah gave him a slow smile. 'What do you think?' she asked.

Alison was beginning to think she didn't know anything about anyone. First of all, she'd had a strange conversation with David in which, quite randomly, he'd asked her if Leah was seeing anyone. And then, when she told him Leah wasn't but they both knew he *was* and they were very happy for Merrily, he had looked at her, given her a hug and charged off. And just now she'd seen him and Leah eating each other, to use Nathan's very graphic jargon, and it didn't surprise her at all to see them subsequently slink off towards the car park.

Well, Alison thought, she had obviously been wrong about David and Merrily. She did seem to be wrong rather a lot of the time at the moment. Her eyes widened as she saw Eva and Gordon come in from outside. They were holding hands and looked very happy. There was obviously something in the air tonight. Over by the fire escape door, she saw Harry with that nice girl, Ginny, sitting on his lap. And over by the wedding cake, Phoebe and Lennie had their arms round each other. Alison supposed she should find out how old Ginny was, and she should try to remind Eva about the importance of condoms, and she really should stop Nathan from climbing onto the platform and getting out his guitar.

And then she saw Felix. He smiled at her from across the room and she smiled back. His words were wrapped around her like a warm winter coat. Just for tonight, she wouldn't allow herself to worry about her friends or her children or her own inadequacies. Just for tonight, she would revel in the fact that her husband loved her.